MW01135132

# Warta

# Retribution

By Tammy L. Sonnen

Step into my dreams with me
Join me in my world
Of heart felt fun and fantasy
Of stories yet unfurled

--t/s--

This book is a work of love written during long car rides to far-off destinations and unexplored adventures. Its beginnings entertained my three young sons as they rode in the back of whatever vehicle served as the transportation of the moment. Their ideas added flavor, their criticisms added texture, their laughter added joy, and their enthusiasm helped flesh things out.

As each boy grew, he left the story behind, checking in on it occasionally and urging me for more. Life often took precedence over the tale, but Ru-Lee and her family waited patiently, their own lives pulsing through my veins asking to be shared.

I dedicate this story to my sons, Johnathan, Benjamin, and Timothy, without whose urgings Ru-Lee may never have found breath. I also dedicate it to my husband, David, whose patience is unsurpassed.

I ask you, dear reader, to read with your heart. Enjoy the tale and let the adventures unfold.

T.L.S.

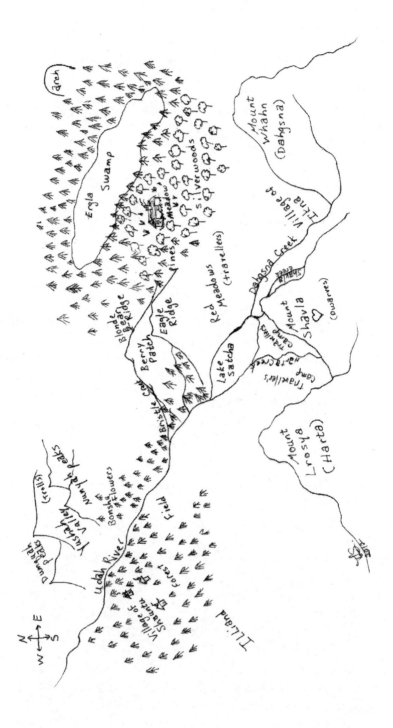

## Chapter 1

Among humankind, there have always been a lucky few who are born with the ability to hear the song of the magic of the worlds as they overlap. Most lose that ability as they grow into puberty and adulthood—some retain it, but the song is squelched to a barely audible hum as their lives become filled with concerns and responsibilities. A blessed few manage to sense the gateways into other realms; even fewer ever pass through them. Sophie Nanos was one of those who heard the song of the gateways and passed through them many times. She had been kissed by magic, as had her child.

As dusk closed in on the woods near her childhood home, Sophie guided four children, her daughter and three nephews, towards such a gateway, its magic singing to her heart as it drew her to it. Using her mind and the small talent available to her in this human world, she wove a protective net of spells around them. She had to get them to the gate and safely through before she was discovered—before the gates were sealed. Her world was besieged by war; she was hunted; her sister already dead; her husband in danger—a danger he did not fully comprehend.

The Council of Keepers was sealing all of the gates to prevent the evil that pervaded her world from entering theirs. This gate had been left open for her to get the children through to safety. Friends and family on the other side would protect and care for them once there.

Sophie's mind drifted to memories of happier times as she tread on the overgrown paths of her childhood. How many times had she passed through the gates while her family worked or played around her? They barely even noticed her absence, such was the time difference between the worlds. A few seconds here, could be hours, days, or more there. Yet aging was slowed to a near crawl. Time didn't run the same there. There was no logic to it. She had long-ago concluded that the magic inherent in the other worlds was the reason for the differences.

1

In her travels through the passages over the years, she had met others like herself—born of one world, but able to pass to another. Some stayed in the other, feeling as if they belonged there more than where they were born. Many who stayed formed a nomadic band, taking care of each other and traveling from place to place. Sophie wondered if the boys might join them over time. Her daughter, Ru-Lee, might not. She had power, Sophie could sense it in her and had seen its spark. The power was latent in her birth world but blossomed forth in this other realm.

Sophie had introduced Ru-Lee early in her life to the "magic land". The two had spent full and wondrous days there. Many years before, Sophie had built a cabin in a clearing. It was protected by spells she had learned and friends she had made. Now it would belong to Ru-Lee and the boys.

Twigs and brush snapped behind them and to their left, jolting Sophie out of her reverie. The children heard it too and the group halted abruptly. Peering anxiously into the darkening shadows of the trees, Sophie saw movement—a beast of some sort. Moving quickly, she placed herself between the oncoming animal and the children, picking up a large stick as she went. The brush directly in front of her shook violently as the beast forced its way through, panting heavily. Suddenly, a furry head burst through followed immediately by shouts of joy from the children and an enormous amount of wiggling and hairy-tail wagging. The 'beast' was Dawg, D.G. for short, Ru-Lee's pet and best friend. He had been out roaming the brush when they had left and Sophie hadn't thought to call him. She should have known he would find them—he was never far from Ru-Lee for long.

Lowering the stick, Sophie took a second to breathe before quieting the group and continuing on. They were almost there; she could feel the pull strong on her heart.

A shadow of worry crossed her mind as she went. In order to pass through the gates, one must possess an almost childlike belief in the *possibility* of being able to pass through. Ru-Lee would be able to; Jace, at the age of seven, would pass through easily; as would Davlin. Even though he was twelve years old, he possessed a strong belief in what could be. Relmar, however, concerned her. He was fourteen and beginning to show outward signs of the skepticism that comes to most young adults. Glancing back at him with Dawg prancing by his side, however, dispelled her doubts. He was still a child at heart, and the heart, after all, is what matters most where magic is concerned.

Concentrating, she mentally tightened the invisible magical shields she had placed around the children. These would stay in place, unseen, long enough to see them safely to the cabin. She had spoken to Ru-Lee about the plan. Ru-Lee knew what to do; even the oldest boy would follow her and listen. At the age of twelve, she was self-possessed and wise beyond her years.

Nearing a bank of thorny brush to the right of the trail, Sophie's body vibrated with the magic of the gateway. Turning to the children, she smiled reassuringly and stepped backwards through the brush, disappearing in the blink of an eye. The boys gasped and curiously watched Ru-Lee and Dawg follow Sophie. Jace looked back at his brothers questioningly. Davlin shrugged, Relmar raised his eyebrows and, moving forward, they shoved their youngest brother ahead of them through the brush.

Once they were all through the gateway, Sophie went over the plan with them again. They were to follow the trail until they met with Ru-Lee's grandparents and some of Sophie's friends who would take them to the cabin and stay with them awhile. Sophie would return for the children when it was safe; when the wars were over and the gateways were unsealed--she hoped it would not be long.

Her heart broke—she couldn't stay. Her husband was in the human world, her birth world. She had to go back and try to shield him if she could. Her love for her husband and child tore at her. One she could save, the other she hoped to shield. Once the gates were sealed, she wouldn't be able to come back to her daughter until the danger from her world had passed. She shared a heart-thought with Ru-Lee. A last good-bye filled with love and strength. Ru-Lee knew she had power here. It would only grow with her time in this place. Sophie's friends and family would guide Ru-Lee and the boys. "This is right," she told herself. "It will be okay."

Gently, Sophie kissed each of the children, then turned and passed back through the gateway. She hoped she wasn't too late to protect her husband from what she sensed was coming.

XXX    XXX    XXX    XXX    XXX

Once Sophie had disappeared through the gateway, the boys turned to Ru-Lee who smiled engagingly at them. Reaching out her hand to Jace, she began to hum a tune. They turned and walked down the path through a wood filled with soft laughter and silver trees, starlight filtering down on them, a soft mist swirling around their feet.

They had only gone a short distance when they rounded a bend in the trail to find two men, a woman, and a young boy blocking their path. The woman was less than five feet tall with short curly hair and a quick bright smile. She wasn't slight, but she wasn't stout either—her physique was somewhere in between. One of the men, obviously attached to the smiling woman, was taller than her and solidly built with a full, bushy beard and twinkling eyes. The other man wore tanned leather clothing. He was tall with a lithe strength that was evident even in his stance. The young boy looked to be about Jace's age, also dressed in tanned leather. His eyes were filled with curiosity and he wore a mischievous smile. As soon as Ru-Lee could make out their features, she squealed with delight and ran to embrace the woman. "Aylon! I am so glad to see you!" Releasing Aylon, she hugged the stout man saying, "Nevlon! Mama said you would be here!"

Laughing, Nevlon hugged her back, lifting her up so that her legs swung out. "Yes, we are here! Wouldn't miss you all for the world!" Placing her feet back on the ground, he turned to the tall, lithe man and said, "You remember Rannue and his son, Trieca, don't you?"

"Yes! I didn't know you would be here, but I am glad to see you," Ru-Lee said, smiling up at Rannue and giving Trieca a curious look. "I think you grew, Trieca!" She said, eliciting a blush of color that fled up to the peaks of the young elf's ears.

Nevlon turned to the boys, who had been watching in silent curiosity, and said, "Come on, then. Let's get you all to the cabin so you can get rested up before you explore your new home!"

As they turned to walk on down the trail, Nevlon whispered to Ru-Lee, "Ru, I think you had better start humming again before these trees start getting ornery!"

Ru-Lee giggled, but started humming as directed and the group walked on into the evening towards their new home.

## Chapter 2

The warm, late-summer air, filled with the buzzing of flies and the delicious smell of ripe berries. Sunlight filtered through the pine trees and brush to land on a deep purple cap as it bobbed up and down, in and out, of the dense Mountain Berry bushes. A large, white spider swung from a strand of web attached to the brim of the hat, and reached out its long legs to latch onto some of the strawberry –blonde hair that tufted from beneath the cap. As she dropped a handful of berries into a can, the young woman lifted a heavily-laden branch and peaked beneath. Smiling, she turned hazel-gold eyes to her companion; a splotchy white and gold colored mutt with a great puff of hair on top of his head between his floppy ears. He ran a berry-stained tongue over his muzzle and wagged his tail appreciatively.

"You like these berries, don't you, D.G.?" She asked him. One could almost see him smile broadly in response. "Well, get your fill, I think they are a bit early this year. That, or we are a bit late. Most of these are over-ripe and won't make it home in the bucket. Guess you get more than you bargained for today, eh?" Continuing to pick, she contemplated her hairy companion. His true name was Dawg, but she had called him D.G. for so long now that she wasn't sure he would respond to his original name. He had been her constant companion and protector since her parents adopted him when she was five. They were inseparable, unless D.G. found something good to chase, but he always returned.

A slight breeze rustled through the trees above them and she turned to look up at the sky. Clouds quickly drifted to blot out the sun causing a shiver to run down her spine. D.G. stood sniffing the air. Dark shadows glided past overhead. The young woman and her companion exchanged concerned looks as she bent down to gather her can of berries, a pit forming in the bottom of her stomach.

"Time to go, D.G.. I don't like the looks of those shadows." Her brows knit together as she thought of the dreams that had haunted her sleep over the past month. It had been a long time since her dreams showed themselves in the conscious realm, but it had been known to happen. Usually, it was something small and easily dealt with. If this was going to show itself, as her dreams and other signs seemed to indicate, it would not be small or easily finished. Taking a deep breath to steady herself, she began to fight the brush towards the trail down the mountain following the sounds of D.G. tearing through the underbrush.

They reached a creek winding through a gulley at the foot of the trail. She bent and washed the purple berry juice from her hands as the spider dangled down to her shoulder. D.G. splashed happily to the middle of the creek and lay down with the shallow water rippling past his fur. He lay there, tongue lolling to one side, watching her rinse the bucket of berries.

Once finished, she carefully placed the lid on top and rose to stretch her back. Suddenly, the hair on her neck raised and her spine tingled as the woods went still. An unpleasant odor drifted on the wind. She signed to D.G. for silence as her eyes widened with recognition of the familiar stench. Ergla!! Grabbing the berry bucket, she sprang into motion. Leaping across the creek with D.G. on her heals, she sought to get downwind of the creature. What was it doing in her woods and why was it outside of the swamp, she wondered as she quickly made her way uphill through the thick brush. It amazed her how quietly a person could move when necessary.

She was out of the gully now and running along the ridge through the sparse trees. Even D.G. was striving to move with as much silence as possible. Erglas were known to devour anything they came upon, alive or dead. Their lack of preference for either might account for their stench, which was a cross between skunk, smelly feet, and rotten potatoes. They ranged in size from a mid-sized cat

7

to a large cow with patchy gray and black fur. Their long teeth and sharp retractable claws lent an evil bent to their temperament which rivaled that of a teenager forced out of bed too soon. It was always best to avoid them whenever possible, which was usually easy to do, as they seldom left the swamp. What this one was doing here was a puzzle that might lead to unpleasant answers. The one they had just missed was, by the sounds of its movements, about goat-sized and it appeared to have stopped around the vicinity of the berry patch so recently vacated.

Satisfied that their unwelcome visitor would not bother them now that it had found something to eat, Ru-Lee slowed to a quick walk and began to angle down the ridge on the opposite side from the Ergla. D.G., tongue hanging out, loped along at her heels, testing the wind with his nose.

The two dropped down into a patch of pine trees that filtered the sunlight through their boughs and blocked most of the thicker brush from growing beneath them. Mushrooms, mosses, and a few ferns could be seen growing here and there as they neared another small spring. The ground became spongy and Ru-Lee stepped onto a fallen log to cross the worst of the wet ground. Mosquitoes whined past, stopping to snack on them as they continued through the marsh. The ground began to rise slightly, pine trees thinned, brush began to thicken, and the sunlight could be seen in broader patches. It slipped through the tree branches offering its warmth and brightness to the afternoon. The scent of sun-warmed earth, pine, and wild honeysuckle filled Ru-Lee's nose bringing a smile to her lips

That smile faded as she caught the sound of voices on the wind. She quickened her pace, concern etched in her eyes. Turning her head slightly to glance down at the tufted head of her companion she asked, "Who is up ahead, D.G.? I don't recall sending out an invitation, do you?" D.G. blinked in answer and swayed his head side-

8

to-side as they continued on the now-visible path through the trees.

As they closed in on the sounds, it became apparent that their visitor was not happy. The wind carried a steady stream of swear words mingled with child-like giggles. The swearing voice sounded familiar and Ru-Lee's face broke into a broad grin as it dawned on her what must be happening.

Laughing, she reached down to rub D.G.'s ears and said, "I believe our visitor is entangled in the Silver Forest." D.G. leaned his head towards her leg and bobbed it up and down in answer and enjoyment of the ear rub.

The trees around them had changed as they walked. They were no longer the thick pine and fir trees, but were tall and willowy with silver bark. The branches waved gaily in even the slightest wind, causing the slender leaves to make a constantly-moving, sunlight-dappled pattern on the ground below. The roots seemed to cause the ground to ripple and, indeed, popped up occasionally to trip an unwary traveler. D.G. and Ru-Lee often had to step high and quick to avoid being tangled in them. The sound the wind made blowing through the leaves was a bright and happy giggling that grew louder as they neared the unexpected visitor. They had entered "The Giggling woods", as Ru-Lee so often called it.

No one knew exactly what caused this strange portion of woods to be as it was. Ru-Lee had her suspicions, of course. Long ago, this area was said to have been home to a large population of wood sprites. Ru-Lee believed they had not left, but had somehow joined their spirits with the trees, becoming one with them, thus giving the trees the teasing, mischievous qualities of the sprites themselves. She had long ago learned how to pass through them without mishap, but strangers often became entangled, as the current visitor demonstrated.

Her thoughts turned again to the traveler struggling on the trail ahead of her. He was about four and a half feet tall, though it was difficult to tell for sure due to the fact that he was flat on his back at the moment. Dust and leaves clung to his clothing and bright blonde hair. As he rolled onto his stomach and righted himself, she could see that the laces of his large brown boots were entangled with the roots of one of the trees. Every time he took a step, the tree roots appeared to yank on the laces causing him to topple over into the dirt and release a new stream of swear words fit only for the Travelers or trappers. A blue cap lay in the path, and he appeared to be attempting to retrieve it when he hit the ground yet again. As Ru-Lee approached, she saw a branch stealthily dip down and lift the cap just out of reach while the traveler roundly abused the roots of the silver tree that held his laces captive.

Ru-Lee stopped to watch, stifling a giggle herself, as D.G. sat next to her grinning his lopsided grin. The traveler had discovered the cap's position and removed his boots to better achieve the goal of returning the cap to his possession while it bobbed just out of reach. The leaves were outright laughing now, mingling their cacophony with his abuse; the noise was like being surrounded by noisy squirrels and sea gulls.

Finally, Ru-Lee stepped forward onto the trail and began to hum a traveling tune. It began softly, growing into a strong and happy ditty. The roots around her seemed to tap the ground to the tune she hummed, the hat dipped down in front of her and she plucked it from the branch as if it were a ripe fruit. The giggling changed to a hum that blended with her tune. As she reached the traveler, who watched her with a face red with rage, she took him by the elbow, picked up his shoes, and steered him on down the trail without changing her tune. He sputtered a bit at being steered like a child, but allowed himself to be moved along until they broke from the silvery trees and entered a clearing. At the center of this clearing, surrounded by soft purple wild flowers, stood a cabin nearly hidden by its coloring, which blended so well with the forest one could easily have walked past it without noticing.

Ru-Lee stopped just inside the clearing and released the traveler's elbow, dropping his shoes at his feet. D.G. left her side and set off to sniff around the perimeter of the clearing and cabin, apparently making sure all was well and safe. While D.G. did his search for unwanted intruders, Ru-Lee turned to the traveler. Her face crinkled with happiness at the sight of him putting on his shoes, face still red and jaw set with anger from his encounter in the forest of silver trees.

"To what do I owe the joy of your pleasant company, Jace?" she asked, barely able to keep the laughter out of her voice.

# Chapter 3

"Well, it's not to see that infernal forest of yours, that's for sure! You know there isn't anything more infuriating in all these lands, don't you?" He replied as he dusted off his hat and jammed it unceremoniously on top of his blonde head.

"I count on that to deter unwanted visitors. You should know by now that swearing at them only makes it worse for you. They love to get a rise out of people, and animals for that matter. Just last week they were tormenting a squirrel that wandered in there. You ask me, I think they lured it in for fun; had a few nuts they were dangling around while yanking its tail. Poor thing. It finally managed to skitter away scolding the whole time."

"Oh, and I am sure you enjoyed the scene tremendously!"

"I just find it interesting how easily even the animals are bated to frustration. Only a few can get through without getting irate."

"Including me! Blasted ?*?@!! Trees anyway!"

"Now, you know full well that all you have to do is ignore them and hum a bit and they will let you pass in peace."

"Yeah….I'll remember that next time they trip me a dozen times over," Jace replied scowling.

D.G. returned to Ru-Lee and scratched absently at his ear with his hind leg. As the white spider crawled up a renegade hair to the top of the purple cap, Ru-Lee chuckled and said, "I swear, you still look put-out by your 'ordeal'. Come on in and we will get you settled with some of my fabulous cooking!"

"Poison me is more like it! I'll just have a big bowl of those berries you've got there and call it good—I remember your 'fabulous cooking'!"

The color in his face was returning to normal, although his forehead was still creased with frustration.

Together, they walked through the tall purple flowers and grass to the cabin door.

From the small ledge of the upper door sill, a pair of yellow eyes set in a fluffy ball watched their approach with interest.

Ru-Lee seemed not to notice as she raised her hand above the door latch and muttered something under her breath.

"Still using magic to seal things, eh?" Asked Jace.

"I find it useful," she said with a grin.

At that moment, the ball of feathers-with-eyes spread delicate wings and dove for Jace's shoulder.

Jace, startled, jumped sideways, but wasn't fast enough. The feathery puff landed on its target and nipped the edge of Jace's ear.

"Ouch! Pug, you ornery bird! Why do you keep him around, Ru? He's a menace!"

In spite of the harshness of his words, his mouth had twisted into a half smile as he winced from another nip to his ear.

Smiling broadly, Ru-Lee pushed the door open and stepped through.

The inside of the cabin was dimly lit by the light filtering through two windows on one side and one on the opposite wall.

A small stove stood in the far left corner; a bed stood against the wall near it under the single window. Along the back wall stood a neat stack of wood. Different herbs were hung along the wall and in the far rafters drying. Along the short wall near the door and along the wall under the other two windows was a counter with cabinets under and above it. There were various bottles, bowls, pots, and pans stacked on the shelves and the counter. Each bottle was carefully labeled and organized. A small sink with a pump-handled faucet was sunk into the counter near the windows. A small table with stools stood off-center in the room. It was a comfortable space—the scent of drying herbs giving it a safe, earthy feeling.

Jace sat at the table and deftly scratched Pug, the pygmy owl, on top of the head. Pug, for his part, half-closed his eyes and seemed to thoroughly enjoy the attention.

Ru-Lee poured some of the berries into a bowl and placed them in front of Jace. D.G. curled up under the table, eyes shut, appearing to sleep. Ru-Lee knew he would be listening intently to whatever conversation took place above him.

As she sat down next to Jace, arms folded on the table in front of her, the white spider skittered down her back, off the chair and into a corner of the room near the stove.

The door stood open to take advantage of the cool evening breeze wafting through the clearing carrying the scent of the flowers into the cabin.

Ru-Lee eyed Jace as he quietly nibbled at the berries before him. It had been a year since he and his brothers, Davlin and Relmar, had last been here. Jace looked older. There were lines around his eyes that came from traveling long and worrying much. In spite of his apparent ease at the moment and the bright smile he flashed her, she suspected something troublesome weighed on his mind. Unexplained fear passed over her heart as she wondered if Jace's concerns could have anything to do with the dreams she had been having. She fervently hoped not.

# Chapter 4

Jace pushed back his chair licking his lips and fingers of the last drops of berry juice. He sighed contentedly and closed his eyes, a soft smile playing at the corners of his mouth.

Ru-Lee rose to start a fire for tea. She knew Jace would tell her why he had come soon. Sensing his news was not good, she let him enjoy the moment and memories before being forced to return to whatever troubled him.

Once she had set the water to heat on the stove, she returned to the table to find Jace watching her. The smile was gone from his face and concern tugged at the corners of his mouth.

"Have you noticed anything strange the last month or so, Ru?" He asked.

Her face clouded as she thought of the Ergla and the strange shadows she and D.G. had seen earlier in the day. She relayed her account of the day's events to Jace, but did not mention her dreams. She wished to hear what he had to say first so she might have a better idea of what might be happening.

As she spoke, a furrow formed across Jace's forehead. Once she finished he swore softly and let out a low, bear like growl.

Ru-Lee recalled other times she had heard that growl as she ran from a berry patch and a great blonde bear. Jace would often take this form to steal berries when he was younger. Before she knew it was him, she lost a great many berry harvests to that big bear! Despite her current feelings of apprehension, she smiled at the memories.

Turning her mind back to the present, she watched Jace rise and begin to pace the cabin.

"Something is very wrong," he said. "The Erglas are leaving the swamp! What would make them do that? They have been seen as far south as Red Meadows. It's out of character for them to travel so far from their home territory! These shadows are an even bigger mystery. The

Travelers have lost horses to them, or so they say. They haven't seen them taken, but the horses disappear without tracks or trace when the shadows are around. What could they be? And why are they taking horses? For food?... I just don't understand, it feels a bit sinister to me."

Ru-Lee shuddered and gently rubbed the goose bumps that had risen on her arms as she recalled the sense of dread she had felt when the shadows passed overhead earlier in the day. She stood to add wood to the fire in the stove, her mind reeling with the implications of what Jace was saying.

As she stirred the fire, she glanced into the corner and spied the silver webbing that always hung there. In the center sat the white spider watching her. She finished stoking the fire and closed the door to the stove. Addressing the spider, she said, "Well, Sheila, have you any insight to share with us?"

As if in answer to her question, the spider began to shimmer, grow, and change shape to reveal a delicate, petite, female child of about seven years old. In truth, the girl, Sheila, was about 30 years old and young for her species. She was a Mist Elf, so named because of their ability to change shapes like the passing mist. They were not true elves, but a close cousin somewhere between a brownie and an elf. When she spoke, her voice was like the soft tinkling of water in a small pond.

"I have no insight, Ru-Lee, only more questions to add to the pile."

"What questions might those be?" Jace growled. He had never much cared for Sheila, who had come to Ru-Lee shortly after their arrival at the cabin many years prior. Sheila knew of his dislike for her and believed she was being unjustly treated due to his near-death experience with a Trog-Lace Spider before she arrived. Since she had no control over the form her shift took, she felt unfairly judged, and the two had remained at an icy impasse for years.

16

Tossing her flaxen hair over her shoulder, she replied, "One would be to ask where your brothers are? Someone must think something serious is wrong to have sent you here. Or were you planning a visit and just discovered these things along the way? Another would be, does anyone know if the dragons still sleep? I caught a murmur on the wind today that felt like dragon wing."

Jace curled his lip and glared at Sheila. Ru-Lee was sure he wanted Sheila to take her shift form again so he could "accidentally" step on her. It had always been so between them. In the past few years, Jace had taken to ignoring her spider form; the girl-form was more difficult to ignore.

"My brothers and I were with the Travelers a fortnight ago when rumors of Erglas came our way and the shadows began showing up and taking the horses. It was decided that the elves, dragons, and Ru should be contacted. I was sent this direction. We were just South West of the Silver Woods and it seemed to be the least dangerous of the routes. That is also the reason I came alone, it seemed fairly safe. Davlin went with a party of six to the elves; Relmar and six others went to the dragons. To answer your second question, no….no word has been heard for certain regarding the dragons---good or bad."

"Wait a minute," Ru-Lee interjected as the teakettle began to whistle. "I am confused as to why I am being called upon in this. My only connection is to you, Relmar, and Davlin. I am not a Keeper of the lands as the elves and dragons are. Why were you sent to *me*?"

Jace looked at Ru-Lee and furrowed his brow pondering the question. "I don't know for sure, Ru. All I know is they sent me here telling me to find out what I could and to warn you of the possibility of danger. I assumed it was both to keep me out of danger and to truly warn you because of your proximity to the swamp and the Erglas. If they have started to leave their swamp in numbers, you could have real trouble."

Sheila's voice drifted softly to them. "We may have more information soon, another guest comes."

D.G.'s head was already up, ears perked, and nose testing the wind that slipped through the still-open doorway.

Ru-Lee looked at him and ask, "Who, D.G.?"

D.G. made some growly-guttural sounds in response. Ru-Lee smiled. D.G. only did that to indicate one particular person---Nevlon. Even Jace was familiar with the signal. There was often much that passed between Ru-Lee and D.G. that Jace didn't understand, but he knew this signal.

"Well, if Nevlon is coming, you had best make some of those hard discs you call pancakes. You know how he loves them."

Ru-Lee laughed and rose to begin the suggested meal.

# Chapter 5

Before long, the base notes of a traveling tune carried through the woods to the meadow and cabin beyond.

Ru-Lee had added some of the berries to the pancake batter as well as having mixed up some berry syrup for the finished pancakes. The smell filled the cabin and wafted into the meadow invitingly to welcome the new guest.

Soon after the last of the batter was poured into the hot pan, a man of medium height and rough appearance entered the clearing. He wore a wide-brimmed traveling hat unceremoniously pulled down to his bushy eyebrows. A long-handled moustache and full red/blonde beard filled his face and accentuated his sparkling eyes and quick smile. He was stoutly built and strong as an ox with solid legs that could go for days trekking the countryside. This was Nevlon, Ru-Lee's grandfather, advisor, and surrogate parent. He strode through the tall flowers, nose flaring as he caught the scent of the food being prepared. Poking his head playfully into the open doorway, he grinned and said, "Hello there, girl! Can an old man join you, or is this a private party?"

Ru-Lee's grin spread across her face and lit her eyes as she gave him a welcoming bear hug.

"Come and eat! You know you are always welcome here!"

"Hello, Jace! Heard you might be here! Glad you made it safely!" Nevlon said as he patted Jace on the back and took the stool next to him.

"Good to see you again, Nevlon! What brings you this way?" asked Jace, sliding his stool over to make room. He smiled warmly at the newcomer. Although Nevlon was his grandfather as well as Ru-Lee's, Jace hadn't known him until entering this world. The two had bonded instantly, forming a warm and jovial relationship.

"I came to check on Ru-Lee, in part...as for the rest, I would prefer to eat before getting to that," Nevlon replied with a grin.

"Well, then, dig in," put in Ru-Lee as she placed the steaming pancakes and syrup on the table with plates and forks.

"You're welcome to some as well, Jace. I think you will find they are at least edible these days!"

"You know I have to have a couple at least---you put the berries in there!" teased Jace as he heaped a plate full of the fluffy discs.

Ru-Lee ate little during the meal, preferring instead to listen as the two males bantered and shared stories covering the year's time since they had last shared a meal. The information brought by Jace, her own premonitions, and now Nevlon's appearance caused her emotions to be far too stirred up to eat.

Evening had fallen, the kitchen door closed, dishes done, tea steeped, and Nevlon's pipe lit before the three allowed their conversations to return to the reason for the old man's visit.

"Okay, Nevlon...care to tell us exactly what has brought you here?" asked Ru-Lee, refilling Nevlon's teacup. "I am pretty sure it isn't my cooking!"

"Oh, now, you know no one in the land makes pancakes like you do, Ru!" Nevlon Joked as he winked at Jace.

"Yes, I know...most do much better!" Ru-Lee knew her cooking often left much to be desired; it had been a standing joke with the boys.

"I disagree, but you are right. There are other reasons for this visit; more serious reasons. I am sure Jace has informed you of the strange shadows that are snatching the Travelers' horses, right?" asked Nevlon as he glanced at Jace.

Both Jace and Ru-Lee nodded.

"And you are aware that the Erglas are leaving the swamp in some numbers, correct?" he paused as the two nodded again. "Ru, have you had any strange dreams that could give any light to what is happening?"

Ru-Lee hesitated. She hated to give voice to her dreams; it always seemed to make them more real when she did so. She sensed that, in this case, she was going to have no choice. Nevlon seemed to know about them already and was only asking as verification. He had often done this when she was younger. Even when she didn't tell him what she sensed or had seen, he seemed to know.

She took a deep breath, avoided Jace's quizzical gaze, and began to explain what she had seen over the past few months.

Her dreams had been infused with heart-racing fear and winged shadows that consumed and chased. She had sensed a weakening of the defenses of safety and peace. There had been pain, darkness, and terrible evil. She had been unable to discern where the evil came from or what defenses were being challenged. Only that the evil was coming and their world was in peril. In her dreams, she had the feeling that she was supposed to do something to stop the evil, but she had no idea what. She usually woke feeling helpless and confused.

Her eyes had glazed a bit as she relayed her dream experiences to Nevlon and Jace. Now, her body shuddered as she brought herself out of her dream-thoughts.

Jace's blue eyes watched her with concern. He had never liked her dreams; they always seemed to be followed by trouble. Usually the trouble was manageable, but he had the feeling that this time things might be different.

Nevlon took a deep puff on his pipe and stretched his legs out in front of him. He considered Ru-Lee a few moments before slowly turning his gaze to the corner of the room where Sheila sat cross-legged on the bed. She had been there since he arrived, quietly listening and watching. She hadn't eaten with the others, she seldom did. The food she consumed in her spider form sustained even her humanoid form.

"Have you any insight to add, Sheila?" he asked.

"I know only that my spider sisters are troubled," she replied in her melodic voice. "There seems to be a weakening somewhere, as Ru has alluded to. Unfortunately, I am only a half sister. Thus, I am not fully connected to my eight-legged sisters and cannot be exactly sure what is weakening or where." Fixing his gaze with her gray eyes, she said, "I do think, however, that it is time you told us the full measure of why you are here…as well as what all this has to do with Ru-Lee."

Nevlon snorted, a puff of smoke escaping his nostrils causing him to look like a round, hairy dragon. "You sound like a stern governess, Sheila! Very well, I will tell you, but it requires a bit of a history lesson first."

# Chapter 6

Jace and Ru-Lee glanced at each other, then back to Nevlon. It seemed to both of them that they had always been a part of this world, even though they had only lived there for the past nine years. It was odd to be reminded that they didn't yet know everything about it and its history prior to their coming.

Nevlon seemed to understand this and gave them time to settle their thoughts before beginning to speak again. After a few moments and a drink of tea, he began the lesson.

"Many long years ago, the four elemental powers that rule this world were combined as one and kept safe deep within the heart of the earth in a place called the Life Cave. They were guarded by the Trolls and Dwarves, as that is their domain. The two races were allies and worked together to guard the powers.

"As the races developed, the Elves, Dragons, Stone Spiders, Trolls, and Dwarves came together and decided that the powers should be divided among them so that no one race would ever have control over all of the powers at the same time.

"The Trolls wanted none of the great powers or the responsibilities that went with them. They preferred to keep to themselves in their mountains. Likewise, the Dwarves chose not to take on the Elemental Powers and their burdens. The Dwarves' sworn duty to keep the Life Cave safe as well as their love of the treasures hidden deep within the earth was all that they desired. Both races held earthbound magics as their birthrights. These were enough for them.

"As guardians of the Elemental Powers and keepers of the Life Cave, only the Trolls and Dwarves, together, could disperse those powers to the other races. None could hold the Elemental Powers without first being aware of the risks and willing to take on the responsibilities. Second, they must be approved, and blessed, by the guardians before the powers could be bestowed upon them.

"It was decided that the Elves would wield the powers of the waters. Since their gift was to help living things grow and thrive, this power suited them well. The Stone Spiders, being earthbound and having the ability to bind and hold things together were given the powers of the earth. The Harta Dragons were given the powers of fire. This suited their nature; being strong, courageous, and fierce when necessary, they were also wise and patient. This blend of qualities would help them control the unpredictable nature of this power. The Dahgsna Dragons, with their gift for the breath of life and their strength, grace, and love of the skies, were given the powers of the wind.

"These four races became the keepers of the land and had the burdens of the land and its people upon their shoulders. All members of each race had the powers given to their kind to be used for the good of the land and its inhabitants. For many years, the four Keeper races kept the lands safe and peaceful.

"During that time, both Harta and Dahgsna Dragons had the ability to fly. This trait alone they shared. Their differences were many ranging from wing size to temperament. Harta Dragons were strong, fierce, and courageous. This was tempered with deep patience and wisdom. Their bodies were large with bulky muscles, small wings, enormous mouths, jagged fangs, and wickedly sharp claws made for digging deep into the mountains they loved. Dahgsna Dragons were strong and graceful. Their bodies were long with elegant, but short legs, retractable claws, and short snouts that held row upon row of efficient teeth. Their wingspan often spread as wide as their bodies were long. They loved the skies and spent most of their time riding the wind. They held the gift of life-breath and could, if absolutely necessary, return a soul to the world of the living. This was seldom done because of the rules of nature that apply to it....but their gift was often used for healing. Dahgsna tended to be flighty and unpredictable by nature. The two species seldom interbred as their temperaments were very different and they tended to irritate each other.

"There did come a time, however, when a Harta Dragon named Fe-ah and a Dahgsna Dragon named WheeLan mated. During that time, dragons could produce thousands of eggs and offspring. However, many of their young often died. The union between Fe-ah and WheeLan produced a new and dangerous breed of dragons called Warta--nearly all survived.

Warta had the powers of both wind and fire blended within them in a combination for destruction. Their parents' attempts to tame their souls were futile. When the brood reached puberty, they devoured their parents. They plotted and worked to gain control of the other dragons as well as all the land. The Harta and Dahgsna defended themselves from the Warta attacks and a war began that lasted many years. These dragon wars threatened to consume our world.

Elves and Stone Spiders joined forces with Trolls, Dwarves, Harta, and Dahgsna to stop the Warta and restore peace. They combined their gifts and powers in an effort to entrap and contain the Warta. The races were able to bind the Warta to the earth and douse their flames. Unfortunately, they were unable to calm the Warta's fiery hearts. Their thirst for power and mayhem could not be quelled.

"It was decided that the Warta would be banished from our world and sent to the world of man. There, they would be contained in human form, for that was the form most dragons took when they passed through the gateways.

"It was believed that this would prevent the Warta from wreaking havoc and causing pain in the human world. They wouldn't have their powers while in human form. There was hope that this would be enough to keep all around them safe.

"To help prevent this problem from recurring, the leaders of each of the four races that held Elemental Powers, along with the leaders of the Trolls and Dwarves, chose the wisest of their members to act together to protect the races and assist in decision-making for our world. This group became known as the Council of Keepers. It was decided that it was unwise for both remaining races of dragons to fly. If one race of dragons was earthbound, the two would be less likely to mingle and the Warta race would not be born again.

"Since the Dahgsna were keepers of the wind, they retained their ability to fly. To this day, they spend more time in flight than on the ground, keeping to their nests on high cliffs and crags.

"The Harta had always been cave-dwellers and lovers of the treasures deep within the earth flying only as a quicker means to reach a destination. The loss of flight was not a concern to them, so they were bound to the earth. Over time, their wings shrank to the point of nonexistence.

"The gateways were sealed to the Warta, and to all of their offspring, by means of a magical marking upon their souls. This marking emitted an energy that was recognized by the magic protecting the gateways.

"Even though all memory of the Warta birth world was wiped out upon their banishment, their offspring were drawn to find a way back to their ancestral home. They longed always to feel the wind beneath them and the heat of fire spewing from their maw; even without fully realizing what it was that they desired.

"It was hoped that the Warta would mingle and mate with humans, causing a weakening of the fire in their hearts as the bloodline was diluted. To an extent, this has been so, but the strength of that fire was misjudged.

"The Warta, in human form, have been the cause of much suffering and many tragedies in the human world over the years. Their kind were the catalysists for the wars that took your parents, Jace, and forced Ru's mother to bring you all here for protection.

"When those terrible wars threatened to destroy the human world and weaken the gateways, the Council of Keepers decided to seal the gateways completely. This would make it impossible for anyone to pass through."

Nevlon paused, taking a long puff on his pipe. He seemed lost in thought and memory, gray smoke swirling around his head.

"What does that have to do with what is happening now?" Jace asked, leaning forward, elbows on the table.

"I'm coming to that," replied Nevlon, blowing a large smoke ball towards Jace.

"When Ru-Lee's mother, Sophie, left you here, she hoped that the Council would re-open the gateways once the wars ended. This would allow her to come back for you.

"The wars have lasted longer than anyone thought possible. A few of us are still able to connect with the human world and keep watch over events. Things do not look good. The human world is imploding upon itself. The Warta are, again, threatening to bring destruction to our world, though unwittingly at this point.

"In the quest for treasures to fund their war machines, the Warta and humans have been excavating the human side of Mt. Shavla. This is weakening the walls and protections surrounding the Life Cave. If they gain entry there, they will assume dragon form and could, conceivably, gain the powers of wind and fire. Those powers are latent now and unknown to them. In most, they are diluted by years of mating with humans. However, upon their entrance to this realm, some measure of the powers will return as well as the memories of their banished ancestors. The proximity to the Cave of Life will pull the Warta towards the Heart of the Earth hidden deep within. If they reach it, they could become nearly undefeatable.

"The dwarves who guard the Life Cave and the Heart are working to shore up their defenses, but they have asked the Council to send help in case the Warta are able to break through."

Confused, Jace queried, "What has all this to do with the shadows that steal horses and the Erglas leaving their swamp?"

"There is a gateway near the swamp that was, at one time, fairly large—it was called The Arch. That is where the defenses are weakest," continued Nevlon, ignoring Jace's question. "The Keepers were simply unable to make it as strong as the other seals due to its size. It is thought that something has passed through that gateway. Something that is unpleasant enough to drive the Erglas from their home. I leave here in the morning to try to find out if our suspicions are correct and see how we can fix the problem."

Nevlon finished and poured himself another cup of tea. He pondered the tea leaves swirling in his cup giving the others time to digest the information he had given them. Somewhere in the distance a wolf howled and was answered by its brothers.

Jace spoke first asking, "Do the Travelers know of all of this?"

"Some of the Old Ones know the history. However, only those with the gift of Sight are likely to know the rest. That is fairly new information and has not been shared openly yet. The Council has been called to meet in three day's time at Illiand. I hope to have information about the Arch by then and we can decide what to do about both problems."

"Have my brothers reached their destinations safely?"

"Yes. In fact, it was their reports coupled with reports of others that spurred quick action by the Council."

"Why? What did they report?" asked Ru-Lee, rising to pour more tea.

"Davlin and his group met with a large party of Elves who were hunting Ergla. It seems that a few had made their way to the Elven woods and caused some problems by eating a young Unicorn. That is a good way to find yourself at the wrong end of an Elven arrow.

"The Elves had thought there was only one or two rogue Ergla that had wandered too far from home. The information brought by Davlin and the other Travelers set off alarms. The elves have sent a message to the Stone Spiders to find out what they can from them.

"Relmar, it seems, had a bit of excitement on his trip. When they came to the village, Ikna, they found the villagers preparing to attack the Dhagsna. It seems that the shadows had passed that way and taken several animals from their herds. No one saw the animals taken, but since no tracks were left behind, the dragons were the immediate suspects. The people of Ikna have always had an innate distrust of the dragons. This situation does not help matters.

"Apparently it took a lot of convincing, but the villagers finally agreed to hold off their attack until Relmar and the Travelers returned from meetings with both the Harta and the Dhagsna dragons.

"The group split; half climbing the crags of Mount Whahn to the Dhagsna and half continuing on to Mount Lrosya and the caves of the Harta. Of course, Relmar was with the crag-climbing group! You know how he loves that sort of adventure! The two groups agreed to meet at Mount Shavla to share their news with each other as well as the Dwarves and Trolls before reporting to the Council.

"Both groups found the dragons still sleeping; not really surprising since this is the time of year that they tend to rest. Had they not been awakened by the Travelers, they would have slept for another month or so. The Dhagsna have sent out patrols to see if they can spot anything. The Harta will help the Dwarves in the Cave of Life."

"Was Relmar able to calm the villagers and let them know what is happening?" asked Jace.

"Yes. He and some of the Travelers are with them now helping to devise ways to protect their livestock from the shadows and the possibility of wandering Erglas; the rest reported to the Keepers. I was with the Council when the reports came in and was sent out to see what part, if any, the Arch gateway plays in all of this."

"You certainly got here fast!" Interjected Jace.

"Being a shape-shifter has its advantages, as you well know! Travel is much faster in my eagle form, and I am able to get a bird's-eye-view of things as I go," replied Nevlon.

"True," put in Ru-Lee, "but why did you take human form before entering my woods? Wouldn't it have been quicker to fly to the meadow and transform there?"

"Yes, but I enjoy the Silver Woods and desired a stroll through them," he replied with a grin. "There is too little joy in life to miss an opportunity like that."

"Hmph!" Grunted Jace, crossing his arms across his chest. "We do _NOT_ see eye-to-eye on where to find joy!"

"No, we seldom do!" Chuckled Nevlon.

Sheila's soft, melodic voice came to them as she chimed in saying, "Now that we are all up to date, wizard,...."

"Part-time wizard!" Cut in Nevlon as he turned to look at her.

"Fine, part-time wizard. Could you please tell us what part Ru is to play in all of this?"

Ru-Lee had risen to light the lamp that stood on the counter near the sink. At the sound of her name being spoken, she stopped and turned to focus her gaze upon Nevlon.

In the dim light of the candle on the table, Nevlon returned her gaze as if seeing her for the first time. He seemed to be contemplating what to say next.

"Ru," he spoke, his voice low and serious, "please be so kind as to light the lamp...without a flint."

Ru-Lee caught her breath. "But, I haven't done so in ages, on your order!"

"I know. I need to see if you still possess the skill. Please, Ru….?"

"Wait a minute!" Interjected a puzzled Jace. "Only Harta can control fire like that. It isn't even one of the gifts anyone has ever had!"

Still watching Ru-Lee, Nevlon replied, "Ru used to be able to do some small things with fire, Jace. I discouraged her from using this ability and from telling anyone about it."

"Discouraged???!" inquired Ru-Lee, sharply. "More like ordered! You indicated dire consequences if anyone ever found out about it! What changed?"

Nevlon heaved a heavy, exasperated sigh, "Please, Ru---humor an old man?"

Ru-Lee's brows furrowed and her lips drew into a tight line. She had worked hard for many years to control her abilities, on Nevlon's orders. Why did he want her to use them now?? She knew she could still command fire. Although she only used it when she was completely alone, she found it a very useful ability. Briefly, she wondered if Nevlon knew of her use and wanted to confirm it before chastising her. She quickly discarded this thought, though. Her intuition told her there was a much deeper reason for his request, and she wasn't sure she wanted to know what it was.

Turning to the lamp again, she focused her thoughts on the wick and snapped her fingers. Quickly, a small flame sparked to life engulfing the tip of the lamp wick and spreading a warm glow over the counter. She glanced over her shoulder at Jace's dumbfounded look before meeting Nevlon's eyes.

"What other little surprises have you been hiding all of these years?" sputtered Jace with a note of irritation in his voice.

Nevlon answered for her saying, "Jace, our dear Ru has many gifts and powers; some she may not yet know herself. Don't hold our secrecy against us. It was necessary to protect everyone involved."

Jace growled unhappily at this somewhat cryptic answer. He settled deeper on his stool clamping his arms over his chest and furrowing his golden brows as he eyed Nevlon suspiciously. He had never liked surprises and, as the youngest of the group, had always felt out of the information loop. This little demonstration seemed to prove him right regardless of the fact that his brothers didn't know either.

A gust of wind swirled dust near the door into tiny dust devils. "What do you mean, 'gifts she may not know herself', Nevlon?" asked Ru-Lee, feeling anger rise within her chest. "Tell me what is going on and how I am involved!" Ru-Lee's eyes flashed gold, as if tiny sparks were crackling within them. Another gust of wind caused the lamp wick to sputter.

Speaking calmly, Nevlon asked Ru-Lee to sit. She obliged, closing her eyes as she did so and forcing herself to calm down. When she opened her eyes she found that the wind had receded to its out-door realm; all eyes patiently watching her. Looking under the table revealed D.G. also watching expectantly. He thumped his tail at her and licked his muzzle. She grinned a cock-eyed half grin and chuckled slightly.

"Alright, Nevlon," she sighed. "Tell me what I need to know."

## Chapter 7

Darkness filled the meadow outside the cabin. Insect sounds floated on the breeze and bats swooped by the light of the waning moon as Nevlon began his tale for the small group. Pug, still perched upon Jace's shoulder, blinked sleepily as he tried to listen.

"To tell you what you need to know, we must look again at the history of this world and see where it intersects with yours. As I stated earlier, the Warta found mates in the human world and produced children. Their offspring inherited some measure of the Warta powers. These powers remained latent, and would stay that way unless the offspring were to enter our world, something they could not do since the gateways were locked to them.

"Over many generations, the powers became so diluted they were nearly non-existent. Every once in awhile, an offspring would be born who held a strong power for fire or wind, but the bonds of the human world kept those contained. These individuals often found themselves drawn to these certain elements, that is all.

"Offspring born with both wind and fire lived fast, hard, violent lives. They were often the driving forces behind human wars and other acts of violence and discontent. As you can see, even diluted this is a very dangerous mix."

"That explains a few things," grumbled Jace under his breath.

Ignoring him, Nevlon went on, "Now we come to your part, Ru. Far back in your ancestry, we find one of the first Warta. He was named Sha-he, and he took for wife a flaming-haired woman with a fiery temper named Ellana." Behind him, Sheila gasped.

"What!?" Exclaimed Ru-Lee. "You mean I am a Warta?"

"Not exactly," replied Nevlon patiently stirring his tea. "Let me finish."

"Sha-he and Ellana had many children," he continued, "some with wind and some with fire in their blood. Only two had both elements; Rena and Oran. Rena took a war captain for husband whose name has been lost over time. Both were killed in battle, but not before she gave birth to twins, Himshaw and Rahwn. Himshaw had both elements in his blood, and he wed the woman, Neahna, who gave him several children. None of which held both elements. Some had fire, some had wind, and some had neither. One of those with no elements within him was named Daniel.

"All this time, beings passed between the two worlds. As you know, going from one world to the other causes changes. Dragons entering the human world take on human form; humans coming here discover gifts hidden from them or kept latent in their world. For some beings, the human world suppresses their powers, while some humans coming here discover unknown powers. Elves are the least affected by these changes. Being closely related to humans and strongly tied to the earth, they neither change form, nor lose much of their powers.

"During Daniel's time, a female elf named Ahnya passed through the gates. She and Daniel wed and produced two sons, Rohar and Callon. Again, there was no sign of either fire or wind in the boys, but both sons held water powers in their blood. Daniel died of illness and Ahnya returned here with her sons.

"I thought the offspring were marked so they couldn't come through the gates," queried Ru-Lee, confused.

Jace rose to stoke the fire, agitated by what he was hearing.

"It appears that the gateways are not as strongly guarded as was once believed." Answered Nevlon. "We do not know for sure why Ahnya was able to bring her sons through. Most likely it was because they did not hold fire or wind in their blood. It is possible that the Warta bloodline was diluted so much at that point that the gateways were, in essence, tricked into letting them slip through."

"What happened to them when they came through?" Asked Jace as he returned to his seat.

"The eldest, Rohar, discovered he could shape-shift into a Stone Spider. He spent most of his time in this form, eventually falling in love and mating with a Stone Spider named Gretin. Their union produced hundreds of offspring. All held the element of Earth in their blood, but none received wind, fire, or water powers from their parentage. Only a handful could shape-shift. One who could shift to human form was Annelle. She left this world to live with humans. Her husband was a man named Duho. Each of their six offspring had elemental powers in their blood. Some held water, some earth, some fire, some wind. All married humans....a trend that continued for several generations. Each generation saw fewer offspring with any traces of Elemental powers; most had none at all, and none returned to stay in this world.

"It was believed that the powers had disappeared in that arm of the Warta line. That belief was wrong, as seen in you, Ru."

"Are you saying that, because of my ancestry, I am related to the Warta and hold their power for fire?" Ru-Lee asked.

"Yes." Replied Nevlon.

"How can that be? Wouldn't I have been unable to enter the gates if I were marked by the Warta lineage?"

"I am not sure why you were able to slip through, Ru. I know that you had only exhibited your connections to the water powers at the time you passed through the gates. The other Elemental Powers remained hidden. That fact, coupled with your mother's protective spells, may have been enough to allow you through. I simply don't know for sure."

# Chapter 8

Ru-Lee's head was spinning. She closed her eyes to shut out the others so that she could come to grips with this new bit of information about herself.

She had always known she possessed the powers of water and earth. When she was fifteen, she discovered she also held wind powers. These, she found, were nearly impossible to control and seemed to come to life mostly when she was angry. She found she could not truly use them, but had learned to contain them...for the most part. A year or so later, when caught near the swamps in a snow storm with Nevlon, she discovered that she could start a fire by concentrating very hard on bringing a flame to life. She had been thrilled, but Nevlon was far from pleased and forbid her to use this new power saying that it was a matter of life or death. He swore her to secrecy. She had not understood his reaction, but had sensed his urgency and honest fear for her life, so she had promised. She had told no one and had used it only seldom, though even that small use had been more than Nevlon would have approved of.

She had never done more than start a small fire or light a candle or lantern. She didn't know if she could, or even if she wanted to. Fire was a difficult thing to control once it took to life---it always seemed to do as it pleased.

Now she understood Nevlon's caution and concern. Only those in her make-shift family knew she possessed even a small amount of three of the Elemental Powers of this world. Only she and Nevlon had known about the fire element. If the Keepers knew that she possessed all of them, it was quite possible that they would deem her too much of a danger to be allowed to come of age...something that would happen soon.

She knew that, when those born in this world with the Elemental Powers came of age, there were ceremonies and time spent training with the community elders. Individuals were also guided throughout their lives as they learned to use and control their powers. She had received only the small wisdom that Nevlon and his wife, Aylon, had been able to give her over the years.

Most of those who came from the human world to here did not possess any Elemental Powers. Some discovered gifts and abilities that had been hidden from them in their home world, and some gravitated towards magics, as did Nevlon. Only a few with ancestors from this world held any amount of Elemental Powers. Some, over the years, had held more than one power, but Ru-Lee did not know what had happened to them when they came of age. In truth, she had never really given the matter much thought. She had simply assumed that, since she was not born of this world and did not belong to any of the Keeper races, nothing would happen out of the ordinary when she 'came of age'. The information about her ancestry meant that she could be very wrong.

Her thoughts were broken by Jace's voice. He was glaring at Nevlon as he asked, "Nevlon, you said you had been checking on things in the human world--how?"

"I, and a few others, have the ability to leave our bodies and send our spirits into other realms. It is in this manner that I have been able to pass through the gates--they don't block spirits." Nevlon replied with a grin.

Sheila eyed Ru-Lee from across the room as if her friend had suddenly sprouted wings. When she spoke, her voice was barely above a whisper, as if to herself.

"Ru, what will become of you?" she asked.

Ru-Lee opened her eyes in response, and, looking to Nevlon, she replied, "I don't know, Sheila. Do you, Nevlon? What will happen when I 'come of age'?"

"That, my dear Ru, is a mystery. You see, it is rare that someone from the human world comes to our world possessing much, if any, of the Elemental Powers. At least, none that the council is aware of that stayed long enough to come of age here. They usually come as children and return to their families in their home world after a short time. A few come as adults, but are already

37

past the age of concern. Any powers they possessed were minor and posed no problems to themselves or others.

"You and the boys are among only a handful of people who came as children and stayed."

"What happens to members of the Keeper races when they come of age?" Ru asked.

"That depends on their race and power," replied Nevlon rising and walking to the stove to tap the ashes out of his pipe. "Each race is pulled to and into their element. They must learn to master it without allowing it to overtake them. It can be a difficult, dangerous time not only for the individual, but for those around them as well." After tapping his pipe out, Nevlon stirred the coals and added some wood before returning to his seat.

Turning to Ru-Lee, he continued, "You hold four Elemental Powers in your blood. You may struggle with each in turn or all at the same time. However, your lineage being what it is, you may not experience much of a struggle at all. The powers may be diluted enough that you will barely notice a change. I don't know.

"I need to consult with friends regarding this issue, but I need to do so cautiously. I am sure you understand why. If the Council were to find out about you, they would consider you very dangerous. They know of the two elements you showed when you first came, but are unaware of the wind and fire elements. If they knew of either of these, they would guess at your lineage and you would not be safe.

"It is because they, and the Travelers, know of some of your powers that Jace was sent here. The Traveler's seer has predicted that you have an important roll to play in the upcoming events. She says no more than that, but they wished to make sure of your safety."

## Chapter 9

Ru-Lee lay awake most of the night. She had given her bed to Nevlon and rolled out bedding on the floor near the stove for both herself and Jace. Sheila, returned to the form of a silver-white spider, had settled onto her web while Pug burrowed in under Jace's chin, glad to have him back in the cabin. D.G., curled into a ball in the middle of Ru-Lee's back, snored contentedly.

The hard floor caused Ru-Lee to toss and turn. Regretting having dismantled the bunk beds when the boys left, she decided to re-assemble them so she would have 'guest quarters' in the future.

The night had been half over by the time they all settled in to sleep. So much had come to light in such a small amount of time—Ru-Lee was amazed that the others could rest...she could not. When she did doze off, she slept fitfully, her mind filled with ominous dreams and drifting shadows.

As the pale glow of morning began to fill the sky, she gave up the struggle, slipped on her boots and softly stepped outside. Into her outstretched shirt, she gathered fragrant, dew-filled blossoms from the flowers around her cabin. This was the best time to harvest them, their petals still heavy with dew. These ones were best in a gentle tea, but could be used to cure headaches or cleanse the skin. She brought them into the cabin and spread them on a cloth near the sink to dry.

Sensing she was being watched, Ru-Lee turned to meet Nevlon's gaze. Without speaking, he rose and walked outside. She followed. He didn't need to say anything; she knew what she needed to do. It had always been this way—they understood each other.

In the midst of the sea of purple flowers, there stood a large boulder; Nevlon headed there. Once he and Ru-Lee were seated upon the cold stone watching the morning unfold, he took her hand and spoke quietly to her.

"Aylon sends her love. She is in Shauntu gathering some herb or other that she needs. It only grows there for a few days out of the year so she could not come to you. Besides, she can't fly, so the trip would have been much too slow," he said, grinning. "I want you to go to her. She will be looking for you. Take Jace, D.G., Pug, and Sheila. Aylon has been figuring out how best to help you when you come into your powers. She has worked with healers and members of the Keeper races over the years in helping others through their 'coming of age' transition. I am sure she will be able to help you as well. Listen to her and be _very_ careful along the way. Avoid contact with others outside of our circle if possible. I don't want anyone to know where you are, understand?"

Ru-Lee swallowed and answered, "Yes, I understand. I will be careful, and I won't use my powers. You don't have to tell me."

He smiled at her and replied, "No, I suppose I don't. As I said last night, the Council will meet in three day's time to decide what course of action to take in light of the information they can gather together. I will be there and will come to you and Aylon as soon as possible."

They rose and Nevlon swept her up in a warm, strong hug.

Nestling into his chest, Ru-Lee breathed in Nevlon's scent. She had always felt safe and protected with him.

"Don't you want food before you leave?" She asked, already knowing the answer.

"No. I need to get moving so I can return sooner. I'll grab something on the fly!" He chuckled. "Be safe!"

Releasing her, he began to shift. His form shimmered and shrank until, in his place, stood a large golden eagle. The eagle cocked his head to one side and blinked at Ru-Lee before spreading his wings into the air.

She watched him disappear into the distance, then returned to the cabin to rouse her friends and pack for their journey.

# Chapter 10

Ru-Lee and Jace packed quickly and efficiently. Ru-Lee had a store of dried cakes, meats, and fruits that she put in a leather case Nevlon had given her many years earlier. She also filled a bag with smaller pouches of various herbs. She tied this to the belt at her waist along with a skin filled with water and a smaller skin filled with Loushah, a strong drink with excellent healing properties. A short knife joined her tools as well as a small wooden cup attached to her belt with a special loop.

Jace, having lived with the travelers for the past year or so, had become adept at speedy departures. He slipped on his boots, strapped his bag to his shoulder, wrapped his cloak over his back and waited in the meadow with Pug and D.G. while Ru-Lee closed up the cabin.

The morning air had a slight chill as it whispered of the coming cooler seasons. Summer would end all too soon.

They had eaten a quick breakfast of cold left-over pancakes and dried jerky while discussing the route they would take. Ru-Lee had relayed Nevlon's directions to Jace who felt it best to travel to Shaunta by way of Blond-Bear Ridge. The ridge had gotten its name from the blonde-haired bear that used to chase Ru-Lee from the large berry patch that covered most of it. The name had stuck even after it was revealed that Jace was the bear! Ru-Lee agreed to the route, hoping that the Ergla had moved on and wouldn't be a problem.

As her friends waited, Ru-Lee raised her arms and murmured a spell, bringing her hands down to encompass the cabin and meadow in a protective seal. They would be able to leave, but none would be able to enter without knowing the words to allow them in. The spell would nudge the mind of passers-by to avoid this area. Most would pass without even seeing it, a few might see, but 'decide' not to enter.

With Sheila perched on top of her hat, Ru-Lee joined Jace, D.G. and Pug. She began to hum as the group left the meadow for the Silver Forest. The giggling trees swayed with Ru-Lee's tune adding their voices to the melody. Only once or twice did a branch bend low to give Jace a playful shove. It was all he could do to refrain from a nasty retort as he was propelled forwards into his companions. He succeeded in keeping his mouth shut, however, not wanting to have a repeat of the previous day's events. Ru-Lee could sense Sheila's enjoyment of the trees' treatment of Jace and had to suppress a grin herself. She knew Jace did not appreciate the trees' sense of humor, even if she did.

Once through the Silver Forest, they made their way southwest through the pine trees towards the ridge that would drop down into the gully where Ru-Lee had washed her berries the day before. This ridge was known as Eagle Ridge and offered a reprieve from the mosquitoes that plagued them in the marshy lowlands. They decided to stop and eat an early lunch on Eagle Ridge. The vantage from this ridge allowed a being to see for miles around; thus, its name. One did not need the eyes of an eagle when viewing from Eagle Ridge. Jace and Ru-Lee hoped to use this vantage to spot any Ergla that might still be lurking in the area. Ergla tended to dislike high places. The one from the day before had, most likely, been lured up Blonde-Bear Ridge by the scent of the large berry patch that covered most of its top. The scent would have been nearly irresistible.

The midmorning sun had risen high and bright causing Ru-Lee and Jace to shed a few layers as they hiked. Once on top of the ridge, they stood drinking water from their skins and surveyed the area below. D.G. nudged Ru-Lee's leg with his head to get her attention. When she looked down, he smacked his mouth open and shut twice, indicating he wanted some water. She smiled and squirted some into his open mouth.

"Sorry, D.G.," she said with a grin. "I didn't mean to forget about you!"

Licking his lips, D.G. bobbed his muzzle up and down and appeared to grin at her.

"Looks as if you're forgiven--this time," Jace said, chuckling at the interaction between the two. "He's got you trained well, doesn't he!"

"I suppose so!" replied Ru-Lee, still smiling as she returned the water skin to her belt and rubbed D.G.'s ear.

Returning her gaze to the land below them, she said, "I don't see, hear, or smell a thing, do you?"

"No. D.G. doesn't seem to see any cause for concern either," Jace said as he watched D.G. scratch his other ear with his hind foot.

"I guess we can head down, then. I just wish I knew where...," Ru-Lee trailed off, her body going rigid, brows furrowed. She turned her head side-to-side, her eyes quickly scanning over the land below and around them.

"What is it?" asked Jace in alarm.

"Shhh!!" Ru-Lee hissed. Then, slowly, her gaze shifted up to the northeast corner of the sky.

Jace followed her gaze to shadows forming in the distance. They seemed to mass together before beginning to glide in their direction.

When he looked back at Ru-Lee, he found she had gone into a defensive crouch.

"Hide!" she whispered as she grabbed his hand and jerked him beneath a large stone outcropping. D.G. and Pug wedged themselves in also, causing Jace to have a difficult time making sure nothing was poking out and visible. He couldn't see Ru-Lee's face, but he could feel her body taut against his; her heart beating wildly. Neither breathed as the shadows closed in on Eagle Ridge.

The shadows hovered directly above them for a long time blocking the sun and its warmth. Finally, they glided away to the west leaving the small group to tentatively crawl out of hiding.

Jace, Pug, and D.G. were out and stretching the kinks from their joints before Jace realized that Ru-Lee hadn't emerged yet. Peaking beneath the stone, he found Ru-Lee, eyes closed, skin ashen, attempting to slow her heart and breath normally.

"You okay?" He asked.

"I will be," she breathed.

"What was that all about?" he asked, lifting one eyebrow. "It's not like you to panic like that."

"I didn't panic!" she snapped. "If I had, I wouldn't have been able to move. That 'thing'—whatever it is—is looking for something. I didn't think it would be good for it to find us, that's all."

"What do you mean, 'it was looking for something'? What something? And how did you know?" asked Jace, concerned.

The color was returning to Ru-Lee's face as she slowly crawled out, eyes casting about to be sure the shadows were gone. She didn't reply right away causing Jace to snarl and ask, "What is going on, Ru? I don't like secrets, you know that! Tell me what just happened here!"

Apologetically, Ru-Lee replied, "I'll tell you, Jace. I don't mean to be secretive. It's just that I am not sure myself yet—and I would like to get off this ridge before I explain things. I feel very exposed here."

Jace started to snarl something about not moving until he had some answers, but the troubled look on Ru-Lee's face stopped him. "Fine," he grumped. "We'll get down into some cover first, maybe even into the berry patch. Then you spill!"

He turned and led the way down towards the gully with Pug on his shoulder. Ru-Lee followed wordlessly, casting worried glances towards the sky as she went. Sheila dangled a bit of webbing at the back of Ru-Lee's hat, using her senses to gather information as she went. D.G. brought up the rear, testing the wind. Ru-Lee's reaction to the shadows on Eagle Ridge had put them all on edge.

The bubbling sound of Bristle Creek drifted up to them as they neared the gully. Continuing on in silent vigilance, the group eventually waded through the shallow creek and began the ascent up to Blonde-Bear Ridge. Here, among the thick brush, mosquitoes were far fewer than in the pines or the marshy grounds. Flies buzzed past on their own business, butterflies flitted in and out of the filtered sunlight, and the smell of crushed Mountain Berries filled the air.

As they continued on, it became apparent that the Ergla had trampled several berries and plants while it foraged. Ru-Lee could hear Jace growling softly about the wastefulness of some creatures and she grinned in spite of herself. Jace had always been quick to anger and just as quick to forgive. She knew that, when they stopped again, he would no longer be upset with her. However, he would still want some answers. She struggled with what she could tell him. So much of her earlier premonition was not even clear in her own mind. Yet, she had known that they must hide or they would have been in grave danger. She had been filled with fear that nearly rooted her in place and she had barely managed to force herself into action. As they neared the deepest part of the berry patch, she decided to be completely honest with Jace. Maybe he could help her sort this all out.

The berries here were thick and untouched. Apparently, the Ergla had filled up on the lower berries and moved on. The climb was steeper from here to the top, which was also a probable deterrent to the Ergla. At any rate, it was gone and had left enough berries for a lunch.

D.G. had already climbed a bit higher to a flat spot where he could lay down and slurp berries from the low-hung branches. Pug flew from Jace's shoulder to D.G.'s head. Settling in the nest-like tuft of fur there, he began to nibble at some of the higher berries that D.G. was ignoring.

Ru-Lee sniffed the air and said, "At least the Ergla take their stench with them when they go."

"Mmhm," was the only response Jace made as he filled his mouth with a handful of berries. He closed his eyes and chewed slowly, letting the juices glide down his throat, a pleased smile playing upon his lips.

Ru-Lee shook her head—Jace was truly a bear at heart. She gently picked some of the berries and popped them into her mouth. As the flavors burst and blended she could almost understand Jace's bear-like attitude.

Once their bellies were filled, Jace approached Ru-Lee and spoke. "Okay, we're safe, it seems, and we are rested. You want to fill me in on what happened back there?"

Ru-Lee sat on a log watching Pug and D.G. snoozing in the shade of the now-empty berry bushes. She glanced at Jace wondering how to put her feelings into words.

Nibbling on her lower lip, she began; "Those shadows had substance, Jace. They don't always, but these ones did. I don't know what they were, but they were searching for something. The past few times they have passed overhead, a pit would form in my stomach and the hair on my neck would stand on end. I would feel a sense of foreboding, nothing more. This time was different. I was overcome with fear! My instincts told me to take cover, but I was so afraid that I had to force myself to move! I have never felt fear like that."

"Do you have any idea why?" Jace asked, raising an eyebrow.

"No. There was so much anguish and pain filling those shadows, Jace! I don't understand it, but my gut tells me I can't be out in the open when those shadows are around."

"And you haven't felt this way with the other shadows?"

"Not really—I have felt dread and foreboding; that sort of thing, but no threat to me personally. The shadows

46

we saw today were different somehow—stronger; almost malevolent."

"Well, then, I guess we should move out so we can get to Shauntu before they show up again," Jace said, shouldering his pack as he rose.

He let out a small, chirp-like whistle as he moved, causing Pug to open his eyes. The small bird lifted his wings and quickly flew to Jace's shoulder. D.G., feeling the shift in weight from the top of his head woke and slowly stretched.

"Come on, D.G.—Aylon will become impatient if we don't show up on time," Ru-Lee sighed. She adjusted the purple cap on her head, careful not to squish Sheila, who rode in the middle of the cap crown.

They made their way down the hillside watching for signs that the Ergla might still be in the area. Occasional signs of the Ergla's passage could be seen, but these were several hours old. They found nothing fresh and, eventually, no signs at all. The Ergla had taken a different direction from theirs, which suited them fine. Remaining watchful, they continued down the northwest side of Blonde-Bear Ridge.

## Chapter 11

The sky glowed amber-orange as the sun began to set on the small group trudging through the brush towards Udah River. Jace had set a steady pace down from Blonde Bear Ridge. Planning to camp on the East bank of the Udah, he was searching for a good site to spend the night. As they walked, he told Ru-Lee of a place he remembered where the trees came down nearly to the river's edge. He was looking for this spot, as it would afford some protection from prying eyes. In keeping with their goal of reaching their destination undetected, they planned to forego fires. However, people on the open river banks were easily seen from a distance so a place that offered some cover would be ideal.

Crossing the river in the morning would allow their clothes to dry as they traveled in the sun. This was preferable to an evening crossing which would mean sleeping in wet undergarments. Both Jace and Ru-Lee had agreed that this was a very unpleasant idea.

Eventually, Jace located the spot he was seeking and ushered his friends into the relative safety of the overhanging boughs. Though physically exhausted, both he and Ru-Lee found the events and information of the past few days swirling around in their heads keeping them awake. They talked in hushed voices deep into the night discussing each bit and trying to uncover the mystery of the shadows and their portent.

Finally, the two drifted off to sleep with their furred and feathered companions nestled against them.

XXX    XXX    XXX    XXX    XXX

As the faint hint of pink tinged the edges of the clouds, the smoothly running waters of the Udah River began to swirl. Gurgling softly the water rose up in a column near the bank where Ru-Lee, Jace, Pug, Sheila, and D.G. slept beneath the trees. Slowly, the light of the coming dawn glinting off its surface, the column began to take the shape of a woman. The features were fluid and held only the colors of the river water, but a woman, nonetheless. She glided towards the shore and stretched forward to peer at the sleeping group. D.G. watched her approach with interest, but no alarm or fear. A slender, watery arm reached out to smooth a strand of hair out of Ru-Lee's face, leaving behind a faint, moist line on her cheek.

Pug, snuggled beneath Jace's chin, popped open his eyes and watched in surprise as the woman-figure smiled at him and gestured for silence with her finger to her lips. As the morning light slid across the sky, the liquid woman diminished and disappeared into the river.

Pug looked quizzically at D.G. as if to ask, 'What was that about?' D.G., cocking his head to one side, grinned his lopsided grin, and closed his eyes. Sheila, still perched on Ru-Lee's hat, had watched the event with confused interest. Like D.G. and Pug, she had felt no fear or concern, but she had no idea what it meant or could have been. Only D.G., it seemed, was in on the secret, and he wasn't sharing.

Pug puffed out his feathers and worked his head back and forth scrunching it down into his fluffed-up body in irritation. He clacked his beak at D.G. who ignored him completely. In frustration, he shivered his feathers and closed one eye, apparently deciding it was best to be watchful.

Sheila smiled as she observed Pug's reaction to D.G.'s indifference. Sometimes the bird was quite entertaining. She settled in atop Ru-Lee's hat to await the full coming of dawn and the sun's warming rays. Jace and Ru-Lee had decided to wait until full-light to cross in hopes that the air might be warm enough to dry them quickly once they emerged on the opposite bank. The smell of the sun on the dawn breeze held the promise that their hopes were well-founded.

## Chapter 12

Early dawn birdsong faded away, replaced by the hum of river-bank insects harmonizing with the song of the river. The sun's warmth penetrated the small band's hiding place causing them to blink, yawn, and stretch their sleep-stiff muscles.

Sheila shot a string of webbing onto a low-hanging branch and quickly crossed over it before Ru-Lee stood up. She crawled to the thickest part of the branch near the trunk and began to shift into human form.

Jace saw her shimmy down the tree trunk as he stood with his back to the river.

"Decided to make the swim across under your own steam?" He snarled at her.

"Yes," she answered, adjusting the large leaves she had linked together for clothing. She didn't usually bother with such things, but Jace's presence brought out the modesty in her. "I decided I would rather swim than try to hang on as you attempted to drown me."

"Hmph!" Was Jace's only reply, as he turned to survey the riverbank. D.G. was already drinking at the water's edge. Pug launched off of Jace's shoulder, diving into the tall brush. He rose a few seconds later with a small, gray mouse in his talons. Flying to a large stone jutting out of the middle of the river, he landed and began his morning feast.

"Thanks, Pug!" Grumbled Ru-Lee as, she bent to splash cool water on her face from the river. "I have officially lost my appetite!"

"That's okay," remarked Jace. "I think it would be best if we waited to eat until we reached the other side anyway. I never liked swimming on a full stomach."

"Sounds good to me. Is there some way to float our things across so they stay dry?"

"Yeah~ There are a couple of small logs lying around," answered Jace, glancing around him at the debris on the riverbank. "I think we can tie them together, lash

50

our stuff to them, then pull them along with us. The current doesn't seem to be too strong here, but the water is pretty deep. I know you can swim longer, but I think I am the stronger swimmer, so I will pull the load."

"I have some rope in my pack," Ru-Lee offered, rummaging through her bag. She soon pulled out a good length of rope and handed it to Jace.

The two worked quickly lashing small logs together and were soon ready to add bundles to their make-shift raft. Sheila brought their packs and helped Ru-Lee tie them down. Once the raft was ready, Jace and Ru-Lee stripped down to their underclothes and poked their clothing beneath the pack lashings on top of the raft. Having grown up together, neither felt any sense of discomfort or self-consciousness as they prepared for their swim, but Ru-Lee did notice that Jace had grown some muscles since she had last seen him.

Jace checked the ropes once more before tying a loop around his chest and entering the cool water. Ripples formed around him as he began to angle towards the opposite shore. Sheila entered next with D.G. close behind. Ru-Lee brought up the rear. She wanted to keep an eye on her friends and be available if anyone had problems. Sheila had many strengths, but swimming was not one of them. D.G. could offer immediate assistance, but Ru-Lee wanted to be ready if more was needed. Pug watched the approach of his companions from his mid-stream perch ready to give the alarm if anyone showed signs of distress.

The initial plunge into the frigid waters of the Udah River caused Ru-Lee to catch her breath. Her body quickly acclimated to the temperature, however, and she found the swim calming to her frazzled nerves. As she glided through the water, she noticed the fish and other creatures that shared the river with her. She felt her spirits lift to a nearly giddy level when she saw some otters playing just beneath her. Without realizing she had dived, she found herself beneath the surface joining the otters in their twisting, twirling play. They, for their part, didn't seem to notice her at all as she danced with them in the current. She felt so free and happy here beneath the water that it was several minutes before she realized she didn't seem to be holding her breath. Slowly, a sense of confused amazement crept into her mind. Twisting onto her back, she stretched her arms out in front of her and was alarmed to see that they were translucent! Startled, she darted towards the surface for a better look hoping that what she saw was just a trick of the underwater lighting. Water showered away from her head and shoulders as she shot up from below, but she didn't stop there. Before she knew it, her entire body was rising above the river held in a plumed column of swirling froth.

"Yikes!" She yelped, thrusting her arms out to her sides. This movement slowed her upward momentum until she held level.

Heart pounding, she looked around for her friends as she tried to figure out what was happening. She heard Pug's screeched alarm sounding loudly and found he was circling the water's edge on the opposite shore a little ways upstream, eying her suspiciously. Her playful interlude with the otters had carried her farther downstream than she thought should have been possible. She could see Jace dragging the raft out of the water and D.G. assisting an exhausted Sheila to the shore.

D.G. looked around for her, letting out a sharp bark when he saw her high above the river. She was wrestling with a strong feeling of panic as she came to grips with the fact that she was suspended by a column of water thirty feet in the air. D.G.'s bark caught her attention, drawing her out of her panic. She closed her eyes and allowed his calmer mind to enter hers. She sensed him willing her to be still and knew that she must do so if she wanted to get out of her current predicament. Taking several deep breaths, she focused on forcing herself back down into the main body of the river. The column of water slowly receded and she found herself safely returned to the Udah River. Without hesitation, she made for shore.

Jace had spied her by this time and ran to meet her as she dragged herself from the water, suddenly drained of energy. Still several feet away, he came to a sudden halt, his mouth hanging open.

"What happened?!" He sputtered.

Looking down at herself, Ru-Lee realized she was completely translucent. This was definitely strange! "I …..I don't know," she whispered.

"Are you solid?" Jace asked, his eyes nearly bugging out.

Flexing her water-clear hands, she placed them on her stomach. Closing her eyes, she felt her ribs and realized she was indeed solid. The flip-flopping of her stomach was, most likely, _not_ fish, as she had begun to imagine.

"Yes, I'm solid,' she assured him.

Sheila joined Jace, flanked by D.G.. Pug circled down slowly to them, landing on top of Jace's head, and eyeing Ru-Lee quizzically. Sheila had been adjusting her leaves again, not yet aware of her friend's condition. When she caught sight of Ru-Lee, her eyes popped wide.

After a moment of stupefied silence, she asked, "Do you think this is a symptom of your water powers beginning to come through, Ru?"

"Maybe," Ru-Lee mused.

"Hey! You are starting to look normal where the sun has dried you off, Ru!" Jace blurted out in surprise.

"I like the look," Sheila noted, smiling. "It is quite pretty."

Looking at herself again, Ru-Lee realized that Jace was correct; wherever the sun had dried her, she looked normal~ where she was still wet, she was translucent.

"Thanks, Sheila," she replied, "but it is pretty weird."

Pug clacked his beak and looked accusingly at D.G.

"What's your problem, Pug?" Jace asked.

Sheila looked from Pug to D.G. curiously for a moment, catching her breath as she suddenly remembered the water lady from earlier that morning.

Jace, noticing the exchange, glared at her and snapped, "What? Do you know something about this, Sheila?"

Sheila told Ru-Lee and Jace what she had witnessed in the pre-dawn light, relaying Pug and D.G.'s reactions as well as her own impressions of the event.

"I don't know what it means, but it does seem related, doesn't it?"

"Yes, it does---touched by a 'water-woman' while sleeping, huh? Not good, Ru," stated Jace, irritated.

"Yeah, like I had any say in it!" Ru-Lee groused. "Why didn't you mention this earlier, Sheila?"

Sheila shrugged and replied in her sweet, melodic voice, "Slipped my mind, I guess."

"Convenient," growled Jace.

"Stop it!" Snapped Ru-Lee. "It doesn't matter now."

Looking down at herself, she found that she was nearly back to normal.

"Well, at least it doesn't seem to last long. The weird thing is, I felt so at home in the water, like I could stay there forever. If I hadn't noticed I was see-through, I probably would still be there."

"You were clear as water, and the only thing you find weird is that it felt good??? *You* are weird, Ru!" exclaimed Jace.

"I think we need to move on, no matter what we find strange. I think we need to tell Aylon and see if she has any idea of what is happening," Sheila said. Her voice had a calming effect on both Ru-Lee and Jace.

"Stop that!" Jace barked.

"Stop what?" chimed Sheila innocently. "You know I can't help the effect my voice has; it is innate and subconscious."

"Yeah, sure it is," Jace retorted, but he let it go. This was an argument the two had repeated many times and he never got anywhere with his end of it.

Sheila's voice sometimes had a calming effect when those around her were distraught. It was truly not something she could control; it was just part of who she was. Jace, however, felt that she had some control over it and he resented it every time he felt the effects~ even to the point of fighting it. Ru-Lee believed he fought it mostly because of his dislike for Sheila, but she knew better than to try to talk sense to him where Sheila was concerned.

During this exchange, D.G. wandered over to Ru-Lee. He sniffed curiously at her feet, still somewhat clear, and at the water that had followed Ru-Lee onto the riverbank. No one else noticed how it trailed after, reluctant to release Ru-Lee from its grasp.

As the group moved off towards the small raft, dry clothes, and food, the wayward tendrils of river could be observed retreating into the current.

# Chapter 13

Two spotted fawns romped in the large field of tall grasses and wildflowers that lined the bank of the Udah River. Their tawny-coated mother, grazing vigilantly nearby, flicked her ears to fend off the flies that hummed about her head. She was alert and aware of the visitors near the water, watching them warily. When D.G. ventured, nose down, into the grass' edge, she stopped eating and stomped for her young to come closer. As the grasses waved in the breeze, she picked up D.G.'s scent, raised her tail, and loped off into a close stand of trees, her spotted miniatures dashing after her.

Pug's shadow could be seen gliding across the flora as he hunted for small rodents to fill his stomach. Jace, Ru-Lee, and Sheila followed D.G. into the rolling sea of plants, headed towards the trees the deer had disappeared into. Each member seemed lost in their own thoughts. Jace, leading the way, was distracted from his usual vigilance by the events in the river as he tried to puzzle through what was happening to his cousin. Sheila, having chosen to remain in human form, was enjoying the sun's warmth on her silvery hair and the feel of the breeze tickling her skin. As a spider, she seldom gave such things much notice. This was such a nice change for her that it brought a blissful smile to her lips. Since transformations were a part of her everyday existence, she wasn't concerned about Ru-Lee's "water changes." Her only thought was that it might be nice to have some water-powers of her own that could help her swim better. She giggled a little at the thought of riding the waves and ripples of the Udah River in her spider form, commanding the waters as she went.

Ru-Lee walked behind her friends trailing her hands across the tops of the grasses and flowers. She noticed with interest the way they tickled her fingertips, and marveled at the fact that, not long before, she would have been able to see the grass through her palms. She wished she understood what had happened in the river. What did the "water woman" have to do with her transformation? She had known from a very early age that she held water powers. As a child, she had delighted in using those powers to create mini fountains in various puddles and pools, as well as in her bathwater. Knowing she had some amount of control over water, she had always felt safe in or near it. However, she had never *become* part of the water. She was sure that was exactly what had happened, and she longed to talk to Nevlon about it. Maybe Aylon would know if this had anything to do with the coming of age process.

Sighing, she raised her eyes from the grasses and blossoms around her to the tree line ahead. What she saw caused her to stop and catch her breath. An enormous feline figure was emerging from the forest edge.

The large cougar moved slowly, but without caution or concern~as if it was traveling a well-known trail in a safe area. It had neither seen nor smelled them yet. The wind was in their favor.

Sheila, having heard Ru-Lee's sharp intake of breath, looked up quickly but found she could see nothing over the tops of the ocean of plants that surrounded her. Swiftly changing form, she scrambled up to Ru-Lee's hat for a better view, discarding her clothing-leaves as she went.

Jace, the breeze in his face, came to a halt as he caught wind of the big cat. Looking up, he spotted it immediately. It was still near the tree line, not yet in the grasses where it would be nearly impossible to see. Jace's mind raced. Where was D.G.? He couldn't see Pug either. A glance behind showed Ru-Lee rooted in place, holding her breath. He would have to act fast, before the cat realized they were there. It was probably on its way to the river for a drink after a night of hunting. He needed to make sure it didn't get another meal on its way to water.

He dropped to the ground amidst the plants. Shifting shape as he went, he shrugged off his pack and clothing.

Jace's crouched form grew to a hulking size, sprouting yellow-blonde fur all over. His face grew a snout with a mouth full of razor-sharp teeth; hands and feet formed into huge paws ending in four-inch long, vicious claws; small, round ears sprouted from his now-furry head, cocking forward as they checked for sounds of the feline ahead of him.

Shaking his now very bear-shaped head, he sat back on his haunches and looked over his shoulder to check on Ru-Lee. Finding her nowhere in sight, he grunted and hoped she had the good sense to stay put.

Assured that Ru-Lee was out of the line of attack, (and not the least bit worried about Sheila), Jace, the bear, sniffed the wind. Cougar scent filled his sensitive nostrils. With a loud snort and a growl, he rose up on his hind legs to face his foe.

As the shortest member of his family, Jace always reveled in his size when in bear form. He truly was huge! The cougar looked small and frightened as it crouched low to the ground glaring at him in surprise. Even so, Jace knew he must be careful. This cat was large in its own right, and experience had taught him that its kind were both strong and quick. He was hoping he could scare it off without the need for a fight. The thought of those sharp claws and the deep scratches they could leave brought up some unpleasant memories of his last tussle with a young mountain lion several years earlier. He bore the scars of that lion's claws across his rear-end. It was definitely not a pleasant memory for him. Although Ru-Lee and his brothers had enjoyed a good laugh at his expense, once it was clear he would survive. He shook his head to remove the distracting memory the cougar smell had aroused in his mind, a wry smile on his bear face as he recalled how the others had teased him about his inability to sit down while his hind end healed.

# Chapter 14

When Jace disappeared below the grass-heads, Ru-Lee snapped out of her initial trance and followed suit, quickly guessing what his plan was. She now hunched in the grass listening to the sounds of Jace changing form.

Probing with her mind, she tried to find D.G. She knew he was somewhere ahead of them, and guessed that he, too had become aware of the feline's presence. D.G. had never been able to resist chasing cats regardless of their size or species. She hoped to touch his mind and restrain him before he charged in. When she finally found him, however, she knew she was too late. His thoughts were focused on the cougar as he crept to the edge of the grass.

"D.G., No!" Ru-Lee commanded with her mind, her thoughts loud in her own head.

D.G. ignored her. He was on the hunt. She would have to do something more drastic if she was going to stop him.

Placing her hands, fingers splayed, firmly on the ground by her knees, Ru-Lee began to call forth the powers of the earth. She focused her thoughts on the plants near D.G.'s feet, calling forth bindweed vines and commanding them to wrap around his paws. The energy of growing things pulsed in the earth and she directed it towards D.G.'s paws.

The vines had just begun to respond to her when her concentration was broken by a flurry of small clawed and furry creatures bombarding her chest and head. She felt restraints being wrapped around her torso and was pulled over sideways, landing with a thud. Her hat flew off her head, sending Sheila into the grass stalks.

Ru-Lee struggled against her bonds, twisting her head in an effort to see her attacker~or attackers, as it seemed to be. She could hear war whoops, growled orders, and other military-like sounds, which seemed very small and low to the ground.

Her hands were bound and she was forced on her back. Still unable to locate her assailants, she was beginning to panic when she felt a sudden light pressure on her stomach. This pressure began to move up her body, as if a very light creature were walking up her. Looking down her torso, she saw a very brawny black mouse standing on her chest glaring at her.

"Thickna whatna bianta!" It commanded.

Ru-Lee had no idea what that meant having never spoken to a mouse before.

The mouse repeated his command with more force, "Thickna whatna bianta!"

When no answer was forthcoming from his bemused captive, he raised a very dangerous-looking, small sword, which appeared to have been honed from stone, and yelled something unintelligible. Ru-Lee's chest was immediately swarmed by various sizes of angry-looking black mice brandishing stone swords and spears. They whooped and hollered, bouncing up and down on their captive's chest, then charged towards her throat.

Shutting her eyes tightly, Ru-Lee thought, "Oh, great! Death by militant mice!" She was trying to scrunch her chin to her throat in an effort to protect her jugular when her chest was slammed by what felt like a small explosion. At the same time, she sensed a presence near her head. Small, furry, black bodies flew everywhere and scattered into the shadows of the grass forest surrounding them. All except two~one of which was firmly held captive in Pug's clawed feet, apparently begging for its life. The other dangled by an ear which was pinched in Sheila's delicate fingertips, squealing loudly.

"Shagud!" Sheila commanded her noisy dangler. The tiny creature's eyes widened upon hearing its own language from this strange creature that, only seconds before, he had been about to eat. He appeared completely mystified by this turn of events.

"Okay, you two~quit playing with your food and untie me, please," asked Ru-Lee, with a relieved sigh. "And please don't eat that one while you are on my chest, Pug~mouse guts leave an awful stain."

Pug cocked his head sideways at Ru-Lee and blinked, then spread his wings and hopped, with his whimpering passenger, to the ground beside her. Still holding her prisoner, Sheila picked up a discarded miniscule sword and cut Ru-Lee's bonds.

"Now, what just happened here?" Ru-Lee asked as she sat up, brushing leaves and twigs from her chest.

Pug only blinked at her, but Sheila replied, "We were attacked by Shaooganas."

"Shoegans??" asked Ru-Lee. "What are those?"

"Sha-ooo-ga-nas," Sheila corrected. "They are a particularly fierce, territorial, war-like breed of mice~at least as far as mice can be fierce and war-like. We must have wandered into their territory. Normally, they would have let us pass, given our size and numbers. Your earth powers must have done something that caused them to feel threatened."

"Are you sure that is the only reason they attacked?"

"No, I am only guessing from what I heard and what they asked you."

"What *did* they ask me?"

"They wanted to know what you were doing."

"Oh. Well, ask your little friend there why they attacked. I want to be sure."

"Okay," replied Sheila with a shrug. Turning the mouse to face her, she said, "Okna lou ak mogat ute?"

The reply was squeaked out immediately, "Beyetay nos waaken viers. Nose tula ne oos pleadon?"

Sheila grinned and used her other hand to take hold of the mouse's tail before releasing its ear.

"What?" Asked Ru-Lee.

"Oh, he wanted me to let go of his ear. It was probably hurting."

"Okay. Did he say why they attacked?"

"Yes. Apparently, you woke up the vines. The vines run through their lairs underground and your efforts made them move. This, most likely, scared the mice half to death!" Sheila shook her head and snickered a bit picturing the panic that must have ensued below ground, causing the mice to grow bold enough to attack Ru-Lee.

"Hmm. Tell him I am sorry we frightened them. It was unintentional."

"Meyekna toos mien ta foota oos," Sheila relayed to the mouse.

"Mmhm," came the grunted reply.

Ru-Lee heard a loud crash from the area of the cougar and Jace. Feeling the ground vibrate beneath her, she hoped the cause was Jace moving, and not falling.

Hearing Pug's warning screech, she jerked her head in his direction to find him standing on one foot while holding his hostage out in front of him in the claws of his other foot menacingly. She immediately saw the cause~at least fifty black mice were massed on the ground, advancing towards them.

"Uh-Oh!" Breathed Sheila.

"What now?!" Whispered Ru-Lee in alarm.

Sheila's captive was rapidly speaking to her in his own language.

"Pug has their leader," she said. "If we don't give him back unharmed, we risk a war."

"What?! Seriously?"

"Yes~Seriously. These ones we see are only the 'parlay' troops sent to give us this warning message. We are surrounded and there are millions more in this field alone."

Ru-Lee peered into the brush and found that there were, indeed, thousands of tiny eyes watching her from the ground and up the stalks.

"But, what could they do in a war?"

"Ruin crops, spread disease, spoil food stores.....they can cause a great deal of devastation," replied Sheila matter-of-factly.

"Okay~Pug, give them their leader," Ru-Lee ordered shaking her head.

Pug spun his head around and looked at Ru-Lee as if she had lost her mind. Mice were food, not a thing to be bargained with. He blinked one eye at her, then the other, contemplating her sanity.

"You heard Sheila. Has she ever been wrong before? Come on. Do it, nicely, or I will tie your ankle to Jace's wrist for the remainder of our journey!"

Pug clacked his beak, screeched, and spread his wings in protest as he lifted off without the mouse who fell forward face first, unmoving.

"Oh, good grief! He killed it already!" Moaned Ru-Lee.

"No, look," said Sheila, pointing.

As Ru-Lee and Sheila watched, the mouse leader slowly began to breathe deeply, gingerly picking himself up.

"He was playing dead," grinned Sheila. "A very useful ruse for rodents."

Ru-Lee looked up at Pug circling above her head.

"You are soooo lucky!" She told him quietly.

The leader looked at Ru-Lee, Sheila, and Pug. Noticing his fellow captive, now sitting on Sheila's palm, he began speaking. The two mice exchanged words, which ended with the leader walking off with his subjects. The masses of mice melted into the grasses and weeds, leaving the lone mouse with Sheila.

"What's up now?" Asked Ru-Lee, eyeing the mouse Sheila held.

A bemused Sheila replied, "He says his name is Hafart (Ha-fart), of the River Field, Once-Favored Brother of the Ruler, Ute. He thinks I am some sort of god and feels he is duty-bound to escort me safely to the edge of the grasses because I didn't kill him. It is, apparently, a matter of honor."

"What exactly happened with you two?" Ru-Lee asked, dusting herself off to hide her consternation.

"He tried to eat me," replied Sheila casually.

In response to Ru-Lee's puzzled look, she explained, "When you fell, your hat was knocked off and I went flying. I grabbed a flower stem. Hafart was up there as a scout. Seeing me, he thought I would make a good snack and grabbed my front leg. Just as he was about to pop me in his mouth, I shifted shape, grabbing his ear with my other front leg—or rather, my hand--as I went. It must have been rather traumatizing for him!"

"Yeah, sounds like it," chuckled Ru-Lee. Looking up, she asked, "What's going on ahead, Pug?"

"Um, Ru, I think we should move~quickly!" Sheila warned, sniffing the air.

"Why? What's coming?"

"Ergla!" Sneered Sheila, as both she and Hafart covered their noses.

At that moment, the scent also reached Ru-Lee. 'Oh, No!' she thought, covering her face. 'What's going on with Jace?'

Pug had flown off in Jace's direction. Hoping the small bird would be able to help her cousin, she began to crawl through the tall plants, following Sheila and Hafart as they angled towards the trees away from the Ergla.

# Chapter 15

Jace reared high, extending his body to its fullest height. He pawed the air in front of him, and roared loudly at the cougar hoping to intimidate it.

Tail twitching, ears flat to its head, the big cat coiled its muscles ready to spring. Focused on each other, neither opponent saw the lightning-fast streak of fur as D.G. charged in, low to the ground, striking the feline full-force in the side. Flying sideways, the big cat slammed its head into a tree trunk and lay motionless. D.G. stood over it, a deep growl rumbling in his throat, teeth bared, hackles rigid along his spine.

Jace still stood high, one paw extended in midair, gaping at the scene before him. As he watched, the cougar's body began to shimmer, changing into that of a young man!

Recognizing him, Jace was about to change form and make sure the man was alright when a new odor drifted his way. D.G., who was nosing the body and whining, raised his head to the wind, curling his lips in a disdainful grimace. The smell was Ergla, and it was coming their way!

Quickly, Jace dropped to all fours and sped to the unconscious man. Using his front legs as arms, he scooped up the downed male and carried him into the grasses, angling away from the direction of the Ergla scent. D.G. followed and lay down near the man as if to protect him.

Jace nodded appreciatively, then turned and made his way back in the direction of his discarded clothing. He planned to stay in bear-form until the Ergla had passed, just in case it posed a threat. Not knowing where Ru-Lee was, he didn't want to take any chances. He had heard a ruckus in the grass, as well as Pug's screeches a few times. He hoped they were alright. He even felt a mild twinge of concern for Sheila.

As he neared where he had hidden his clothes, the Ergla emerged from the tree line. It was quite large—almost the size of a cow—its fur matted and splotchy. Unaware of Jace, the creature snuffled its way to where the fallen man had lain. Lifting its grizzled muzzle into the air, it appeared to be trying to find where this being had gone. Catching the scent, it slowly changed direction and headed towards the position of D.G. and the man.

Jace, still somewhat hidden in the grasses and flowers, stomped his front feet and snorted in an attempt to draw the Ergla's attention without revealing himself. The beast stopped, turned its head, and sniffed. The small-minded creature appeared to process the sounds, but, finding nothing to attach them to, chose to ignore them and continue on its chosen path.

Jace would have to be more blatant if he was to protect his friends. Stepping out of the grass, he growled loudly and pawed at the ground, his long claws scraping deep trenches in front of him.

This got the Ergla's attention. Bears, especially big bears, were one of the few things Erglas tried to avoid. However, this Ergla was quite large, a fact that it seemed to be well aware of as it turned to face Jace.

Knowing Ergla to be extremely slow-moving as well as slow-witted, Jace hoped to use his own speed and claws to convince this smelly creature it had taken on more than it could handle. He earnestly hoped he would not have to use his teeth. The thought of getting his nose that close to something so nasty was very unappetizing to say the least.

Staying low to protect his underside, Jace stalked closer, stomping, growling, grunting, and tearing up the ground as he closed the distance between them. The Ergla snarled at him, baring nearly black fangs and emitting breath that smelled of rotten flesh.

Shaking his head to dispel the cloying odor of death, Jace charged, struck, and danced out of reach before the Ergla was able to react. Jace's claws had raked the side of its neck up to its jaw line. Blood beaded up in the wounds, running down the Ergla's neck and dripping onto the weeds below.

Emboldened by the success of his first strike, Jace repeated the tactic on the Ergla's other side. He barely escaped the Ergla's jaws as they snapped shut just inches from his head. Roaring in pain and anger, the beast charged. Still slightly off balance from his last strike, Jace was bowled over by the Ergla's weight. Instinctively, he curled his body into a tight ball, using the momentum of the attack to carry him a safe distance away towards the woods.

As he attempted to untangle himself, the Ergla charged again, claws extended, fangs bared. This time, it meant to take flesh. Jace, bracing himself for the onslaught, lowered his head, squared his shoulders, closed his eyes, and readied for impact.

The impact never came. Surprised, Jace opened his eyes to find his opponent face-down about two feet in front of him, an Elven arrow in its neck. Swinging around, he searched for the source.

It was too late to try to hide or shift—whoever shot the Ergla obviously could see him as well. He quickly spotted a group of four Elven hunters coming towards him, bows raised, arrows directly aimed at him. Keeping them in his sight, he began to back slowly away in hopes of reaching the tall weeds where he would be somewhat camouflaged. Once there, he could shift, find his clothes, and, with luck, stay hidden until the hunters left. This was assuming, of course, that they went directly back the way they had come.

Jace hoped they wouldn't shoot. Elven hunters rarely missed and their bows and arrows were known to be deadly to even the largest animals. Even dragons could be brought down by one Elven archer, provided that archer knew where to aim.

His heart jumped to his throat as he noticed that the archers had stopped walking. Three had lowered their bows, but the fourth was taking careful aim in his direction.

He wondered what they would think if he dropped to his knees and started to pray! He grinned slightly in spite of himself, briefly picturing his bear form praying. Instead, he chose to turn tail and run!

Just as the enormous bear turned, Trieca (Tri-Ay-ka), one of the hunters, called out to his companion to hold his arrow. There was something familiar about this creature. Although he hadn't seen it in three or four years, it looked remarkably like the shifted shape of an old friend—bigger, maybe, but the same. He signaled for the others to stay back as he walked out of the woods to the edge of the grasses the bear had slipped into. He was quite tall, even for an elf, and was able to see well over the tops of the field. As he watched, the passage of the bear could be marked by the fevered movement of the plants. He noted that the areas of movement suddenly became smaller, confirming his suspicions.

Calling out over the field, he yelled, "Did you lose your clothes again, Jace?"

The movement stopped and the yellow-blonde head of Jace popped up—shoulders bare above the seed heads.

"No—just momentarily discarded. I thought a bear would have better luck against the Ergla than I would."

Laughing, Trieca replied, "Yes, I suppose so. What are you doing here? I thought you were visiting Ru-Lee."

"Is there anything you nosey people don't know?" Snapped Jace, irritated that Trieca would know the nature of his business.

"Not much—where is Ru-Lee?" Pressed Trieca. "I haven't seen her in quite awhile."

"Back at her cabin where I left her, I suppose," Jace replied as he continued towards his clothing. "I needed to visit Aylon before heading back. She has some herbs I can't get near the Red Meadows. What are you doing here?"

"Hunting Ergla. They have been causing some problems. This one was trailing a young cougar. Did you see it?" Trieca walked along the edge of the grasses, parallel to Jace's course as he talked.

"No," lied Jace. He had found his clothing and bent to slip on his pants and hide his face from Trieca.

"You should be more careful, Jace. Cougars are dangerous and so are Ergla. What made you try to fight this one?"

"I was feeling tough," Jace replied with a grin as he gathered his things and headed out of the field. "It isn't every day I get the chance to wrestle an Ergla."

"Tough, or stupid? You always were a little crazy!" Responded Trieca. "Are you sure Ru-Lee didn't follow along?"

"Yes, I'm quite sure. She much prefers her little protected valley to the rest of the world. Why?"

"Nothing, I suppose. It's just that, we all thought we felt the earth magic in this area awaken a bit. It was brief and could have been our imagination, I guess."

"Yeah~probably was," replied Jace, covering his surprise and wondering what would have caused Ru-Lee to use her powers.

Changing the subject, he asked, "Are you hanging around, or headed back?"

"Headed back. We need to report what we've seen and that this Ergla has been eliminated. We haven't seen any others in the past few days. Would you like to travel with us a ways?"

"No, thanks. I think I may swing back to the river to fish a bit before going on. Fighting always makes me hungry."

"Really? Where is your fishing equipment?"

"I don't need any, remember? A bear does fine on its own," Jace parried as he walked out of the grass to join Trieca. Dropping his pack, he finished dressing.

"Ah," nodded Trieca, assessing his old friend. "I will bid you farewell, then. Take care of yourself and be safe."

69

As Trieca turned to go, Jace asked, "Are you going to do something with the carcass?"

"Like what? The crows are already circling—it won't last long."

Looking up, Jace saw that Trieca was right. A large number of crows had begun to circle above, spiraling slowly towards the carcass.

"Thanks for your help with the Ergla. I think I would have won, but it might have been a bit painful. Tell your friends I appreciate the assistance," Jace said, gesturing towards the three hunters waiting patiently just inside the trees.

"No problem. We were after the Ergla anyway. You're just lucky I recognized you, or you would have been next! You shouldn't make a habit of battling large, dangerous animals for fun. I won't always be there to save your hairy butt!" Laughed Trieca as he slapped Jace on the back.

Jace smiled, remembering another time Trieca had saved him. He was thankful that it had been Trieca's party to stumble upon them. He knew his friend did not fully believe his story, and that Trieca would set a watch on him for awhile. He would have to be careful not to meet this or any other Elven hunting parties between here and Shauntu. Not everyone would be so willing to let things go.

# Chapter 16

Jace returned to the field.   He meandered back towards the river, retracing his previous steps through the sea of plants.  Bent stalks and trampled weeds guided him until he reached a spot that was smashed down in a much wider area than the rest of the trail.  It was as if someone had lain down and rolled around.  Bending, he picked up a small, toy-like spear and eyed it curiously.  He had hoped to find Ru-Lee near here.  This odd discovery, coupled with the compressed area in which he now stood, raised several concerned alarms in his mind.  A familiar brush of wing-tip on his head broke his train of thought.  Pug, who had been watching and listening from a safe distance above, landed softly on his shoulder.

"Do you know what happened here?"  Jace asked his feathered friend.

In response, Pug stretched his body to its fullest height (not very impressive), spread his wings, and bobbed his head quickly up and down.

"Okay then~where are they?"

Pug launched into the air in the same general direction as D.G. and the traveler.  Jace glanced over his shoulder at the woods, and wondered if the Elves were still watching.  If they were, and he shifted shape now, they might think he was preparing to fish and they would head out.  It was worth a try.

Stripping for the second time that morning, Jace shifted to bear form and trundled towards the river.  He reached the edge of the grasses in no time and checked Pug's position in the sky.

Pug, who had circled around and followed him, now wheeled back in what Jace hoped was the direction of Ru-Lee.  Walking a few feet down stream along the shoreline, Jace shifted again and re-entered the field, careful not to disturb the surrounding plants more than necessary.  Angling back through the itchy tendrils and stalks to his clothing, he redressed and hoped he would not have to get naked again soon. He stayed low, following the barely-visible trail that led away from the crushed area, being sure to keep Pug in his sight as he made his way slowly towards his companions.

It was close to midday when Jace came upon Ru-Lee and Sheila, half dozing, back-to-back. In Sheila's lap, a black mouse sat, as if keeping watch. When Jace poked his head through the brush and tapped Ru-Lee on the shoulder, the mouse, squeaking in alarm, jumped up and drew a miniscule sword.

Instantly alert, and finding the cause of alarm to be Jace, Sheila spoke rapidly and calmly, using the mouse's language. Ru-Lee shook her head, as she had many times since their little black fur ball had joined them. Jace, for his part, sat back on his heals and blinked in surprise. He had never before seen anything quite so strange to him as what he now witnessed, and he had seen quite a few of strange things.

Turning to Ru-Lee, he asked, "What is that all about?"

Ru-Lee sighed and answered, "Apparently, Sheila spared his life and he feels honor-bound to escort us safely out of this field."

"Really? Where did you find him?"

"He was with a band of others like him. Sheila says they are called Shaooganas. They attacked us."

"What?? Why?" Exclaimed Jace in surprise.

"Oh, I stirred up some vines in their lairs. I didn't mean to!" Ru-Lee replied. Catching Jace's startled look, she explained "I was trying to stop D.G. from going after that cougar, but I wasn't close enough to grab him, so I tried to use the vines to do it. The mice got frightened and attacked. Pug helped us escape by capturing their leader. He had to give back his prisoner, however, to prevent a war." Glancing up at the still-circling owl she added, "I think he is still kind of mad about that."

Jace stared at her a moment before asking, "A war? With who?"

"Oh, the mice. They were threatening war if their leader was harmed."

"Really?" Jace replied in disbelief.

"Yes, really," came Ru-Lee's irritated response. "We were surrounded. According to Sheila, the devastation the mouse population could have caused for humans would have been significant."

Smirking, Jace stifled a chuckle. "Okay, now I've heard everything! Attack mice, mouse wars! Who'd have guessed! And all of this in such a short amount of time!"

"Whatever!" Snorted Ru-Lee. "Scoff if you want. What happened with you and the cougar?"

As they sat huddled amongst the flower stems, Jace quickly related the details of the cougar battle, the Ergla's arrival and death, and the encounter with the Elven hunters and Trieca.

"Wow! You were lucky Trieca was there," breathed Ru-Lee. Her heart had skipped a beat when Jace had spoken of the hunter aiming an arrow at him. Jace was like a brother to her, and the thought of him in harm's way upset her deeply.

"I know," Jace grinned, bringing his legs out from under his body and crossing them in front of him for a more comfortable seat. "It bothers me that he knew so much about where I had been, though. It feels like I have been watched for awhile and that makes me uneasy."

"I know what you mean," answered Ru-Lee thoughtfully nibbling on her bottom lip.

"I hate to interrupt, but shouldn't we check on 'cougar-boy'?" Sheila inquired, still holding the mouse in her lap.

"Oh, yeah! I almost forgot about that!" Jace exclaimed. "He should be close. Ru, can you connect with D.G. to find them so we aren't wandering blind?"

"Sure," replied Ru-Lee closing her eyes. Focusing her thoughts, she breathed deeply and reached out with her mind to D.G.'s. Her eyes suddenly flew open and she glared accusingly at Jace.

"When did this happen?  Why didn't you say something earlier?" She demanded.

"I don't know when it happened!  And I didn't tell you because I forgot.  I was a bit busy, you know!" Jace snapped defensively.

"Fine," growled Ru-Lee.  "They're straight ahead. Let's go."

As the group began to crawl ahead through the grasses, Sheila shrugged, looked at Ha-Fart, and remarked, "I think we missed something."

The mouse grunted a reply and scrambled up to her shoulder.

# Chapter 17

A lone bull elk walked cautiously out of the woods. His coat glistened in the sun as he sniffed the still, midday air. Apparently deciding it was safe, he crossed into the field and slowly began to graze his way towards the river, unseen by the small group moving just inside the edge of the grasses.

The heat of the sun caused sweat to trickle down into Ru-Lee's eyes as she crawled towards the spot where D.G. lay with the downed man. She fumed, her mind filled with questions; questions that may go unanswered if 'he' was hurt too badly to respond.

She felt a small measure of relief upon seeing D.G.'s tail softly thumping the ground in front of her—at least D.G. did not seem too concerned. She was about to break through to the unconscious man and D.G. when Jace's order of "Wait, Ru!" brought her up short.

"What?" She snapped, sitting back on her heals.

"I think it would be best if you let me go first to cover up certain….ah…areas—okay?" Jace asked, blushing.

"Why? …. Oh, yeah. That would be good," chuckled Ru-Lee, as she nodded and moved over a bit for Jace to get past.

Sheila, who had retrieved her own leaf-clothing after their encounter with the Shaooganas, cocked her head at this comment, puzzled.

Jace jostled past Ru-Lee, fishing his cloak from his bag as he went. Not wanting to chance being spotted by any elves who might still be watching, he continued to stay low.

Sheila, Ru-Lee, and Ha-Fart waited patiently until Jace whistled for them to come forward. Parting the thick stalks revealed the inert form of a strong, slim young man with thick dark hair---Davlin. D.G. lay protectively by his side, tail softly beating the ground as it spun in gentle circles. Sheila let out a startled "Oh!" as she peered over Ru-Lee's shoulder.

"How…? When…?" She stuttered, glancing at Ru-Lee.

"I don't know," shrugged Ru-Lee, irritated by that fact.

Sheila, with Ha-Fart still seated on her shoulder, crawled carefully past Davlin's head to kneel on his opposite side, a look of concern on her face. Ha-Fart watched the humans with cautious curiosity.

Gently slipping her hand beneath Davlin's head, Ru-Lee felt for injuries and found a large spongy knot on the back of his skull. Marveling at the fact that there was no bleeding , she recalled that Davlin had always had a hard head; this time, it may prove to be a good thing. Since the knot protruded outward, she thought there might be no internal brain damage or hemorrhaging.

Pug glided down to perch on Jace's head as Ru-Lee untied the smaller pouch from her belt, removed the cork, and lifted Davlin's head to trickle a small amount of its dark liquid through his lips. Under D.G.'s amber gaze, she gently lowered Davlin's head, and massaged his throat to encourage him to swallow.

There was an immediate response of "Unh!" from Davlin as he groaned and rolled his head from side-to-side, as if trying to rid himself of something unpleasant.

Ha-Fart looked quizzically at Ru-Lee.

"Loushah," offered Ru-Lee in response. "It's strong and not particularly tasty. It also tends to burn all the way down," she grinned, "but its healing properties are unmatched. He'll come around quickly now."

Davlin began to cough and sputter his way to consciousness as the Loushah burned through him. Blinking rapidly, he looked around in confusion at the small cluster of faces.

"Uhh----what happened?" He asked, closing his eyes again.

D.G., who had lain still until now, suddenly grinned and happily thrust his cold nose deep into Davlin's ear.

"Yikes!" Yelped Davlin, jerking sideways and bringing his hand up to cover his ear.

"Good one, D.G.!" Laughed Jace, sitting back on his heals near Ru-Lee.

"Umh! Don't encourage him!" Growled Davlin, attempting to sit up.

"Careful," cautioned Ru-Lee, reaching to support his shoulders. "You took a nasty blow to the head."

"What happened?" Davlin asked again, closing his eyes and reaching up to rub the back of his head. "Feels like I was kicked by a horse.

"Yeah---you can blame D.G. for that, too—although it could have been worse," interjected Jace.

"Shhh! Not so loud, Jace!" Put in Sheila nervously as she slipped around behind Davlin to lean her back against his as support.

The group had kept their voices low and hushed as they crawled through the flowers and grasses in an effort to remain undetected. Their relief at Davlin's apparent recovery had caused them to be less cautious.

Jace glared at Sheila, but held his tongue. Ru-Lee, watching the two, wondered how long his silence would last.

"Um—Jace?" Davlin said, tentatively.

"Yeah?" Growled Jace, still shooting daggers at Sheila.

"You got an extra pair of pants in your bag?" Davlin asked, inspecting the cloak covering his lower extremities and realizing he had nothing to replace it with.

This brought chuckles from everyone as Jace replied, "Yeah, but they won't fit those long legs of yours too well!" He dug some out of his pack and tossed them to Davlin.

"That's okay---just need my bum covered until I can get to....wait! Now I remember what happened! We were about to go at it when…Something hit me! What was it? It wasn't you, was it?" Davlin asked, raising one eyebrow quizzically at Jace.

"No----that was D.G.," Jace responded with a nod in the dog's direction. "Mind telling us how you came to be facing me as a cougar, brother?" He added, his eyes boring into Davlin's.

"Oh, that," Davlin responded sheepishly.

"Yes, 'that'," put in Ru-Lee. She was growing impatient with the brothers' banter and wanted some answers. "How long have you been able to shift, and what are you doing here?"

"Many years, and walking," Davlin sneered tersely as he struggled to keep covered by the cloak while wriggling into the pants Jace had given him.

Ru-Lee's eyes flashed and the once-light breeze picked up speed. It began to swirl around them as Ru-Lee growled through gritted teeth, "Davlin, you know what I mean; why in shifted form and why here? What were you doing?"

Still struggling with the pants, Davlin smiled a crooked grin, heaved a sigh, and answered, "Fine. The shift was necessary to pass through the area unobserved. The elves are not aware that I can shift, so they would not bother me in cougar form—or so I thought. I was looking for you and Jace. Something funny is going on and Relmar thinks it has something to do with you. We decided it was best if I came alone and tried to keep an extra pair of eyes on things."

"Wait—Relmar knows you can shift??" Asked an astonished Jace.

"No," replied Davlin slyly. "He just believes me to be incredibly skilled in slipping past people unseen."

"I might have killed you, you know," said Jace, grimly glaring at his brother.

"Right! You tried that a few years ago and got your butt whipped...literally—remember?" Responded Davlin, a devilish twinkle flashing in his eyes.

Realization and understanding spread across Jace's face, followed quickly by flaming red anger, as he recalled his encounter with the mountain lion several years earlier.

"That was you?! I oughta' smack you right now!" He snarled, balling up his fists and lunging towards his brother.

"Stop!" Ru-Lee ordered, grasping Jace's arm so hard that her fingernails dug through his sleeve. The hair on her neck prickled sending shivers of fear down her spine— her chest constricting as she froze in place.

"Ow! What?" He snarled in surprise. Turning to her, he was startled to see her holding her breath, eyes wide and wild, skin pale, body stiff. The skin on his arms prickling with goose bumps, he grabbed his bag, eyes darting to the horizon.

Screeching loudly, Pug launched himself skyward; Ha-Fart leapt from Sheila's shoulder, drawing his blade and shouting orders in his language, oblivious to the fact that most of them did not understand him. D.G. flattened his ears to his head and whimpered, nosing Ru-Lee's elbow urgently.

As shadows passed over the sun, Sheila slipped behind Ru-Lee, put her slender arms around her friend's neck, and whispered, "Ru, Run!" into her friend's ear.

It was enough. Ru-Lee gasped, released Jace, leapt up, and charged out of the grass with Sheila clinging to her back. Jace and D.G. kept pace on either side. Ru-Lee's fear spread through them like a contagion. A puzzled Davlin brought up the rear with Ha-Fart clinging to the long hair on his right leg. The mouse brandished his sword wildly, shouting at the shadows that scudded across the sky towards them.

As they entered the sheltering canopy of the trees, a blood-curdling scream pierced the air. Ru-Lee spun around and dropped to a crouch behind the trunk of a large pine tree, her slender fingers gripping the rough bark. Her nostrils flared, filling with the scent of sun-warmed pine pitch, needles, and something else.....terror. The air was thick with it, but she couldn't tell if it came from her or those around her. Heart pounding, blood thumping in her ears, scalp tingling, she scanned the field trying to find the source of the scream. Her eyes settled upon the source of her fear about three-fourths of the way through the field.

Shadows had descended and were swirling around the terrified and defiant bull elk. His eyes rolled and narrowed as he slashed his antlers repeatedly through the threatening darkness that was enveloping him.

Ru-Lee's breath caught in her throat as the elk screamed again, rearing up to strike ineffectively at his foe. Suddenly, the shadows disappeared, leaving the bull confused and shaken. He stood heaving ragged breaths through flaring nostrils, casting his head from side to side. White foam formed on his flanks and around his mouth as Ru-Lee watched from the trees. The others had come to huddle around her; Sheila still clung to her back, unnoticed. All held their breath, waiting. For what, Ru-Lee did not know, but tension hung thickly in the air.

Afraid to breathe and upset the balance of the scene before her, Ru-Lee gripped the tree trunk harder, pressing the side of her face into the bark in an effort to blend with it. The elk shook his antlers, raised his head, and bellowed his defiance. It was an unearthly sound—a roar filled with rage, pain, and despair.

A loud rumble filled Ru-Lee's mind as her vision became engulfed by flames. Her breath came in ragged gulps as smoke filled her nostrils and she felt heat rise in her body. Unable to control herself, Ru-Lee threw back her head and screamed with the elk as he reared up on his hind legs and trumpeted forth his challenge to the world. She was vaguely aware of Sheila's yell as the mist elf sprung from her back. A hot wind swirled through the trees around Ru-Lee, picking up speed and intensity as it swept into the meadow. Suddenly, the elk burst apart in a cloud of ash, the wind rising to a roar that tore through the trees, scattering ash and shadows across the meadow, bending the grasses to the ground before it.

As the wind abated, Ru-Lee collapsed against the base of the tree, unconscious and barely breathing, surrounded by her stunned friends. Wisps of smoke curled unnoticed

from her smoldering handprints scorched into the tree's
bark.

## Chapter 18

Voices played at the edges of Ru-Lee's darkened mind. She couldn't quite make out what was being said or who was speaking, but she could hear Sheila's voice weaving an unfamiliar tune through the murmured cadence of conversation. The strands of music drifting around her calmed her senses allowing her to slip deeper into the darkness. She felt safe here; safe from the anguish, pain, rage, and fear that had engulfed her entire being. She longed to stay in this cocoon, burrowed in the inner peace of her mind. But her peace was not to last. Sensing a presence encroaching upon her haven, she pulled her consciousness protectively around herself. She tried to hide, but as it came closer, she realized that this presence was familiar to her---it was D.G. He was probing her mind with his consciousness. As he gently slipped in around her battered psyche, Ru-Lee began to relax her protections, allowing the darkness to begin to dispel.

She and D.G. had many ways of communicating with each other mentally. One way was to simply 'read' each other's thoughts and emotions (more emotion than thought where D.G. was concerned). This was a sensing of the other's motives, opinions, and ideas. Another way was for both of their minds to be together in the same head; each retaining their own sense of being and essence, but residing together and understanding the other. This was useful when one needed to see or hear what the other saw or heard without being in the same place. The third way was what D.G. was attempting to employ now—merging minds. In this way, their minds merged into one--- allowing them to not only 'read' each other, but to actually 'feel' the other's thoughts and emotions. While D.G. could feel Ru-Lee's darkness, she could also feel his strength and brightness as he tried to draw her out.

As the light of D.G.'s mind washed through her and consciousness began to return, pain crashed over her. She screamed and twisted in agony, her body making its presence known. She attempted to bring the black walls of protection back around her mind, wrestling against D.G's light; but the light was stronger and the pain would not be denied.

Her screams pierced the small cottage as they ripped forth from her body. Cold beads of sweat ran down her forehead into her eyes; her body burned with fire; her hands engulfed with pain. D.G. whined in shared agony as their link was severed.

Clenching her teeth, she tried to force her eyes open, but candlelight from the room beyond shot rays of pain directly into her brain causing her to scrunch them tightly shut. Her hands throbbed, muscles ached, and body burned. What had happened? What was causing all this? She remembered running from the field, the elk, the terror.....then...nothing, only flame and anger.

In the room outside her mind, she heard shouted commands of, "Put out the fire!"; "Here, put this cloth at the base of the door!"; "Sheila, cover the cracks around the window!" There were sounds of frenzied movement; furniture crashed and someone swore---the singing had stopped.

Wind caressed her body, slightly cooling the flames on her skin—or was it fanning them? Loud hissing and acrid smoke filled the air, mingling with her agonized screams. Someone lifted her head and pressed a cup to her lips. Bitter, strong smelling liquid slid down her throat causing her to cringe and cough. Her mind filled with the memory of her child self standing by a table in Aylon's cabin learning from her grandmother how to mix the right herbs for the deep-sleeping, pain-numbing medicine.

The effects were immediate. A haze filled her mind and numbed the pain in her body. She groaned thankfully allowing herself to sink into drug-induced slumber. With her last vestiges of conscious strength, she retreated deep within herself, pulling the dark protective walls tight around her psyche. As she drifted into oblivion, her mind attempted to ponder where she might be and who could have given her the blessed draught—then she ceased to care.

# Chapter 19

Doves cooed their gurgley love songs in the late summer dawn as mice and other small creatures rustled about the thatched roof of a small cottage on the outskirts of the village of Shauntu. Pink-edged clouds slid lazily across the sky, and morning light peaked into the window to kiss Ru-Lee on the cheek where she slept fitfully on a low cot. The light slid across the room, caressing slumbering forms as it went. Jace, snoring loudly, slumped in a wooden chair near the fireplace, a bucket near his feet; D.G. breathing softly, stretched out on his side near the cot that held Ru-Lee; Sheila curled up in the opposite corner with a small pile of candles and the household lantern beside her, a dark mouse nestled on her neck gently snoring. In the rafters of the cottage, untouched by the seeking sunbeam, Pug kept watch over his friends as he listened intently to the furtive movements of the creatures in the thatching.

Slumped over manuscripts and sheets of paper scattered on a square table in the center of the room, was the form of a woman. Her head rested upon folded arms; a bright stripe of gray ran through the curly hair, shimmering in the morning light; large eyeglasses, twisted sideways, sat low upon her narrow nose.

Pug cocked his head and eyed Ru-Lee as she suddenly began to groan and toss on the cot. Flames burst forth in the fireplace and a breeze picked up inside the cabin; rapidly forming dust devils began to swirl across the floor seeking the flame. Pug screeched a warning to the cabin's inhabitants, startling most of them awake.

Sheila jerked up to a sitting position, launching Ha-Fart against the wall. He jumped up, dazed, shaking his head and cursing.

"Sorry, but there is no need for that kind of language about it!" Sheila chastised groggily as she blew out the candles that had popped to life in front of her. She had drained the lantern of oil and removed the wick during the night, but she noticed it was still attempting to spark to life—sending small puffs of smoke curling up into its chamber.

D.G. jumped up and poked his cold nose into Ru-Lee's ear attempting to wake her. If they could rouse her, even a little, the spell would be broken causing the fire and wind to die down. D.G. whined and gently pawed the blankets on Ru-Lee's chest. She gasped, opened her eyes for a moment, then settled down—her breath coming in shallow, ragged whistles. Instantly, the flames died and the wind ceased—the dust devils slowly dancing to a stop and sinking onto the floor.

Aylon rose from the table to mix another sleeping draught. This was the third one in as many hours--it was not working as long as it should. One dose should last most of the night. This one would be the last she would be able to give to Ru-Lee without concern for her safety. Shaking her head, she smiled down at Jace as she passed to Ru-Lee's cot. He hadn't even stirred this time. It had been a very difficult night, especially for a growing young man. Placing her hand beneath Ru-Lee's fevered head, Aylon lifted it up and brought the cup of medicine to Ru-Lee's lips.

"This situation cannot go on, Sheila," she said as she laid Ru-Lee's head back against the pillows. "Her body is on fire and the medicine is only helping a little. Things are getting far too dangerous for Ru-Lee and everyone else. This should not be starting until she comes of age!" Her brows knitted together in concern and frustration.

"Why is it happening now?" Sheila asked, yawning and stretching her sleep-stiffened limbs.

"I don't know for sure, but I suspect it has something to do with those shadows. Their presence seems to have caused the changes to speed up."

"What can we do to help her?"

"The herbs that will help the most will be ready tonight, at the height of the full moon. I had planned on going alone to gather them, but now I am not so sure. Her condition is worsening too quickly. I think we will have to move her tonight. Until then, we must try to reach her where she hides in her mind. If we can rouse her, she may be able to exert some control herself."

Turning to D. G. she said, "D.G., do you think you can try again?"

D.G., who had been listening intently, nodded in answer to Aylon's question, his ears flapping up and down.

"She will be groggy because of the medication, but that might be a good thing—she won't be able to fight you quite so hard and maybe it won't hurt you so much." She reached out to rub his ears sympathetically.

D.G. grinned, then placed his head next to Ru-Lee's on the cot and stared at her intently. Slowly, Ru-Lee's breathing became calm and soft; her toes stopped twitching beneath the blanket; she ceased grinding her teeth, her jaw becoming loose.

# Chapter 20

The light was back, illuminating her mind. The pain was still there, but dulled—as were her senses. She tried to retreat deeper inside herself to hide from the light, but it followed her. It surrounded her, relentlessly tearing away the dark walls she had worked so hard to build up. She was like a child hiding in the closet, only to be found out and forced into the light.

With a thick, heavy tongue, she tried to moisten her lips and open her sluggish eyes, attempting to shake off the thick drug-induced slumber. Her eyes refused to respond. She recalled drinking something bitter---a scent and taste she knew to relieve pain and bring on sleep. That must be why she felt this way. *'Aylon,'* she thought, *'I must be in Aylon's cabin—but, how?'* Moaning, she tried to raise her arms above her head and stretch her fingers, but the movement sent pain shooting up her arms. Gasping, she rolled her head from side to side and listened to D.G.'s thoughts in her head.

*"Yes, D.G., I am awake—I think,"* she thought, in response to his unspoken question in her mind. *"I don't want to be, though—please go away, it hurts too much to be 'awake'."* But he would not relent. Forcing his mind around her, he dragged her from her dark corner into consciousness—or something akin to consciousness.

*"Why do you need me awake so badly, D.G.?"* She thought to him. *"What has happened? Where are we? Why do I hurt so much?"*

In response to her questions, her mind was flooded with images: An elk in a field, surrounded by shadows; her screaming—no, not screaming, roaring—head back, crouched at the base of a tree in the forest; the elk exploding; wind tearing through the woods and field; her collapsed form unconscious on the forest floor.

She saw herself being carried at a run between Jace and Davlin, Sheila carrying her pack, Ha-Fart sitting upon her chest. Wind bent the trees around them as bursts of fireballs exploded in their wake. She was dropped several times—*'That explains some of this pain!'* she thought. The brothers swore, yelling orders and insults at each other, apparently no longer concerned about being heard. Each time she was dropped, the mouse bounced off, leapt back to her chest, and watched her closely.

Finally, Jace shifted into bear form and hoisted her across his back. Sheila, using ropes from one of the packs, tied Ru-Lee to Jace's hairy body before he began to move again. Davlin shifted also, running ahead through the darkening forest. Sheila, carrying both Jace's and Ru-Lee's packs, placed Ha-Fart upon her shoulder and raced after the large four-legged brothers.

The fireballs and wind had died down by the time they neared the edge of the forest, but Ru-Lee could sense from D.G. that they had not trusted this respite to last. A cloaked figure met them just before they burst free from the canopied cover—Aylon. She quickly muttered a cloaking spell before ushering them into the open and on to her cabin.

Once there, Ru-Lee's wounded hands were bandaged and a decoction was given to help her rest; but the wind and the fire had followed them, even to within the walls of the hut, causing constant chaos and disruption for her friends. The last image D.G. showed Ru-Lee was an image of the brothers conversing near the door, then Davlin shifting to cougar form again and slipping out into the night.

These were only images—like a chopped-up movie in her mind—but it was enough for her to have an idea of what had taken place after she passed out. *'Where did the balls of fire come from?'* She wondered, but there was no answer from D.G. If he knew, he wasn't sharing.

*'All right, D.G., I will come out, but it is under protest....remember that,'* she thought as she slowly rolled her head from side to side and attempted to open her eyes again.

# Chapter 21

North east of Shauntu, on the far side of the swamp, a small female Ergla rooted and dug for grubs beneath a rotting log. Nearby, perched atop a twisted archway of tangled wild rose vines, a large golden eagle studied her patiently. As he listened to her snort, snuffle, and claw, he realized that the morning sounds were quieting. Cocking his head to one side, he listened as the symphony of animals and insects grew still. The air began to pulse with a nearly audible thrum, and the Arch of roses shivered and rocked precariously causing the eagle to lift his wings and use his tail for balance.

The open space within the Arch shimmered and rippled, like waves on water. The Ergla stopped her snuffling and eyed the arched roses curiously. Squinting her beady black eyes, she sniffed the air and inched closer. The Arch shuddered as a dark shadow began to emerge from its depths.

The eagle, crouched low among the brambles, grabbed a branch with his beak to keep from falling off, and watched. From his perch, he could see a writhing mass deep within the dark, smoky depths of the shadow, as if there were many souls contained within it. The air vibrated with the emotions of pain, remorse, guilt, and anger emanating from the mass. A foreboding shiver ran through his body as he watched, transfixed.

Before the Ergla understood her danger, the shadows settled upon her and disappeared within. Her muzzle curled back, showing her blackened teeth, and she screamed in pain, fear, and anger. Clawing at her face with her front paws, and digging at her ears with her back ones, she rolled around on the ground snarling and howling. Suddenly, she stood up and charged at the base of a nearby tree, bursting into ashes upon impact.

Startled, the eagle released the branch he had been holding in his beak and stared, blinking in consternation. He raised his wings as if to fly from his vantage point, but was forced to latch on again as the Arch began to quiver and shake once more. As he watched, another shadow pushed through, rose to the sky, and sailed off in the direction of the Udah River. He stayed crouched down for a long time, the air pulsating with the emotions the passing shadows had left in their wake. As the life-sounds began to return to the surrounding forest, the majestic bird spread his wings and floated down to the ground in front of the Arch, his body shimmering and shifting form in mid-air.

"Umph!" Nevlon exclaimed softly as his hunched form landed with a thud, arms outstretched. "I really need to practice that move a bit more," he muttered to himself. As he stood upright, he ran his hands across his pockets and the pouches around his waist, checking to be sure everything was in place. Having long ago mastered the ability to shift from one form to another with whatever he might need in place upon his person.....such as clothing, he still always checked to make sure he wasn't missing anything. He watched a squirrel dash to the safety of a nearby tree, chattering angrily at him and chuckled as he thought, *'I really should teach Jace how to do that someday so he doesn't end up naked all the time, not that he seems to mind.'*

He fingered a dark pouch hanging at his waist as he contemplated the Arch of wild rose vines before him. This Arch was extremely large, ten feet across and at least twenty feet tall. Over the years, the brambles and branches of the rose vine had twisted and tangled upon themselves, narrowing the Arch's opening to nearly half its original size. Soft pink blossoms scented the breeze that brushed through them.

Heaving a sigh, Nevlon untied the pouch and poured out its contents. Three tan-colored runes and one black one tumbled into his waiting palm. Positioning himself at what appeared to be the center of the Arch, he paced out five steps towards one outer corner. Once there, he bent down and began to remove the debris that had accumulated at the base of the rose. It was slow going and he was pricked a number of times as he attempted to find the base of the mother plant.

*'Finally!'* He exclaimed, when his fingers found the small stone bowl seated at the base of the original plant. Sitting back on his heels, he sorted through the runes in his left hand until he found the one he wanted. Holding it between his right forefinger and thumb, he lifted it up high, closed his eyes, and uttered a barely-audible incantation as he slowly lowered it into the waiting bowl.

Rising, he returned to the center of the Arch, turned, and repeated the process with the other side. Returning to the center once again, he knelt down and began to dig in the weeds until he found a third stone bowl filled with dust. Using his, now reddened and bleeding fingers, he dug out the dust. The rune he chose for this bowl was larger than the others had been and he repeated the incantation twice before placing it into its seat.

*'Getting too old for this nonsense,'* he grunted as he straightened up and brushed the dust from his pant legs. He placed the black rune in his mouth and began to utter another incomprehensible incantation as he shifted form and flew to the top center of the Arch. Once there, he burrowed his head into the mass of brambles until he found the stone bowl hidden there. With an audible *'clink'*, he dropped the stone and flew back to the ground. He once again changed form as he went, though landing was a bit smoother this time.

Straightening up, he watched as the air within the Arch began to hum with vibrations and a rainbow of color filled the opening. A large white boulder materialized, filling the space within the Arch. *'Good,'* he thought, relieved, *'the Guard Stone is still in place.'*

His relief was short-lived. As Nevlon watched, the boulder became translucent and he was able to see several long cracks and deep crevices running through its surface. On the other side of the stone, he could see an abandoned and overgrown park, littered with debris. He could also make out what appeared to be several dark shadows drifting about and coming together.    As they came together, they appeared to merge, growing larger and, he assumed, stronger—strong enough to pass through.  Other smaller shadows hovered around the edges of his vision as well.    He exhaled, swearing beneath his breath---- *'Not good!  Not good at all!'*

Sweeping his arms across the opening in a wide circle, Nevlon broke the spell.  The boulder, rainbow, and visions disappeared instantly leaving no sign that they had ever been there.  The only thing now visible on the other side of the Arch was more woods and a slightly confused-looking rabbit.

Shaking his head and muttering under his breath, Nevlon gathered the runes from the stone bowls.  Using a long stick, he tipped the rune out of the bowl at the top of the Arch and returned them all to his pouch.    For a moment, he stood contemplating the Arch.  Then, heaving a heavy sigh, he shifted form, spread his wings, and exploded into the air launching himself over the swamp in the direction of Illiand.

# Chapter 22

Bats filled the sky as dusk crept through the sleepy village of Shauntu. The full moon smiled down upon a small cluster of cloaked individuals as they slipped cautiously out of a darkened cottage on the village edge. Quickly melting into the nearby trees, the group disappeared from sight, seen only by the canopy's night-eyes.

They travelled in silence through the woods, towards the gentle sound of the Udah River. More bats swooped through the air, brushing the travelers' hoods with their wing tips, as they searched for their dinner. As they swept near the dark hat of the young woman, aiming for the shiny spider crouched there, the bats were lifted high in the air--caught in an updraft that seemed to encircle the woman. None of the hooded figures noticed, and the dog that travelled with them only sniffed as the flying hunters passed. The leader of the group stooped now and again as she went. Gathering various herbs and flowers that glowed in the filtered moonlight, she tucked them into a pouch at her waist.

Since waking early that morning, Ru-Lee had fought a battle with her body and mind. She felt as if she were flying apart at the seams, unable to contain or process everything that had happened since Jace had arrived at her cabin. She knew that the meeting at Illiand should have taken place earlier that day but there had been no word as to what had transpired there. Aylon and the others had determined that it was not safe for Ru-Lee to stay within the confines of the cottage so near the village. The cottage was far too flammable with too many eyes and ears nearby. They had decided to travel to the Desolate Valley near the land of Yushah. Nothing grew there amongst the stones, so there would be nothing for Ru-Lee to set on fire. *'Nothing except my friends and family,'* Ru-Lee thought grimly, setting her jaw against the fresh wave of frustration and anger that threatened to flare up at this thought.

Ru-Lee could feel the fire-powers moving through her system: her skin was hot; her eyes, burned--tingeing everything she viewed with red-orange flames; her mouth, dry; her breathe, heated; her temper, short and volatile. All day long, she had been setting things aflame and causing balls of fire to burst forth from thin air within the cabin. Her handprints were burnt into Aylon's table where she had placed them during an argument with Jace about something trivial. Her hands, blistered by the fire that smoldered within her, were now wrapped in bandages soaked in flame-retarding ointment to keep them from blistering further. According to Aylon, an herb that would help her body heal itself and cool the heat growing within grew on the opposite bank of the Udah River, blooming only during the full moon of late summer--tonight.

Aylon had spent most of the day teaching Ru-Lee various spells meant to assist her in holding onto herself as the elemental powers began to overtake her. During practice of a particularly tricky spell, she had mispronounced a word and caused Sheila to be drenched by a localized raincloud. Jace had collapsed in fits of laughter as Sheila scampered about the cottage attempting to hide under pieces of furniture, shifting form from spider to girl and back again in her attempt to elude the persistent cloud. She ended up in spider form hiding in a very tiny mouse hole while Aylon corralled the cloud beneath a large wooden bowl, scooted the bowl across the floor to the door, and released it outside. For over an hour the cloud had continued its attempts to re-enter the house. It finally ran out of rain and was gently blown away by the breeze.

"Why must I learn all of this?" Ru-Lee had growled, scowling at Jace as he continued to snicker.

"So you can get paid as a rainmaker!" Jace quipped, nearly falling off his chair as he collapsed into another fit of giggles.

Ru-Lee had lost her temper at this, suddenly causing Jace's hat to burst into flames. Jace had removed himself to the farthest corner of the kitchen and had glared at her for the rest of the day. Still angry when they left the cabin, he had jammed the charred remains of his hat upon his head, blonde hair poking up through the blackened band.

Aylon had explained to Ru-Lee that when members of the keeper races came of age they had to give themselves over to the power in order to merge with it and make it a part of themselves. If they could not maintain a hold upon their essence as the powers filled them, they were consumed—turned to ash by fire; blown away upon the wind; absorbed into the waters; become one with the earth. This seldom happened to members of the keeper races, but Aylon had no way of knowing what would take place with Ru-Lee.

Before leaving the cabin, Ru-Lee had tried to place a shield around herself to contain any flammable or windy outbursts from harming her companions. It had not worked well. The wind gusts had been tolerable within her bubble, but the fire was another matter. The bursts of flame had rebounded off the shield, singeing her hair as they bounced around. Dropping the shield, she had decided to rely upon her own self-control and had asked D.G. to assist her if necessary.

The scent of pine filled Ru-Lee's nostrils as she followed Aylon through darkened woods, D.G. walking reassuringly beside her. Sheila, again in spider form, rode upon her hat. Once the shield had been removed, Sheila had felt this was the safest place for her since Ru-Lee usually remained untouched by the wind and fire. Aylon had argued vehemently against this arrangement. "You could burst into flame at any time!" She had growled disapprovingly; but Sheila had insisted and Ru-Lee had been too tired to argue the point. Jace brought up the rear, casting his head back and forth as he listened for sounds that they might have been followed. With Pug on one shoulder and Ha-Fart on the other, he almost looked like a three-headed creature moving through the darkness. The mouse had decided to stay with them stating through Sheila that he had not had such a grand adventure before and he was curious to see where it would lead.

The sounds of frogs and night-bugs filled the air as they neared the river's shore. Aylon parted the branches in front of her and stopped suddenly, causing Ru-Lee to stumble and step on D.G.'s foot. Yelping, he leapt sideways and disappeared, crashing through the parted branches in front of Aylon as if falling into a hole. The crash was almost immediately followed by a splash and the sounds of D.G. struggling back up the muddy riverbank.

"Sorry, D.G.," Ru-Lee whispered, peering down upon her wet friend.

Shaking vigorously, D.G. bobbed his head and made small grunting noises; his way of saying he was fine.

"Goofy dog," muttered Aylon as she gingerly stepped forward and began to slide down to join D.G. "You could wake the pixies with all that racket!"

Once everyone was standing on the slippery, muddy bank of the river, Aylon led them to a small boat that was tied to, and hidden by, the drooping branches of a downed tree. Ru-Lee helped D.G. into the boat, then stood on the bank while Jace seated himself in the rear and Aylon started to untie the mooring.

"Come on, Ru. We have to get to the Bonshu flower while the moon is at its strongest. After that, it closes and won't open again this year," Aylon said over her shoulder as she worked the ropes free.

Ru-Lee couldn't move. Her knees had begun to shake uncontrollably at the thought of actually getting into the boat! *What is wrong with me! I have never feared boats or water before!* She thought, trying to get control of herself as the others waited patiently.

"What's wrong, Ru?" Asked Jace, his brows knitting together with concern as he watched her quivering on the shore.

Ru-Lee shook her head and weakly responded, "I don't know....I am...uh.....afraid. I can't make my feet move!"

Jerking her head around, Aylon took in Ru-Lee's panic-stricken face.

"Oh, dear. I was afraid something like this might happen," she said, shaking her head, the gray stripe flashing in the moonlight.

Ru-Lee's heart thudded as her chest constricted in fear. "What is going on, Aylon?!" She asked, her voice edged with panic.

"It is the fire power. Fire is killed by water—it is as if your power is a sentient being. Sensing this truth about water, it imbues you with fear in order to preserve itself." Pausing in thought, Aylon mused, "I wonder......"

"Wonder what??" Ru-Lee snapped, heat gathering in her fearful, impatient mind.

Waves gently lapped the side of the boat, rocking its passengers, as Aylon quietly contemplated the situation for a moment longer before speaking.

"Ru, try to call up your water powers...the ones you have always had access to."

"Okay," Ru-Lee breathed softly. The water powers had always come so quickly and easily to Ru-Lee---it came as a bit of a shock to realize that they weren't immediately accessible. Her eyes widened as she looked to Aylon for help.

"Not right there, eh? Okay....Take a deep breath, close your eyes, and take your mind deep within yourself. The power is there, it just hasn't awakened fully yet, so the fire and wind are enveloping everything—hiding the water powers from you." Her blue eyes gently watched Ru-Lee as she added, "I know you can do this, Ru."

Jace and the others watched as Ru-Lee followed Aylon's directions. Closing her eyes, Ru-Lee swallowed the lump in her throat and began to breathe deeply, inhaling through her nose, filling her lungs, then slowly releasing her breath. In her mind's eye, she slipped into

98

the depths of her heart and found a small pool of water, shimmering blue and invitingly cool. This pool was surrounded by a wreath of fire. Ru-Lee assumed this was the fire power's way of preventing her access to the water. Taking another breath, she began to hum softly, calling to the pool. It rippled and stirred to life, pushing through the wreath of fire to make an opening for her. Fighting the fire's fears, she let her mind move forward and slip into the pool. Sighing, she opened her eyes, and smiled to her companions. Her skin had begun to cool and, although she was still shaking, she was able to stumble into the boat, anxiously gripping the edges.

# Chapter 23

Aylon deftly guided the small craft through the current towards the opposite bank, the rhythm of the oars and the waves soothing to most of her passengers. Ru-Lee, however, could not enjoy the momentary serenity or the beauty of the moonlight on the water. White-knuckled, she gripped the edges of the boat. Forcing herself to close her eyes and breathe deeply, she attempted to hold on to that small pool of safety and control deep within her heart.

When the group was just past the middle of the river, the smooth, rhythmic movements of the boat were interrupted by a jolt, as if they had hit something---or something had hit them.

"Oh, Piffle!" Aylon exclaimed, drawing in her oars and cautiously peering over the side. D.G. brushed against her as he leaned over the edge of the boat to sniff curiously at the water.

"What?" Ru-Lee and Jace demanded together, Ru-Lee's voice edged with barely-controlled panic.

The boat jerked sharply to one side, throwing Aylon into the bottom. Ru-Lee gripped the sides tighter, gasped, and hunched over her knees, eyes wide with fear, her hands throbbing. Sheila, crouched flat to the top of Ru-Lee's hat, swayed with the motion of the boat. Jace toppled backwards onto D.G., who grunted and scrambled quickly to his feet attempting to avoid stepping on Pug and Ha-Fart as they tumbled around in the boat, having lost their hold on Jace's shoulders. Once upright, Pug shot into the night sky, apparently deciding that rolling around in a boat was definitely *not* where an owl belonged.

"A Naiad," Aylon answered irritably.

"A what?" growled Jace, grimacing as D.G. stumbled again, digging claws into his hand.

"A Naiad—a water nymph! She has taken this section of the river as hers," growled Aylon as the boat rocked again, rolling her onto her back. "I had hoped she wouldn't notice us crossing in the middle of the night."

"What does it..er....she...want??" Jace asked, trying not to hurt D.G. or Ha-Fart as he struggled for a grip on the boat's edges.

"I don't know....we will just have to hang on and wait until she is ready to talk to us," Aylon replied as the boat jerked again and D.G.'s tail slapped her in the face.

Ru-Lee closed her eyes and put her head down, hanging on while her companions rolled about the boat. After what seemed like an eternity, she realized they were not jolting about any longer, but seemed to be listing a bit to one side. No one spoke.

The hairs on the back of Ru-Lee's neck stood up, and a shiver of foreboding ran down her spine. She cautiously opened her eyes and raised her gaze slightly to see Jace, D.G., Ha-Fart and Aylon jumbled about the bottom of the boat. Jace's eyes were wide and soft, a goofy, rapturous grin spreading across his face as he looked at something to her left. Aylon was also looking in that direction, but with something less than rapture in her eyes. Her brows were knitted together in a scowl, and her jaw set stubbornly. D.G. lay on his side in the boat's bottom with Ha-Fart leaning against his stomach. Both looked glad to have the boat moving in a gentler manner and seemed quite content to stay put.

Ru-Lee slowly turned her face to the left side of the boat and found herself peering into the curious, emerald-green eyes of a beautiful, young, dark-haired girl. The Naiad hung onto the edge of the boat, tipping it towards the water. She blinked slowly and smiled at Ru-Lee who gulped and smiled back. Without considering what the implications might be, Ru-Lee felt herself sinking slowly into the depths of the Naiad's impossibly green eyes, her fears and pain momentarily forgotten.

The Naiad's water-soft voice cascaded over them as she said, "This one is of the water, Aylon. Why is she in a boat?"

"She has not fully come into her own, yet," Aylon replied, a hint of irritation in her voice. "What can we do for you, Neyana?"

"Nothing," the Naiad responded flippantly, tilting her head to one side while keeping her gaze on Ru-Lee.

Pug's warning screech pierced the night as dark shadows slipped across the moon, breaking the Naiad's spell. Suddenly, Ru-Lee's breath caught in her chest, her eyes widening with fear. She felt the heat rising within her as flames again crept into the edges of her vision. Her mind filled with a now-familiar roar, and wind began to whip the river into white froth. She could not force herself to look away from the Naiad's mesmerizing eyes completely, but she could sense the presence of the shadows as they swept closer through the night erasing the peace she had found in the Naiad's eyes.

Moving more nimbly than her age would indicate possible, Aylon slipped close to Ru-Lee, and placed a calming hand on her arm.

"Neyana, we need your help," she said, her voice startlingly close to Ru-Lee's ear. "This one is of the water, but other forces are keeping her from it. Please take her into the water with you while the shadows pass by?"

"And if I do not return her once they are gone?" Ru-Lee heard Neyana ask mischievously.

"Then I will find you..." Aylon hissed, tightening her grip on Ru-Lee.

"Hmmm....What will be my payment?" Neyana inquired, now tilting her head to look at Aylon.

"I will bring you a Bonshu blossom," answered Aylon quickly. "They are blooming now, but I must hurry to gather them. What is your decision?" Aylon urged, glancing anxiously at the sky.

Ru-Lee's breathing was coming in ragged gasps as she fought to maintain control of herself. As the shadows drew nearer, small sparks began to flicker around her and the wind grew stronger, spinning the boat in a lopsided circle.

"Alright, I will accept her," grinned the Naiad. "This should be fun!" She pushed herself away from the boat, propelling backwards and causing the boat to rock violently. "Come and join me, sister," she said to Ru-Lee. Her head floated above the water surrounded by the dark mass of her hair as it skimmed the surface. The image looked surreal to Ru-Lee, edged as it was with the bloom of fire that tinged her vision.

Ru-Lee barely heard the nymph through the roar in her mind and stayed welded to the spot. Sheila, feeling the panic running through Ru-Lee's body, quickly began to slide down Ru-Lee's back, shifting form as she went. As her toes touched the wood of the boat, she placed her lips near Ru-Lee's ear and urgently whispered, "Get in the water, Ru."

The sound of Sheila's voice displaced some of the panic from Ru-Lee's fevered mind. She released her grip on the edge of the boat and turned her body to face Neyana, but she couldn't make herself climb over the side into the water. Panic gripped her again and she frantically looked to Aylon and Jace for help.

"Jace, push!" Aylon ordered, as she readied herself to assist Jace in getting Ru-Lee into the water against her will.

Ru-Lee's eyes widened further and she started to protest, but it was too late. She felt Jace's boots upon her backside, Sheila's hands on her back, and Aylon's hands upon her elbow propelling her overboard. D.G. let out a yip of surprise. As Ru-Lee's feet cleared the side of the boat, he scrambled up to the edge and peered over, whimpering. Ha-Fart, whose head had bumped the bottom of the boat when D.G. moved, sat up and rubbed his head in bewilderment.

Steam rose from the rippling surface of the river where Ru-Lee had entered as her hat bobbed along the current. Aylon again turned to the sky and watched as the shadows, which had passed overhead, stopped and reversed course. She looked to the shore they had recently vacated and saw three figures standing on the muddy riverbank, their cloaks billowing in the wind.

"Figures!" She grumbled.

"What figures?" Jace asked, following her gaze

Ignoring his query, Alyon reached for the oars, tossed one to Jace and ordered, "Row!"

Jace missed the oar and Sheila fished it out of the bottom of the boat for him.

"Thanks," he snarled, snatching it from her and immediately dipping the wrong end into the water.

"You might want to use the other end....it would be a bit more efficient!" She quipped.

"Yeah, and you might want to put some clothes on! That hair of yours doesn't cover everything, you know!" Jace replied, his ears reddening as he dipped the right end of the oar into the water and pulled furiously, refusing to look at her.

Looking down at herself, Sheila gasped—her body was no longer that of a small girl, but a teenager! She lunged for Ru-Lee's discarded backpack from the front of the boat beneath Aylon's seat, nearly tipping the vessel over.

"Careful!" Aylon warned, nearly losing the oar as she grabbed the boat to keep from falling overboard. "What is going on?" She asked, turning her gaze to Sheila as she pawed through Ru-Lee's bag. "Oh,...dear," Aylon exclaimed softly, shaking her head and sighing deeply.

Producing a dark blouse, Sheila swiftly pulled it over her head and dove into the bag again. She immediately emerged with britches. Quickly donning these, she wrapped her arms around the bag and drew her knees protectively in towards her chest. Her silver hair fell forward around her face, but it couldn't hide the fact that she was blushing profusely.

"What now?" Asked Jace. He scowled from Sheila to Aylon as he dipped his oar into the water, pulling a bit harder than necessary and causing the boat to turn slightly.

"It appears changes are coming for our dear Sheila as well as Ru-Lee, Jace," Aylon answered as she turned back to her rowing.

The wind picked up and began twisting the trees along the river, spinning the tops out of a few of them and sending them flying. The waves grew larger and more violent and the task of rowing the small boat safely to the other side of the river became quite difficult. Though Jace burned to ask Aylon who it was on the shore behind them and exactly what changes were taking place with Sheila, he was preoccupied with keeping their vessel upright and headed in the right direction. Aylon would not have heard him over the rush of the wind and water anyway. As the boat tipped, rocked, and twisted, he chanced a backward glance in time to see one of the figures change form and rise into the sky---Nevlon!

## Chapter 24

The river hissed and roiled as Ru-Lee plunged beneath its surface, blood pounding in her ears; bubbles drifting from her clothes. Fish scattered, fleeing the heat that emanated from her flesh. The normally frigid water felt cool to her overheated system. Frantically opening her fevered eyes, she cast about looking for the Naiad. Glancing upwards, she could see the shadows coming closer. From her angle beneath the waves they were distorted, but the fear they brought to her was not. Panic settled around her heart. She looked down as she caught a glimpse of movement below her. The Naiad, Neyana, flipped her tail at Ru-Lee and grinned, diving deeper into the river.

Ru-Lee stretched her hands out in front of her and kicked away from the surface, noticing that she was, once again, translucent. This time, however, her watery skin had the pale cast of reflected flames. Unfortunately for her, the peace and joy she had felt during her previous experience in the water were not repeated.

'*Strange,*' she thought, as she followed Neyana through the darkening gray-green waters. It seemed they were diving straight down past large, moss-covered boulders. She hadn't realized the river was this deep in places. Pressure built up within Ru-Lee's ears. She opened her mouth to release it, marveling at the fact that she didn't choke on the mouthful of water she gathered in. Her neck tickled as large air bubbles brushed her skin and floated towards the surface. Curiously, she felt her neck and gasped when her fingers slid over gently fluttering gills.

The shadows were directly above her now. The waves on the surface seemed to be bringing their turbulence down below as the current became choppy and uneven. Pain seared Ru-Lee's mind, blinding her. Her heart caught and missed a beat. She stopped her downward motion and jerkily curled in a ball, clutching at her chest. *'What is happening??'* Her mind screamed. *'What do you want???'* Her frantic thoughts and emotions swirled within her. Fear, anger, pain---they all mixed within her mind and heart. Reeling with frustration, she threw back her head and screamed, emitting nothing but bubbles and gurgling silence beneath the waves. The shadows drifted closer to the river's surface.

Ru-Lee's body arched and lengthened, wracked with pain—as if it was being stretched from within. She closed her eyes against the pain. As it ebbed, she opened them slightly and attempted to breathe, cautiously looking around for help. The Naiad, Neyana, peeked out from behind a slimy green slab of stone, her eyes wide.

*'What is her problem? I am the one in danger here!'* Ru-Lee thought, irritably. Bringing her hands up to rub her aching head, Ru-Lee was shocked to find she no longer had hands---she had claws! Big, translucent, claws---- dragon claws! Shaking her head, she looked at Neyana again and blinked disbelievingly. *'What is that on my face??'* Directly in front of her, way out past where her nose should have been, was a snout! Carefully feeling the snout with her claws, she was able to discern that there were fangs within the snout---fangs attached to her!!!

*'What is happening? Oh, help!!'*

She caught Neyana's eye pleadingly, but the look on the Naiad's face told her there would be no help there. With a quick flash of her shimmering tail, Neyana darted away upstream, leaving Ru-Lee alone, deep in the river, in a body that wasn't her own.

Another surge of pain ripped through Ru-Lee's body. Angrily fighting the pain, she shook her head, clenched her dragon-like jaw, and growled, *'Fine! Change is what you want? Then change is what you'll get!'* She had no idea who she was speaking to in her mind, but with this thought, she stretched out her body to its fullest and gave herself over to whatever changes were coming her way. Roaring in pain and anger, she twisted and screamed silently beneath the waves. Her body stretched and enlarged, ripping her clothes to shreds which drifted away with the current. Writhing one last time, she whipped her body through the water. A grim satisfaction filled her enraged mind as she shot towards the surface in the form of a full-sized, translucent, dragon---a water dragon.

*Original artwork by Tammy L. Sonnen--2011*

# Chapter 25

Rocks grated against the bottom of the small wooden boat as Aylon and Jace tossed the oars into its hull and jumped out onto the shallow, rocky shore. Ha-Fart clambered up onto D.G.'s back as D.G. followed Sheila over the side of the boat into the shallows.

Wind whipped and howled around them, tearing through the trees and whipping up the river which threatened to pull the boat away with it. Sheila and Aylon's hair swirled around their faces obscuring their vision, and Jace's hat lifted off his head, nearly escaping before he jerked what was left of it tightly around his ears.

"Sheila!" Aylon yelled over the din of the wind and waves.

Pulling her hair away from her mouth, Sheila replied, "What, Aylon?"

"Take D.G. and Ha-Fart to get the Bonshu blossoms! Get as many as you can!" Aylon replied, pointing towards a cluster of trees about twenty feet from the shore. "You know where they are and what they look like! Hurry!"

Nodding, Sheila struggled over the rocks and boulders on the shore towards the clump of trees, D.G. and Ha-Fart on her heels.

As Jace wrestled the boat to safety, Aylon reached into it and pulled out the rope that was tied to the bow. Glancing around the shoreline, she spied a large boulder with a foot-long point jutting up into the air like a Unicorn horn. There were twisted marks around it that looked as if they had been worn there over years of use. Aylon worked her way to it against the raging wind and wrapped the rope around the point several times before tying it off securely.

Just as she finished, a large, golden eagle swooped down out of the sky, wobbling slightly in the wind. He descended towards her, shimmering and shifting in the air. Nevlon stumbled slightly on the rocky river bank as he landed in front of Aylon.

"You really should wait to shift until your feet are firmly planted, Old Man! You'll break a leg this way!" Aylon shouted over the wind.

"I know, but this way has so much more finesse!" Replied Nevlon, grinning wolfishly. Then, gently gripping Aylon's shoulders, he gazed at her beseechingly and said, "Aylon, you have to call Sheyna!"

"Wha...? NO!" She yelled, shaking her head and grabbing at his hands attempting to wrench herself free of his now-tight grip. Realizing he would not let go, she glared at him and asked, "What for?"

"We need her help---Ru-Lee needs her help. She is the only one who will be able to contain Ru now," Nevlon responded gravely, his voice so low that Aylon had to struggle to hear him.

Jace had finished securing the boat and now stood leaning on the boulder a few steps behind Alyon. He had heard only snatches of what Nevlon was saying and could not see Aylon's face, but the set of her shoulders spoke volumes. Anger seemed to radiate from her in waves, and her hair appeared to crackle with sparks. Jace had only seen Aylon angry once, when he and his brothers had stolen some chickens and fed them to the village pigs. Although he was painfully curious about the conversation between Nevlon and Aylon, he did not wish to be in the line of fire when she lost her temper. Cautiously feeling his way over the rocky ground, he slipped a few steps backwards and edged around the boulder, ready to duck if needed.

Shaking her head and scowling at Nevlon, she asked, "How do you know? What has happened to Ru?"

Nevlon gently steered Aylon to the water's edge as he replied, "It appears that our grandsons have some special gifts they have been keeping from us."

Glancing at the two figures standing on the opposite side of the river, buffeted by the wind, Aylon asked, "What do you mean?"

Taking a deep breath and releasing Aylon's shoulders, Nevlon replied, "Well, Relmar has apparently developed the ability to read people's hearts. He has sensed that Ru-Lee is changing as we speak. He also told me that those shadows could cause tremendous complications for Ru-Lee once she surfaces, which she will do rather soon, I fear. He is not sure exactly what they want with her, but it does appear to be her they are after."

Aylon closed her eyes and brought the palm of her left hand up to rub her forehead. She allowed her shoulders to slump forward momentarily before gathering herself up and walking knee-deep into the churning, icy river. Looking back at Nevlon, she said, "I don't think she will come for me alone, Nevlon." Then, looking over his shoulder, she called out, "Jace! Come here! I need your help!"

Puzzled, Jace stepped out from behind the boulder where he had been watching the exchange, and cautiously made his way into the water beside Aylon, catching his breath as the chill of the river shot through his shoes.

"What do you need, Aylon?" He asked, brows furrowed in a wary scowl.

"Do you remember your mother, Jace?" Aylon asked, watching his face intently.

"Yeah....sort of, why?" He asked, confused.

"I need you to place your hands in the water with me and concentrate on your mother as if she were here. Can you do that?"

"Maybe, but why??" He asked, slightly irritated.

"There isn't time to explain now—I will tell you once we are done. For now, just trust me and do it, okay?"

There was a slight note of fear in her voice that kept Jace from pushing the point. Thinking to himself that there had better be a lot of explanations coming soon, he nodded. Following her lead, he bent forward and plunged his hands into the cold, turbulent water. Immediately, he was drenched as the water swirled and splashed around him. His feet slipped on the mossy rocks, pushed by the unruly current, but he was able to stay upright.

"Okay, close your eyes, take a deep breath, and concentrate on your mother, Jace," Aylon directed, as she closed her eyes also.

He could barely hear her before the words were snatched away by the wind, but the idea was conveyed. Closing his eyes, he breathed deeply of the spray-filled air, and tried to bring up memories of his mother. It had been a long time since he had attempted this, and he wasn't sure if it would work. When he was younger, he would often spend hours sitting high up in the pine trees, eyes closed, dwelling on his memories of his parents. He had missed them furiously when they died, and even more so after he passed through the gates with his brothers and Ru-Lee. Aylon had shown him how to call up the memories to help him feel closer to his parents and to ease his homesickness. Over time, the need to be with them in this way ebbed, but the memories had not faded away.

A smile slipped across Jace's lips as he brought up his mother's face in his mind, as if from a moving-picture book. She was laughing at something he had done, her green eyes dancing, honey-blonde hair tossing softly about her shoulders. He could almost feel her warmth as she wrapped her arms around him. The memory seemed so real....as if he could actually feel her hand as she brought it up to caress his forehead----he felt a warm, wet finger trail across his forehead! Gasping, he opened his eyes and stumbled backwards, landing on his rear in the water. Before him extended up from the tumultuous river, hovered a 'water-woman'----his mother! Her right hand was outstretched, finger extended to a point in the air where his forehead had been moments ago. A loving smile played upon her lips.

Jace shook his head, blinking---it couldn't be! He turned to Aylon and croaked out, "What the...."

"I told you I would explain later....there isn't time now," Aylon muttered out of the corner of her mouth, cutting him off. She was watching the womanly spiral of water cautiously.

"Sheyna, your sister's daughter needs you!" She said firmly, as if giving an order.

The water spirit, Sheyna, who had been dreamily watching Jace, whipped her head around and glowered at Aylon. She started to sink into the waves. Aylon's eyes went wide with fury and she jerked her head around to Nevlon who was standing on the bank, watching patiently.

"I told you, she wouldn't help! She is too stubborn!" Aylon yelled to her husband.

Jace, being young when his parents died, had not really known that his mother had any name other than "Mom". However, it was clear to him now that this spirit, somehow, was his mother and her name was Sheyna. It was also clear that it was very important that she not leave. As he watched her slowly descending into the river, his heart broke anew as it had the day she had died. Without even thinking, he yelled, "MOM! Please stay!!"

The water spirit stopped and turned her gaze upon him. She regarded him for a moment before nodding slightly. He took this to mean she would stay, and looked to Aylon for the next step, his heart pounding in his aching chest.

Aylon stood her ground, the river splashing about her knees, an incredibly sad look upon her face. Nevlon stepped into the water and placed a hand gently around her waist before speaking.

"Sheyna, daughter, your niece is in grave peril. I am sure you are aware of her below the waves. She is struggling to maintain a hold upon herself, but she will lose the battle if she cannot be contained when she surfaces. Your other sons are on the opposite bank. I know you can sense them there."

At this, Sheyna turned for a moment to regard the young men standing in the wind. After she had returned her gaze to Nevlon, he continued, "Please call upon the waters to contain Ru-Lee. She will be difficult to control,

114

but I think you can do it. You may have to attempt to connect with her somehow so that we can draw her true essence back out. Will you do it?"

The water spirit looked at them all with the moon reflected in her penetrating, watery green eyes. Jace felt his heart settle in his throat. He remembered that gaze....it could weed out lies and hidden hurts alike when he was younger. Holding his breath, he watched as the water spirit, his mother, inclined her head forward indicating that she would help.

Heaving a sigh of relief, Jace struggled to find purchase on the slime-covered, rocky, river bottom so that he could stand. As Nevlon and Aylon turned towards the shore, the river erupted around them.

## Chapter 26

Though half hidden by the shadows, the bright full moon lit the way as Sheila and D.G. raced clumsily over the rocky shore towards the tree line. Ha-Fart clung to the hair atop D.G.'s head, digging in all four paws and making D.G.'s eyes water. The ground rose abruptly where the rocks ended, revealing scrubby brush and bare tree roots. Wind pushed and shoved them, tearing at Sheila's hair and clothes as she scrambled up the dirt embankment, grasping at roots and brush. Tree tops cracked, swayed, spun and groaned all around them. The top of one tree was wrenched from its home and thrown into the cradling branches of another, just feet from Sheila's head causing her to gasp and jump back, nearly stepping on D.G..

Once inside the trees, the howling voice of the wind changed to a loud, roaring moan. Sheila slowed and began to count her steps in an effort to measure the distance she had travelled. Once she had gone about twenty steps, she turned right towards a large wild-honeysuckle bush. She attempted to push through, but was unable to part the tangled brush enough to wriggle through the vines. Shifting to spider form, clothes falling to the ground around her, she tried to crawl through the tangled vines at the base. After several attempts, it became clear that she would not fit; the changes her body was going through meant that her spider form was larger than she was used to. Shifting quickly back to human form, she sat on the ground near the bush, tears of confusion and frustration sliding down her cheeks. Her silvery hair draped softly over her now-womanly form, falling nearly to the ground around her gently curving hips. Sighing heavily, not realizing the changes her last shift had brought about in her physique, she slumped forward and placed her head on her knees.

Ha-Fart detangled himself from D.G.'s fur and slid to the ground. Walking over to her on his hind legs, he looked up, placed his front paws on his hips, and, in his native tongue, asked if there was anything he could do. Sheila raised her head and wiped the tears from her face, contemplating the furry creature for a moment. D.G. came up and sat on his haunches on her other side, cocking his head and pondering the honeysuckle that blocked their way.

"Apparently, I am unable to pass as I usually would, Ha-Fart. You will have to get the Bonshu blossoms for me," Sheila said, thinking that it was useful that Ha-Fart had been quick to pick up an understanding of her language, even if he could not speak it yet.

At this, Ha-Fart puffed up his chest and nodded.

"Okay, you have to go through these vines; they block a very small, short tunnel that comes out on a narrow ledge hanging out over the river. Just over the edge of the ledge, are the flowers. They are pure white, with seven petals. Bring as many blossoms as possible, okay?"

"Yuh!" Ha-Fart replied as he pulled out his small sword and swung at the vines near the base. He quickly made an opening large enough to squeeze through and disappeared into the thicket.

Sheila and D.G. could hear him hacking away, cursing the vines as he went. They knew he had passed into the tunnel when his sword went silent. However, Ha-Fart did not become silent. Apparently, mouse though he was, Ha-Fart did not like dark tunnels. He cursed the dark, swearing loudly in his own language, his voice echoing back to them from the tunnel. Once on the other side, they could no longer hear him and could only hope for the best. Sheila dressed again, and D.G. paced back and forth in front of the honeysuckle, looking back towards the river often and whimpering.

"It will be okay, D.G., Ru is tough. I am sure everything will be okay," reassured Sheila soothingly. She had her own concerns which she kept to herself as she wondered what all these changes meant, and would mean, for their little group and herself.

Shortly, they could hear Ha-Fart returning through the tunnel. There was far less cursing on his return trip through the vines, the passage having already been made. When he emerged, Sheila giggled in spite of herself. There he stood, framed in the vine doorway, a wreath of gleaming white Bonshu blossoms draped around his dark neck, a sheepish grin on his usually gruff visage.

Gathering the mouse up in her hands and placing him on her shoulder, Sheila snickered and said, "Okay, lets get these back to Aylon."

D.G. shook his head and followed as Sheila broke into a run back towards the river. In their haste to return to Aylon, they burst from the trees, lost their footing, and slid unceremoniously down the embankment, Sheila first, with D.G. nearly landing on her head.

Sheila leapt to her feet rubbing her backside as D.G. scrambled upright. Ha-Fart, clinging tightly to Sheila's ear, squeaked loudly—a sound he seldom made. The noise startled Sheila and she peered quizzically sideways at him just as D.G. barked sharply causing her to jerk her head towards the river as it burst from its bed.

# Chapter 27

Wind roared through the trees above the muddy river bank raining twigs, pinecones, leaves, and needles down on the heads of two young men. The dark-haired one, Davlin, cloak snapping in the wind, paced restlessly between his brother and a downed tree that stretched out into the turbulent waters, anchored to the shore by a large bundle of tousled roots. The blonde, Relmar, absent-mindedly brushed debris from his hair as he stared across the river, intent upon the activity on the opposite shore.

They had arrived on the shore, sliding down the embankment through the underbrush as Ru-Lee was shoved overboard into the roiling Udah River. Nevlon had taken immediate action, leaving them to wait impatiently for a way to get across.

"Stay here—Help if you can!" Nevlon had ordered as he shifted form and took flight.

Davlin had shouted, "Help? How??" to Nevlon's rising form, knowing there would be no answer. "What are we supposed to do from here?" He asked, as he turned his glowering gaze upon his brother.

"I don't know for sure," Relmar had muttered, his brows furrowing into a scowl as he watched the shadows changing course in the bright night air.

Glancing up at the dark, wispy forms, Davlin asked, "Can you sense what they want from this distance?"

"Not really. They seem to be mostly emotions--anger, sorrow, guilt--but there seems to be a firm purpose with these particular shadows. I haven't noticed that with any of the others before. Those had always been seeking something---these ones seem to have found what they want." Relmar closed his eyes. With clenched jaws and knitted brow, he concentrated his energies on the shadows sweeping closer to the turbulent river.

Davlin had watched quizzically as his brother exercised his newly burgeoning gift to sense the intentions of the ominous presence overhead before asking impatiently, "And just what do they want?"

Opening his eyes, Relmar had turned his hazel-blue eyes to look at his brother. Fear and concern mingled on his face as he replied softly, "Ru—they want Ru."

Davlin's breath caught in his throat. "What do you mean, they want Ru? What for?"

"I don't know. Some kind of vessel maybe? At least that's what it seems like," Relmar replied, shaking his head. "I am new at this, you know. Couple a' weeks doesn't make me an expert! Maybe I've got it wrong—I hope so." He sighed and returned his gaze to the opposite shore.

The watching and waiting quickly chafed on Davlin, and he began to pace. His boots squelching, making barely audible sucking sounds as he wore a slimy path between the log and Relmar. With each turn, he stopped momentarily to watch his brother and glance across the river before resuming his restless vigil.

Rooted to the spot, mud and cold oozing in around the sole-seams of his boots, Relmar stood watching across the turbulent waves. Wayward leaves and twigs caught in his hair as they flew through the air, ripped from their rightful places in the canopy. He gazed intently at the opposite shore, seemingly oblivious to everything else.

Relmar's sudden gasp caused Davlin to jump and slip on the sloppy path he had trod. As his eyes met a watery image rising from the river, he completely lost his footing and landed on his rear, mud splattering up into his hair. In an open-mouthed daze, he scrambled to his feet and made his way towards Relmar, his gaze never leaving the scene unfolding in the river. The wind had picked up to a deafening roar and seemed to be intent on pushing him backwards as he kept his eyes on the woman-shaped column rising from the water. He stopped for a moment to watch in consternation as it bent forward to touch Jace's forehead. Stumbling and slipping, he finally reached his brother, grabbed Relmar's right arm for balance and yelled over the wind, "What is it?"

Relmar's reply came back to him as a barely audible, somewhat stunned, question, "Mom....?"

This response caused Davlin to jerk his head around and stare round-eyed at Relmar wondering if his brother had lost his mind. "What?? What are you talking about?"

Raising his left arm, wind pulling at the sleeve of his cloak, Relmar pointed at the column of water, and replied in a dumbfounded voice, "That is Mom....or...her spirit at least."

"You're nuts!" Davlin retorted.

"No I'm.....Whatever! Don't believe me, but I know what I am talking about! That is Mom out there!" Relmar growled back, glaring at him.

"How?? Mom is dead! We saw her body buried, remember??! Whatever that is, it can't be Mom! It has to be a trick of some kind...Maybe the shadows are doing something...??" He searched Relmar's face, his eyes begging for any other explanation, his heart suddenly constricting in his chest. In Relmar's eyes, however, he saw only the truth of his brother's words. Relmar, who could sense a being's emotions and had recently developed the ability to read thoughts, was telling him that this.....this creature....was their dead mother---or her spirit.

'How can that be?' He asked Relmar. 'If that is Mom, why hasn't she made herself known to us before now?'

Relmar only shrugged in answer watching as those on the opposite shore appeared to talk to the water spirit. Davlin's heart skipped a beat as the figure turned to look in their direction, her watery gaze flooding him with love and warmth—the kind of love that only comes from a mother for her child. When she turned back to the group on the opposite shore, the warmth went with her.

His chest heaved as he struggled with the emotions left in the wake of his mother's gaze. Tears pricked the edges of his eyes as the pain of losing his parents seeped into his heart anew. He squeezed his eyes shut, grit his teeth, and forced himself to be reasonable. There had to be an explanation for this. If his mother had been able to come back, she would have. She would not have left them alone if there had been any other way.

Opening his eyes, he found Relmar, tears streaming down his cheeks, watching him. "You okay?" He asked.

With a heavy sigh, Davlin lied, "Yeah."

Smirking, Relmar replied, "Liar."

"Cheater," Davlin growled, his dark eyebrows knitting together as he glowered at his brother.

Relmar, eyes twinkling, replied, "Yep, I know." He paused, placed his hand on Davlin's shoulder, and continued, "Look, I need you to get a grip on your emotions for a few minutes so I can figure out what is going on. Your thoughts and feelings are too loud! I can't make out anything else."

"Whatever! Maybe I should move a few feet away, huh?" Snarled Davlin.

"Just calm down a bit and don't touch me for a few minutes, 'k'?" Relmar asked. "I know what you're feeling—I feel it, too---but we need to know what is going on over there if we are going to be any help at all."

"What do you mean, 'help'? We can't do anything from here!" Mud flew from Davlin's body as he jerked his shoulder free of Relmar's grip.

Making a disgusted face and wiping mud from his chin, Relmar answered, "Maybe—let's see if I can find anything out before we jump to that conclusion, okay?"

Stepping back towards the embankment and gritting his teeth, Davlin snapped, "Fine!"

Relmar turned back to the river, clenched his fists at his side and swore softly. Swinging his head back towards the embankment, he yelled over the din of the wind, "Trieca, get out here and stop thinking! My elvish isn't that good, you know!"

Startled, Davlin spun and looked up the embankment as two soft-booted feet slid down through the brush and splatted into the mud beside him—Trieca.

"What....?" He began but was cut off by Relmar's order of, "Both of you, keep your thoughts calm and your mouths shut!"

Trieca shrugged at Davlin and they both turned to watch Relmar. Wind whipped his blonde hair and tore at his cloak as he bent his head, closed his eyes, and forced his concentration across the river. He had only been at it for a few seconds when he jerked his head up, eyes wide, swore loudly, and covered his head with his arms as the river shot skyward.

# Chapter 28

Water, fish, and debris shot into the air, shimmering in the moonlight, as Ru-Lee burst from the river's depths. Driven by the amazingly strong spiked tail she now wielded, her scaled head and body exploded from the surface. She roared, screaming her defiance at the forces working within her. Her enormous, translucent body, now gray-green, was tinged with red-orange flames that glowed and moved beneath her skin, almost as if there was living fire fused within her liquid form.

The force of the river leaving its bed swept up Jace, depositing him at the edge of the embankment to sit, drenched, at Sheila's feet near D.G.. Nevlon, still embracing Aylon around the waist, was carried across the rocky shore and slammed against the stone where the boat was tied. Grasping the spiraled horn, he pulled Aylon to safety as the main body of water ebbed back to its home. Driven against the tangled roots and dirt of the embankment on the far side of the river, Relmar, Davlin, and Trieca were forced to grapple for a hold on anything handy as the river surged and roiled, threatening to pull them under the waves. Glimmering fish and huge drops of water rained down around them all, flying away from Ru-Lee's water-dragon body and tossed about in the furious wind.

Ru-Lee's right claw found purchase on the rocky shore, the wicked talons scraping the stone loudly as she began to leave the water. Acting quickly, Sheyna used the river to encircle Ru-Lee in a flurry of foam and waves that spiraled around her raging dragon form and drew her away from the shore. As Sheyna brought the tornado of water up to encompass Ru-Lee's snarling head, the shadows dove into the snapping jaws. Ru-Lee's roar of defiance changed to one of agonizing pain as the cage of spiraling water closed, trapping her within.

# Chapter 29

Inside the swirling tornado of water, Ru-Lee's dragon body curled in upon itself. Her mind screamed in fury and pain as a loud, high-pitched whine filled her ears sending shivers down her spine-encrusted body. She fought to maintain a hold on that small part of her mind that was still Ru-lee, but she felt herself being pushed into a small corner of her being—held there as if by chains, forced to watch and listen to that which she did not wish to bear witness to.

She struck out at the watery walls with her claws, striving to rip them open so she could escape into the night and attempt to shed the chaos in her brain, but her claws only slid across the surface as if it were made of ice. She slammed her snout and fangs into the walls again and again—an effort which only added to her pain and frustration.

Finally, her breath coming in heaving rasps, she stopped fighting and allowed her dragon body to slip back down into the water thinking that she might be able to slide beneath the impervious tornado tube. It followed, churning the river as it went—even beneath the waves, her body was cocooned within its solid walls.

Closing her eyes, she gave in to the sounds and emotions of the shadows that had entered her. *'So much regret and guilt!'* She thought. Her mind filled with images of destruction, murder, and revenge---flashing through her mind's eye as if each were an unruly child vying to be seen and heard over all the others. What she saw caused bile to rise up in her throat. She wretched, her body convulsing violently. Emotions burned through her—anger, despair, guilt, sorrow. As each new wave of images engulfed her, her mind and body spasmed, recoiling against the onslaught. She was held within their grasp and could not escape. Her only defense was for her soul to retreat deep within herself; to bring up the walls that had served to protect her in times past. She retreated, her essence curling into a ball at the back of her mind, hiding as best she could, but the walls could not keep the shadows out. Each time the walls rose up to protect her, the images—the shadows---tore them down, shattering them into dust around her embattled soul. Despair gripped her heart. There would be no escape—no hope for her. She would die here, beneath the waves, in a body not her own. *'The shadows will take this body and use it as they wish,'* she thought, *'I will cease to exist and no one will even know I am no longer here.'* A silver tear slid from her dragon eye and travelled slowly down her snout.

Her breath was shallow now as she drifted beneath the waves in her turbulent cocoon, no longer able to see or hear that which filled her. Numb now, almost destroyed, she slowly became aware that the voices of the shadows had changed. They were quiet, waiting. The images had stopped berating her. They were waiting on her. *'Why?'* She wondered, retreating deeper within herself, fear coiling around her heart. *'Why don't they take this body and leave me be?'* Her soul felt battered and bruised—damaged beyond repair. *'Let them wait! I am done!'* she thought angrily as she prepared to let go of her hold on life. *'It should be so easy to just stop 'being'—stop living; stop feeling,'* she told herself. But she couldn't. The fire within her soul flared, fed by a burning anger that refused to be quenched. As she sat seething, huddled in her mind's darkest recesses, she heard a new voice slip softly into her mind, soothing the pain she felt; cooling her fevered thoughts.

*'What now?'* she wondered, cautiously uncurling herself, curious about the voice that slid past the shadows. Recognition registered in her memories and she thought, *'I know this voice—but it's been so long since I've heard it. How can it be here now?'*

"*Ru-Lee,*" the voice hummed softly, murmuring with the soothing sounds of a calm and gentle stream, drowning out the sounds of the shadows. Ru-Lee's soul felt light and strength wrap around her as the voice continued, "*I* am here to help you. You must control the shadows. You must maintain control of yourself! Draw from my strength—come out of hiding and take hold of this form your body has taken!"

'How are you here? Where are you?' Ru-Lee asked, puzzled and distrustful. 'How do I know you are truly the one I think you are?'

"I am she—your mother's sister. When I died in the human world, I gave my spirit to the river near where I was killed. Those same waters run through all worlds in some form or another. For a time, I lost myself within the river waters---it happens often and time slips away from me—but I have watched those I loved while I lived; your mother, my sons, you, Nevlon, Aylon. It was they who called me here."

'Are you responsible for the cage of water?' Ru-Lee questioned, allowing her aunt's strength to fill her. As she tentatively spread her essence out from its hiding place within her mind, the shadows retreated slightly.

"Yes. It is necessary until you come back to yourself. The forces within you will consume you and harm others if you are not contained," answered Sheyna, her voice filling the cavern of Ru-Lee's mind, pushing out the voices of the shadows. There was quiet for a moment before Sheyna continued. "The shadows grow restless. Do you know yet who and what they are?"

'No. Do you?"

"I believe they are spirits, like myself. They are displaced, and have no home, but seek to find one. You must speak to them—find the answers you need to control them," Sheyna replied.

'And if I refuse?' Ru-Lee thought, resisting the urge to recoil back into herself again.

"They will consume you and all will be lost," Sheyna said in a matter-of-fact manner.

'Full of sunshine, aren't you!' Ru-Lee shot back sarcastically, fire flaring in her mind. 'Don't you think you

are being a bit melodramatic? I would be gone, but ---
they are only shadows. What can they do?'

"Have you so quickly forgotten what they showed
you?" Snapped Sheyna, her voice becoming harsh with
impatience—the walls of the tornado-like cage spinning
ever faster.

Cowed, bile rising anew in her dragon-body's throat,
Ru-Lee replied, 'No.'

"Then you know what can happen—what will
happen—if you give up. You must find out what they want
of you. You must take control of yourself or others will be
destroyed through you!"

Heaving a heavy sigh, Ru-Lee asked, 'If I gain control
somehow, will I return to my human form—will I ever be
myself again?'

"I cannot say," Sheyna replied, mysteriously.

'Fat lotta' help you are!' Ru-Lee growled as she
completely uncurled her essence, pushing the shadows
further down into a cramped and narrow part of her mind.
They roiled and compacted in upon themselves and she
could feel their strength and determination.
Apprehensively, she thought, 'Fine, Sheyna! I'll do what I
can, but if I do regain my human form, I had better not
have any stretch marks!' She heard Sheyna's spirit
chuckle as she gathered her courage, and called out to the
shadows with her thoughts, 'What do you want?'

The answer was instant and fierce, the voices of many
answering in unison "You!" The sound reverberated
within her causing her dragon form to wince and recoil,
thrashing her tail against her cage and curling her claws.

'What do you mean, 'me',' she asked. 'You already
have my body—such as it currently is—and you nearly
crushed that which is me in the taking of it. What more is
there? Who are you?'

The answer shocked her more than she had thought
possible.

# Chapter 30

The light of the bright, full moon sparkled off the turbulent froth of the angry Udah River, falling gently upon the fractured group of friends and family standing watch upon the river's shores. The savage wind that had raged at them earlier was now nothing more than a gentle breeze. Pug, the pygmy owl, having survived the ordeal of being tossed about as he tried to maintain a grip within the violently dancing canopy of trees, now soared and dipped cautiously through the night air watching the river intently for any sign that might indicate what was happening below its surface.

On the northwest riverbank, D.G. and Sheila, with Ha-Fart on her shoulder, stood huddled near the boulder where their boat was anchored watching as Aylon carefully divided Bonshu blossoms into three separate groups, then tied them with strips of twisted twine. Nevlon stood nearby intently watching the figures on the opposite shore. When the shadows had entered Ru-Lee, Relmar had gone down to his knees as if in pain, clinging to the exposed and twisted tree roots of the riverbank. Helpless to offer any assistance other than physical support, Davlin and Trieca now stood watch over him, ready to lift him up should he lose his grip on the roots.

Beneath the wild waters of the Udah River, encased within a solid tornado of water that was now floating horizontally in the current, lay the enormous form of a translucent, gray-green water dragon, red-orange flames dancing beneath its shimmering skin—Ru-Lee. Within her mind, her soul conversed with the voices of the shadows seeking answers only they could give. Her dragon eyes glowed red with fire when their answers came, loud and echoing within her being.

*"We are the ancient Warta—your ancestors,"* they said, their multitude of voices rattling through her mind.

*'How can that be?'* she growled, gnashing her jaws. *'The ancients died long ago in the human world.'*

A wizened voice, rough with age and bitterness, emerged and rose above the rest. *"True—our forms died, but our souls stayed within the world of humans---stuck in a void of non-existence."*

*'Why—why did you not move on to the spirit world? What happened?'* Ru-Lee snorted, small puffs of steam rising from her dragon nostrils.

*"When each of us died, our memories returned to our souls—memories of who and what we had been, where we came from, and what we had done in our lifetimes before we were forced into human form and after. Our souls were tortured by our deeds. We could not move on to the spirit world until we found a way to right the evil we did while alive.*

*"This would seem a simple task, but our evils were great and many, and did not all take place within one world. It soon became apparent that we would have to return to where we began if we were to ease our tortured souls, but we were barred from that world, even in spirit form."*

The shadows roiled in the corner of her consciousness where she had contained them, their whispered voices rising angrily within their dark mass.

*"After many years of searching and testing, we discovered that the defenses that kept us out of our home world were weakening enough to allow the strongest among us to pass through. Those of us who were the oldest souls had retained the largest measure of strength. We came through singly, where and when we could, but we could do nothing to relieve our suffering or change the course of our existence—we realized we would need to work together to affect any change. We returned to the void, gathered others to us, and pushed through as a group hoping to use our combined strength. We did not know exactly what we needed to do, but we felt we must inhabit a living beast in order to accomplish our task.*

*"The beings most readily available where we crossed were Ergla. Their minds were small and easily overcome,*

130

*but their bodies could not contain us---they incinerated. Each of these efforts weakened us, forcing us to return to the void to gather our strength. Others joined us, growing our numbers and lending us their strength. Those newly dead who had been born in the human world were filled with fury and confusion. Their emotions were, and are, difficult to contain, but their strength is useful."*

The shadows convulsed and growled in the background, stretching and trying to slip around Ru-Lee's defenses. She snarled and pushed back with her mind as the voice went on, unperturbed.

*"We tried larger beasts---but had no success. All perished, taking a measure of our strengths with them. We had begun to despair that we would forever inhabit the void, never to be free of our own guilt and shame."*

Fearing the answer, Ru-Lee whispered, *'What changed?'*

The voice sighed and softly breathed, *"You."*

A shiver ran the length of Ru-Lee's body and angry heat rose within her. She stretched her claws and flared her nostrils, sending wisps of smoke into her water-walled cage. Within the vortex, void of water, she could hear her pounding heart echo off the surrounding walls. She did not respond to what the Ancient had said, waiting instead for the Warta to continue. When it finally did, she closed her eyes and listened, letting the information wash through her.

*"We could sense your presence in this world as you began to come of age—sooner, perhaps, than you would have had we not been present here. It has been difficult to find you, as we were not sure exactly what or who we were seeking. However, once you shifted to this form, there could be no doubt. This form will be of use to us, as will you."*

The tumultuous shadows again pushed against her mind and Ru-Lee felt a measure of wicked delight emanating them. She gritted her teeth as she held them in their confinement and asked, *'What do you intend?'*

131

"As you may know, some young of our line are on the verge of entering here from the human world. They will enter near the Hart. When they break through, the collective memories of their ancestors will return to them. Some may even take the Warta form, or some semblance of it. They will be confused, filled with fury, and insatiable in their new-found powers. The forces that drive them will cause them to destroy everything in their path...that is the nature of our kind. Total destruction---it is what happens when fire and wind come together....it is what we are--- destruction incarnate."

Becoming impatient, Ru-Lee pressed the Ancient saying, 'I am aware of these things. What part do you intend to play in this, and how do you plan to use me?' For she strongly suspected that the use of her powers was the true intent of these long-dead, body-less beings.

"We would use you to prevent these young ones from wreaking the same havoc we once did. They must be stopped! The evils they have committed in the human world are terrible, but the damage they would do in their true form would be far worse. We must make them see the harm they do to their souls.

"Our understanding came only after our own deaths. This may be the case for them also. If it be so, then we will bring about that death all the sooner."

Snarling, Ru-Lee growled, 'You would make a murderer of me?'

"Only if we must--but it is likely that this will be," the Ancient answered, indifferently, its gravelly voice grating through her mind.

Furious, Ru-Lee spat out, 'Do you truly believe that more killing will free you?'

The shadows bulged and surged towards her from their corner, pushing against her mind and soul; expanding within her. "If it is to save others, yes!" The voice answered, filling her mind and causing her to shake her dragon head vigorously.

132

The walls of the watery cage spun and swam around her, swooshing gently in her ears as the soft voice of Sheyna whispered to her, *"Careful, Ru—they are not all of one mind on this."*

Scowling, Ru-Lee's soul thought for a moment before asking the Ancient Warta, *'What of the souls of the younger dead? Do they, also, wish for retribution---or would they use my powers and this body to live again in our world and destroy those other beings that dwell here?'*

The Ancient chuckled from the darkness of the shadows, a dreadful, mournful sound. *"You are perceptive. It is true, some wish these things. But they are young and do not fully understand all that we Ancients have suffered. They are also not as strong as we are, their strength having been diluted over many generations. They will not be a problem,"* the Ancient answered. The shadows, however, seemed to give a different answer. They surged and roiled, the voices of many disgruntled souls growling and gnashing within. Ru-Lee struggled to contain them, holding her ground.

*'Do you expect me to allow you to control my body, to do as you wish with it, while I huddle within the recesses of my mind?'* Ru-Lee snarled, her dragon growl matching the growls within the shadowy mass, her soul stretching out to fill the body that was now hers. As she spoke, she rose to her feet, spiked tail lashing angrily from side to side, the flames within her skin leaping to life and dancing across her body.

The Ancient answered menacingly, *"You must work with us to obtain our goal. Allow us the free use of your body and powers---or perish. We will succeed----your resistance will only lead to your destruction."*

As the Ancient spoke, the shadows expanded and began spreading throughout Ru-Lee's body, crowding against her soul as they went; pushing it out of the way. Ru-Lee roared her defiance. She reared up as far as her cage would allow, gnashing her teeth, and clawing at the walls, smoke now billowing from her nostrils.

A wild wind began to rush within the cage as Ru-Lee fought for control of her limbs and powers, bellowing, *'You will NOT use me for your purposes! I will assist you, but I will NOT be USED by you!!'*

Sheyna's voice whispered again to her, slipping softly into her fevered and furious mind, *"Ru, they are too strong to resist on your own; they will overpower you. We have a plan---Aylon has gathered some Bonshu blossoms into a bundle. When I bring the mouth of the cage up out of the river, I will open up the top. You must thrust your head out and open your mouth so that Nevlon can fly over and drop the bundle in. The blossoms should counteract the changes taking place in your body, expelling the shadows at the same time. The Bonshu is pure life-force--the dead cannot dwell where it is; it will destroy them if they do not leave your body. Can you hold them off long enough to get to the mouth of the cage?"*

Tossing her head and squeezing her eyes shut tight, Ru-Lee ground her teeth together and groaned *'Yes!*

*"Good. Once the changes are complete, and the Warta gone, I will take you safely to shore. Hang on, Ru,"* Sheyna whispered, her voice a soft caress and boost of hope to Ru-lee's embattled soul.

The shadows, perhaps sensing something was amiss, pushed forward, filling Ru-Lee's mind and twisting her body with pain and agony that burned through her brain. Her soul screamed and her dragon voice roared, as she tried to clear her mind and remember what she was supposed to do. Her heart felt heavy and shriveled in her chest.

The darkness of the shadows surrounded her, filling her mind with numbing, searing anguish. *'Please, stop! I cannot bear it!'* She thought.

*"Then give up the fight!"* The Warta yelled within her.

*'Never!'* She moaned as she gathered her strength to her heart's core and pushed back against the shadows that wrapped around it. A small fire sparked to life within her

and her tortured soul nurtured it, seeking any source of light available to dispel the darkness the shadows brought.

Outside her body, she felt the liquid cage tilting upwards and vaguely remembered a need to climb to the mouth. Clawing and scraping her way upwards, she bellowed her defiance to the shadows, belching flames from her fang-filled mouth as she went, her body operating separately from her soul, which sought to stay alive within it. The cage filled with the acrid stench of scorched flesh, searing her nostrils; was it her own? She could not be sure, for her entire being was consumed with agonizing pain.

Opening her eyes, she saw the bright white of the full moon peering into the mouth of the cage. Forcing her soul to battle the shadows and fill her dragon form, she struggled towards its light.

The shadows became molten tar within her, dragging her down—making each step torturously slow. Her body struggled on as her soul battled within. Nearly there, the eerie cry of an eagle met the screech of an owl in the night and pierced her mind reminding her of her task.

As her claws grasped the watery edge, she felt the swirling coolness, rush over and around them. The shadows, perhaps believing they were to gain freedom from the liquid prison, cheered and surged through her body with such force that she lost her grip and slipped a few feet down the hard, swirling surface. The darkness of the shadows engulfed her mind; the small spark within her heart sputtered and faltered. Forcing the shadows back with every ounce of her strength, she snarled, gnashed her jaws, and leaped towards the opening—the light—her body contorting as if demon-possessed.

Opening her mouth wide to the night—she no longer remembered why, just that she must—she thrust her head through the opening. Her fangs brushed the wingtips of a passing eagle, which screamed and dropped his cargo---a small bundle—into her gaping maw.

Snapping her jaws shut, Ru-Lee released her grip on the opening, and gave up the fight allowing the Warta to fill her body and mind. Darkness and despair swept through her being; her body shuddered. The cage of water closed in around her once more, as she swallowed the sweet bundle of Bonshu blossoms—her serpentine body sliding to the bottom of the cage and curling in upon itself.

Ru-Lee moaned softly as the Bonshu blossoms took affect within her. Cool, soothing, liquid light poured through her body--a balm to her fevered mind. Light burst within her and a loud crack filled her ears. Every synopsis in her brain snapped. The light burst throughout her mind and soul, shooting through the shadows---bursting them apart. She gasped; her body convulsed, then became still. The flames and anger that had consumed her for days, died down, her breathe coming soft and easy. Her fiery dragon eyes turned a soft shade of gold-flecked heather green, and fluttered shut. The flames that had danced beneath her skin disappeared as the skin itself began to shrink and change color.

Too late, the Warta realized their peril. They screamed, twisting and retreating into themselves. Ru-Lee's body began to shrink as she drifted into unconsciousness, filled with numbing peace—a gift from the Bonshu blossoms. The Warta screeched in anger, pain, and frustration. Unable to stay connected as a group, they fractured. The cage filled with thousands of small black clouds as the shadows left Ru-Lee's body, dispersed and slipped through its closed, watery mouth into the night.

Curled in the apex of the swirling tornado cage, lay the unconscious, naked, human form of Ru-Lee, her pale skin raw, blistered, and glistening with sweat--disheveled blonde hair covering her face.

# Chapter 31

Water lapped gently upon the shore, pooling around Relmar's knees where they sunk deep into the mud. His agonized scream split the air like an ax as his body convulsed and pitched forward, face-first, into the river. Davlin gasped and leapt to his brother's side. Trieca joined him as they pulled Relmar back against the riverbank's tangled mass of roots, so intent on their task that they did not notice the wisps of shadow leave the funneled cage of water and scatter into the night.

Seating Relmar upright, Davlin grasped his brother's shoulders and peered into his face. The shock of the frigid water seemed to have roused Relmar slightly, but he appeared dazed and confused, his breathe coming in heaving gasps.

"What happened?" Davlin asked, the urgency in his voice unmistakable.

Relmar's eyes slowly focused on Davlin's face, his head wobbling loosely on its axis. Haltingly he said, "She is free….Ru-Lee….the shadows have left her. She is unconscious, but safe…I think."

Brows furrowed with concern, Davlin searched his brother's face and said, "You sounded like you were hurt. Are you—is she—in pain?"

Relmar weakly shook his head and swallowed before answering, "No….not anymore. There was pain…a lot of it, but….not now."

"Anyone care to fill me in?" Trieca asked.

Relmar, struggling to stand, shook his head and responded, "No. Not right now anyway. We haven't much time and we have a lot to do."

"What do you mean, we have a lot to do? What can we do from here?" Davlin asked, helping Relmar to his feet.

His strength returning, Relmar answered, "I was able to hear everything that went on in Ru-Lee's mind---the conversation that took place between her and the shadows—they are Warta, by the way! I am not sure exactly what we can do to help her or to fight off the Warta that are breaking through from the human world, but I think Ru is going to have to get to the Dragon Mountains as quickly as possible."

Davlin raised his eyebrows and sarcastically responded, "How? In case you haven't noticed, she is still underwater."

"Wait just a minute," interjected Trieca, "what do you mean, you could 'hear' what was said in Ru-Lee's mind? Where is Ru-Lee?"

Apprehensively, Relmar met Davlin's gaze. Trieca did not know that Ru-lee had changed form or what powers she possessed. If he knew, could they trust him not to report this information to his king? With an ever-so-slight shake of the head, Davlin warned Relmar not to reveal the truth.

Unfortunately, lying to an elf is extremely tricky, and Trieca had known them most of their lives, so he might know they were being less than truthful. Relmar probed Trieca's mind briefly, hoping to find some grain of information to build upon that would lend credence to the lie he must tell. Finding nothing useful, he sighed with exasperation and opened his mouth to mislead his friend.

However, before Relmar could speak, the funnel, which had been hovering half-in and half-out of the water, collapsed, sending waves washing once again over their water-logged feet. He caught his breath and grasped Davlin's shoulder in shock as a female-shaped column of water rose gently from the surface of the Udah River bearing the naked, unconscious form of Ru-Lee.

# Chapter 32

Pale moonlight sparkled on the frigid water as it streamed off of Ru-Lee's hair, her unconscious body draped in the arms of her aunt's liquid spirit rising from the midst of the Udah River. Gently, Sheyna bore Ru-Lee to the river's rocky shore where Nevlon, D.G., and Aylon stood waiting to receive her. D.G. watched anxiously as Sheyna placed Ru-Lee into Nevlon's arms. Aylon draped a cloak around the inert form of her granddaughter and looked up into the watery eyes of her daughter's spirit. A tear slipped from her right eye to glide slowly down her flushed cheek—pride and gratitude glowing in her face.

"Thank you, Sheyna," she whispered. "Thank you."

Sheyna bowed her head, her shoulders slumping slightly as she turned to go back into the river.

"Wait!" Jace yelled as he leapt over the anchoring boulder where he had been watching with Sheila and Ha-Fart.

Sheyna turned and smiled at him as he splashed into the river's shallows.

"You can't leave yet! We still need your help!"

"What do you mean?" Questioned Sheila, who, with Ha-Fart still clinging to her shoulder, had followed him to the edge of the water. "What more can she do?"

Scowling at Sheila, Jace sputtered, "Well, ah…you know….um…--I don't know for sure! But I KNOW she has to stay awhile longer until we get things sorted out!" Turning back to his mother's spirit, his voice almost pleading, he said, "We have to get everyone together on one side of the river or the other so we can figure everything out---make a plan!"

Ru-Lee groaned in Nevlon's arms, causing D.G. to whine and sniff at her dangling arm in concern. Nevlon watched Ru-Lee tenderly for a moment, then turned his gaze to Sheyna and said, "Jace is right, but we need to move quickly and get Ru to the Dragon Mountains before things get out of hand again."

"What are you thinking, Old Man?" Aylon asked him cautiously, brows knitting together across her high forehead.

A mischievous smile played upon his lips as he glanced at his wife, wiggled his eyebrows, and answered, "I was thinking Sheyna could help us get to our destination."

Confused, Jace asked, "How?"

But Aylon understood completely, and she did not appear to like it. Her face drained of color and she slowly shook her head. "You are nuts! Ru-Lee needs her rest, and I am NOT getting into anything like that!!" She growled, glaring at her husband.

"Aylon, you know as well as I do that those Bonshu blossoms won't last long, and..."

"I have more, remember?" Aylon interrupted.

Shaking his head, Nevlon continued, "Yes, I know--- but you don't have enough for a prolonged trek from here to the Dragon Mountains. Unless I miss my guess, that is exactly where Ru-Lee will need to be when the Warta from the human world break through to ours."

Aylon closed her eyes and set her jaw, letting her head fall back so that the moonlight illuminated her face and sparkled off of the white stripe that ran through her hair. Breathing deeply, she drank in the late-summer night air.

Pug landed on Jace's shoulder, gently nipping his ear in greeting. Jace reached up and ruffled the pygmy owl's head feathers absently, frigid water swirling around his ankles. He watched the exchange between Nevlon and Aylon impatiently. He had still not received an answer to his question, a fact that irritated him, but he was reluctant to interrupt them. Sheila stood behind him, listening, curiosity painted on her face. Ha-Fart sat on Sheila's shoulder, alert, as if ready for action at a moment's notice. The once-turbulent waters of the Udah River now lapped softly around Sheyna's liquid form. She listened to Nevlon and Aylon, but let her eyes glide over the others in the party. As her gaze fell upon Jace, a gentle smile tugged at the corners of her watery mouth, and her face softened tenderly.

After a few moments, Nevlon asked, "Well, wife---will you do it?"

Aylon sighed heavily, raised her head, opened her eyes, and glared daggers at her husband as she answered, "Yes. I suppose you will not?"

Nevlon's eyes danced as he chuckled and answered, "No. I think it best if someone goes on ahead to see how things are going on the other end."

"Naturally," Aylon sneered as Nevlon bent to kiss her cheek.

"Okay...enough of this cryptic nonsense! What are you two talking about?" Jace asked, unable to control his irritation.

Looking at Sheyna, Nevlon asked, "Sheyna, daughter, will you carry our group upriver to the Heart the way you carried Ru-Lee in dragon form?"

At the sound of her name, Sheyna tore her eyes from Jace and looked at Nevlon, then Aylon. Sorrow seemed to flow from her, rolling off into the river like a living thing. She moved towards the shore, coming almost to the water's edge and reached her hands towards Aylon. Her soft voice filled with regret and love as she spoke saying, "Forgive me, Mother. I was foolish."

The anger in Aylon's face melted away as she reached for her daughter's watery hand. Tears filled her eyes as she responded, "There was never anything to forgive."

Jace could stand it no longer and burst out, "You mean we are going to be imprisoned underwater?? No way! I love you, Mom, but I am NOT doing that!"

Sheyna turned to him and laughed, the sound falling around him like a waterfall. "Always the stubborn one, and still uncomfortable in tight places---don't worry, Jace, I will make sure you have plenty of room to breathe!"

With that, Sheyna released Aylon, turned, and dove into the Udah River. The droplets from the splash she made had barely returned to their home before the river began to churn wildly.

Jace quickly splashed to shore, startling Pug who flapped his wings and dug his sharp claws into Jace's shoulder.

"Ouch! Pug, be careful!" Jace yelled, grimacing as he stumbled and slipped on the rocks.

Pug replied with a reproachful screech in his ear. Jace jerked his head away from the ruffled owl and glared at him.

"Knock it off, you annoying ball of fluff, or I'll stew you up!"

Pug nipped Jace's ear and scrunched down on the boy's shoulder, settling his head deep within the neck feathers and clicking his beak.

D.G. barked and Jace turned to find a massive water tornado lying on its side in the river, mouth open towards the shore.

# Chapter 33

There was no wind now, only the watery whirring sound of the sideways tornado as it spun in the river, the water it displaced sloshing through the rocky crevices on the river's shore. Jace stood, shaking his head, trying to convince himself that this funnel of water was not in front of him awaiting his entrance. Pug, still irritated at Jace's harsh words to him earlier, squinted at the funnel and clacked his beak noisily in Jace's ear. Sheila let out a soft breath behind them, glanced sideways at the dark mouse perched on her shoulder, and shrugged. Ha-Fart shrugged back, and scratched his ear in confusion.

Nevlon stepped forward first, D.G. on his heels. Carrying the inert form of Ru-Lee, he splashed through the shallows and stepped tentatively into the water tornado's open end. Finding the inner surface to be strong and solid, he carried his burden halfway to the apex and gently laid her inside where D.G. laid down beside her, resting his head upon Ru-Lee's chest.

Nevlon returned to the shore to find Aylon glaring at him; eyes flashing; sparks snapping from her hair into the moonlit night. Her jaw was set in a rigid line, and her high forehead crinkled into a dozen angry ripples that came to a point between her brows. He shrugged and grinned sheepishly.

With laughing eyes, he kissed his wife on her pursed lips and said, "I'll see you on the other side. I am going over now to let the others know what is going on." His form shimmered in the moonlight as he shifted to eagle form and lifted off into the night, winging towards the opposite shore.

Aylon snorted loudly through her nose as she watched him go. Behind her, Jace said, "I do NOT want to get in there! What if it caves in?"

Irritated, Aylon turned to him and snarled, "Oh, pull up your big boy pants and quit complaining! If I have to, you have to!" Then, her voice softening slightly, she sighed heavily and said, "Besides, the old man is right. It is the best solution to our travel problem---it will be quicker, easier, and safer." She turned back to the sideways tornado of water, sucked in her breath and let it out slowly as she walked into the shallows towards it. She stepped cautiously inside saying, "Okay, Sheyna…Make it an easy ride, please?"

With his head down, refusing to look directly at the funnel, Jace trudged towards it. Growling and grumbling, he swore, "#@@%&^! I really hate this, Pug!"

Pug clacked his beak tauntingly in Jace's ear as if to say, "Serves you right!" However, as they neared the opening, Pug sidled across Jace's shoulder and nestled next to his neck, eyes wide and wondering. Jace stepped inside and went to sit next to Ru-Lee and D.G., a constant stream of profanity flowing from his lips.

"That is quite enough, Jace! You know how I feel about that kind of language," Aylon chastised from her position near Ru-Lee's head.

Jace fell silent, but his jaw muscles worked of their own accord as he glanced warily around the enclosure.

Sheila had followed quietly and walked softly past Jace to sit near Ru-Lee's feet, her own legs curled delicately beneath her. Ha-Fart jumped from her shoulder and strutted past Ru-Lee to curiously inspect the inner lining of their transportation, fascinated by the solid nature of the inside of their swirling water-funnel.

Jace's sharp intake of breath caused them all to face the entrance in time to see the mouth of the water tornado close, sealing them in.

# Chapter 34

It took only a short time for the funnel of water to reach the opposite shore where the three young men waited with Nevlon. Sheyna hadn't bothered to lower the tornado below the river's waves as she carried her passengers between the shores. It was with amazement and trepidation that Relmar, Davlin, and Trieca watched its approach. Once the wide end faced them and opened, they were able to view the others of their party seated safely within. Relmar and Davlin smiled broadly to see their youngest brother's discomfort, knowing how he felt about anything resembling an enclosed cave, and splashed through the shallows to climb aboard. Trieca, however, was less than enthusiastic.

"What is this?" He asked Davlin as Relmar entered the tornado, sat beside Aylon, and curiously eyed the beautiful silken-haired woman seated at Ru-Lee's feet.

"You heard what Nevlon said," Davlin answered, glancing sideways at him with amusement. "This is our ride." Grinning, he followed his brother.

"You'll be fine, Trieca!" Nevlon chuckled, roughly patting the elf on the back and propelling him forward. "Load up!"

Trieca ran his hand gently along the inside edge of the water tornado, shook his head, and trailed wonderingly after his friends. Aylon greeted him with a curt nod, her own discomfort etched upon her face. Trieca sat near Jace, his eyes falling on the still form of Ru-lee.

"Is she okay?" He asked, concerned.

"Yeah," Jace replied. "Just resting," he added, evasively.

"Resting from what?" Trieca asked as he watched Ru-Lee's breast gently rise and fall beneath the cloak.

Warning flashed across Aylon's face as Jace caught her eye. There was also a question in her look---how much did Trieca know? She glanced surreptitiously at Davlin and Relmar who, still preoccupied with the woman near Ru-Lee's feet, did not notice the exchange. Davlin covertly poked his older brother in the ribs causing Relmar to jerk his head around in irritated alarm. Before he could speak, however, Nevlon intervened.

"I think you ALL need to debrief each other about recent events and activities," he said. He allowed his eyes to travel meaningfully over each member of the party, finally settling on his still-irritated wife. "I need to get to the Dragon Mountains to find out how things are going and let them know what I can of our situation, Wife. Be safe. I will see you all there soon."

Aylon grinned a slightly wry grin and nodded, replying, "Be safe, Husband. I will see you soon."

Nevlon shifted form and took flight in one swift movement, the moonlight shining on his eagle back as he quickly disappeared into the night.

Sheyna's soft, watery voice filled the funnel saying, "Hang on, everyone. I will get us there as quickly as possible."

Trieca Gasped and jumped backwards into Jace, his head darting back and forth as he tried to discover the origin of the voice, which was now laughing softly at his confusion. Jace grabbed Trieca's shoulders and gently sat him upright again, chuckling.

"It's okay—just my mom," he said, smiling into Trieca's stunned face.

# Chapter 35

The light of the late summer moon reflected off the surface of the gently rolling waters of the Udah River. The occasional swelling of the waves as they were displaced by the submerged tornado was the only sign of the passage being forged upstream beneath the waves. Occasionally, where the river was shallow, one might see the funnel rise from the depths and skim across the surface. The view was only momentary before it descended below the surface once again, small ripples slipping across the waters in its wake.

Inside the horizontal water twister, Ru-lee woke from a dreamless sleep to the soft murmurings of conversation. She felt peaceful and lighthearted—her earlier experience a cloudy dream in her mind. Opening her eyes and slowly rolling her head from side to side, she found her friends and family seated around her, watching her and speaking in low whispers. Soft blue light reflected and danced upon the walls of the enclosure, illuminating her surroundings and showing concern etched on every face. Though her body no longer ached, she could feel the fire burning deep within her, waiting to rise again. Had it really come so close to consuming her, or had she imagined it? Slowly pressing her hands to the cool smooth surface of the water-enclosed cage they travelled in, she sat up blinking. The cloak covering her naked body slid down, draping over one shoulder to cling lightly to her chest. D.G. rose to his feet, his whole body wriggling joyfully as he nuzzled her neck and grinned at her.

"Where are we?" She asked in a raspy voice as she wrapped her arms around D.G.'s neck, smiled at him, and affectionately rubbed his velvety ears. Her throat felt hot and raw, a remnant of the heat that had filled her body earlier. *'It must have been real,'* she thought, bemused. She blinked as she looked into D.G.'s amber eyes and fleetingly wondered why she felt so peaceful if her 'dream' was real. The corners of her mouth dipped down slightly and her brow furrowed as she tried to grasp the implications of the events that hazily drifted in her head. Her thoughts were like smoke in the wind, however--gone before they could take hold in her mind. Her smile returned quickly as D.G. curled his legs beneath his body and lay down beside her, resting his head in her lap.

Aylon pulled a small bundle of Bonshu blossoms from the pouch at her waist, removed one petal, and handed it to Ru-Lee, ordering, "Eat this." Eyeing Ru-Lee, she said, "We are inside a tube of water created by Aunt Sheyna. She is carrying us to the Dragon Mountains." Her answers were short and concise, and she watched Ru-Lee's face as she spoke.

"Aunt Sheyna? How can that be?" Ru-Lee asked. Her rough voice taking on a note of amused confusion as she took the petal from Aylon's outstretched hand. Deftly, she placed the soft white blossom into her mouth, smashed it with her tongue, and swallowed. The heat in her throat cooled instantly as the Bonshu juice slid down. Her smile widened as she closed her eyes, enjoying the relief.

Sighing, Aylon answered, a note of sadness in her voice, "When Sheyna was wounded, she was near a river—one that runs in both worlds. She slid her body into the river and gave up her spirit to water." Aylon looked down at her hands sitting restlessly in her lap and smiled ruefully. "Water was Sheyna's element—she was connected to it during her life, and now she is linked to it for eternity."

"So I *did* hear her voice speaking to me—I thought I had imagined that! I dreamt that I changed form—was that real, too?" Ru-Lee asked, perplexed.

"Very!" Jace answered, nodding and scratching Pug's neck feathers.

Aylon shot him a warning look. He met her penetrating gaze and chanced a sidelong glance at Trieca to see if the elf had taken note of his slip. Trieca sat watching the exchange with growing interest and furrowed brows—he had definitely caught the slip!

"Why was I imprisoned?" Ru-Lee continued, oblivious to the undercurrent of tension surrounding her.

"Because you were not in control, Ru," Aylon responded patiently. "The Shadows had entered your body. You needed time to deal with them and manage your emerging powers without being consumed by either. It was the only way to keep you safe."

Davlin sat next to Relmar, only half listening to the conversation. Amusement played on his face as he watched Trieca's discomfort and confusion. As children, Trieca had always seemed to be one step ahead of him in everything. It was sadistically satisfying to have the upper hand for once. He glanced at his older brother and shook his head. Relmar's preoccupation with the young woman seated near Ru-Lee's feet was almost comical. The girl looked familiar to him, and he was sure her identity would come out soon.

Trieca listened with growing concern and consternation, his gaze passing between Ru-Lee, Aylon, and Jace. "Wait--Am I to understand that Ru-Lee has the ability to change form?"

Aylon chewed on the inside of her lip as she glanced to the other members of the group for help. Each shrugged, not wanting to be the one to spill the beans to Trieca. They had refrained from discussing anything of any importance while they waited for Ru-Lee to rouse, but they had all known that a confrontation was inevitable.

Though usually helpful and resourceful, Ru-Lee was no help at all in her current state. The Bonshu blossoms calmed her system and counteracted her powers, but they also short-circuited her brain to the extent that she could not fully grasp the gravity of the situation around her. She sat rubbing D.G.'s ears, a dazed grin playing on her lips.

Growing impatient, Trieca turned to his old friend, Jace, and demanded, "Well---can she, or can't she transform?"

Ru-Lee felt the hair on her neck prickle as the tension within their enclosure thickened. She stopped petting

D.G., who regarded the others with lidded eyes. Her mind felt foggy and, for some reason, this made her giggle. She turned from the group of males to look at Sheila, who sat quietly absorbing the scene that played out before her, Ha-Fart lounging in her lap.

'*Ever thoughtful,*' thought Ru-Lee fondly--then she blinked and looked again at her friend. Sheila had changed! Or had she? Ru-Lee stared harder at Sheila, trying to discern if her friend had really changed, or if her own mind was playing tricks on her.

Sheila cocked her head and locked her eyes with Ru-Lee's, smiling. Suddenly, the veil of haze lifted from Ru-lee's mind, and she gasped at the clarity of her memory and understanding of their current situation. She had always been aware that Sheila had the ability to see straight to the heart of things, but she had never dreamed that her friend could bring such clarity to others. She held Sheila's gaze for a moment longer, amazement etched upon her face.

'*How did I deserve to be so lucky in my friends,*' she thought. Blinking, she looked around at the others. No one appeared to have noticed her sudden 'awakening'. She held her breath and watched as they tried to figure out how much they should confide to Trieca. If he were to share their secrets with his king, as was his duty, their lives would all be forfeit. They had spent much of their childhood with Trieca and his family--he was their friend. However, since he had entered the king's service, they had rarely seen him. There was no way to be sure where his loyalties were now. She shook her head and lowered her eyes sadly.

Ru-Lee did not know when Trieca had shown up, or how he had come to be with them, nor did she know how much he knew, or guessed, already. Her stomach clenched and she bit back the nausea that threatened to wash over her as she thought of what would happen to her if the council were to find out about her powers.

Something needed to be done immediately, though. Soon they would reach the Dragon Mountains. They needed to find out what was going on and make plans. That would be impossible to do if they had to keep Trieca in the dark.

Finally, Aylon heaved a heavy sigh drawing all attention to her. Locking Trieca's grey eyes with her own hazel ones, she paused before saying, "Trieca, we must have your word that what you hear will go no further. It is a matter of utmost importance and safety. Our very lives depend on it."

Narrowing his eyes at her, Trieca asked, "How can I make that promise, when I don't know what I will hear?" His voice edged with distrust.

"I don't know," Aylon responded, shaking her head, "but you will have to find a way. If you do not promise, I will have the boys hold you down while I administer a potion to knock you out so we can discuss things." Aylon continued. She cocked her head to one side, a sly grin on her face.

"You'd do it, wouldn't you?" Trieca said, his eyes moving from Aylon to survey the three brothers who each bore a sadistic smirk. Remembering a time years earlier, when the brothers had used some of Aylon's concoctions to trick him so they could sneak a ride on his father's racing steed, he snorted, "Wouldn't be the first time, would it?" The others watched as he appeared to mull over his options; Ru-Lee licked her lips and waited, her throat suddenly tight and dry.

Finally, Trieca looked at Aylon, shrugged, and said, "Fine--I give you my word that I will say nothing of what I hear this night."

"Are you sure? No word will be given to the king?" Aylon pressed.

"I am sure—but you are putting me in a very unpleasant position! I hope it is worth the dishonor I will bring if things don't work out."

"So do I," Aylon replied, her voice grave.

Ru-Lee breathed a sigh of relief. She had not been looking forward to a physical altercation between the brothers and their long-time friend, though Jace appeared to be a bit put out to miss the chance to wrestle Trieca. She shook her head and smiled affectionately at him. Her heart swelled as her eyes travelled over the faces of those around her. Blinking, she thought, *'That Bonshu flower must make a person mush-brained!'* Behind her, she could see Relmar sneaking glances in Sheila's direction. Catching her friend's eye, she raised a questioning brow. Sheila met the question with a shrug and blushed.

"Aylon," Ru-Lee said, a confused smirk on her face, "I think maybe we should *all* share our information. There appears to be a lot going on with more than just me!"

"Yeah," Jace agreed, leaning back and watching Trieca. "First, I would like to know what *you* were doing following us."

"Fair enough—I'll go first," Trieca shrugged. "I didn't buy that bull about you fishing, Jace. You always preferred berries over raw fish--it was a poor lie on your part. After we made our report, I hung around the meetings at Illiand watching Relmar and Nevlon. Relmar seemed to be acting strange, so I tailed him when he left. I watched him meet up with Nevlon and slip away--I followed thinking they might lead me to you. I was right," he finished, stretching his legs out in front of him, a self-satisfied look on his face.

"Just as nosey as always!" Jace snorted.

"If that's what you want to call it. Some call it following a hunch," Trieca grinned, then turned unexpectedly to Ru-Lee. "Your turn."

Ru-Lee met Trieca's gaze, contemplating where to start and how much to reveal. A lump formed in her throat and her stomach churned at the thought of reliving her recent experiences.

"I don't think so," Relmar's strong voice filled the space around them. "Let's give Ru a bit more time to process what has happened to her."

Trieca replied, "Okay—how about you, then."

"What do you want to know?" Relmar asked, evasively.

"Why were you acting so strangely in the council meetings? Why did you and Nevlon sneak off? Why are you here and not with the Travelers?"

"Is that *all* you want to know?" Relmar questioned, his eyelids half closed, hiding his sky-blue eyes.

"We'll start there," Trieca answered.

"Okay." Sitting up, cross-legged, Relmar folded his hands in his lap and looked at the expectant faces of his friends and family. He closed his eyes and looked down at his hands, then spoke, saying, "As you know, I have always been able to sense when someone was hurt, lying, or needed help."

Everyone nodded. The soft sound of wings caused Relmar to look up and watch Pug flutter from Jace's shoulder to the top of D.G.'s head. The small bird nestled down in the fluff between D.G.'s ears, hooting softly when he was settled. Relmar smiled and continued. "Well, it seems as if that was just a pre-cursor to another, rather annoying ability. Around the time of my twenty-first birthday, I discovered that I could *feel* what others feel. Not at will, mind you. Their feelings and emotions would just wash over me! It wasn't too bad when I was with the Travelers or in a small group. I could usually distance myself enough to manage. After some time went by, I found the ability to be a useful asset.

"Unfortunately, the empathic nature of my ability was not meant to stay—not on its own, at least." He stopped a moment and looked up, meeting Trieca's gaze. "When I went to meet with the dragons, something changed."

"So close to the Heart—it is not unheard of for one's powers and abilities to become enhanced," Trieca said, unflinchingly returning Relmar's stare.

"So Nevlon said, later," Relmar replied, dryly.

"How did they change?" Asked Jace, curiosity shining in his eyes.

Without taking his eyes from Trieca, Relmar answered, "I can hear thoughts."

Trieca's eyes widened, and he asked, "Is that why you were acting strange in the meetings?"

"Yes," replied Relmar. "It was hard enough being around the villagers, hearing all of their thoughts milling around in my brain. So close to the mountains and the Heart, I felt like I was losing my mind! It was nearly unbearable speaking with the Dahgsna dragons. The lead female knew I could hear her thoughts and refused to communicate any other way. Unfortunately, I can still feel emotions as well. Did you know that dragons, Dahgsna at least, think of food nearly every second when they first wake? They are not particular about what they eat, so long as it is alive when they start. They are extremely articulate at describing what it smells, tastes, sounds, and feels like—I think she enjoyed making me ill!"

Ru-Lee cringed, remembering her own encounter with dragons and the gore they seemed so intent upon in the visions they showed her.

Relmar touched her shoulder and whispered, "Sorry."

Drawing a deep breath, she pushed the memories down and said, "It's okay. What happened at the council meetings?"

Speaking to Ru-Lee, Relmar continued, "All those people in tight quarters—upset, worried, angry. It was too much for my senses....overwhelming. I had to get out of there. Nevlon guessed what was happening and suggested we leave on the sly. We had done what we came to do—give the keepers information. Nevlon wanted to get back to Aylon and you. He was worried that we wouldn't get back in time to be of any use." The corners of his mouth turned up in a wry smile as he said, "He was right to worry, wasn't he."

Ru-Lee nodded. Nevlon, Davlin, and Relmar had not arrived in time to be of much help when her powers and the shadows overtook her at the river. She squeezed

Relmar's hand and said, "I am glad you made it, though. I am sure we will have need of you yet."

Turning to Davlin, she asked, "Where did you disappear to when you left Aylon's cabin?" She did not mention the form he had taken when he had departed in the middle of the night. Although she knew they were sharing secrets and information, she did not want to be the one to give Trieca the secret of Davlin's transformation abilities.

Davlin shrugged and looked at Aylon before responding, "Aylon sent me to hurry Nevlon along. She was very worried about you, Ru. You nearly burned down her hut on more than one occasion! She knew I was fast, and a good tracker, so she asked me to see if I could find out what was keeping Nevlon. I met him and Relmar just outside of Illiand."

"I thought maybe you had been waiting for them!" Trieca interjected.

"Nope…..I met them just as they entered the forest. I could hear them coming! Sounded like a heard of Ergla!"

"No, it didn't! Ergla don't move that fast!" Defended Relmar, his temper flaring.

"No, but they *are* noisy!" Davlin countered, smiling, "And so were you! I am sure Trieca found you easy to follow."

"We were in a hurry!"

"I could tell!"

"Okay, boys, enough!" Ordered Aylon, striking the smooth surface of the water tornado with the palm of her hand.

The slapping sound echoed through the chamber, and the older brothers fell silent. Jace, sitting across from them, smirked slightly. He seemed to enjoy the fact that it wasn't him in hot water.

Trieca eyed Relmar for a moment longer, mulling over the information he had heard so far. He seemed to decide that none of what he had heard was of any consequence, and he allowed as his gaze to travel over to Ru-Lee.

She sat, avoiding his eyes, and holding her breath. Her fingers found D.G.'s velvety ear and she closed her eyes, willing Trieca to ask for someone else's input next. Her mind slid over the names of her friends and family members that were gathered with her. Who else could he ask? Trieca now knew of the involvement of each member, except for Aylon and herself. He would never dare to ask Aylon--Trieca had always harbored a deep fear that Aylon would turn him into a toad if he displeased her. Ru-Lee was sure that his fear had not abated with age and maturity.

She opened her eyes to meet his gaze and prepare her answers, but found him looking elsewhere. Sheila—he was looking at Sheila! Trieca was watching Sheila with a mixture of intrigue and confusion on his face, which made Ru-Lee nearly burst out laughing. Finally, Trieca looked to Ru-Lee.

"Not to be rude," he said, tilting his head in Sheila's direction, "but who is she?"

Relmar perked up, also interested to hear the answer to this question, a fact that confused Ru-Lee. *'If he can read minds, shouldn't he already know?'* She thought. Davlin cocked his head, curious, but with the look of someone who thinks they have something figured out. Sheila doubled over giggling, nearly upsetting a drowsy Ha-Fart from his seat in her lap.

A wide smile slipped across Ru-Lee's face as she answered, "That's Sheila."

Relmar looked startled and puzzled, but said nothing. Jace grunted, a look of utter disgust on his face that caused Ru-lee to stifle a snicker. Davlin grinned and nodded as if confirming his own guess.

Trieca, however, looked more confused than anyone. Cocking his eyebrows, he looked to Ru-Lee and asked, "How? I thought she was a mist-elf-spider being---no bigger than a child!"

"She was," Ru-Lee responded, amused. Out of the corner of her eye, she saw Relmar listening intently.

"What happened?"

"I don't know," she shrugged. "She was like this when I woke up—you were here. I haven't seen her since I was pushed out of a boat in the middle of the river!" At this, she looked accusingly at her friend. "Sheila can answer better than I can about the changes we see here."

Sheila sat up attempting to control her laughter. Her shoulders shook causing her silvery hair to shimmer and dance as it cascaded down her back. Relmar seemed mesmerized by the light playing off of its silky strands.

Sheila grinned at Ru-Lee and said, "I don't know any more than you do. I shifted in the boat and came out larger than before—I shifted again on shore, and came back this way. I really don't know what is going on." Sliding a sly glance sideways to Relmar, she grinned and softly added, "I'm not complaining, mind you." She looked to Ru-Lee again and said, "At least your clothes fit me." Then, glancing ruefully down at the fabric stretched to nearly bursting across her chest, she whispered sheepishly, "Well, sort of."

Ru-Lee shook her head. She had thought Sheila's clothing looked familiar. Looking down at the cloak that clung loosely to her chest and shoulder, she vaguely wondered if her backside were showing, and tucked the cloak's edge around her hips in the hopes of covering up her tush.

Relmar's voice cut through her thoughts, "Aylon, care to share what you know about Sheila's 'condition'?"

"Well, you probably already know my thoughts, but I will voice them for the others," Aylon responded, a note of irritation in her voice.

Relmar nodded.

Looking to Sheila and Ru-Lee, Aylon spoke saying, "Mist Elves live their lives as helper beings. They come into existence only under extraordinary circumstances. Your mother, Ru-Lee, created a part of those

157

circumstances when she gave you up so that you could be safe."

At Ru-Lee's look of confusion, she explained, "When you were born, a Seer foretold that you would be needed in this world one day; that you would have powers and abilities unseen before; and that those powers would come to light no matter where you were. When things began to get really bad in the human world, your mother tried to convince your father to come with her and bring you here for safety. He couldn't. The magic fire had long been quenched in his heart. He *wanted* to believe and follow her, but he just couldn't. Even if she had passed through right before his eyes, he would not have found the doorway into this world. She was torn between her love for you and her love for your father. She knew you would have us, so she returned to the human world to protect your father, leaving as many protections as possible in place for you here.

"The night you arrived, there was a slight mist in the silver forest—you passed through it. That forest, as you know, is filled with magic. You were a magical creature, protected by magic, and shielded by love. As you passed through the mist, the love mixed with the magic, and a mist elf was born—Sheila."

"Wait a minute!" Jace interrupted, shaking his head. "That would make her about nine years old! I thought she was older than that!"

"Well, she is," Aylon explained. "First of all, Mist Elves don't age the same as we do...they gain several years of wisdom and maturity for each of our years. Secondly, they are 'contained' in the mist during the first several years of their lives. They only gain corporeal form when these special conditions are met—that is what I meant when I said she was 'born'....it was the easiest way to explain it."

"But she didn't find me right away," Ru-Lee interjected, perplexed.

158

"Not that you were aware---but she found you. She was your helper being. She would take the forms that would best be able to assist you. Her forms of child and spider were the best forms for your needs at the time."

"So, she is changing now because I need her to be something else?" Ru-Lee asked.

"No, I think she is changing now, because you no longer need her. She is becoming that which will be most helpful to someone else."

Ru-Lee looked to Sheila and the mesmerized face of Relmar and asked, "Who?" Even though she felt she knew the answer.

"I am not sure," Aylon answered, watching the pair also. "Sheila does not even know yet. Only time will tell."

Unconvinced, Ru-Lee asked, "How much time?"

Her friend and her cousin did not seem to be paying any attention to the conversation, but Davlin, Jace, and Trieca were listening intently.

"I don't know. She is changing quickly. I imagine she will know by the time we reach the mountains." Shaking her head, Aylon added, "This could be a long ride."

Murmuring her agreement, Ru-Lee turned from Sheila and Relmar to find Trieca watching her expectantly.

# Chapter 36

Ru-Lee ran her fingers through the silky soft fur around D.G.'s ear, his head still resting in her lap. The soft whirring rush of the spinning tube of water in which they rode filled her ears, blocking out all else as it gently spun through the river's current. Her mind mulled over the events that she recalled from the past few days. Organizing her thoughts was difficult, since the Bonshu blossoms muddled her brain. The clarity Sheila had given her earlier now waned considerably, and she found it hard to focus. Her attention kept flitting through images without really acknowledging what they were—flipping through memories that she wished she didn't have.

Trieca had asked for an explanation of how she had come to be delivered, unconscious, from the depths of the Udah River. She did not know where to begin, or how much information to give him. He sat watching her, patiently. She could feel his eyes boring into the top of her bowed head. The others waited in silence, not wanting to give away more than she was ready to share. Even Jace held his tongue, though he had removed his hat, and sat fidgeting with the blackened brim as he dangled it over his bent knee.

D.G. gazed at her with lidded eyes. She felt his calm presence enter her mind, assisting her as she sifted through information--helping her find the right starting point for her tale. She smiled her thanks to him, and he gently nodded his head in response. His jaws rubbed her knee as he did so, and a wide grin crinkled the corners of his eyes. In her mind, an image came into focus--the shadows, dark and ominous against a summer blue sky. This was the place to begin.

She looked up to find Trieca's grey eyes regarding her intensely. His gaze softened, when he saw the smile sitting peacefully upon her face. Shifting his position, he slid his legs out of the way and lay on his side, propped up on an elbow, preparing to hear her tale. She chuckled softly, recalling how she used to entertain Trieca, Jace, Davlin, and Relmar with stories she made up for their enjoyment. The look on Trieca's face was the same as it had been when he was younger, stretched out near an evening fire with his friends.

She glanced around to find Davlin and Relmar also waiting patiently. Jace pretended indifference, but she was certain he was listening closely to see where she would start and what she would share with their elven friend. Aylon met her gaze with a nod of encouragement, a hint of sorrow in her eyes. The sad tinge rimming Aylon's eyes worried Ru-Lee. It was as if she was missing a vital piece of information—information that concerned her. However, her muddled mind, unable to get a handle on whatever it might be, flitted back to the task at hand.

Breathing in deeply, she began, "For months now, I have had disturbing dreams concerning the dark shadows. They always left me feeling uneasy—even frightened. That fear has become heightened and now invades my waking hours as well whenever the shadows came near. They fill me with terror and dread.

Ha-Fart stirred in Sheila's lap, softly attesting to the fear the shadows brought to him as well.

"A few days ago, Jace came to my cabin with his own concerns about the shadows. He said that the Travelers had experienced animals disappearing and that Ergla had been leaving the swamp—they had been seen quite a ways from their home. His brothers had sent him to check on me because I lived so close to the swamp—they were worried that the Ergla might cause me problems."

Jace nodded, but did not look up from his hat.

Ru-Lee ran a hand through her hair, and vaguely wondered, 'What happened to my hat?' The thought was fleeting, however, as Trieca interjected, "Erlga were in the forest near Illiand. That was what we were hunting when we found Jace in the field near the river."

"I know—I was hiding in the field," Ru-Lee responded.

"Why were you hiding?" Trieca asked, suspiciously. "Why did you leave your cabin?"

"Nevlon came to my cabin shortly after Jace arrived. He asked us to go to Aylon's and not let anyone know where I was. He told us about the Warta coming through from the human world—then he said he needed to go to the Arch to check out a hunch of some sort. He didn't say what, exactly."

"Wait!" Trieca interrupted. "*What* did you say the Warta are doing?" He had not been *in* the meetings at Illiand, having only been allowed to view them through the gallery openings that surrounded the meeting halls. He had not heard all that had been said, and had left to follow Relmar and Nevlon before the information discussed there could be shared with him.

Relmar broke in explaining, "A few Warta descendents, the ones running the war in the human world, have begun digging through the mountains on the human side--apparently looking for resources to use or sell to fund their war efforts. They are dangerously close to the Heart and will break through soon. The dwarves, trolls, and dragons are doing their best to shore up the defenses on our side. Pixies, brownies, and other beings have been called upon to delay the work on the human side."

"How have they been 'called upon'?" Trieca asked Relmar, puzzled. "There is no communication—no way to get through the gates!"

"I don't know, exactly," Relmar shrugged, "I only know that, according to Nevlon and the Elven leaders---your king among them---contact has been made, and an understanding established."

Trieca sat up, a dazed look on his face—as if he had been hit in the head by a brick, and his brains had been slightly addled.

"Wow..." he breathed softly.

"Yeah," Davlin agreed.

After a few minutes of stunned silence, Trieca returned his focus to Ru-Lee. "Okay....now I know why you were hiding and where you were going—at least initially. But, what were you doing in the river? Where were you headed then? And how does you transforming come into play?" he asked.

Ru-Lee slid her arms beneath the cloak and pulled it up around her neck, shuddering slightly as the coolness of their funnel swept over her. Pug blinked at her and shook his head, his neck feathers ruffling around his face.

She looked to Aylon, then Sheila before replying wryly, "Things are a bit fuzzy here. We were headed to the other side of the river…I think…I was kind of out of it, though. I know that one minute I was in the boat looking at something---the next minute, I was in the water." She cocked her head at Trieca and waited, wondering if he would push for more information.

"Really?!" Jace snarled, irritation flashing in his eyes as he glared at her.

'Great!,' Ru-Lee thought. She should have known that Jace would not allow any more secrets and game playing than was necessary, but she did not really wish to speak of what had happened to her---not out loud anyway. She hadn't had much of a chance to mull things over and come to grips with the events that had swept her along. How could she put them into words if she didn't even understand them herself? She glared back at him, almost willing his hat to catch on fire again---almost. Fortunately for Jace, the effects of the Bonshu blossoms still held sway in her system, and she couldn't raise so much as a spark— couldn't even feel much more than deep irritation towards him.

"Do you know more, Jace?" she asked, daring him to call her out.

"A bit!" Jace snapped at her, glowering.

"Look, I don't care who tells me, but I would like a bit more information!" Trieca interjected as he watched the tense exchange between Ru-Lee and Jace.

Ru-Lee's chest tightened at the thought of attempting to explain what had happened to her. Most of it was still fuzzy in her mind, and the Bonshu blossoms weren't helping her focus any. She could not speak out loud about things she wasn't sure of in her own mind!

Aylon came to her rescue by saying, "I think we need to give Trieca as much information as possible, Ru. It won't do any good if he doesn't know what he is dealing with, and I believe I can fill in some gaps for you." She patted Ru-Lee's shoulder gently, her eyes soft and understanding, before she turned to Trieca and continued, "Trieca, Ru-Lee is coming of age—coming into her powers. This is happening much sooner than it should, and I think it has something to do with the presence of the shadows. They are having an adverse affect on her. Since she has more than one elemental power to contend with, she is struggling more than others I have seen.

"We were crossing the river to gain access to the Bonshu blossoms that grow on the opposite shore so that I could use them to help her. The shadows came upon us in the middle of the river. I felt they were a threat to Ru and asked one of the Naiads that live within the Udah to take her into the water and keep her safe until the shadows passed. Ru-Lee, however, was not herself and had to be pushed into the water against her will."

Nodding contemplatively, Trieca said, "Okay. That gets her into the water, which should not have been much of a problem anyway, given that one of her powers is water, right?"

Aylon looked ruefully at Ru-Lee before continuing. "Yes—one of her powers is water----but it was being overshadowed by another elemental power; one, I believe, that was being pulled to the forefront by the presence of the shadows."

A look of confusion crossed Trieca's knitted brows as he processed this information. "Ru-Lee's powers are water and earth. They can *blend*, but I have never heard of either one suppressing the other.....what am I missing here?" He asked, suspicion creeping back into his voice.

164

With a deep sigh, Aylon shook her head and answered, "Fire. Ru-Lee holds the element of fire in her blood."

Astounded gasps echoed through the chamber as this fact pummeled Relmar and Trieca. The information came as no surprise to Davlin and Sheila, who had seen the effects that this emerging elemental power had on her and those around her—their wild flight through the forest still fresh in their minds.

"That can't be!" Trieca announced, bolting to an upright position. "If she had the element of fire in her blood, she would not have been able to pass through the gates years ago!"

"We don't know exactly how she was able to come through, Trieca—maybe the protections her mother gave her shielded her powers from detection," Aylon countered. "But, let me assure you, she does hold the element of fire. In the boat, I realized that the presence of the shadows made those powers stronger. We had to get her into the water for her own protection. It was obvious that the shadows wanted to control her somehow."

"What could they want with Ru?" Trieca asked, blinking incredulously at her.

"They want to use me," Ru-Lee answered softly, bowing her head as if she would like to curl in upon herself and disappear. "They are the spirits of Warta who have died in the human world. They have returned to this world to find peace, something that will elude them unless they can make retribution for the evil they committed while they lived. If they cannot, they will remain in limbo—stuck in a void forever."

"How, exactly, do they hope to make retribution for evils hundreds of years past?" asked Davlin, cautiously, dreading the answer.

Raising her eyes to meet Trieca's, Ru-Lee replied, "By inhabiting my body, and using my powers."

Ru-Lee's revelation caused Ha-Fart to squeak in shock and surprise, nearly falling off of Sheila's lap.

Trieca, Jace, Sheila, Davlin, and Aylon sat in stunned silence.   Jace and Trieca looked almost comical—their mouths hanging open, eyes wide with shock at the news Ru-Lee had just imparted to them.   Davlin, and Sheila blinked in disbelief.   Sheila had not shared Ru-Lee's thoughts or feelings since Ru-Lee had awakened, having been absorbed with her own issues.   Now, a hint of pity entered her eyes as she regarded her friend.   Though taken aback, Aylon stoically bore the look of one who had just had her worst fears confirmed.   Relmar shook his head sadly.   He had 'heard' bits and pieces of what had transpired between Ru-Lee and the Warta while he stood on the river's shore, but he had only guessed at the rest---this was far worse than he had thought.

After taking a few moments to absorb what he had been told, Trieca took a deep breath and pushed on, "Okay...so these spirits want to use you and your powers---powers that are considerable, I might add—to, um, somehow atone for their sins??   Do I have that much right?"

"Yes," Ru-Lee replied, calmly watching him.

Suddenly frustrated, Trieca burst out, "You still haven't told me what form you take when you transform, or how that comes into play with the Warta, or how these spirits intend to use you and your powers!"

Pug flared out his wings, and clacked his beak at the sudden outburst, glaring accusingly at Trieca.

"Sorry, Pug, but I am getting kind of sick of the run-around!"   Trieca apologized to the flustered bird as he glowered at Ru-Lee.

Shaking his head and ruffling his feathers out, Pug softly hooted his acceptance of Trieca's apology, and settled in again on D.G.'s head.

"What form *do* you take, Ru?"   Trieca demanded.

Ru-Lee tilted her head to one side and regarded Trieca contemplatively.   How would he react when she revealed to him the form she believed she had taken?   She still wasn't positive herself—it all felt so much like a bad dream. But, Jace had confirmed that she *had* transformed, hadn't he? She recalled how it had felt to be in that body for the few moments beneath the waves—before the Warta had invaded her—before she had been imprisoned and filled with their vile visions. What had Aylon said was the reason for her imprisonment? 'For her own protection'? *'Probably—and to protect everyone else as well!'* She thought sardonically. She ran her tongue over her teeth— *'teeth, not fangs,"* She reminded herself---but for how long?

"Water Dragon." The words escaped her body on a breath she hadn't meant to release. Trieca blanched, eyes widening further than Ru-Lee had thought possible. The color drained from his face and she thought for a moment that he might pass out. He blinked at her, as if seeing a mirage—as if her very presence was an impossibility.

Slowly, as if rousing from a dream, he moved his head from side to side. His voice came as a barely audible rustle to her ears, "Not good! Definitely not good!"

# Chapter 37

Insect mating calls filled the night, inadvertently luring in leather-winged bats that swooped hungrily through the air. Nocturnal hunters padded softly down to the river's edge to slake their thirst. The brilliant full moon briefly reflected in their vigilant eyes before they faded back into the brush and grasses lining the banks of the Udah to continue their search for food.

A raccoon fastidiously nibbled crawfish in the rocky shallows. He suddenly halted his work, sniffing the air. The night sounds went deathly still around him, and he crouched low to the slime-covered rocks, sidling towards the cover of some nearby overhanging brush.

High above the dark treetops, shadows swept towards the river. Palpable fear engulfed the fields and forests surrounding the waterway as all its residents held their collective breath. The only sound left was the soft sloshing of unfeeling waves upon the ancient stone-strewn shores.

The shadows hovered high above the river for a moment before dipping low towards the rippling water, appearing to sniff out a trail like a hunting hound. Beneath the waves lay their quarry—found, but not cornered.....not yet.

Leveling out above the water, the cloud of darkness and fear began to snake along the river's route. Travelling a few feet above the cool rippling water, it followed the liquid trail, as if tracking its prey.

# Chapter 38

Safe within the spinning tornado of water, deep beneath the rolling waves of the Udah River, the small group of friends and family were carried against the current towards the Dragon Mountains. Trieca, now satisfied that he knew all that he needed, and certainly more than he wanted, sat mutely contemplating the ramifications of what he had been told.

Everyone seemed intent on planning what they should do when they arrived at their destination. Ru-Lee, however, watched Relmar, a nagging question gnawing at the edge of her mind. Finally, after mulling the possible answers over in her sluggish brain and finding no satisfactory response, she decided she would have to ask directly.

"Relmar?" She said, interjecting herself into his strategic conversation with his brothers and Aylon.

"Hmm?" He responded, slightly irritated at having his thought process interrupted.

"Why could you not read Sheila's mind when you first saw her?"

"Oh," he said, his face coloring slightly as Sheila turned her gaze on him also. "I could—or can---sort of."

"What does that mean?" Ru-Lee asked, brows knit in confusion.

Relmar looked to Davlin, but found no assistance as his brother regarded him with amused curiosity.

"Well, she doesn't think in words, exactly," he continued, sheepishly.

"What does she 'think' in then?" Ru-Lee snorted. "I've heard her voice in my head—she uses words then..."

"Maybe so, but when she is just thinking, she thinks in pictures and emotions. And she has other minds loosely connected to hers."

"Those are the minds of my sister spiders," Sheila interjected.

"That's why I didn't know who she was right off....she was thinking about.....other things," he said, his face turning a deep scarlet that crept slowly down his neck. "I couldn't work out who she was from what I saw in her mind."

"Ahh, I see," sighed Ru-Lee, an understanding smile sliding across her lips as she scratched D.G.'s back gently.

Coloring deeper and becoming agitated, Relmar asked, "You see what?"

"You know what," Ru-Lee teased. She widened her eyes and wiggled her eyebrows playfully at him as she projected several insinuating thoughts into her head pertaining to possible entanglements that included Sheila and Relmar.

Relmar glowered at her, but did not respond.

Davlin snickered and shook his head at his older brother's discomfort. Jace, however, watched Sheila as she smiled slightly and lowered her eyes. Her reaction concerned him--he wasn't sure he completely understood the insinuations being made, but he was fairly certain he didn't like the direction they were going.

"Enough, you two!" Aylon ordered. "We have a lot to do, and...."

Suddenly, Ru-Lee gasped and clutched the cloak to her chest, her eyes wide with shock and fear. The sound filled the watery tornado and sent shivers down the spines of its passengers.

She breathed, "The shadows are here!"

## Chapter 39

The roar of fire filled Ru-Lee's ears, muting all other sounds within her mind. Deep within her chest, heat swelled, overcoming the waning effects of the cooling Bonshu blossoms. Her vision blurred as everything in her line of sight turned crimson. A serpentine dragon stirred at the base of her spine, twitching its tail and threatening to stretch itself into her limbs—drawn from its resting place like iron to a magnet. Ru-Lee's breath came in shallow, ragged gasps, as if there wasn't enough oxygen in the funnel to fill her lungs. A scream shattered the air—her scream?—she could not be sure. Her body lurched and twisted sideways, recoiling upon itself, writhing in pain as she tried to maintain control. Her soul recoiled from the pain and terror overtaking her body—curling up in a corner of her mind as it cast protective walls around itself.

Faint voices, muffled and far away, floated through her consciousness. Strong hands restrained her thrashing body, pinning her to the cool floor. She screamed again and something soft was placed upon her tongue. She lay, mouth open, panting, eyes closed tight. D.G.'s cold nose was thrust into her ear, causing her to jerk sideways, startled. His calm mind insinuated itself into her fevered thoughts. He showed her a Bonshu blossom on a tongue— her tongue.

The fire within her rebelled against the vision and flared. Fireballs burst into life throughout the tornado, bouncing off the smooth sides and causing the other passengers to duck and dive for safety. Sparks flew and danced, stirred by a scorching wind.

Muffled orders were urgently shouted around her and someone pinched her nose and forced her jaws shut on the blossom. A soft moan escaped her as the Bonshu blossom was crushed in her mouth, releasing its healing juices to spread throughout her system.

## Chapter 40

The coolness of the water tornado permeated Trieca's shirt where his left shoulder and arm lay pinned beneath Ru-Lee's thrashing, feverish legs—his right arm wrapped over the top of them in an attempt to pin them down. His legs twisted around her ankles and his head pressed down hard on her abdomen. As sparks smoldered in his hair, he gritted his teeth and growled, "Anyone mind telling me what is going on *now*??"

Davlin held Ru-Lee's shoulders as Jace pulled closed the strings of the bag holding the Bonshu blossoms. Both ducked fireballs and deftly brushed sparks away as they worked. Aylon held Ru-Lee's jaw closed, pinching her nose to force her to swallow the blossom that had been placed there. Relmar sat near Ru-Lee's head, holding it tightly in his hands as she tossed and turned. His eyes were closed, and he appeared to be attempting to read her thoughts. D.G. stood near Sheila, allowing the others to work and whining with quiet concern. Sheila had jumped back, startled, when Ru-Lee had begun to thrash about. Now, she sat back on her heels and watched, waiting for her turn to help her friend. She placed a reassuring hand on D.G.'s back and murmured softly to him. Ha-Fart had climbed up to Sheila's shoulder for safety and sat watching the scene with interest, one paw clinging tightly to her earlobe. Pug flew agitated circles around the group. Ducking and diving to avoid the sparks and fireballs that filled the space, he screeched and hooted loudly, expressing his irritation at having had his nap disrupted.

Aylon, Davlin, Jace, and Sheila had seen this happen before, if not to this degree. During their trip through the forest and their stay at Aylon's cabin, they had seen the damage caused to Ru-Lee and her surroundings as she struggled with the fire and wind powers within her. However, this was new to Trieca and Relmar. While Relmar had the advantage of being able to 'read' Ru-Lee's mind, Trieca was working blindly, and he did not appear to appreciate it much.

Jace answered him, "The shadows must be close....probably above the river. They seem to draw out Ru-Lee's powers. When they do, she isn't able to control them very well. I'm guessing that, since they know she can transform now, they are probably trying to draw that out, too."

"And the wind??" Trieca questioned as another fireball narrowly missed his head.

Shrugging his shoulders, Jace replied, "Yeah....she has wind powers, too."

Trieca sucked in his breath and slapped at a spark that had ignited his eyebrows.

"The powers coming so soon, so fast, and together is overwhelming—they could consume her if we don't find a way to help her, and soon," Aylon added tersely. Releasing Ru-Lee's jaw, she watched her granddaughter begin to relax.

Relmar's eyes opened and met Aylon's gaze. "She is doing better now," he said releasing his breath.

Davlin released his grip and sat back. As Trieca untwisted himself from Ru-Lee's lower extremities, he asked, "What happens if she shifts form while we are in this tube? Does she become a *little* dragon, or a *big* one? Will she know who we are?"

Davlin shrugged and replied, "She becomes a *very* big one. If she shifts while we are travelling, we are in big trouble!"

"We don't know how much she will or will not know when she shifts. Usually, when an individual shifts, they retain their mental state—at least for a time. However, I am not aware of anyone ever shifting to a water dragon before—or any other dragon!" Aylon said. "With all that is going on within her body and mind—it is hard to tell what part of herself she will be able to retain. If the Warta spirits would just leave her alone, I think she would be okay. They are complicating things considerably. I don't know if she is strong enough to handle the combined powers as well as the Warta--we could lose her!"

Sheila leaned forward and touched her friend's forehead. A peaceful smile slipped across Ru-Lee's face at Sheila's gentle touch. Looking up to the expectant faces of those around her, Sheila said, "We won't lose her. She is very strong—and stubborn. She can master the forces within her—if we allow her time to do so without being possessed by the Warta."

"Can we give her that time? Can the Warta get in here?" Trieca asked.

The water tornado filled with Sheyna's soft voice, causing the small entourage to glance upward when she spoke, "They *can* penetrate this space, but they *won't* so long as we stay submerged. While they lived, entering deep water would have doused their flames and muted their winds. Fear of water was instinctive—that fear has stayed with them in their death. They may follow, but they will not enter until we rise above the waves—maybe not even then."

"Can we stay submerged for the rest of the journey?" Davlin asked.

"There are no shallows between here and our destination. We should be able to stay below the surface until we arrive," Sheyna replied.

"What *is* our destination?" Trieca questioned. "Has that been decided yet?"

"This river originates deep within the Dragon Mountains.....near the Heart. We will surface there," Davlin answered.

Aylon nodded in agreement. "We need to bring Ru around enough that she can begin working with her powers before we get to the mountains," she said. Looking meaningfully at the three brothers, she added, "She will need *all* of our help."

Jace narrowed his eyes at her and asked suspiciously, "What kind of help?"

Aylon regarded him for a moment before taking a deep breath and responding, "D.G. obviously has a close link to her mind. He can use his presence to help her maintain control. However, if she pushes him out or ignores him, it won't be enough."

D.G. grunted his agreement as he curled his legs beneath his furry body and lay down next to Ru-Lee, his claws tapping lightly on the funnel's surface.

Aylon continued, "Sheila can use her link with Ru to keep her calm and help her see things clearly. It may help keep her mind clear and help her find the controls she will need within herself, but the link may not be strong enough to withstand Ru-Lee's powers—she may be pushed out as well."

Davlin furrowed his brows and exchanged a confused look with Relmar as he listened to Aylon.

"Okay, I get how they can help---but you said *all* of us. What are the rest of us supposed to do, exactly—other than stay out of the way and try not to get burned up in the process?" Jace growled, becoming impatient.

Pug, finally calm, fluttered down to land on Jace's head. Jace ignored him.

"Staying out of the way will, most likely, be left to Trieca, Ha-Fart, and Pug," Aylon quipped, passing Trieca a sideways grin. "You and your brothers, however, will have a much bigger part to play."

Before Jace could respond, Relmar broke in, "What are you saying, Aylon?"

"You can see, can't you?"

"Yes, but I am afraid I don't fully understand."

"Okay, I will explain it---for all three of you." Settling back on her heels, Aylon bit her lip and considered the brothers before beginning her explanation. "We must call upon the elemental powers. This is what is done when an individual comes of age—they go apart from the population with a master, someone who can control that element. When their powers come upon them, the master calls upon that element also and assists the individual in making it their own."

"But none of us are masters of any of the elemental powers!" Interrupted Jace, incredulously.

"I am aware of that, but I believe we can work with what we have," Aylon answered, patiently bowing her head towards him.

"How?" Davlin asked a puzzled expression on his face.

"First let me explain what needs done, then I will tell you how," Aylon replied as she brought her legs in front of her and stretched them out. "Ru has fire, water, wind, and earth within her—as well as the water dragon. The water has manifested itself, I believe, as the water dragon. I have never heard of this happening before, but it could be due to her Warta heritage. It could be the way the dragon part of her comes through. The fire—well it is obvious how that is manifesting itself." She brushed a weak spark from Ru-Lee's cloak as she continued. "Ru will need a lot of help with that one—especially with the Warta hanging around. The wind is also obvious as to how it manifests itself.

"There have been times when an individual coming of age into the wind powers has been carried away by that element's manifestations. They become one with the wind and are swept away, literally. It hasn't happened often, and I haven't heard of it happening recently. I think the earth powers that Ru possesses will keep her grounded, though, so I am not too concerned there. We have not yet seen the manifestations of the earth powers, and I have no idea how they will show themselves. However, I am sure they will show up when we reach the Heart."

"Why?" interrupted Jace as he cast a sideways glance in Relmar's direction.

"The Heart sits in the Life Cave where *all* life, human and otherwise, was birthed. The Heart is the key to the elemental powers as well as all other gifts that are bestowed upon individuals in this world." Aylon paused and smiled at Relmar. "That is why your powers expanded when you were near the Heart, Relmar—the Heart draws them out."

"Why didn't they fade when I left the mountains, then?" Relmar asked.

"Because that isn't how it works," Aylon responded patiently. "Once bestowed, they cannot be returned—they are permanent."

"Will they change again when I return?" he asked, concerned.

"I don't know. You weren't within the Life Cave—not even that close to it really....they may change again—I can't really say," she said, shaking her head.

"Wait..., um," Jace interjected. He sat watching and listening, a look of dawning concern spreading across his face.

"Yes, Jace?" Aylon asked.

"If we don't know how the Heart will affect Relmar, and we aren't really sure what affect it will have on Ru-Lee—and Ru isn't in control of the powers she has yet---is it really a good idea to get her near the Heart??" Jace questioned, incredulously. "Seems like a dumb move to me!"

"Maybe—but what choice do we have?" Aylon shrugged. "The Warta are coming through near the Heart. Ru will have to be there if she is to be of any use in the fight against them, and it seems clear that she must be. All powers will be heightened near the Heart. That is why it is so important that Ru gain at least *some* control over them before we get there."

"Okay," Jace continued, raising his eyebrows and regarding Aylon intently. "What about the Warta? They are coming through from the human side; their powers have been diluted—we hope—by generations of interbreeding with the humans. If I understand things correctly, they are unaware of their lineage and the possible powers that they may or may not have. How will the Heart affect them?"

"I don't know," Aylon answered sadly. "We can only guess at what will happen to them when they enter our world near the Heart. We know the Heart will draw out whatever powers they do have, but we have no way of knowing how that will happen. The only thing we can be sure of is that their ancestors' collective memories will flood through their psyche. Some may process that information fine—others may be driven mad by it.

"What will happen to them physically is unknown. They may revert to dragon form but hold no powers; they may find they have some form of wind or fire powers, but stay in human form; they may be ripped apart by drastic changes to their body and mind; or they may revert to dragon form complete with all powers intact. We won't know until they come through. I am sure that they can feel the pull of the Heart and the Life Cave as they dig closer to it. They may even be experiencing some changes before they come through. We have to be prepared for the worst."

Jace heaved a sigh and hunched his shoulders as Aylon continued.

"Right now, however, our immediate concerns are the shadows—the Warta spirits—and helping Ru gain some control over her powers and her transformed body." She glanced around at each of the brothers and said, "When you were younger, I taught you three the simple spells needed to shield and protect yourselves and others, and...."

"Yes, but we weren't all good at them!" Jace broke in, jerking his head up, eyes wide with a sudden inkling of Aylon's plan. "Ru-Lee was always the best at those things."

"I know, but your skills will have to suffice. I can help, as can Sheyna and Trieca. Sheila can help some also—she has some earth elements within her. She is also linked with the stone spiders—this will enhance her earthbound powers."

Jace opened his mouth to protest, but Aylon cut him off, irritated. "We have to work with what we have available, Jace! Arguing about it won't change a thing!"

Jace's mouth snapped shut and he glowered at Aylon, but he knew better than to force the matter further. Davlin watched the exchange thoughtfully, processing the information Aylon had given them. Relmar screwed up his face and looked at his brothers as if trying to figure out what part each one would be playing in this next venture.

"Hand me my pack, Jace," Aylon ordered, extending her hand towards him.

Sheila removed Ru-lee's pack from her back and prepared to open it as she asked, "Shouldn't we clothe Ru before we wake her up, Aylon?"

Aylon smiled and replied, "Nope—I doubt she will be in human form for long once she wakes up, Sheila!"

Trieca jerked his head around and stared in shock at Aylon as she took her pack from Jace and began purposefully rummaging through it. As she worked, Aylon ordered, "Sheyna, you know what to do--get started with Ru-Lee while I prepare things here."

# Chapter 41

Sheila's soothing touch and the cooling effects of the Bonshu blossoms brought a troubled peace to Ru-Lee's embattled system. Her soul cautiously uncurled itself from the protected corner of her mind where it lay hidden—slowly lowering its protective walls.

A voice like water pouring over a fountain, softly slipped into her mind and ran trickling down her spine—Sheyna.

*"Ru-Lee, you must not hide yourself,"* Sheyna gently chided. *"You must take control of your body and your powers."*

*"But how? I feel I control nothing—I am at the mercy of the Warta. They control my powers now. They draw them out of me and fill me with pain,"* Ru-Lee's soul whimpered.

*"You are allowing that to happen, Ru. The powers are yours to command—they always have been,"* Sheyna replied, her voice becoming a waterfall that rushed softly down Ru-Lee's spine to form a cool green pool at the base.

The flames that had earlier filled Ru-Lee's fevered body now lay quietly smoldering in the pit of her stomach. As the green pool spread, the fire subsided to nothing more than a flicker.

*"I know I have commanded them before, but they threaten to consume me now. Why?"* Ru-Lee's soul asked the spirit.

*"It is just the way of things...each seeks domination. You must make them your own. Assign them each a place in your being—where each can live within you so that you can call upon them as you need them and blend them when necessary. Right now, they each want all that you have. You cannot allow that, or you will lose yourself within them—they must become one within you."*

The protective walls disappeared as Ru-Lee's soul began to spread out, filling her body once again with her essence. Her mind uncurled, and her breath evened out as she asked, *"How do I do that? Can you help me?"*

*"Yes, I can help you with some of the process. I have already begun. The base of your spine is a good place for the water to dwell. It can travel up and down your spine from there--it likes to travel. It does not like to be still, because it can become stagnant. Can you feel it there?"*

Ru-Lee breathed deeply feeling the water rise up her spine and spill softly over the top to travel back down to the pool at its base.

*"How do I keep it there and not allow the fire to dry it up?"* she asked.

*"You must relegate the fire to a place of its own so that it does not dry up your wells,"* Sheyna replied simply.

*"But when the fire fills me, where will the water go?"*

*"Deep within your core--you will always keep it there---watch,"* Sheyna ordered.

The rise and fall of the water rinsing Ru-Lee's spine slowly ebbed; the pool at the base of her spine shrunk to a puddle and receded deep within the core of her belly. Here it sat, awaiting her command.

*"Call upon the water, Ru,"* Sheyna's spirit commanded Ru-Lee's soul.

Ru-Lee concentrated upon the small green puddle, willing it to expand and fill the empty pool at the base of her spine. Slowly, the water began to rise in the pool. As the pool filled, she drew the cool water up her spine with her mind, and let it spill over the top to trickle back down to the pool.

Smiling to herself, she thought triumphantly, *"That was easy!"*

*"Exactly!"* Sheyna congratulated her. *"Now comes the hard part—Aylon believes your water powers, when they take over, are coming out as the water dragon. Does that sound right to you?"*

*"I don't know,"* Ru-Lee answered. The flames within her belly danced. *"I think, maybe, but I also think there is fire within the dragon."*

*"That is what I wondered. It is strange that fire and water would blend, but they seem to when you transform. Your skin dances with flames, yet it is liquid—liquid fire. Is that how it felt?"*

*"Yes."* Ru-Lee recalled how her skin had danced with flames, her vision blurred with fire. *"How can I control the fire? It feels like it melts my brain!"*

*"I am not sure—when Aylon awakens you, we will see what we can do."* Sheyna's voice was silent for a moment, leaving Ru-Lee to listen to the peaceful sounds of the waterfall trickling down her spine.

Finally, Sheyna spoke again, *"Can you call upon the dragon within you? Do you know where it sleeps?"*

Ru-Lee considered the serpent she had felt unwinding itself at the base of her spine before the Bonshu blossom was given to her. Her soul quivered and she replied, *"I know where it sleeps, but I am afraid to awaken it!"*

*"See if it still sleeps where you believe it to be—look for it, Ru,"* Sheyna commanded, gently.

Her soul followed the green water down her spine to the quiet pool at its base. She looked around the pool and in it, but did not locate the serpent. *Where was it hiding?* Taking in a deep breath, she waited and listened, slowly scanning the edges of the pool. As her soul's eyes travelled again to the base of her spine, she gasped. Wrapped around the spine, twisted within the bundles of nerves, water washing over it, coiled the dragon. Water shed off of its gray-green scales as it regarded her with flame-rimmed golden eyes. Ru-Lee caught her breath and attempted to swallow the lump that rose into her throat as the dragon grinned widely, showing its fangs, and slyly winked at her.

## Chapter 42

The first kiss of dawn's soft light crawled over the mountains and across the crimson blossoms that filled the Red Valley, appearing to set them ablaze. The morning's light sparkled on the gently rippling waves of Lake Satcha—the lake that the Udah River ran into on one end and out of on the other. Reflected in its steel-blue surface, the waves of blossoms seemed to dance across the ripples, blighted only by the cloud of dark shadows that hung suspended a few feet above.

Deep below the reflected shadows, the sideways tornado of water slowed to a near crawl and angled towards the depths of the lake. Ha-Fart sat upon Sheila's shoulder, urgently speaking to her in his native language. The sound of his voice and her murmured responses bounced off the walls of the funnel. Pug cocked his head to one side and watched the duo with wide, attentive eyes. The rest of the group sat in silence, their attention split between the unconscious form of Ru-lee and the increasingly urgent sounds of Sheila and Ha-Fart. Ha-Fart had become so agitated that he was now standing on his hind legs and gesturing wildly with his front paws while Sheila shook her head slowly and appeared to be attempting to calm him down.

Aylon looked up from Ru-Lee, her brows furrowing as she asked, "What does he want?"

Sheila held up a hand to Ha-Fart and spoke to him saying, "Wait! Let me talk to the others and see what can be done, okay?"

The black mouse glared at her, grunted, and plopped down on her shoulder once more, a definite air of disgruntlement surrounding him.

Addressing Aylon, Sheila responded, "He wants out so he can raise his brethren to assist in the coming battle."

"What?!" Aylon asked as every face turned to stare at Sheila in disbelief. Pug clacked his beak loudly and ruffled his neck feathers in alarm. "We can't surface to let him out," Aylon continued. "If we do, we allow the shadows access to Ru-Lee!"

"I know! I have tried to explain that to him," Sheila answered, an unfamiliar note of annoyance in her voice.

"And?" Aylon pressed.

Sheila took a deep breath and puffed it out her nose in disgust before replying, "He says, if we let him out below the waves, he can swim to shore." She looked sideways at her furry companion and raised an eyebrow in his direction, setting her jaw as he jerked a nod at her.

Aylon regarded the large mouse, contemplating the possibilities. "It would be useful to have more warriors at hand when the battle starts—if it hasn't already," she mused thoughtfully.

"What?! Now way! You are not actually considering this silliness, are you?" Jace burst out. "He's a MOUSE! NOT a WARRIOR!"

Instantly, Ha-Fart leapt from Sheila's shoulder and charged Jace—pulling his mouse-sized sword and yelling fiercely as he went. Before Jace could react, the sword was thrust through the toe of Jace's boot and deep into his left big toe. Pug dove from Jace's head towards Ha-Fart. Jace screamed and kicked out, flinging Ha-Fart and his sword into D.G.'s furry ribs. Pug missed his mark and smacked hard against the cool floor of the funnel, momentarily unconscious. D.G. grunted and growled, but Ha-Fart leapt up, ready to charge again. As the mouse ran forward, D.G. twisted around and grabbed Ha-Fart's tail in his teeth. His muzzle curling in a warning growl, he snapped his head and flung the mouse into Sheila's lap. Sheila quickly pinned him down and removed the sword from his grasp. Ordering him to be still, she turned her attention to Jace.

Pug roused to consciousness and shook his head vigorously, unnoticed by the group. Screeching like a banshee, he burst from the ground towards the pinned and struggling mouse in Sheila's lap. Yelling, Sheila pulled Ha-Fart to her chest and turned her back on the attacking owl. Pug clawed briefly at her back with his talons before angrily returning to inspect Jace's wounded foot, screeching his disgust as he went.

Blood soaked the soft leather of his boot and oozed out of the hole made by Ha-Fart's sword. A wild string of swear words flowed from Jace, piercing the air, ringing off the walls, and filling the water tornado. Aylon shook her head, cringed, and waited patiently for the noise to subside.

Jace quickly worked the lacings, yanked off his boot, and peeled off his blood-soaked sock. After surveying his injured toe, he grabbed his hat and threw it at the restrained mouse shouting, "D*#@ mouse!! What the *#^%! do you think you are doing?? You want out?? Fine! I think we can arrange that!" Leaping at Ha-Fart and Sheila, he ordered, "Give him here, Sheila! I can let him 'out' real fast! Pop his *&*#8#$ head off, that's what!"

Trieca grabbed Jace around the waist, dragging him down as Davlin and Relmar bounded over Ru-Lee's inert form to pin Jace down. Jace flailed and cursed, but to no avail—the combined weight of his brothers and Trieca was too much for him. Finally, he calmed down and lay still beneath them. Through gritted teeth he growled, "Please get off of me."

"You gonna behave?" Davlin asked, grinning.

"Sure," Jace snarled back.

"No killing the mouse?" Relmar questioned.

"Fine," Jace conceded, glaring at his brothers.

"Okay, let him up," Relmar ordered, lifting his weight off of his youngest brother.

Trieca unwound himself from Jace's midsection and sat up, eyeing Jace suspiciously. It had been his experience that Jace did not usually give up so easily. Sure enough, as soon as Davlin began to lift his weight, Jace made another lunge for the captured mouse, kicking Trieca hard in the knee as he did so.

185

"D*#@, Jace!" he swore as he grabbed Jace's flailing legs. Davlin dropped his full weight back onto Jace's midsection and Relmar rolled around to get Jace in a headlock, growling fiercely at his brother at he went. "Jace! Leave the mouse alone! You would have attacked, too, if you had been as insulted by him as he was by you!"

Jace stopped struggling, snorting loudly through his nose, chest heaving, and glaring furiously at Ha-Fart. His face and body slowly relaxed as he considered the truth of Relmar's words. Finally, he grunted and shrugged his shoulders.

"You good now?" Relmar asked. "I don't want to have to take you down again."

"I'm good," Jace answered, the pupils in his eyes beginning to return to normal size.

As Davlin, Relmar, and Trieca began to release their holds on Jace, Aylon interrupted, "Wait! Hold him, please while I have a look at that toe! You know how he is about these things!"

Jace's eyes grew wide with comprehension and he began to struggle anew. Grinning widely, his brothers and friend renewed their positions and held on tight—Jace hated to have people touch his feet, no matter the reason!

# Chapter 43

Bright morning light illuminated the cloud of dark shadows that continued to hover patiently a few feet above the waves of Lake Satcha. They seemed completely oblivious to the soggy, furry, dark head of a black mouse as it surfaced silently and paddled furiously for shore. Finding footing in the muddy bank, the exhausted mouse scrambled out of the water and collapsed in the tall blades of grass that lined the river. After a few moments of rest the creature grunted, hoisted itself up, and scurried off into the tall stalks of red-blossoming flowers, glancing back at the shadows as he went.

XXX    XXX    XXX    XXX    XXX

Deep beneath the lake's surface, the water twister had come to a halt suspended just shy of the murky floor. Within its walls, Aylon had used a black piece of charcoal from one of her pouches to draw a wide, dark circle around the still-unconscious Ru-Lee. Another circle had been drawn with white sandstone about three feet outside the black circle. D.G.'s toenails clicked softly on the floor of the enclosure as he slowly paced the perimeter in between the two circles, keeping a close eye on Ru-Lee as he made his rounds.

Inside the dark circle, Relmar and Sheila knelt on either side of Ru-Lee's body, each laying a hand upon the inert girl's forehead. Relmar's job was to monitor what was taking place within Ru-Lee's head. Sheila was to connect with Ru-Lee's mind and soul to try to help Ru-Lee stay in control of her faculties when she transformed. By then, Relmar would be outside of the black circle, in relative safety. Sheila would stay within, shifting to spider form if needed—Aylon felt it would be safest that way.

Both of their tasks required a great deal of concentration, however, Relmar found his attention straying to the soft touch of Sheila's fingertips as they brushed against his hand on Ru-Lee's forehead. The contact sent electric sensations throughout his body that seemed to short-circuit his brain waves, relegating Ru-Lee's thoughts to a whisper in his mind. He tried to focus and push Sheila's mind out of the way so he could hear Ru-Lee's, but it was a half-hearted attempt at best.

Looking up, he found himself falling into Sheila's deep grey eyes, his senses lost in her musky earthen scent—like pine, moss, and sunshine intermingled. Sheila's breath quickened when their eyes met and she blushed deeply. Sliding her hand over to Ru-Lee's temple and lowering her gaze, Sheila broke the contact that held Relmar mesmerized. He blinked and cleared his throat, returning his attention to Ru-Lee.

Outside of the dark circle, positioned near Ru-Lee's feet, Davlin watched the interaction between his brother and Sheila with amusement, a smile playing upon his lips. Aylon had placed a smooth blue stone at his feet on the cool, damp surface of their enclosure. She had mumbled an incantation as she placed the stone and taught Davlin the words to use to invoke the powers of water from its depths. He could feel the power radiating from the stone. Aylon had assured him that he would be able to draw out that power when needed because of the blood connection with his mother, who would also be assisting him to contain the water powers. He was doubtful of Aylon assertions. Although he had always enjoyed the water, he had never been able to control it the way he had seen others do. Further, he did not remember his mother ever using her elemental powers, and sincerely doubted that any had been passed on to him. However, he had nodded and agreed to his task, eyeing the stone with trepidation before turning his attention to his older brother and Sheila.

To Davlin's right, also standing on the outside of the dark circle, Jace fidgeted from one foot to the next, apprehensively watching Aylon as she placed a stone at his feet that shimmered with rusts, browns, and greens--the colors undulating as if alive. Perched on Jace's shoulder,

Pug twisted his head to one side and watched the stone with interest.

Jace had replaced his boot on his now-bandaged foot and the pain in his toe had subsided to a dull throb. He was thrilled when Sheyna had agreed to release Ha-Fart into the lake without rising closer to the surface, and he sincerely hoped the mouse had drowned or been eaten during his swim.

His mind wandered recalling how Sheyna had ordered Ha-Fart to lean against the wall of the funnel in which they rode. Once the mouse had made contact with the wall, Sheyna allowed the point of contact to thin enough for the mouse to slip through and out into the lake, re-sealing the surface behind him. Only a small amount of water had seeped in, slightly dampening the floor on which the company now stood.

Aylon's voice now filled the chamber as she chanted an incantation, charging the stone with the power of the earth and bringing Jace out of his reverie. She had explained to him that he possessed an earth-bound soul that would connect easily with the earth-powers within the stone. Once she had finished her incantation, she lifted the stone and met his gaze.

"Hold out your hand, Jace," she said, her voice soft, but commanding.

Jace cautiously held out his hand and Aylon placed the stone in his palm. He gasped and his eyes went wide as the stone's warmth and power filled his hand and spread up his arm. Aylon smiled at him and gently removed the stone, placing it at his feet once again. Jace blinked incredulously at his still-outstretched hand.

"It still tingles!" he declared and looked questioningly to Aylon.

"As I explained, you have an earth-bound soul—practical and solid. The powers in the stone recognize you. You won't have any problems raising them."

"If you say so," he responded, wiggling his fingers and looking at the stone with mixed awe and apprehension.

Moving around the circle to a point directly across from Davlin, near Ru-Lee's head, Aylon removed a smooth red stone from the brown pouch at her waist that had held the other's. Bringing the stone close to her mouth, she murmured an incantation and breathed upon it. At the touch of her breath, the reds in the stone flared to life, giving off light and heat. Glancing at Relmar, she shook her head and placed the stone near the spot where his feet would be. Relmar looked up to meet her gaze, raising his eyebrow to her in consternation.

"Why so concerned?" he asked.

"Look into my mind and you will see why," she responded wryly.

Puzzled, Relmar watched Aylon's face for signs of deception that would belie what he saw in her mind. Finding none, he asked, "But why weren't we told this before?"

"Told what?" Jace asked, instantly interested in what was being said.

Taking in a deep breath, Aylon let it out in a puff and replied to Relmar, "You weren't told, because it did not appear to touch you."

"What didn't touch us?" Jace persisted, his eyes boring into Aylon's.

"I don't understand," Relmar answered, shaking his head. "Wouldn't we have known? Wouldn't something have shown up in at least one of us?"

"Not necessarily," Aylon continued. "The bloodlines are terribly diluted. Ru-Lee is an anomaly—no one could have predicted that she would be affected the way she is, or that she would carry all four of the elemental powers. The lines are just too mixed up!"

"What are you talking about!?" insisted Jace, a slight growl in his voice.

Davlin tilted his head to one side and listened intently to the exchange. As he watched and listened, tentative comprehension began to dawn on his face and he interjected, "You think one of us may have some elemental powers also, don't you?"

Glancing at Jace, Aylon answered, "Yes, Davlin, I am wondering if that is possible."

"Wouldn't we have known by now?" Jace asked, startled by this new information.

Shaking her head and meeting his gaze, Aylon said, "Not necessarily. It is possible that the powers are latent. They might not arise unless they are forced to."

"Forced? How?" Davlin asked, his brows furrowing deeply as he crossed his arms.

"By being called upon," Aylon responded, her gaze drifting to the stone at his feet.

Looking down at the blue stone, Davlin's face twisted thoughtfully; Jace glared at his earthen stone wondering what sort of thing might be called up from its depths; and Relmar's gaze travelled from Aylon to the dancing flames of the red stone, then back again before he asked, "But you aren't really that worried about my brothers, are you Aylon?"

Shaking her head sadly, Aylon answered, "No."

"Why?" Relmar persisted.

"They have a connection to the element they will be working, as do you, but the fire element is so much more difficult to control. It is deeply connected to the soul. If not properly contained, permanent damage could be done to you—to your soul. If this process awakens a spark inherited from your father, things could get out of control quickly."

Jace's head jerked up, startling Pug from his mesmerized inspection of the stone. Jace glanced quickly at Davlin before blurting out, "Wait! What??"

Pug clacked his beak at Jace and fluffed his wings in irritation at having his concentration broken.

Sheila raised her head at Aylon's words, and turned troubled eyes to Relmar.

Davlin returned Jace's confused look and turned to Aylon saying, "What do you mean 'spark inherited from our father'?"

Shrugging her shoulders and fiddling with the pouches at her waist, Aylon slowly answered, "Your father was also a descendant of the Warta, but the line was much diluted. There had been no signs of any elemental powers for generations. Unfortunately, that was where the dilution stopped short—powers. In all other ways, the Warta blood showed true."

Raising one eyebrow accusingly, Jace glared at Aylon and asked, "What are you saying?"

"I am saying, Jace, that your father seemed to carry the destructive nature of the Warta in his veins. Once the bloodlines have been diluted as much as his was, offspring don't often show much of the destructive nature of their ancestors. However, your father was an exception." Seeing Jace and Davlin bristle at her words, Aylon continued, soothingly, "Your father was a wonderful man, don't get me wrong! He just had a tendency to lean to the destructive side of things. That is what got your parents killed."

Sheila gasped, her free hand jumping to her mouth, eyes wide.

"What do you mean?" Asked Davlin before Jace could jump in. Jace's face contorted in anger as he struggled to control himself and listen to Aylon's explanations for smearing their father's good name.

Trieca sat outside of the circle and off to one side, silently watching and listening to all that was being said.

"Really, we don't have time for these explanations right now!" Aylon huffed, flustered. Looking quickly to Relmar, she asked, "How is Ru-Lee doing?"

"She's doing fine," Relmar responded. "I think we had best make time, Aylon."

Looking around the circle, Aylon nodded sadly and explained, "Your father was attached to a military team that was charged with hunting down anyone they believed had anything to do with 'magic' or what they called magic. Somehow, our family became prime targets even though the gifts we have here were not the same there--- imperceptible, really. No one knows how they knew about this world or how they were able to track us.

"Your father bought into their rhetoric. He claimed he did not believe in powers or magic, but he felt that any connection—or perceived connection—to such things would damage his children and his chance to advance within the ranks. He convinced your mother to denounce her heritage—her family. He demanded that she not speak of this place—said it was for her own protection. He truly did love her.

"She stopped coming here and refused to bring you here, believing that the propaganda was right and that this place would corrupt her and her children. She turned her back on her gifts. It didn't help, however. She was still drawn to the water, even if she chose not to call upon it.

"Your father did not realize that he himself held the power for fire—not much, really, just a spark. He could coax a fire out of just about anything—it seemed to dance for him. He used this ability—skill, he called it—to entertain soldiers and lift their spirits. Being connected to the soul, the gift of fire--if used correctly--can spread a great deal of good cheer.

"It was his bad luck, that one of the men he entertained decided that his 'skill' was a gift for elemental power. They turned him in to the authorities. Before he could be apprehended, he ran to warn your mother. She was with friends just outside of the military encampment. They ran, but were found and murdered as they tried to cross a nearby river in a small canoe.

"You were staying with Ru-Lee's parents at the time. Your mother had a premonition before she and your father left on that trip. She feared for your lives, but could not let your father know why. After much coercion, your father agreed to allow you to stay with your aunt, believing that your mother was experiencing womanly hysteria. He had a great deal of respect for Ru-Lee's father, however, which tipped the scales in favor of the visit.

"After your parents' death, your aunt shielded and protected you, calling you her own sons to elude those who were looking for you. The ruse lasted a few months before word came to your aunt that the trackers were on your trail. That is when she decided to bring you all here for safety," Aylon paused, a tear trickling down her cheek.

"I remember where they died," Davlin put in, softly, his eyes glazed with the memory. "We used to go there for picnics and paddle around in the river in that canoe. No matter the weather, the water was always smooth for us."

"That would have been your mother's doing—she always wanted to keep you safe," Aylon responded, wiping away the wayward tear and sniffing as she smiled fondly at her grandsons.

"And now you are afraid that the 'spark' our father had was passed on to us unnoticed?" Jace asked, nudging the stone at his feet with his injured toe.

"Yes—actually, I am mostly concerned for Relmar, since he is the one who will be calling upon the fire element and since his gift for mind reading and empathy is closely connected to the soul. It is highly likely that he has a spark of fire in his veins."

"Sounds like this could get very interesting," Trieca interjected from his place near the wall, an ironic grin on his face.

Nodding, Davlin added, "Yes, Very!" Turning his gaze to Relmar, he regarded him as if seeing him for the first time. "You up for the challenge, Brother?" he asked, a slow smile dimpling his cheeks.

Shrugging, Relmar chuckled and responded, "Guess so! I think I am as ready as I will ever be to wake up a dragon, and start a fire inside a water tornado while in the depths of a lake!

"Let's not start any fires, if we can help it!" said Aylon, shaking her head. "Do you remember the spells I taught you, Relmar?"

Relmar grinned and nodded, pushing his blonde hair out of his eyes.

"Good, then let me finish preparing so we can wake Ru-Lee and get started." Dipping her fingers into the stone-carrying pouch once more, Aylon produced a pure white stone and carried it to a point directly across the circle from Jace. She murmured an incantation over the stone, placed it at her feet, and removed a small vial of Laousha from another pouch at her waist. "Okay, Relmar, give this to Ru-Lee," she said as she stretched out her left arm to hand the vial to Relmar.

Reaching for the vial, Relmar asked, "Won't this be too much?"

"No—we have to counteract the Bonshu blossoms."

Sheila, having recovered from the shock she had felt upon hearing of Relmar's heritage, returned her focus to Ru-Lee as Relmar gently slipped his hand beneath the unconscious girl's head.

"Okay, here goes," he said as he lifted Ru-Lee's head and tipped the burning liquid down her throat.

## Chapter 44

Mesmerized by the golden eyes of the dragon, Ru-Lee's mind and soul were only mildly aware of her head being tipped back and something warm passing her lips.

*"Brace yourself, Ru,"* Sheyna's soft voice whispered to her.

Curious, Ru-Lee asked, *"Why?"* Her question was answered immediately as the burning presence of Laousha made itself known, spreading throughout her body and burning down her spine. The dragon's grin widened and it began to uncoil itself, stretching its limbs through the running water, and beginning to grow.

Gasping, Ru-Lee's mind shrieked, *"What do I do? How do I stop it?"*

*"You don't stop it,"* Sheyna replied calmly. *"You accept it, make it part of yourself--since that is what it is. So long as you accept this part of you and make it your own, you will control it. Let it fill you, embrace this part of your being."*

Waves of panic washed over her as Ru-Lee watched the dragon comically wiggle its eyebrows; its serpent-like tongue flicked out of its maw and across its muzzle, and it flared its nostrils at her. *'A sense of humor?'* she thought. *'Who would have guessed?'* The panic ebbed slightly.

The dragon arched its back and softly unfurled glistening blue wings—she hadn't noticed those before. *'Did I have wings when I transformed before?'* she wondered.

Sheyna's voice filled her mind, *"Approach it, Ru....remember--it is a part of you, but you are in control."*

*"Easier said than done,"* Ru-Lee responded, trying to slow her racing heart. *"What if it wants to 'come out and play'?"*

*"Then you bring it out, carefully,"* Sheyna responded.

The dragon shook its head and puffed hot air through its nostrils. Eyeing its reflection in the pool of water near the base of Ru-Lee's spine, it dipped its muzzle in. As it stretched its nose and neck up high, it reveled in the blue-green liquid washing over its head to slide off its body just behind its wings. Returning its gaze to Ru-Lee, it snorted and a distinct rumbling sound, like that of a large cat purring, filled her mind.

"*It's waiting,*" Sheyna prodded.

Ru-Lee heard herself whimper as she whispered, "*Will it hurt? Last time, it hurt.*"

"*It may pain you some,*" Sheyna soothed, "*but not in the same way—you won't be fighting it, and it isn't being forced out by the Warta. It should not be as bad this time, but I cannot be sure.*"

"*Ru?*" A new voice intruded upon Ru-Lee's mind, and her spirit lifted at the sound.

"*Sheila?*" Ru-Lee asked.

"*Yes. I am here to help you—so you don't get lost within the dragon.*"

As Sheila's melodic voice filled her mind, Ru-Lee felt herself relaxing slightly and was thankful for this gift that Sheila had.

"*You are not in this alone, Ru—we are all here to help you as best we can,*" Sheyna added.

As she watched the dragon gazing at her hungrily she responded, "*Thank you—I think I am going to need all the help I can get. Is everyone safe?*"

"*Yes—as safe as we can get. Are you ready?*" Sheila answered.

"*I don't know—Sheyna, what happens to the water when I shift? Does it join the dragon? Do I call on it separately?*"

"*I don't know, Ru....you are going to have to ask the dragon, I think.*"

"Great," Ru-Lee quipped. "*I am not sure I can get a straight answer, if that is the case. I think I will have to find out as I go along maybe.*"

Gathering her courage and strength, Ru-Lee nodded to the waiting dragon. *'Wanna play?'* she asked, sending the thought to the patiently watchful creature.

Grinning widely, the dragon nodded and stepped into the pool at the base of her spine. Ru-Lee groaned, as the weight of the dragon settled at the base of her being like a stone. Her eyes shot open to find Sheila seated next to her. Her body arched upward and her breath came in short, quick pants as she struggled to hold on to herself. Her wild eyes found Sheila's calm grey ones and she gasped, *"Help!"*

# Chapter 45

The morning sun rose slowly in the sky above Lake Satcha, illuminating the brilliant flaming red blossoms in the surrounding valley. Thick silence filled the air, heavy with pulsating emotions that emanated from the cloud of dark shadows that hung a few feet above the softly lapping waves.

A light breeze rustled the tops of the flowers in the fields, rippling across the lake and seeming to disturb the cluster of shadows. They expanded, spreading over the lake with their roiling darkness. The draft of air picked up speed and heat, stirring the waves to soft foamy peaks. A low, frustrated moan filled the valley, rumbling into its recesses and bouncing off of the water's surface.

The shadows cautiously dipped lower, nearly touching the waves--like an inexperienced animal sniffing curiously at fire for the first time. Rambunctious whitecaps flicked up and passed through the dark cloud. A roaring screech split the air and the shadows recoiled, pulling in towards their center and returning to their previous height above the lake as if burned, churning furiously.

A hot wind rushed through the valley, frying the crimson blossoms to a dry brown, and laying the plants low to the ground in a swath. Small furry bodies scurried to find safety outside of the path of the blistering air.

After several minutes, the roiling within the cloud slowed to a mild churning, and the angry winds died down to a gusty hot breeze. A wide swath of burned, dead plant matter on either side of the lake bed showed the extent of the Wartas' frustration.

# Chapter 46

Within the cool water tornado, deep beneath the waves of the lake, Aylon's voice cut through the tense silence that Ru-Lee's breathless plea left behind.

"Relmar—Move! Now!" she commanded raising her arms high and wide in the air, encompassing the space around her.

Relmar blinked, gently released Ru-Lee's head back to the floor, and leapt to his position outside of the dark circle. Sheila began to sing, her soft, melodic voice draping a veil of calm over Ru-Lee and the others. The serenity was deceptive, however, charged as it was with the overlaying tensions of their tasks.

Ru-Lee squinched her eyes closed tight and clenched her teeth. Her body arched upwards, a guttural growl escaping her throat.

"Begin!" Aylon's voice rang out, crossing over Sheila's song.

Relmar, Davlin, Jace, and Aylon began their chants as one. Though the words varied slightly for each, the cadence matched perfectly, weaving together and merging with Sheila's song beautifully. Pug bobbed his head to the rhythm, adding his own calls where the melody needed them. The stones placed at the feet of Relmar, Davlin, Jace, and Aylon began to pulse. Light and color danced around them, radiating up and outwards until each stone's color united with the ones on either side, filling the space and creating a colorful shield around Ru-Lee and Sheila. D.G., still marching deliberately in the space between the black and the white circles, added a low, rumbling sound that emanated from deep within his throat, serving as an anchor for the music and the magic being produced by the others.

Trieca crouched outside the dual circles, his hands firmly in contact with the cool, smooth surface of their enclosure. His job was to assist Sheyna in maintaining and expanding their water tornado as needed. Since she would be helping both Davlin and Ru-Lee as well as managing their transportation, it seemed prudent to give her as much aid as possible. There was no way to know how engrossed she might become in her task with Ru-Lee, and Trieca was quite accomplished in his skills with managing water. Although he could never have created their current resting place on his own, he was more than capable of offering support in maintaining it.

When Jace had remarked earlier that it was a stroke of luck for Trieca to be present now when they needed him, a slightly suspicious crooked grin had crossed Aylon's face. Davlin and Relmar had merely shaken their heads, irritating Jace, until Sheila had remarked, "I would imagine Nevlon had something to do with it." Disgruntled that Sheila had been the one to point out what appeared to be obvious to everyone else, Jace had huffed slightly, but agreed.

The colorful shield rose to the ceiling, settling into place on the lines of the black circle. As the musical notes of the chants fell silent, the air throbbed with the power emanating from the shield.

Aylon spoke softly, her voice skimming around the edges of the shield, "That was the easy part. Be ready to call upon your powers, boys."

Davlin glanced at the blue stone near his toes and inhaled deeply. Placing his left foot upon the stone, he felt its power surge through his boot and into his body, washing up his leg like a backwards waterfall. He gasped and quickly looked past the shield in time to see Ru-Lee's skin begin to turn a translucent, watery blue.

A cool flood filled his lower extremities and washed up through his torso, filling his limbs. He stretched out his hands and watched in awe as his skin became as translucent as Ru-Lee's. As the watery feeling spread to the ends of his hair, his legs began to feel rubbery, and his arms flopped to his sides like cooked noodles.

He paled and panic filled his face as he yelled, "Aylon! Help!"

Glancing sideways at him, Aylon's eyes widened and she blinked before shouting, "Sheyna! Davlin needs you!"

Suddenly, Davlin was surrounded with the calm warmth of his mother's presence. "Davlin, you must contain the water within yourself, or it will wash you away!" her voice sounded softly in his ears.

"Yeah...And exactly how am I to do that?" Davlin snapped, struggling to remain upright on his wobbly legs.

Relmar watched his brother through the colored shield from the other side, a dark look of concern covering his face. Jace, too, watched in wide-eyed silence, mouth hanging open in shock at what he was seeing. Pug spun his head around to get a better view of the scene, his round eyes filled with curiosity. Sheila, eyes closed, remained focused on Ru-Lee, oblivious to the happenings outside of the shield.

Trieca broke contact with the water tornado and quickly rose, walking over to offer his help to Davlin. Unnoticed, the enclosure walls began to waver ever so slightly. D.G. started past Davlin as Trieca approached the outside of the white circle. As Trieca stretched out his hand towards Davlin, D.G. came to a halt and bared his teeth, a low growl emanating from his throat.

Taken aback, Trieca stopped, jerked back his hand and asked, "What?"

Sheyna answered, her voice filling the cavern, "You cannot pass the white circle or you will break the protective seals. We cannot chance it."

Frustrated, Trieca snapped, "But I can help him!"

"I know, but he will have to do this on his own. Please return to your place and support our structure while I slip into his mind to see what I can do for him," Sheyna kindly responded.

Scowling, Trieca returned to his place and crouched, again making contact with the funnel's smooth, cool floor. A look of puzzled curiosity passed over his face as he watched the structure solidify once more, wondering what had caused it to warp.

"I'd really prefer you stayed out of my mind, mom—if it's all the same to you—one person tinkering around in there is enough!" Davlin grunted as he jerked his floppy arms back and forth beside his jiggly body. A silly grin slid across his face as he watched his hands flop back and forth.

"Really, Davlin! It isn't funny! Focus!" Aylon snapped.

"I can't help it," Davlin replied. "They look funny!"

Snorting with exasperation, Aylon growled, "Sheyna—please fix that so he can focus!"

Sheyna chuckled softly in Davlin's ear, then said, "Davlin, do you have your foot on the water stone?"

"Yes."

Aylon rolled her eyes.

"Please remove it," Sheyna directed.

"Okay—why?" Davlin said as he tried to work his jelly-like body so that his foot would come off of the stone.

Sighing, Aylon answered, "The water energy within the stone is channeling directly through your body—you need a small buffer of space or it will overwhelm your system--as it obviously has!"

Davlin flopped his arms around his body and swung his hips to the left causing his foot to slip and roll off the stone. The stone rolled free of his foot. He felt the rush of water recede from his limbs and his skin quickly lost some of its translucence as his body solidified again.

"Can you control the water within you now?" Sheyna's voice asked.

"Not sure—how would I go about finding out?" he asked, wiggling his fingers.

Sheyna paused a moment before responding, "Call upon the water and see what happens."

"How?"

"Concentrate on water, drawing it to you, and see what happens."

Closing his eyes, Davlin stilled his mind and clenched his jaw, stretching his arms out to the sides as if he were hanging on a cross. Spouts of water shot from his fingertips, narrowly missing Jace and Aylon. Davlin's eyes shot open in surprise at the sounds of their startled yells. His concentration broken, the flow of water stopped instantly. A wide grin spread across his face, "I guess I can control it—though I don't have a clue what to do with it!"

Ru-Lee's sudden screams ripped through the funnel drawing the attention of those tending to the walls of her protective shields. Her body writhed and twisted in pain on the cool floor of the inner circle. There was only a moment for the others to register what was happening to her before the power gathering around Ru-Lee shot across the floor, wreaking havoc outside the edge of the dark circle.

Vines sprouted from the dark stone near Jace's feet. Rooting into the floor, they quickly grew up and out, wrapping around the shield. The heat that rushed through Jace's body caused him to roar in startled pain. Instantly, he dropped to the ground, shifting to bear form as he went, tattered clothes flying off of him. Pug shot into the air, frightened by the sudden burst of activity, but careful to stay close to the inner shield.

Davlin smiled as fountains of water flowed forcefully from his hands to join with a stream of liquid springing up from the blue stone. The fluids fused with the shield in front of him, becoming a wall of solid ice.

Across from Davlin, on the opposite side of the shield, Relmar screamed. Flames burst from the stone near his feet that scorched his face and singed his eyebrows.

Searing winds rushed through the water tornado swirling around the shield, blowing Jace's tattered clothing into Trieca's startled face, and nearly lifting Aylon off the ground.

## Chapter 47

Inside Ru-Lee, the dragon plunged deeper into the pool at her spine, the cool water shot upwards, engulfing the dragon and drawing Ru-Lee into its vortex. Ru-Lee's soul instinctively dug in its heels and struggled against the pull of the water.

*"Don't fight it, Ru,"* Sheyna's voice chided, echoing in her brain.

Breathing hard, Ru-Lee cried, *"Help!"*

Immediately, Sheila's soft, melodic voice filled her mind, washing through her being, enabling her to relax enough to stop fighting against the pull of the water.

*"Call it to you, Ru—don't let it drag you,"* Sheyna commanded.

Taking a deep breath, Ru-Lee gathered her strength and focused on the swirling pool of water, drawing it towards her and bringing it within her soul. She felt the cool liquid swell forth from the pool and wash through her body, drenching her limbs and mind.

*"Good,"* commended Sheyna. *"Now, call on the dragon."*

*"Really? Can't we just settle in like this?"* Ru-Lee's mind asked, reveling in the feel of the liquid running through her system.

*"No, Ru---you know we can't."*

*"Okay,"* Ru-Lee conceded, *"but how?"*

*"Invite it in—it is part of you, but it is still a dragon. It will want to be shown respect."*

*"Hmmm—okay, here goes."*

The dragon sat in the nearly-empty pool, eyeing Ru-Lee with an air of indignity due to the fact that she had taken most of the water. Ru-Lee smiled ruefully at it and thought, *'Would you like the water back?'*

The dragon grumbled and bobbed its head in irritation.

*'Come join with me, and you will have all the water you need.'*

The dragon huffed through its nostrils and rolled its eyes at her. Turning its head sideways, it grinned slyly in the direction of the small flame flickering behind it near the pool's edge.

*'Yes,'* Ru-Lee replied to the dragon's implied request to bring the fire too. *'But can we wait until I am comfortable with just you and the water? One thing at a time, as it were.'*

The dragon emitted a low growl and tossed its head, tail flicking to the side of the pool.

*'Please,'* Ru-Lee asked, patiently pleading her case. She did not think she would be able to handle the fire as well.

Snapping its jaws, the dragon slid slowly out of the pool's hole and curled itself around the rim. It stretched out its serpentine body, nosing into her spine. Winking at her, it swept its tail to the edge of the flame.

Startled, Ru-Lee asked, *'You're bringing it with you, aren't you?'*

A sound like a deep chuckle rolled from the depths of the dragon's body, reverberating in Ru-Lee's bones. As the dragon nodded, a sinister smile slid around its jaws nearly hidden by its fangs.

*"Please, no!"* she cried, but the dragon only grinned wider. Thrusting the end of its tail into the flame, it charged up her spine, coiling around and around her center. It drew the flame with it as it went—joining itself first to the fire, then to Ru-Lee and the fluid that filled her.

Ru-Lee gasped as the heat from the flames spread, boiling the water within her and threatening to melt her mind like candle wax. The dragon, having reached the peak of her spine, arched its body and stretched its limbs, into Ru-Lee's body.

Ru-Lee screamed in pain as her own body began to change, stretch, and grow. The scream turned to an earsplitting growl as her soul embraced the changes taking place, and the dragon began to take over. Reveling in the power that surged through her body, the dragon opened her maw, grinned wide, and roared again.

Ru-Lee's body twisted into a ball. Convulsing in agony, she rolled onto all fours and stretched. Her face began to change, her head to grow; body elongated; fingers grew into claws that scraped loudly on the solid floor; wings sprouted; muscles rippled; flames danced upon her skin, joining with the water; the beginnings of a long, scaly tail sprouted from her backside. Arching her head upwards, mouth gaping, the dragon took control.

# Chapter 48

Glaring through the spreading vines, Jace panted heavily and growled at the dragon taking shape within the colored shield. To his right, he could see Relmar struggling to control the flames in front of him. Fireballs kept bursting forth from his hands, and sparks flew from his hair, burning dark holes in his clothes. His skin looked blistered and raw, and his blue eyes were rimmed with fire.

Glancing left, Jace saw that Davlin appeared to have mastered his element. Expertly wielding the water that flowed from his hands, he fortified the shields in front of him with layer upon layer of ice. He did not seem to notice the crystals building up around him, freezing his feet to the floor.

Jace viewed the thickening vines in front of him with a look of confusion, unsure of what was expected of him. Pug landed softly on his head and hooted quietly, his light weight reassuring.

From the opposite side of the dark circle, Aylon spoke, "Touch the stone, Jace."

Jace vehemently shook his furry head and growled.

Exasperated, Aylon snarled above the roar of the wind, "Would you please change back to human form so I can talk to you!"

Pug fluttered into the air again as the blonde bear's form shimmered behind the vines and Jace shifted back. Standing there in very stretched-out underwear, blushing viciously, he asked, "Happy now?"

"Yes, thank you. I need you to touch the stone lightly with your toes, grip the vines, and pull outwards."

Shaking his head again, Jace refused, "No way! Touching those stones nearly turned Davlin into a puddle! I'm not touching that thing—I might turn into a tree!"

Grunting, Aylon chided, "You won't turn into a tree!"

"But you said we needed a buffer!"

"I said *Davlin* needed a buffer. He was standing directly on the stone! It was channeling straight into his core. If you lightly touch it, it will only give you more control over the element."

"You sure?" Jace questioned, doubtfully.

"Yes, I am sure! Hurry up! We haven't much time to expand the shields!"

Peaking through the vines, Jace could see Ru-Lee's dragon form quickly filling the space within. Sheila had shifted to spider form and clung desperately to the top of the dragon's spiky head.

"Relmar! Have you got a handle on those flames yet?" Aylon yelled as a fireball shot past her ear.

"I think so! Why?" came Relmar's muffled reply.

"Davlin! Are you ready to enlarge your area?" Aylon shouted to her right.

"Yep! Anytime you are!" Davlin answered, calmly.

"We need to expand the shields! She is growing too fast!"

"Will the circles expand with the shields?" Trieca asked from outside the white circle.

"They should! They are infused with magic. Didn't you recognize the spells I used as I drew them?" Aylon asked. "With D.G.'s added magic, the circles will expand and drag the elemental stones with them as we draw them outwards. Ready, D.G.?"

D.G. gave a short, sharp 'yip' in reply.

"All at once, then—one, two, three—Pull!" Aylon ordered, slowly stepping backwards and drawing the cyclone of wind in front of her.

Relmar slowly worked his element outwards, stretching and expanding the flames. Ducking random fireballs and swatting at the occasional spark that bit holes in his clothing, he seemed to have a relative amount of control over the fire that he wielded.

Davlin, however, had discovered that his feet were attached to the floor beneath several layers of ice and was having some difficulty working himself loose. Trieca, noticing Davlin's dilemma, sent a ripple of energy along the floor of the enclosure that quickly turned the ice jam around Davlin's feet to water that instantly fused to the surrounding enclosure. Smiling his thanks in Trieca's direction, Davlin began working the wall of ice in front of him so that it expanded outwards, forming a wider curve that joined Aylon's.

Jace cautiously touched the dark stone lightly with his big toe, feeling the rush of power surge through his body. As he grabbed the vines in front of him, they sprang to life and wrapped themselves forcefully around his forearms. His eyes bulged with panic as more vines whipped out, catching Pug by one leg when he attempted to fly free. The vines whipped out around Jace's legs and torso. Struggling frantically, he stepped back, drawing the wall of plant matter with him. The plant tentacles grew and spread, binding themselves throughout the shield. They wove easily through the water and wind in their natural form. Turning to living stone where they wove through the fire element, they strengthened the shield as they grew, binding Jace to the side of the shield, and dangling a flapping, squawking Pug high in the air.

Between the dark and the light circles, D.G. paced wider and wider, adding his howls to those of the wind. The sound mixed with the wild winds and filled the water tornado with an eerie thrumming. Trieca was pushed backwards towards the opening of the funnel as Ru-Lee's shielded enclosure expanded to hold the growing dragon within.

# Chapter 49

Encased behind the large tubular shield, The dragon Ru-Lee slowly took stock of herself. Her eyes traveled appraisingly over her body. She watched her muscles ripple as her body grew; flexed and straightened her claws; heard the scraping sound as those same claws met the floor of the water tornado; grinned at the spiked ball at the peak of her long scaly tail; and noticed the flames dancing within the scales of her gray-green translucent skin. Twisting her massive head around, she flexed her shoulder muscles and brought beautiful, iridescent blue wings into view. Power vibrated through her body, invigorating her senses. Her flaring nostrils filled with smells she had never noticed before, but recognized quickly as the fear, anger, and frustration of her family struggling to contain her safely. Most of the anger and frustration emanated from Jace dangling just outside the shield.

*'Hmmmm—I think I like this,'* she thought to herself, a wide grin splitting her muzzle.

*"Can you control it?"* Sheila's melodic voice questioned, breaking into Ru-Lee's thoughts.

The dragon had filled her body and pushed into her mind, crowding Ru-Lee's consciousness into a deep corner.

*"Control what?"* The dragon replied, softly snorting smoke from her nostrils. *"Do you think I can breathe fire?"* she asked, puffing again, and marveling at the balls of smoke that were emitted.

*"Maybe--if you can harness the fire within you, you might be able to bring it to bear."*

The dragon closed her eyes and stilled her mind, looking inward for the spark that should be near her core. She found it, but it was much more than a spark—a huge flame snapped and crackled within her, filling her body with heat and the promise of power. Concentrating, she called upon it and felt the flames surge through her system. Opening her mouth wide, she gathered herself and stretched out her neck expecting flames to shoot from her body. Instead, molten lava showered forth from her gaping maw, splattering against the wall of the shield, and quickly turning to stone as it cooled.

She snapped her mouth shut and blinked disbelievingly at the pile of hot black rock in front of her. Pockets of orange heat glowed back at her mockingly.

*"Well, that was unexpected!"* Sheila mused in Ru-Lee's mind.

Confused, the dragon answered, *"Yes, it was—what do you suppose caused that?"*

*"I don't know. It's like the fire merged with the earth powers somehow."*

Opening and closing her jaws experimentally to make sure there was no lava stuck in her teeth, the dragon mulled over the possibility that she would not be able to separately access any of her powers. Disappointment washed through her. She had envisioned herself with the ability to shoot flames, control water, manipulate earth and growing things, manage the wind, and fight like a dragon—each separate from the other. If the powers merged and expanded upon themselves in these odd and unexpected ways, how was she to be of any real use in battle? What would she do, rain molten lava on the Warta? *'Hardly a useful skill against beings who can wield fire,'* she thought.

Realizing she was dealing with the dragon, and not her friend, Sheila began to hum softly, projecting the sound into the beast's shared mind. The melody slowly and gently drew out her friend's soul, pulling on her mind while lulling the dragon's like a drug.

*"Nice tune,"* the dragon purred, closing her eyes to narrow slits.

*"Thanks,"* Shiela murmured, working the word into the music without missing a beat. She could sense Ru-Lee's growing presence swelling slowly to push against the dragon's essence.

The dragon felt it, too and softly growled, *"What do you want?"*

*"We are one in this body,"* Ru-Lee responded, her soul stretching and blending with the dragon as Sheila's voice hummed in the background, maintaining her hold on the dragon's mind.

*"Mmm—why do I need you?"* the dragon grumbled, flames dancing on its skin.

*"Without me, you have no chance to separate the powers or use them to their fullest potential---no way to contain the Warta when they come. We are one—we must work together,"* Ru-Lee persuaded.

The dragon shook her head roughly, nearly dislodging Sheila from her perch on the horned head.

*"Hey! Careful!"* Sheila yelled, swinging precariously around a horn as she scrambled to attach a length of webbing to it, the spell of her song interrupted.

The dragon grunted and slowly opened its eyes to mull over its options, apparently oblivious to the fact that it had been somewhat hypnotized into submission.

*"Will you join with me, or fight me?"* Ru-Lee's mind and soul asked the dragon.

The dragon's sides expanded as it heaved a heavy sigh, grunted, and replied, *"I will join, but it is to be a partnership—none of this controlling nonsense the other spoke of!"*

*"Fine,"* Ru-Lee accepted. She spread her essence through the dragon body, sending a shudder down the spine that rattled the shimmering scales and set the flames dancing once again as she joined herself to the dragon. Her serpentine tongue slid out between her fangs and flicked across her muzzle. A twisted grin split her mouth as her mind joined the dragon's. Its voice went silent and its playful, sadistic nature flooded through her soul.

Raising her dragon head, Ru-Lee turned a tight, slow circle inside her enclosure, catching glimpses of her friends and family struggling outside its walls. Noticing

213

the furious winds that embattled the company, she asked, *"Why are there no winds in here, Sheila?"*

*"I don't know,"* Sheila answered, puzzled. *"Can you call upon the wind—or, for that matter, the earth?"*

*"I don't know—it is easy to do when surrounded by wind and earth in their natural elements. I have never tried to access them where there weren't any."*

*"Well, there is wind and earth here—within the stones. Can you tap into the powers within the stones?"*

*"I don't know—they are outside the shields. I shouldn't be able to access them."* Her eyes travelled around the base of the dark circle and across the floor to her now-large clawed feet. *"Maybe there is a way..."* she mused.

Ru-Lee's settled her mind upon the near-empty pool of water at her core. She could feel the water washing gently through her system, heated by the flames that were fused with it, and wondered if she could tap into the stones outside of the shield using the water in their funnel. Beneath her claws, she felt the cool surface of solid water. Bending her will upon the liquid surrounding her, she watched as the tips of her claws began to slip through the solid flooring. The powerful pulse of each of the elements rippled through the currents of the water tornado, vibrating through her claws into her body.

Focusing her energies on the wind that whipped and buffeted the others, she drew its wildness down from the air surrounding the shield and back into the stone. As the winds surrounding Aylon disappeared, she looked around in confusion. A smile split Ru-Lee's maw behind her fangs.

Carefully pulling the wind powers from the stone, through the floor of her enclosure, and up into her body, Ru-Lee roared triumphantly. A burst of hot air released by her roar rushed forth in the form of a wild tornado that tore through the space within the shield and whipped Sheila from her perch, slamming her hard into the inner wall of the shield.

*"Sheila!"* Ru-Lee's mind cried, startled, as her friend slid down the wall in front of her to land upside down, legs askew. Ru-lee tried to step towards her friend, but when her concentration had broken, her front claws had fused with the floor—she couldn't move.

Inside her head, she heard her friend's feeble groan, *"Ugh! I think I am alright."* Sheila untangled her legs and struggled upright on wobbly spider legs grumbling, *"It's lucky stone spiders are tough and rather bouncy."*

"What did you do, Ru?" Aylon called to her. "You need to replace the power you stole from the stone or the shield won't hold!"

Startled, Ru-Lee attempted to apologize, but the only sound that came out was a series of dragonish grunts. She shook her head and drew it back on her long serpentine neck, surprised—Sheila's chuckle echoed in her mind.

*"You are a dragon now, Ru,"* she explained. *"While in this form, you cannot speak as humans do, just as I cannot speak when in spider form."*

*"I forgot about that!"* Ru-Lee exclaimed. *"Oh well, let's see if I can put the powers back into that stone."*

*"That would be good, but I would retain a bit within yourself, just in case you need it,"* Sheila suggested.

Ru-Lee nodded in agreement before focusing her energies on releasing a measure of wind power back into the stone near Aylon's feet. As the power drained from her, she pulled her claws free of the floor and cocked her head at Aylon, waiting to make sure she had done it correctly. Aylon smiled her thanks as she gathered the unruly winds about herself once more to fortify the slightly weakening shields.

*"You okay?"* Ru-Lee asked Sheila, lowering her head to the floor in front of the white spider so that Sheila could climb back on. *"Nothing's broken?"*

*"No—nothing's broken—I'm okay, but could you hold still for a minute?"* Sheila asked as she made her way back to the top of Ru-Lee's knobby, horned head. Quickly attaching a length of webbing to one of Ru-Lee's horns,

Sheila anchored herself in place so that she would not fly off so easily again.

Suddenly, the air within the water tornado and the shields became thick, and icy cold. Fear and anger prickled down Ru-Lee's dragon spine causing the scales along her back to raise and rattle. For reasons she could not explain, her breath came in enraged gusts that burst forth from her mouth and nostrils. Red crept around the edges of her golden eyes, rimming them with fury.

*"They want in!"* her mind growled to Sheila. She coiled her body in a tight crouch, expanding her lungs as she went. Every muscle in her dragon's body flexed as she thrust her head upwards, filling the cavern with her defiant, challenging roar. Flames exploded through her fangs, spreading across the top of the water tornado to rain boiling lava down the walls of the shield.

Relmar howled in agony as the heat from the dragon flames fused with his own fire, pulsing through him and forcing him backwards, causing him to trip over an unsuspecting D.G.. D.G. yelped, his foot inadvertently stepped on as Relmar fell backwards over him, breaking through the protective barrier of the outer circle.

Hair smoldering, Relmar struggled to his feet, shaking his blistered hands. He reached out to stroke D.G.'s head and apologize, but recoiled as sparks flew from his hands, singeing D.G.'s ears. D.G. yipped loudly and jumped sideways. Landing in a low crouch, he eyed Relmar angrily, a low growl rumbling in his throat.

"Sorry, D.G.," Relmar said, a bewildered look on his face. Shaking his head, he faced the renegade flames that threatened to engulf the entire perimeter of the shield. He quickly returned to his position near the fire stone at the edge of the dark circle. Focusing on the fire emanating from the stone near the edge of the dark circle, he began to bring it back under some semblance of control, ignoring the searing pain in his hands.

Vines whistled and screamed as they recoiled towards Jace. Shrinking from the flames on the inner walls of the shield, their hold on him loosened. He fell to the floor on his hands and knees, panting—contact with the earth stone, broken. Released from captivity, Pug tumbled to land with a thump on the back of Jace's head.

"Ouch!" Jace growled.

Pug attempted to halt his descent, his talons becoming entangled in Jace's thick hair, wings smacking Jace hard in the side of the head. Jace quickly sat back on his heels and grabbed for the frantic bird's fluffy body hoping to pin down the offending wings. Working to loosen Pug's talons, his foot slid backwards and touched the earth stone once again. His body stiffened, his back arched, and he lost his hold on the small bird as power and pain surged through his body again. Pug panicked twisting, screeching, and flapping his wings in fear and fury.

Jace's breath came in quick, hot bursts as he attempted to control the sensations pulsing through his system. Closing his eyes, he willed himself to maintain contact with the stone as he twisted around to face the wall of singed and retreating vines. He knew the vines had to be forced back around the perimeter of the shields to merge with the other elements if they were to maintain a strong protective area around Ru-Lee. Bowing his head, he doubtfully tried to focus his energies on making the vines grow into an impenetrable massive wall in front of him. Suddenly, the scent of brown earth, stones, and growing things filled the air around him. A startled smile broke across his face when he opened his eyes to find a mass of heat-resistant plants he had never seen before springing to life all around him—a wall of unfamiliar, thick, stone-like cactus in front of him.

Heat from the dragon flames ran down the shield, melting the ice wall Davlin had worked so hard to create. Water pooled around his feet making the smooth floor of the tornado funnel treacherously slippery.

Frantic, Davlin yelled, "Mom! Help! What do I do? She's melting the ice!"

Ignoring her son's previous wishes, Sheyna's voice filled Davlin's mind, *"Try drawing the water upwards from the floor around you into a solid wall. You have to infuse it with your strength in order for it to maintain a solid form."*

Struggling for footing, Davlin focused on the water pooled around him, willing it to come together in a wall along the lines of the failing shield. Sweat beaded up on his forehead and ran down into his eyes as he poured every ounce of strength he had into the slowly-forming wall of water.

*"Don't loose your concentration, Davlin, or the wall will fail,"* Sheyna cautioned, her voice liquid-smooth inside his head.

Too busy to argue with the fact that his mother was speaking inside his head, Davlin sucked in a deep breath, nodded and drew his arms upwards, bringing the solid wall up to reinforce the shield.

Hot winds blew Aylon's hair backwards scorching her face and clothes as the dragon fire poured down the inner shield. Tightly closing her eyes, she concentrated on bringing the winds to her and holding them within the shield.

As the others struggled to maintain and reinforce the protective shield around Ru-Lee and Sheila, Trieca felt the walls of their enclosure soften and warp. He forced his will upon the water tornado and felt his hands melt into it—becoming one with the walls. Pushing through his initial shock at finding his arms stuck in a wall of water, he continued to pour his energy into the walls to solidify them as the chill of fear that followed the Warta spirits permeated his body.

## Chapter 50

The dark shadows hovering above Lake Satcha spread and churned like a living beast. Furious screeches and frustrated howls pierced the air. Ice cold fear penetrated every living creature in the valley—a chill so deep, it could not be dispelled by the scorching noon-day sun. Searing winds once again whipped the waters of the lake into a frenzy that sent waves raucously crashing against the shore.

Near the southeast end of the lake, past the flattened path of scorched plant matter, dark furry bodies could be glimpsed moving quickly and stealthily through the red-blossomed foliage towards Mount Shavla and the Heart.

XXX    XXX    XXX    XXX    XXX

Beneath the frothy waves, the twisting water tornado spun its way through turbulent currents towards one of the mountain streams that fed into Lake Satcha from the south. The passengers within struggled desperately to maintain the integrity of the watery walls while attempting to keep Ru-Lee safe from the Warta spirits that threatened to possess her dragon body. Their attempts at both appeared to be failing.

As the liquid walls of the enclosure warped and wiggled like a laughing fat man's belly, Ru-Lee's defiant roar cut through the air, filling the space and echoing off the walls. The dragon thrashed wildly behind the inner elemental shield, her spiked tail crashing through the piles of cooling lava that had built up on the inside.

On the outer edges of the shield, Aylon glanced behind her to check on the protective barrier. Finding it gone, she cursed under her breath. Recalling that Relmar had earlier fallen through the perimeter of the white outer circle that formed the base of that barrier, she grit her teeth in frustration and yelled to the others over the heated howling winds, "The outer barrier is broken! Fortify this one with everything you've got!"

XXX   XXX   XXX   XXX   XXX

Behind the colorful and tangled protective shield, the dragon thrashed its armored tail and dug lethal claws deep into the enclosure's floor. Shattered pieces of lava flew threw the air like shrapnel causing the large white spider to duck beneath a spiny scale protruding from the back of Ru-Lee's elongated head.

The voices of the Warta spirits invaded Ru-Lee's furious and fevered mind. Thousands of spirit voices meshed together, amplified in her head, compelled her to leave the water and become one with them. They promised power beyond measure; freedom to do as she wished; control of all who came near her. They exhorted her to leave behind the fetters of family and friends— promising they would fill that void.

The dragon gnashed her fangs, feeling her hold on reality slip as the spirits wove their hypnotic spell around her soul. She shook her massive head and attempted to flap her huge wings in an effort to ward off the voices in her mind, but the enclosure was too small. She only succeeded in bruising herself and banging her muzzle against the wall of the shield. Anger swelled within her— anger at her confinement; at the voices; at the world.

The spirits laughed at her frustration which infuriated her even more. She roared, filling the air with molten lava that rebounded off the ceiling and bounced off of her armor-like scales.

Sheila's calming, melodic voice whispered around the edges of her mind, *"Hang on, Ru—focus."*

*"Focus on what?"* she snarled.

*"Focus on the water and earth within your soul,"* Sheila calmly answered, her voice barely audible above the rush of flames in Ru-Lee's mind.

*"Why?"* Ru-Lee growled, spitting ground lava from her maw.

*"The water will cool your anger, giving you more control—the earth will ground your soul, enabling you to resist the Warta spirits."*

*"Heed us!"* hissed the spirits, drowning out Sheila's soothing words. *"Draw the powers from the stones, break down the shield, escape! They only wish to use you! We wish to free you!"*

*"They lie,"* Sheila urgently whispered. *"Find the water at your core—call upon it!"*

*"I can help you, Ru,"* Sheyna's voice joined the fray. *"But you must work with me to call upon the water within your soul."*

*"Don't listen to them!"* the spirits howled. *"We can help you realize your full potential! We seek not to hold you!"*

Deep within her soul, Ru-Lee recalled an earlier conversation with the Warta—during the night, beneath a full moon. She heard the voices of Nevlon and Aylon and remembered the peril facing her world. Revolting, gory images imparted earlier by the Warta spirits invaded her psyche—her dragon's body recoiled.

*"LIE!"* her mind shouted. *"YOU LIE! ALL WILL USE ME—WARTA AND OTHERS! I HAVE NO CHOICE! I HAVE NO VOICE! LEAVE ME!"*

Her mind boiled and her vision blurred red; the flames on her skin danced. She dug her claws deeper into the belly of the tornado as it rolled and shook with the turbulence of the lake, its walls rippling and twisting. She drew her soul and mind inward to her core, attempting to pull back behind her protective inner walls and block out the offending Warta voices.

As Ru-Lee's mind pulled in upon itself, she unintentionally began to draw on the powers of the stones surrounding her. The shield surrounding her began to collapse with a domino effect, starting with wind that poured in, whipping around her and cooling her heated body before fading away to a light breeze. The wall of water collapsed next, engulfing her tail and backside; she barely noticed, as she withdrew deeper within herself. Next, hard crusty vines of foreign plants slithered across the floor to twist up her legs, their thorny spines scratching softly across her translucent scales. The last to fall was the wall of fire--flames from the elemental stone snapped and crackled across the floor towards her, surrounded her body, and merged with the fire dancing within her watery skin.

XXX   XXX   XXX   XXX   XXX

Expectant silence impregnated the space within the funnel, hanging heavily in the air. Aylon, Davlin, and Relmar stared at the enormous crouched dragon and struggled to maintain their footing as their conveyance was jostled beneath the waves of the lake, walls rippling and weakening. Sparks still danced around Relmar's head, but the fireballs had disappeared with the stone's flames. Davlin's skin was quickly returning to normal, losing the translucency of the water. Aylon's hair stood on end, jutting out in every direction, the white stripe gleaming vividly in the eerie light of the water tornado. D.G. stood near Jace and whimpered softly to Ru-Lee, his mind unable to penetrate deep enough to break through her mental defenses. Jace sat in baggy underwear, surrounded by the remnants of his tattered clothes and the plants he had called to life. He winced as Pug's talons scraped his head, twisting and pulling his hair. Trieca, arms elbow deep in the funnel's walls, still struggled to maintain the integrity of their transportation, sweat pouring down his face and neck.

Sheyna's tired voice whispered softly in his mind, *"Pull free, Trieca, and get ready to swim."*

Before he could react or respond, the walls failed and icy cold lake water rushed in, engulfing them all.

# Chapter 51

Churning, ice-cold lake water instantly boiled as it washed over the fiery scales of the water dragon, cooking many unfortunate inhabitants in its wake. Ru-Lee's eyes shot open as the chill of the lake water permeated her skin and cleared her mind. The Warta spirit voices still murmured to her, but the roar of the water in her ears muted their sound.

She swung her tail through the wild deep currents and felt the spiked ball at the end strike something hard. She swept her right clawed foot outwards in an attempt to turn her massive body so she could see what she had hit and felt one of her talons rake the length of Jace's ribs. A plume of agitated bubbles escaped from her cousin's lungs as he frantically clutched his bleeding side and fought to distance himself from her dangerous appendages, Pug dangling comically from his head.

Out of the corner of her eye, she saw Trieca swimming away from her towards the surface, his left arm wrapped around the neck of an unconscious and bleeding Davlin. Shocked and wondering if she was the cause of Davlin's wounds, she twisted her body and angled towards her companions, heated water circulating around her.

Suddenly, Sheyna's visage appeared in front of her, a solid form beneath the surrounding waves. *"You cannot follow—not right now, Ru,"* her voice softly assuaged the edges of Ru-Lee's festering mind. *"You need to decide how to proceed. We are nearly at the end of our journey. The Warta will invade your body—human or dragon. If human, they will force you to shift—if dragon, they will simply use you as you are. Can you maintain control of yourself while they are within you?"*

Ru-Lee allowed the weight of her body to drag her down to the depths of the muddy lake bottom, settling amongst the swaying plants and protruding boulders, waves of heat rippling off her back, cool mud oozing into the scales on her stomach. The Warta voices were nearly inaudible here—'*probably too far away for them to project*', she thought to herself. The enormity of her task washed through her mind as she wondered if she would be able to do what was asked of her.

Looking up, she watched the legs and bodies of the others as they ascended: Relmar's booted feet and clothed legs kicked towards Trieca to help raise Davlin's dead weight; D.G.'s four furry legs churned bubbles in the water as he neared the light above; Jace dragged Pug along, trailing a trickle of blood from his wounded side, underwear sliding dangerously low on his hips; Sheila's delicate naked human form struggled frantically, having shifted just as the water flooded their enclosure. Aylon moved closer to Sheila, grabbed the flaxen hair, and pulled her upwards. The elemental stones drifted down through the currents to settle softly in the mud and weeds—lost.

A deep sigh escaped her serpentine body causing a line of bubbles to rise from her nostrils. The fear, anger, and pain that had consumed her earlier were ebbing, carried away by the currents swirling in the lake.

"*I have to, don't I?*" she asked.

"*Yes, I'm afraid so—but can you?*"

"*I have no choice,*" Ru-Lee replied, bitterness dripping from the thought.

Pity filled Sheyna's eyes, and the look inflamed Ru-Lee for reasons she could not explain. "*Don't pity me—it won't do any good!*" she growled.

Rising, she felt soft mud squish between her toes, sucking at her feet and body. Pointing her muzzled upwards, she saw her friends and family reach the relative safety of the edge of the lake. She twisted her head back and forth, watching the surface above her, and was able to make out the reflection of the shadows hovering over the lake. A shudder passed through her.

"*Got any suggestions on how to go about this?*" she asked.

"*Keep your body in the water as long as possible and use the water to help control them—even after they enter you. They will want the fire in you, because that is what they know. If you keep them in the water, you should be able to control them better and I may be able to help in some small way."*

Ru-Lee tested her muscles and felt them ripple as she waited for the others to get clear of the water, not wanting them in the lake when she surfaced. Her courage was bolstered by the reckless nature of her dragon soul as it filled with anticipation for the coming confrontations.

*"Will you stay with me—listen in my head and help me if you can?"* She asked.

*"Yes,"* Sheyna replied quietly.

Ru-Lee chuckled softly to herself as she thought, *'Best not delay the inevitable then.'*

Wings folded tight to her body, Ru-Lee used her strong legs and powerful tail to propel herself upwards. Trailing clusters of fire-warmed bubbles, she launched her massive body towards the surface. In her wake, Sheyna's image faded into the churning waters.

# Chapter 52

The churning cloud of dark shadows stretched itself across Lake Satcha, hovering just out of reach above the waves, and blocking the waning afternoon sun from view. On the southwestern shore of the lake, six human heads, one canine, and one bedraggled fowl broke the surface—some thrashing and gasping for air, others being dragged in various states of consciousness through the waves. Their arrival went unheeded by the shadows as the group hauled themselves and their companions out of the water onto the scorched shore. Overwhelming emotions poured out of the clouds, permeating the air, and leaving the soggy refugees shivering with dread as they attempted to nurse their wounded and catch their breath.

Sheila lay on her stomach where Aylon had left her, coughing and sputtering, her bare body quivering with the shock of her unexpected swim. Her fingers flexed involuntarily, grounding down into bases of the dry stalks of plant matter around her. Under her breath, she softly swore that she would never again enter the water voluntarily in any form whatsoever.

Jace sat in his soggy underwear, his body streaked with mud, attempting to remove Pug's talons from his matted hair with one hand. His other hand clenched his side, blood trickling through his fingertips. Swearing profusely, he cursed the owl and the loss of his knife, which he threatened to use to remove either his hair or both of the bird's feet if he ever found it again. Pug hooted angrily and twisted his body, attempting to snap at Jace's ear, but only managing to tangle himself further.

Trieca crawled over to Jace and offered his assistance in removing the flapping bird from his friend's head.

"Thanks," Jace mumbled, placing his free hand in his lap to allow Trieca to work. Glancing over to where Davlin lay, he asked, "How is he?"

"Don't know," Trieca answered, working one of Pug's feet free of the tangled matt of hair on Jace head.

"Relmar and Aylon are tending to him. It's a nasty cut he has on his head, but Aylon is the best at healing those kinds of things." Noting the look of concern in Jace's eyes, he added, "I'm sure he will be fine."

Wincing as Trieca tugged Pug's other foot free, Jace grunted, "Yeah, sure he will." But the look on his face belied nonchalance. For all their disagreements, Jace would be lost without his brothers. The sight of Davlin laying unconscious with blood pouring from his head, caused his stomach to knot.

Trieca placed Pug on the ground next to him before tearing a strip of cloth from the edge of his soggy shirt and handing it to Jace. "Use this to sop up some of that blood until Aylon can look it over," he said, glancing down at Jace's bleeding ribs.

"Mmm—thanks," Jace nodded, taking the cloth and glancing down as he placed it on the gash Ru-Lee's talons had ripped in his side.

Near the water's edge, Relmar pumped Davlin's chest and arms, trying to expel any water from his lungs—no easy task with Aylon attempting to administer care to Davlin's head wound. Relmar kept bumping Aylon as she worked causing her to glare at him, aggravated at the disruption of her task.

Suddenly, Davlin coughed and sputtered, spewing water and stomach contents. Relmar jerked back and quickly rolled his brother on his side so that the ground would be the recipient of the expulsion and not his own lap. Once Davlin appeared to be finished retching, Relmar gently rolled him onto his back again so that Aylon could continue her ministrations.

"Davlin, can you hear me?" she asked.

Davlin nodded slightly and moaned in response, trying to rise.

Aylon gently held him down saying, "Good--now stay still a moment or two longer while I secure these bandages."

Working quickly, Aylon tore a soggy strip of cloth from the bottom of her blouse, laid it on her lap and removed a large semi-dried leaf and some small milky-white flowers from one of the pouches at her waist. She crushed the leaf in her hands, gently removed the bandages she had placed on Davlin's head to slow the bleeding, and spread the plants across the wound. Lifting the cloth from her lap, she carefully placed it over the gash and wrapped it tightly around Davlin's head causing him to wince.

"Sorry," she said, "but it has to be tight. Stop squirming!"

"Will he be okay?" Relmar asked.

Nodding, Aylon replied, "It is a relatively small cut. A bit deep, but it bled fairly clean. He'll be fine. Doesn't appear to be any internal damage—no apparent punctures to the skull that I can see."

Looking around at the scraggly group, she jerked her head in Sheila's direction and said, "Would you please offer her your cloak, Relmar? I think she would be more comfortable with it on, even if it is soggy."

Relmar turned his head, his gaze falling on the bare back of Sheila as she pushed herself up to a sitting position, her wet hair drizzling lines of water down her back. Color flushed his scorched face, and a smile tugged at the corners of his mouth. Swallowing, he said, "Yeah— Right, she looks a bit chilled."

"Right," Aylon sighed, shaking her head and returning to her task.

Relmar rose and walked to Sheila, removing his cloak as he went, and wincing at the pain in his burned and blistered hands. He had ignored his wounds while working on his brother, but the pain was making itself known. He passed D.G. silently pacing back and forth at the water's edge, staring expectantly across the waves.

"She'll be okay, Dege," he said, reassuringly patting the canine on the head as he passed.

He dropped to his knees to drape the wet cloak across Sheila's shoulders, startling her. She gasped and jolted forward to stand and slip away, but he held her shoulders and spoke, his voice cracking slightly.

"Whoa! It's just me—Relmar. Aylon thought you might want a cloak to cover up with. I know it's not much—wet and all, but…"

"Oh," she sighed, relaxing as the warmth of his hands washed through the wet cloth to her chilled shoulders. Turning her head sideways so she could see him better, she placed her hand over his and whispered, "Thank you."

Her voice filled his ears with its soft melody, and he felt himself melting into her gentle eyes, a silly grin on his face. Beneath her delicate fingers, his hand began to tingle and heal—the ache and burn of the blistered skin disappeared. His eyes widened and a smile spread across his face as the sensation worked its way up his arm and through his body, healing all the bumps, bruises, and burns that had occurred in the past few days. His body relaxed as Sheila's mind filled his with peace. He felt himself slipping away, lost in the warmth of her healing presence. His free hand slid down her side and around her belly, drawing her closer to him and she melted backwards into his chest.

Jace grimaced and shook his head in disgust as he watched his brother and Sheila. He opened his mouth to speak, but before he could find his voice, lake water surged up the shore swamping around him. Huge drops of water rained down on his head, and a large, frightened fish slapped him in the face as Ru-Lee's massive water-dragon head burst through the surface of the frothy waves.

# Chapter 53

Hundreds of angry souls shrieked with fury shattering the air around Lake Satcha as the water dragon shot through the surface of the lake, and punched a hole in the black cloud that hovered above the waves. Cascading lake water rained off her horned head, momentarily forcing the shadows back. As her shoulders breeched the water, Ru-Lee opened her fanged jaws and emitted a roar of challenge so deafeningly loud, it caused the remaining plants in the surrounding meadows to shudder.

Watching from the shore as lake water rained down on them, the small battered company of Ru-Lee's friends and family covered their ears and cringed---all except D.G., who stood tall. Shoulders taut, head thrust high, he joined his voice to the dragon's in a loud, wolf-like howl.

Instantly, the Warta spirits accepted Ru-Lee's challenge, encasing her head in a tight, black ball of swirling, angry souls. They wrapped themselves around her muzzle and twisted around her neck like a writhing snake. A deep, furious growl rumbled in her throat as she shook her head and wrested her mouth open again, allowing the tortured souls to enter her body. As the last wisp of dark shadow slid over her fangs, the dragon flicked her serpentine tongue across her nose and grinned in grim satisfaction. Opening her eyes, she winked across the waves to an astonished Aylon before slipping back into the rolling lake.

# Chapter 54

Deep beneath the surface of Lake Satcha, Ru-Lee dove to the mud-caked bottom, burrowing her claws into the sucking goo and coiling her tail protectively around her body. She squeezed her eyes shut and breathed deeply.

Retreating into her mind, her soul refused to relinquish space to the invading Warta. She stretched her essence into every part of her being and held strong, forcing the Warta into a tight corner of her psyche.

The enraged spirits screamed and howled. Pushing against her soul, they sought room--sought to take over her body. Their voices swirled and buzzed like a swarm of angry black flies in her head, their anger swelling within Ru-Lee. Joining their anger with her own violent emotions, they attempted to slip insidiously into her being through their shared feelings.

The mud beneath Ru-Lee's body began to bubble. The water around her boiled as the flames on her skin grew and changed to a wild orange-red, their blue-white tips flashing across her body in a primal dance. Her muscles rippled as she kneaded the mud with her claws in agitation, working her feet deeper into the ooze. Roaring, her soul thrust against the Warta spirits, shredding their hold on her emotions.

The gills behind her head flapped furiously, her breathing heavy as she fought against the Warta invasion, using her mind to push against the souls that were seeking to intertwine themselves with hers. In their rage at her refusal to allow them further access to her body, they lashed out. Her mind filled with pain so great that her body recoiled upon itself. Screaming beneath the waves, she wretched and thrust the side of her head against the lake floor in an attempt to feel something outside of herself—outside of her mind.

The frenzy of noise in her head subsided as the deep voice of the Ancient One echoed through her body, *"Enough! You must not fight us! We will take over regardless of your efforts! The only one to lose will be yourself!"*

"What do you mean?" she asked. *"If I hold fast, and we remain on the bottom of this lake, you will lose."*

*"Wrong, human!"* the Ancient growled. *"If you 'hold fast', we will break you down. In the end, we will take your body and break your mind. Nothing will be left of you but an empty shell."*

Incredulous, she asked, *"You would use my body for your own purposes, without my input?"*

The Ancient Warta laughed, a sound filled with malice and remorse intermingled. *"What choice would you give us? We must do that which will free us from the void and give us peace. If we must take your body forcibly, so be it. It is your choice."*

*"But to do that would only cause more pain and grief that you would then need to atone for....do you not see the vicious circle you create?"* she challenged.

The voices were silent for a few moments, as if processing information that had not presented itself to them before. Considering the consequences of their actions appeared to be a foreign experience for the Warta.

Finally, the Ancient spoke again, *"You make a point we had not foreseen. We do not wish to be trapped here continuing the cycle. We wish to finish this and move on. We wish to do so without further harm to you, but be warned—we will succeed, even if it is painful for our host. You were made for this purpose—to offer us retribution and release. Do not fight your own fate."*

Ru-Lee opened her eyes a slit and glanced up at the light playing on the surface of the lake above her. *'Was I made for this? Is it my fate to help the lost Warta souls find peace? Is that why I was given all of the elemental powers?'* she wondered.

Sheyna's voice washed gently through her mind, *"It may be your fate to play this role, Ru-Lee---but you must be cautious. The Ancient One may not speak for all the souls with him. I sense dissent among their ranks."*

Closing her eyes, Ru-Lee once again turned her mind inward asking the Ancient One, *"Do you speak for all soul with you?"*

Cautious and coy, he answered, *"Most.....why do you ask?"*

*"Earlier you indicated that some of the spirits with you were newly dead—that they did not all agree with the plan. You said that you, and those like you, were strong enough to control them---that they would not be a problem. Is that still true? Can you still control them?"* she growled, as the Warta spirits pushed against her.

*"There are no guarantees,"* the Ancient chuckled. *"Those who do not fully understand our goals are young souls. They did not live fully as Warta, but a human semblance of us. They have not dwelt long in the void...but they are weaker than we, and we outnumber them. They will be contained until we are freed.....after that, I cannot say."*

Ru-Lee contemplated his answer. Gently probing the dark mass within her mind, she attempted to gauge the truth of his words. *'Too bad I can't read minds like Relmar—it would be handy,'* she thought, irritated by this lack in her abilities.

She flexed her muscles and mentally shoved the roiling dark mass, as if she were pushing a bully she knew she could defeat. *'Must be the dragon in me,'* she thought, a wry smile slipping across her muzzle.

Grunting with disgust, she snarled, *"How does that work, exactly— the freeing bit, I mean? Does your soul just vacate my body and move on once your particular deeds have been atoned for? Or is it a collective thing? Where do you 'move on' to?"*

*"You ask questions that there are no answers for,"* growled the Ancient irritably. *"It may be that we are released one at a time or as a group...where we move to is of no consequence to us---only that we are released from the void."*

*"And if you are released bit by bit, what happens when all of the stronger Warta are gone, and I am left with the newly dead---the ones who only want to gain power and live again through me? Worse yet, what happens if it doesn't work, and you are not released at all?"*

Snarling, the Ancient replied grimly, *"It would be best for you if neither of these comes to pass. If we are released one by one, we will leave you to your fate, be sure of that. You are strong and gaining strength all the time. You may be able to contain them without us."*

*"And if you are not released? Will you leave my body and this world in peace?"*

A low murmur rippled through the Warta spirits as if the thought of failure had not been contemplated. The Ancient's reply forcefully filled her mind, *"We will not fail! You will be released."*

Suspicious, Ru-Lee asked, *"Do all agree to leave me?"*

Deep laughter rolled through her psyche, *"I speak for the old ones and those who seek retribution. You are wise enough to realize that there are some with us who have come for other reasons—we have discussed this already! Their strength is needed in order to succeed. If they choose not to abide by our terms, they are yours to deal with. The true Warta will not dissent."*

Ru-Lee snorted loudly and shook her horned head, stirring up bubbles and debris from the lake bed. Sighing deeply, she replied, *"Agreed."*

A multitude of triumphant roars deafened her as she let down her defenses and allowed the Warta spirits to spread through her body. Their emotions overwhelmed her mind; her stomach lurched; her mind reeled; heat filled her body, spiking a fever in her head—her psyche nearly overcome.

In an attempt to keep from losing herself within the Warta souls, she shoved her snout deep into the mud and clenched her jaw tight—inadvertently calling upon her earth powers. Water plants and reeds growing on the lake bed sprang forth, wrapping around her dragon's body and pinning her to the bottom of the lake.

The Warta souls flexed Ru-Lee's dragon claws, reveling in her strong body. They laughed and she found her mouth open and filled with mud. She jerked her head up and opened her jaws wider, shaking loose the earth that stuck to her muzzle and fangs, and allowing the water to clear her mouth of debris.

*"This will do,"* the Ancient laughed. *"This will do nicely, once we are free of this wretched lake."*

The Warta attempted to raise the water dragon, but the vines held fast.

They turned the water dragon's head to survey their entrapment. *"Nice trick, human—are you ready to join us now, or are we still playing games? Time is running out— our brethren will be through the wall soon. We can sense them."*

Ru-Lee blinked the water dragon's eyes and shook her head again. *"Who steers?"* she asked. *"I would like to control the functions of my body until it is time to battle, if you don't mind."*

Laughing in her mind, the Warta Ancient replied, *"Fair enough. We will simply go along for the ride—for now."*

Flaring her nostrils, Ru-Lee released the vines tying her bulk to the bottom of the lake. Flattening her wings close to her body, she pushed off towards the surface, a trail of bubbles and debris in her wake.

# Chapter 55

The red-orange and magenta sunset flashed off of Ru-Lee's iridescent wings and shot rainbows through the water that streamed off of her scales as she banked towards the small group huddled by the water's edge. Steam rose from her heated body as the moisture upon her back was heated by her internal fire and evaporated into the air. She shook her head and sucked fresh air in through her nostrils. Gill flaps, useless outside of the lake, sealed themselves to her neck behind her ear, blending in perfectly. As she angled in towards the ground to land near her friends, she misjudged the air currents. Her tail twisted wrong, and she landed face first, skidding to a stop on her side in the mud and burnt stubble of the field surrounding the lake. Pushing herself upright, she snorted and grunted. Within her mind, she could hear the sadistic laughter of the Warta souls that lay in wait inside her body.

'*Great! An audience!*' she grumbled to herself.

The others had scrambled out of the way when she nosedived towards them. They now stood huddled together near the edge of the water watching her cautiously. She turned her massive head, blinked in their direction, and opened her mouth to call out to reassure them that it was safe to come near. Grunts and guttural sounds filled the air! She pulled her head back on her long neck and blinked in confusion.

'*What was that?*' she thought as she watched Sheila disengage reluctantly from Relmar and walk towards her, D.G. following tentatively. She snorted at Sheila. Opening her mouth a few times, Ru-Lee again attempted to speak, with the same unsatisfactory results. She narrowed her eyes in irritation as Sheila reached out and gently placed her slender hand high up on her forehead.

"*You can't talk like a human while you are in dragon form, Ru, remember?*" Sheila said, her soft voice cascading through Ru-lee's mind. *"Just think what you want to say and I will relay the information to the others."*

'*This just gets better and better!*' Ru-Lee growled.

'*You could change to human form, if that works better for you—but we would have to dig up more clothing,*' Sheila chuckled.

'*I noticed you don't have much on—whose cloak?*'

Blushing, Sheila grinned and answered, '*Relmar's.*'

'*Ahh,*' Ru-Lee snorted, puffing acrid smoke through her nostrils. She gently fanned her wings as she looked past Sheila to where the others stood waiting. Even D.G., reluctant to move to close while she was in dragon form, hung back a bit. '*What's up with you two, anyway?*'

Sheila shrugged and tipped her head sideways, a silly grin playing gently on her lips. '*I like him,*' she murmured. '*He makes me warm all over.*'

Laughter rumbled in Ru-Lee's throat as she quipped, '*Yeah—I'll bet he does! Is everyone okay?*' she questioned as Aylon approached.

*"For the most part—the injuries seem fairly minor, at least,"* Sheila answered.

'*Why are they so wary?*' Ru-Lee asked. '*I won't harm them.*'

'*We weren't sure it would be you in control of your dragon body when you emerged from the lake—you are in control, aren't you?*'

Warta voices murmured softly in the recesses of her mind. She listened for a moment before responding, '*Yes, for the time being.*'

The slimy mud of the riverbank squelched away from Aylon's feet as she approached. D.G. joined her as she walked past him.

"Are you yourself, Ru-Lee?" she asked, her voice firm and strong compared to Sheila's melodic tones.

Ru-Lee nodded her head, the flames softly rippling along her sides.

Without taking her eyes from Ru-Lee's, Aylon spoke to Sheila. "She can't speak, can she?"

"Not in human terms, no," Sheila responded.

Nodding Aylon replied, "That's fine, we will work with what we have."

D.G. tentatively stretched his head past Aylon's legs, sniffing suspiciously at Ru-Lee's new form.

Smiling, Ru-Lee sent out a thought to him, '*It's me, D.G..*'

The canine whined and tilted his head to the side in confusion. He looked up at her massive body, nose wildly working, trying to find a recognizable scent in the being before him. Finding none, he plopped down on his haunches and whined again.

"*Can you read our thoughts, Ru?*" Sheila asked.

"*I don't know---should I be able to?*"

"*Most dragons can,*" responded Sheila with a shrug. "*Maybe you should give it a try.*"

"*Exactly how does one 'give it a try'?*" Ru–Lee growled sarcastically, shaking her head at Sheila. The others, seeing no harm come to Sheila, D.G., or Aylon, had begun to approach. Ru-Lee watched them, a wry smile sliding across her maw.

Sheila thought for a moment before responding. "*Maybe, just concentrate your energies on hearing my thoughts.*"

"*Won't mean much—I can hear your thoughts already!*" Ru-Lee snorted. Puffs of smoke curled from her nostrils to swirl around Sheila's head.

Sheila coughed and shook her head free of the smoke. "*Okay—how about Aylon, or---Relmar?*" she asked, her face flushing with color.

"*Not sure I want to know what Relmar is thinking— I'll try Aylon,*" Ru-Lee chuckled.

Surreptitiously turning her gaze to Aylon, she tried to concentrate and focus on what might be in her mind. Her head tilted slightly in surprise when a soft murmur— almost a buzzing sound—sifted into her own mind. She blinked and concentrated on the sound, trying to make the words clearer.

*"I hear something!"* she projected to Sheila.

*"Good—can you respond?"*

*"What do you mean?"*

*"Can you send your thoughts to Aylon like you do with me?"*

Ru-Lee glanced at Sheila and raised her right eyebrow at her. *"I can do that??"*

*"If you can hear her thoughts, you should be able to send her yours. Dragons—born dragons—do it all the time. Some can speak, but most cannot. They communicate with their thoughts. Not usually full words though, just impressions, emotions, and images. A lot like D.G. does,"* Sheila replied, glancing at D.G. and gently rubbing his ear.

Ru-Lee took in a deep breath and snorted again, a rumble escaping from her chest.

"What's going on?" Aylon asked Sheila.

"She is attempting to read your thoughts," Sheila answered with a smile.

Aylon furrowed her brow at Ru-Lee. "What if I don't want her to?"

"It won't matter much," Sheila shrugged. "You, yourself, may have the ability to block her a little—but most won't if she has that particular dragon ability."

"Mmm!" grunted Aylon in displeasure as she watched Ru-Lee hunker down for another try.

Jace supported Davlin with one arm while still holding his bloody side; Trieca lifted Davlin on the other side as they followed Relmar to join the group. Pug glided down to rest on D.G.'s head, curiously blinking his large owl eyes at the enormous dragon before him. Relmar stepped up beside Sheila. Reaching out his arm, he encircled her waist and gently drew her to him. She smiled indulgently at him then returned her attention to Ru-Lee.

Ru-Lee lowered her head and stretched her neck out towards Aylon so that they were face-to-face. She squinted hard at Aylon. Her hot breath blew Aylon's hair away from her face. Aylon scrunched up her face, squeezed her eyes shut, and turned her head with a groan.

Quickly, Ru-Lee jerked her head back and up, blinking rapidly. A hurt look filled her eyes.

*"What??"* Sheila asked, concerned. *"Didn't it work?"*

*"It worked fine!"* Ru-Lee snapped.

*"Well, what's wrong then?"*

*"She says I need some mint tea—I have bad breath! Dragon's breath!"* Ru-Lee growled.

Aylon shrugged her shoulders at Sheila who burst out laughing.

Ru-Lee's tail whipped behind her, mowing down damaged foliage in its path. Her eyes flashed, and the flames on her sides flared to life. A barked roar escaped her as she snapped her jaws in anger and indignation.

*"IT'S NOT FUNNY!"* she yelled, projecting her thoughts to all those near.

D.G. barked and Pug screeched, falling backwards off D.G.'s head into the rocks and mud. The others cringed and held their heads.

Trying to control herself, but still chuckling, Sheila attempted to calm her friend. *"Okay, okay! Calm down! You have to admit, it is a little funny—and you are a dragon, so dragon's breath is to be expected, right?"*

"What the *%@#$ was that?" Jace yelled.

Ru-lee grunted and stamped her front feet, claws digging into the earth. She shook her massive dragon head and glared at Sheila.

"Ru-Lee didn't like what I had to say," Aylon replied with a wry smile.

Jace and Davlin looked at each other in confusion, having never dealt with dragons before. Relmar, however, understood only too well. His recent encounter with other dragons still burned in his mind. Trieca also understood, but not from personal experience. Among the elves it was known that most dragons communicated telepathically—most not having the ability of human speech.

240

*"At least it worked,"* Sheila remarked in Ru-Lee's mind. *"Now you know you can communicate, right?"*

Ru-Lee's response was a long, low growl that rumbled through her clenched teeth. Pug struggled to his feet and clacked his beak in annoyance at Ru-Lee. She snorted at him, curling her claws deeper into the mud.

"We have a problem, Ru-Lee," Aylon interjected.

Ru-Lee swung her gaze to Aylon, but did not respond.

"You can't just go flying directly into the oncoming battle in dragon form. The Keepers don't know about this latest development; the other dragons will feel threatened by your mere existence; and we have yet to figure out exactly what will happen to you when you enter battle."

*"What do you propose?"* Ru-Lee asked, tersely, projecting her thoughts to all of their minds. *"There is no time or place to practice for the battle. We will just have to wing it and hope for the best. The other dragons will have to accept my existence and that I am not a threat to them—as will the Keepers. I cannot control their reactions or change the facts."*

Aylon nodded agreement. "True—but we can't have you killed before there is a chance for you to complete your task."

*"What if I can't complete my task anyway? Did you think of that?"* Ru-Lee snarled. *"What if I am just an anomaly with no real purpose in all this?"*

Aylon closed her eyes and sighed deeply. With extreme forced patience, she responded, "That isn't the way of it, and you know it. We are all here for a reason. Some of us have many purposes to fulfill within our lifetimes. Some of us will continue to have a purpose even after our bodies have left this world—we can't know the whole of things. But we do know that you have a purpose here."

Ru-Lee lowered her head and closed her eyes letting Aylon's words sink in slowly. In her heart, she knew that Aylon was right. In her mind, she just wanted to return home and pretend none of the events of the past few weeks had happened at all. She slowly shook her head, a single tear sliding down her craggy face.

Her friends and family stood by patiently waiting for her to accept what she could not change and none of them could control. As dusk settled around them, she resignedly asked, *"What do you propose, Aylon?"*

## Chapter 56

Ru-Lee spread her shimmering wings and lifted off from the banks of the now-quiet Lake Satcha. The first stars of the evening glittered brightly through scudding clouds, their reflection dancing in the column-like watery form of Sheyna as she watched the dragon's ascent. The mating calls of late-summer bugs filled the valley, but the bats who would normally feed upon them were absent. The presence of the enormous dragon flying through the darkening sky deterred these nocturnal predators from their usual rounds.

A smile split her maw as Ru-Lee rode the air currents high into the darkness winging towards the Dragon Peaks and Mt. Shavla. Her heart soared as she reveled in her new-found freedom of flight, barely noticing the weight of her passengers.

It had been decided that they would fly as far as they could without being noticed before landing so that Ru-Lee could shift back into human form. With luck, they would be able to find Nevlon quickly. They hoped the night would give them added cover so they could get closer to their destination before it became necessary to land. The plan didn't go further than that. Everything depended on how dire the situation was when they arrived at the mountain.

In the back of her mind, Ru-Lee wondered if the Warta spirits within her would allow her to change back to human form. If she was able to shift, would the spirits tear her apart as they had so many others? These questions filled her with dread. Unwilling to turn inward and ask the Warta spirits for fear of their answer, she flew on and tried to ignore the ball of terror that had formed in the pit of her stomach. The Warta souls within her did not seem to be aware of her turmoil. Nor had it appeared that they had heard her conversations with the others. *'Is it possible that they exist within me, but separate—gaining access to my mind only when I allow them in—or they force their way in?'* she wondered. The possibility seemed unlikely, but was the only explanation she could come up with as she glided through the silk-soft night.

Aylon, Relmar, Trieca, Jace, D.G, Sheila, and Davlin clung precariously to soggy ropes tied hastily to Ru-Lee's body, gritting their teeth and closing their eyes against errant insects. Her jagged scales bit into their cold, wet flesh as they struggled to stay aboard, but the heat of her body offered a welcome comfort, drying them as they travelled. Aylon, D.G., and Jace were not particularly enjoying the ride, but the others appeared content.

Jace had strapped a reluctant and struggling D.G. in front of him as he straddled Ru-Lee's neck just in front of her winged shoulders. He wrapped a protective arm across D.G.'s mid section and grasped the ropes holding the struggling canine down, hoping his knots held tight. D.G. whined and wriggled, rolling his eyes up to look pitifully at his captor. Jace gently stroked D.G.'s neck with a free finger, trying to instill a serenity to his companion that he himself did not feel.

Pug flew near Ru-Lee's head, angling away from the huge jaws. Every few minutes or so, he could be seen twisting his head to eye her enormous dragon form suspiciously, as if fearing he might be lunch at any moment.

Aylon had bandaged Jace's side and managed to find a spare, if damp, set of clothing in her bag which she had offered to Sheila. The mist elf had argued that Relmar's cloak was enough to warm her, but Aylon had insisted. In the end, she had physically guided Sheila away from Relmar, leaving the young man blinking, a silly smile on his face as he inspected his now-healed wounds.

Once dressed, Sheila had rejoined Relmar and bound herself closely to him straddling Ru-Lee's rump. Before taking off, she had rummaged through their packs and found a few dripping pieces of clothing for Ru-Lee to wear when she shifted. These she had wrung out and tied beneath her legs next to Ru-Lee's body to dry while they were travelling. They now flapped wildly in the wind against Ru-Lee's hind leg as Sheila leaned blissfully against Relmar's chest, a peaceful smile resting upon her lips.

Relmar had eyes only for Sheila, and seemed content with the wind whipping his blond hair wildly around his face. He held her closely to him, his arms wrapped protectively around her slight body, his hands carefully gripping the rope in front of them. A bemused look danced upon his face. It was the look of a man who has suddenly found himself in a very pleasant, yet unexpected, situation—one which he does not fully comprehend, but has no intention of leaving.

Aylon hunched down behind Jace, her eyes squeezed tightly shut and her head pressed between Ru-Lee's winged shoulder blades. The strong beat of Ru-Lee's muscular wings seemed to ease her displeasure at finding herself strapped to a dragon and flying through the air.

Trieca, tied opposite Davlin across the middle of Ru-Lee's back, grinned widely as he watched the shadowy world below him, thoroughly enjoying the experience. He gazed all around, mesmerized by the scenes as they swiftly glided past. As his eyes touched upon the shadowy fields below, his grin faded and his brows furrowed in consternation. Leaning out and away from Ru-Lee's body so he could see around her ribs, he shook his head in confusion, unable to make sense of what he was seeing. He glanced sideways to Davlin, hoping to catch his attention. He caught his friend's eye and pointed downwards, tilting his head. Curious, Davlin leaned out and looked down at the passing countryside. Concern clouded his visage as he took in the vision below. The fields teamed with small dark bodies moving as a wave through the tall plants towards the mountains. The ground had taken on the look of an anthill, swarming with movement. He turned back to Trieca, puzzled. Trieca shrugged and shook his head in answer to the query on Davlin's face. Neither knew what to make of the scene below, and there was no way to communicate over the roar of the rushing wind created by their passage.

Davlin glanced back at his eldest brother hopefully, then shook his head. Relmar's ability to read minds seemed to be diminished greatly when he was in close proximity to Sheila—either that, or he simply didn't care about what he saw in other's heads when she was near. Davlin wasn't sure which was true, but he knew Relmar was blissfully unaware of the developments below. Jace was no help either—he sat stoically staring forward comforting D.G. and refusing to turn his head in any direction that might offer him a glimpse of his moonstruck eldest brother. Davlin shrugged and shook his head at Trieca. Whatever was going on below would have to wait until they landed.

# Chapter 57

The soft orange glow of a lantern slipped around the smooth corners of the cavernous cave, its swaying light illuminating the way as Nevlon strode forward. The warmth of the Heart pulsed around him, filling the grotto with a soft thrumming sound that mingled gently with the echoed voices of dwarves and trolls working deeper in. Trieca's father, Rannue, kept pace, shortening his long strides to match Nevlon's shorter ones, his face grim.

"It won't be long now," he murmured softly, as if reluctant to voice his thoughts.

Nevlon shook his head and sighed, nibbling on his mustache hairs. "No, it won't. Everyone is in place, and all of the defenses we currently have at our disposal are ready."

"Do we know any more of what will happen with the Warta descendants when they pass through?" Rannue asked, glancing sideways at Nevlon.

"No," Nevlon breathed. "Nothing like this has ever happened before—we can only speculate on what will happen and plan for the worst."

Rounding another turn in the path, Nevlon and Rannue suddenly stopped, the tail end of a large, red dragon blocking their path.

"Arnue?" Nevlon asked, brows knit in concern. "What's wrong?"

Sniffing loudly, the dragon, Arnue, squeezed his eyes shut tight. The draw of his breath pulled the flame of Nevlon's lantern towards his nostrils, dimming its light.

*"Rodents,"* he responded—the sound more of a bark than a word.

"Rodents?" Nevlon and Rannue asked in unison. "Here?"

Arnue shook his head and blinked before sending the image of a large black mouse into their minds. *"Coming"* reverberated within both of their heads causing them to cringe slightly.

"Not so loud, Arnue!" Rannue growled. "There's no need to shout, you know!"

A much softer *"Apologies"* quickly followed before the Harta dragon lumbered ahead of them and turned off into a side passage.

Rannue cocked his head to one side and watched the lantern flames dance on the scales of the dragon as it disappeared ahead. "What do you suppose that's all about?"

Nevlon chewed his beard thoughtfully. "I'm not sure. Seems that I recall something of rodents and Warta—but it's like a mist in my brain. I can't seem to grasp hold of the information to pull it up."

The soft slapping sound of bare feet running on stones resonated behind them as a young barefoot boy rounded the corner and nearly ran into the two men. He was dressed in soft-tanned leather pants tied at the waist, his torso covered only by a bright red vest of some rough fibrous material. His tousled black hair hung nearly to his shoulders and looked as if it hadn't seen a comb in days.

Breathing heavily, he placed his hands on his knees and bent to catch his breath before panting "Nevlon! Triya (Tree-ya) must speak with you immediately!"

Nevlon spun around, nearly dropping the lantern. He grasped the boy's shoulder, intently looking into his face. "Why? What did she see?"

Recovering from his run, the boy shook his head and shrugged, eyes wide.

"She didn't tell me—only to bring you quickly."

Nevlon released his grip, handed the lantern to Rannue, and pushed past the boy headed back the way he had come.

He shouted over his shoulder to a puzzled Rannue as he went, "I'll catch up once I find out what this is about."

Rannue and the boy exchanged a baffled look, shrugged, and continued on towards the Heart, the boy's excited chatter echoing through the tunnel as they walked.

XXX   XXX   XXX   XXX   XXX

Nevlon swept through the Travelers' camp with an air of determination that caused those few individuals that he encountered to move quickly out of his way. The seer's tent was pitched on the outskirts of camp furthest from the mountain. When he had asked her why she wanted it so far away, she told him that the energy of the dragons was so strong it gave her a headache. She had also remarked that they stunk to high heaven and she didn't understand how he could stand to be near them.

A small fire crackled near the entrance of the brightly-colored tent, its shadows playing gently upon the figure seated cross-legged beside it. Triya's head was bent forward, rows of flame-red hair spilling around her shoulders and over her breasts. Her cream-colored blouse had slid down her arm to reveal silken chocolate-brown skin that shimmered in the light of the fire. Her strong hands lay still, folded across a dazzling skirt that draped around her form.

As Nevlon approached, Triya slowly rose to greet him, meeting his concerned gaze with penetrating deep brown eyes.

"What have you seen?" he asked, his concern outweighing the need for greetings.

"They will break through before morning," she responded, her voice as silky as her skin.

Nevlon grunted. "Have you seen the outcome or more of Ru-Lee's part in this?"

Triya shook her head, blinking slowly, "The outcome is not clear to me and depends too much on choices yet to be made. Ru-Lee will help turn the tide, if she proves strong enough to maintain control of the forces within her. Without her, there is no hope for us.

"Sheila, with Ru-Lee, must form the lock for which there is no key. In shifted form, she must give her all to contain evil and take the Aged One's place."

"You know I hate riddles!" Nevlon groaned, shaking his head and rubbing his temple. "Who is the Aged One?"

"Gertrude, the Guardian, who has long protected us—her strength is failing. It is her weakening that has allowed openings where there should be none. A new guardian must take her place. The new Guardian will contain the evil that breeches our world as well as guard the gates and the Heart. One has been singled out. She must accept the duty willingly, and knowingly—and Ru-Lee must condemn her to her fate. The two must act together in this, or all will be lost."

"Sheila? She is to be the new Guardian?" Nevlon asked, incredulous. "That explains a few things," he sighed. Rubbing his forehead again with his hand, sadness filled his voice as he asked, "I suppose I am to convince the two that this is what they must do?"

Triya's skirts rustled softly around her bare ankles as she approached Nevlon and gently touched his shoulder. An intoxicating scent of spice filled his nostrils, muddling his thoughts. Her strong, soft, comforting voice slipped through the night, "You know what you must do, as will they. They will not hold you at fault for this. They will come to the choices freely."

Nevlon shivered at her touch—he always did. He told himself it was because her ability to see the future always unnerved him and not because of the smooth rise of her breasts and the intoxicating, mind-numbing scent that lingered around her. Chills raced up and down his spine until her warm hand slipped from his shoulder and she stepped back.

He breathed deeply before asking, "Is that all? Do you know where my family is?"

Triya smiled and her deep eyes sparkled as she nodded, "I know where they are. You will find them where the springs leave the mountain and head to the lake. They will be waiting for you."

"Good, thank you," he turned to leave, but Triya's voice stopped him.

"There is one more thing you must know, but I am unclear about its import."

Nevlon stopped and turned back to her, cocking his head to one side as he waited for her to continue.

"There approaches a horde of small, furry beasts filled with a desire for return to glory—Shaooganah. Do you recall the part they played during the Warta battles years ago?"

Nevlon's brow furrowed and he lowered his head in thought, trying to remember anything about Shaooganah involvement in the Warta battles. He recalled a mention of them, but couldn't come up with the exact context. He shook his head, "No—do you?"

Triya shrugged, "Some. I recall that they worked with and for the Warta. They brought them information and were given status in exchange. There was talk that they may have been involved in assassinations that occurred and in tactical maneuvers done covertly, but nothing was ever proven. They were much larger creatures then. Their size has shrunk much over the years, but it seems their ambitions have not." As she spoke, she walked back to her place by the fire. She spun and sat in one fluid motion--the movement spinning her skirts and rippling her scent through the air.

Quickly shaking off the numbing effects of her aroma, Nevlon smiled and shook his head, "You really need to find a way to control that."

Innocently, Triya asked, "Control what?" a coy smile playing upon her moist russet-colored lips.

"Never mind," Nevlon replied, shaking his head once more. "So we really don't know what these Shaooganah are up to?"

Triya leaned forward and stirred the embers of the fire with a nearby stick. "No, but I feel they may cause some problems. Watch for them, and let the others know."

"Okay. Thank you, Triya," Nevlon inclined his head towards her and turned. "Let me know if you see anything else."

She laughed, a deep, throaty laugh, "I will, to be sure. You know, Nevlon, we could have had a lot of fun together if you weren't so devoted to Aylon."

Nevlon turned back momentarily and smiled before bowing somewhat deeper, "I don't doubt that for a second, my dear—but then you would be turned into a toad or frog, or some-such, and that wouldn't be any fun at all!"

Her laughter followed him back through the camp, for they both knew that he was right. Aylon was a patient, caring woman, but she was very territorial in all things, especially her husband---and she had a raging temper.

# Chapter 58

Like a ghost in the night, Nevlon quietly slipped through the Travelers' camp at the base of Mount Shavla. The smell of roasted meat and vegetables mingled in the air around him making his stomach rumble and his mouth water. He hadn't eaten since morning, and his body was complaining ferociously.

The Seer, Triya, had imparted him with news of his wife and family as well as an unforeseen danger. Her visions on the later had been vague and made no sense to him. As he deftly made his way around the base of Mount Shavla, his mind worked to comprehend the meaning of Triya's vision—what possible real threat could the Shaooganah's pose?

The trickling sound of a stream bubbling forth through the mossy opening of a nearly-hidden fissure met his ears. As he drew nearer, a figure detached itself from the stone and surrounding foliage—Aylon. She was quickly followed by Davlin, Trieca, and a disgruntled-looking Jace. Relmar and a young woman who looked vaguely familiar stayed back, huddled together against the hulking rock with D.G. and Pug.

Curious, Nevlon asked Aylon, "How did things go?"

Aylon rolled her eyes as he caught her up in a huge hug. She responded with a sigh, "As well as could be expected, I suppose." Kissing Nevlon gently, she leaned back to peer up into his face. "And here?"

Nevlon smiled, "The same—Where is Ru-Lee and how is she doing?" he asked, peering over Aylon's shoulder as he spoke.

Aylon twisted her head to look back to where Relmar, Sheila, and D.G. stood. She grinned as Pug launched himself from D.G.'s head and glided silently over to land on Jace's shoulder. The others stood by wordlessly.

Nevlon shook his head and grumbled, "She hasn't shifted—can she? Will they let her?"

Aylon heaved an exasperated sigh, "We don't know. She wanted to wait until you were here to help in case things don't work out right."

"Well, I'm here now, and we should get on with it," he replied brusquely.

Releasing Aylon, he quickly moved past the others and approached Ru-Lee. In the light of the waning moon, with her wings folded close to her body and her tail and head curled around her legs, she looked very much like a piece of the mountain. She lifted her dragon head and watched him approach, her gold-flecked eyes gleaming.

Nevlon approached Relmar, gripped his free hand and drew the young man to him. Patting Relmar on the back, he smiled, "Glad to see you are doing better! I've been concerned about you."

Relmar smiled sheepishly and returned the greeting. "I'm fine, Nevlon," he grinned down at the young woman next to him and continued, "Never better, in fact!"

She blushed and Nevlon's eyes widened with recognition. "Well, things have changed quite a bit for more than just Ru-Lee, it would seem! Triya didn't mention this bit of news—I guess it fits, though," he finished thoughtfully.

Growing impatient, Ru-Lee snorted, surrounding them with wispy smoke tendrils.

Startled, Nevlon continued, "Fine, Ru! We will get on with things. Relmar, will you please join the others? Sheila, I need you to stay in case Ru-Lee needs any assistance during or after she shifts—and I need to have a word with you as well. You can go, too D.G.—I don't know how the Warta feel about canines, but I am guessing it isn't good—they might consider you a snack."

Reluctantly, Relmar detached from Sheila and moved away towards his brothers; Aylon joined him. Sheila turned to Ru-Lee and leaned against her warm, armored side waiting for everyone to get safely away from Ru-Lee. D.G. snorted, glared at Nevlon a moment, then rose and padded softly towards the waiting group. Halfway there, he stubbornly stopped, turned around, and sat on his haunches. Sheila watched him and giggled at the determined look on his furry face. Nevlon ignored him, focusing instead on Ru-Lee.

"This may take a lot out of you, Ru. Can you read my mind and speak in kind?" Nevlon queried.

She tilted her head to one side, *"Yes,"* she responded, *"I can speak in your mind..."* She blinked as she gently stretched her mind out to his, attempting to read, or 'sense', his thoughts as she had done earlier with Aylon. The task was easier than she had thought it would be—she barely had to concentrate at all! As she gleaned information that would have taken far too much time to impart otherwise, she marveled at this new ability. *"This could prove to be a useful talent! Time is running short quickly, though, isn't it?"* she said, more of a statement then a question.

"Yes," he mentally replied. *"Events are progressing far too quickly. Are you able to shift?"*

She blinked thoughtfully before responding *"I believe so, but I haven't tried. The Warta are a part of me now--I am fairly certain they are aware of what is happening, but they haven't made known to me what they plan to do—if anything. How do I go about this shifting business? Up to this point, I haven't had control over any of it—do you have any pointers?"*

Chuckling, Nevlon replied, *"Concentrate on the form you wish to take. If you wish to take human form, you must focus all of your energies on it. It is the same if you wish to take your shifted form. However, sometimes, if our emotions take over, so will the shifted form."*

*"You mean I could change into a dragon against my will?"*

*"Isn't that what has been happening up to this point,"* he asked. *"Let's just say it could take you by surprise from time to time."* Nevlon smiled and gently placed his hand upon her snout. A heavy sigh escaped her as she closed her eyes, shaking her massive head sadly.

The soft sound of Sheila humming a soothing tune floated into the deep night.

*"What have I gotten myself into?"* she asked, a note of despair in her voice.

*"You didn't 'get yourself into' anything. Life just is, and you are who you are at this time and place. You can't feel sorry for yourself—you must, however, work with what you have and do your best with it. No time for self-pity, girl! Are you ready to give it a go?"*

Groaning she snorted, *"I don't suppose I have much choice—let's get on with it."*

*"That's the spirit!"* he responded. Out loud, he spoke quietly to Sheila as he drew her with him to one side, "Let's step back a few feet."

Several feet away, near a cluster of trees, the others watched and waited. A cool breeze stirred the air, filling the night with dewy dampness—its peaceful passing did nothing to quell the concern that hovered over the group, leaving tight knots in their stomachs.

Jace, unable to contain himself any longer, broke the silence, "What's with you and 'spider girl'?" he growled at Relmar, jutting out his chin and puffing up his chest like a tom turkey ready to fight.

"Hmm?" Relmar responded, his eyes still glued to Sheila as her soft tune was carried to their ears by the wind.

Davlin stepped up beside Relmar, clapped his hand firmly on his shoulder and said, "I was wondering the same thing myself, brother—what's going on with you and Sheila? You seem a bit smitten!"

Relmar blinked and turned his head to look at Davlin as if rising from a dream. "I don't know….it's weird."

"Weird doesn't even begin to describe it! Disgusting is more like it! You do realize she was seven years old just a few days ago—and she's a spider!" Jace growled.

Relmar rounded on him, eyes flashing, fists balled, "No, Jace, she was never seven! In fact, she is much older than any of us! I can't explain what has happened to her, or why we are drawn together, but I am glad for it! Back down!"

"Boys! Is this really necessary right now?" Aylon hissed, irritated; but her objections fell on deaf ears. She stepped to the side and hoped they wouldn't end up fighting. She was far too tired and concerned for Ru-lee to break them up at the moment.

"Calm down, Bro," Davlin soothed, tightening his grip on his brother's shoulder and glaring at Jace. "No one meant any harm—we are just a bit confused. Sheila has been like a member of the family—a sister—and now you and she appear to be romantically entangled. You do understand our confusion and curiosity, right? Besides, you are totally out of it when she is near you!"

"I know," Relmar sighed, shaking his head. "I can't explain it….when she touches me or is near me, I stop hearing all the minds around me—all the emotions stop flooding through me. I am free. Does that make any sense?"

"Yes," Trieca chimed in. The others turned to look at him.

"Why? What makes sense about any of this?" Jace asked, glaring.

"Well, that is her nature…to help. You heard Aylon, she shifts to fit the need of the one whose companion she is to be. She has been changing…maybe she is changing to fit the needs of a new companion. Ru-Lee may have outgrown her….maybe Relmar is the new one she is to fit. If that's the case, her ability to calm and soothe might be the reason. Maybe that's exactly what Relmar needs now."

Relmar furrowed his brow thoughtfully, as did Davlin, but Jace continued to glare at Trieca as if he were a traitorous bearer of ill news. They stood there for a moment, contemplating the implications of what Trieca had said, the acrid smell of dragon-smoke wafting through the air.

Suddenly Pug clicked his beak in Jace's ear and nipped his neck causing him to turn his attention back to the base of the mountain. Aylon gasped and Relmar groaned, dropping to his knees as a tortured scream tore through the night that was joined by D.G.'s anxious howls.

## Chapter 59

Near the base of the mountain, Ru-Lee arched her neck, bowed her head, and closed her eyes. She concentrated on her human form—returning to it. In her mind's eye, she saw her human self welcoming her dragon form as it shrunk and cleaved to her spine. She felt her dragon's wings begin to melt into her sides; her scales become smoother; the fire within her skin, begin to cool. She breathed deeply and her dragon lungs swelled. She expelled her breath and billows of smoke surrounded her, the dragon fire containing itself and clearing the lungs for her human body.

*"I can do this,"* she thought to herself. *"It's going to be fine."*

Suddenly, a defiant roar filled her mind, ripping forth from her shrinking maw. Nevlon ducked and Sheila shifted as dragon fire sprang forth from Ru-Lee, spewing lava against the granite skin of the mountain. Flaming black stones ricocheted off mountainous outcroppings and hissed in the trickle of stream sending tendrils of steam to mix with the smoky air.

A half-human scream rent the air. Ru-Lee, the dragon, reared high into the air, clawing and ripping at the mossy rock wall; her now-shortened tail whipped behind her, rending the ground as it went.

Her partially-transformed lungs filled with smoke. She gasped and choked, her now-mutated body crashing to the ground.

*'What's happening?'* she wondered, terror filling her mind. *'It was going so well—what did I do wrong?'*

Every muscle ripped and tore at itself leaving her writhing in pain, tearing up the ground around her. Unable to continue to shift into her human body, her body struggled to go back to full dragon form---but the transformations either way could not continue without her full concentration. The inability to breathe coupled with the excruciating pain that wracked her body left her unable to do anything but gasp, moan, and thrash.

Warta voices echoed through her, *"You cannot contain us in human form! We will not allow it!"*

*"Stop!"* she pleaded. *"You will destroy me? How does that help anyone?"*

*"Not destroy you—convince you,"* the voices growled unconvincingly.

She coughed and struggled to draw in a tight whistling breath, her body twisting in pain. *"You do not understand! I must shift before we join with the others! We will need their help—we must work together with the other peoples or we will fail! If I don't shift, and they realize who and what I am, they will kill me—us—before the real battle even begins!"*

*"We are stronger than they---In your shifted form, we would win any and all battles!"* snarled the Warta.

*"You underestimate your dragon brethren. There are many of them—and the other races have many gifts that they would join together in order to defeat you. Many would die—friends and family of mine—but make no mistake, they would win."*

The murmur of Warta voices thrummed through her body. One voice, the Ancient One, rose above the rest and the pain in her chest eased, *"What do you propose?"*

Drawing a ragged breath, she said, *"Let me transform—if you do not push too hard against the confines of my human body, I believe my dragon self can help contain you. Allow me and Nevlon to explain what must be done to those in charge of our end of things."*

*"Will you inform them of us?"*

Ru-Lee thought a moment, as the pain in her body subsided slightly. *"No. They need not know of your existence---yet."*

The angry voices filling her head swelled to a deafening crescendo. She clenched her eyes shut against the din and waited. The wait seemed long, though she was sure it only lasted a few moments before she had the Wartas' response.

*"We will allow this—but be aware…we won't wait long for our time to battle."*

Released from the Warta's grip, Ru-Lee groaned and pitched forward on the cool grass, damp green blades invading her dragon nostrils. She lay there, sides heaving, eyes closed. As the smoke cleared slowly from her lungs once more, she tried to gather her thoughts and focus her concentration.

A prickly-hairy something rasped against Ru-Lee's outstretched foreleg and Sheila's voice slipped softly into her mind, *"Are you okay?"*

*"Yes…I think so."*

*"Will they allow you to shift?"*

*"They will now.....but I don't know if I can. My thoughts are scattered and I can't concentrate. Pain has a way of muddling your brain, you know!"*

*"That's what I am here for—I think I can help you focus your mind, if you will let me."*

Ru-Lee slowly opened her eyes and was startled to see her image reflected back at her several times over from large multiple eyes embedded in an amazingly oversized spider's head. She snorted and pulled herself quickly upright.

*"What happened to you? Did you grow again???"*

The eyes blinked sheepishly, *"It would appear so. Nevlon tells me there is a reason for it, but he hasn't shared it with me yet."*

*"Yeah…he is good at that—even when I was reading his mind, I felt he was hiding something in that graying head of his."*

Sheila nodded, *"Are you ready to shift?"*

Ru-Lee nodded her snout, slowly lowering her head to Sheila's. Sheila closed her many eyes and leaned the top of her head against Ru-Lee's. *"Okay, concentrate on your human self, and I will too. Between the two of us, we should be able to complete your transformation."*

Ru-Lee took a deep breath and formed an image of her human self in her mind.

*"That's what you think you look like?"* Sheila asked, bemused.

Ru-Lee hesitated and the image wavered. She hadn't actually seen a full image of herself for many years—only watery reflections in slow-moving pools. *"Well...it was....why?"*

*"You have changed a bit over the years. Let me help you,"* Sheila responded.

An image of a full-grown young woman was superimposed over the image Ru-Lee had held in her mind. The hair was honey-gold; the eyes hazel and gold-flecked. The figure was strong and softly curved in womanly places. This was definitely not the image she had held of herself....indeed, she hadn't even really given her own image much thought at all. She had to admit that she wasn't displeased with what Sheila showed her.

*"Is that truly me?"* she asked, fascinated.

Sheila chuckled, *"Well, it was the last time you were truly you!"*

A smile split Ru-Lee's maw, *"Okay, then."* Once again, she breathed deeply and focused on the image in her mind.

She gasped and crouched down low as she felt her body quickly shift—wings melded to sides and back, tail shrank, nose melted into her shortening face. Muscles and bones shifted and shrank to accommodate the smaller frame. Lungs cleared of smoke that belched forth, hiding the two friends from view. In her mind, she saw her dragon self shrink and slip down her spine to sleep at the base. It blinked at her and grinned, seeming to have enjoyed the outing. The Warta souls crowded tightly into her body and her mind. She felt them prickling her skin and stretching out along her limbs. They did not like the confinement of such compact containment, but they were trying. She felt as if her body was a membrane stretched tight and ready to burst. Hoping she could hold together long enough to accomplish the next phase of their plan, she rose to stand next to the enormous shifted form of Sheila—a stone spider whose head now reached to Ru-Lee's shoulder. Together, they waited for the smoke to clear. Ru-Lee kept Sheila between herself and the other members of her group. Nibbling nervously on her lower lip, she hoped Aylon still had her clothes.

## Chapter 60

Jace and Davlin knelt on opposite sides of Relmar's shivering body, supporting him and preventing him from pitching forward as he groaned and writhed in pain. The dew-damp cool grass leached moisture through their clothing, chilling their bodies despite the warmth of the evening. Pug clung tightly to Jace's shoulder, huddled down tightly near Jace's neck.

Aylon cursed under her breath as she crouched near the brothers, soothingly caressing Relmar's head. She could not see what was happening through the screen of dragon-smoke that enfolded Ru-Lee and Sheila, but she could see Nevlon standing on its outside fringes and she watched him apprehensively for any signal for her to come to Ru-Lee's aid. D.G. paced nervously between the small group and his long-time friend, whining and howling.

Trieca stood intently watching the scene across the clearing. With his piercing elven eyes, he was able to penetrate the scene better than the others, though the smoke hampered his efforts considerably.

"What's going on?" Aylon asked, frustrated.

Trieca shook his head, "I can't tell for sure because of the smoke and Sheila."

Relmar moaned and his body jerked forward, tipping Aylon backwards onto her hind end. "Ugh! Well—I don't think things are going well, judging by Relmar's reactions!" she growled as she struggled to right herself. "I thought Sheila's presence numbed his sensitivities…"

"That's what he said, but it seems as if that is only true when she is in human form."

"What do you mean?" Jace grunted as he worked to keep his balance and support his brother.

Aylon picked herself up out of the long grass and stood next to Trieca as he answered, "The moment Sheila transformed, Relmar went down—I don't know if proximity plays any roles in buffering him from the pain of others, but it appears that the form Sheila is in does."

Relmar's body twisted sharply causing Jace and Davlin to lose their balance and drag their brother down into the long wet foliage. Pug screeched and darted off Jace's shoulder just as Jace rolled onto his side, pinned beneath Relmar and Davlin. Aylon sighed, shook her head, and held out her arm as Pug drifted softly towards her. The flustered bird spun his head around to look down at Jace. He clicked and whistled angrily before returning his attention to the hazy scene across the clearing.

Still watching Nevlon, Aylon asked Trieca, "You said that Sheila was blocking your view as well as the smoke....what did you mean?" curiosity edging her voice.

"Well...." Trieca hesitated, "...she appears to have....grown---again."

Shaking her head, Aylon sighed heavily and chewed the inside of her lower lip, "This just gets better and better, doesn't it....I don't like the implications."

Suddenly, D.G. stopped pacing. He stood still and silent, his bushy tail sticking stiffly out behind him as if it was waiting expectantly for the command to wag or droop—ready for either.

Behind Trieca and Aylon, Relmar ceased moaning and thrashing.

"Do you mind moving, guys? This is very uncomfortable," he grumbled, his voice thick and slow from his ordeal.

"Anytime, Bro! Soon as you get off me!" grunted Jace, struggling to free himself from beneath the combined weight of his older brothers.

"Working on it!" Davlin growled as he clumsily righted himself and helped Relmar up.

"Geez! I think you two need to go on a diet or something!" Jace growled, helping to push Relmar up from behind and brushing away wet grass from his torso and legs.

Relmar stumbled forward, falling into Trieca and jostling Aylon, "Whatever.....You're one to talk," he slurred.

Trieca caught him. "You feeling alright?" he asked, concern lining his forehead as he wrapped his arm around Relmar's shoulders to keep him from falling again.

"Yeah...I'm fine. Can you see them?"

Jace and Davlin crowded close to the others and stood silently peering through the night as dragon-smoke tendrils drifted across the small clearing between them and Ru-Lee.

"Not yet, the smoke is too thick still.....I take it Ru-Lee is alright now?"

"She made the shift ok—it was difficult. The Warta spirits fought her for awhile."

In the clearing, D.G.'s tail began to wag, wildly twisting through the air. He pranced and danced with his front feet, head bobbing and shaking joyfully as he realized Ru-Lee was safe.

"We expected as much," Aylon interjected. "Nevlon is moving forward....I hope he got Ru-Lee's clothes from Sheila before she shifted." Glancing at the young men standing around her, she continued, "We will wait here until we get the all-clear from Nevlon."

Puzzled, Jace asked, "Why?"

Davlin slugged his arm hard, "You are so dense sometimes!" he replied. "Neither Ru or Sheila have any clothes!"

Even in the nearly-moonless light, the heat rising in Jace's face was clearly visible, "I....Oh...Uh....Yeah---I knew that!" he stammered, slugging Davlin back.

"Sure you did!" Davlin laughed, shaking his head as he rubbed his shoulder.

Aylon, Relmar, and Trieca mingled their laughter with Davlin's. Jace shrugged and scratched his head smiling sheepishly as D.G., unnoticed by the others, happily darted across the small meadow towards Ru-Lee.

## Chapter 61

A cool summer breeze brushed across Ru-Lee's bare skin causing goose bumps to rise across its surface. Her right leg itched slightly from brushing against the prickly hairs that covered Sheila's long spidery legs. Caustic remnants of dragon-smoke wafted through the air, slowly dispersing on the breeze. She stood with her left hand on Sheila's oversized spider head, hoping she could still speak through her fire-parched throat.

Nevlon approached, his solid form materializing through the remaining wisps of smoke. He stopped several feet away and tossed a bundle to her through the air. It landed with a soft thump near Sheila's feet.

"Clothes for you," he rumbled, averting his gaze. "Let me know once you're dressed. Sheila, would you be so kind as to come over here for a moment—I need to speak to you—there's no need to shift," he said as he turned his back and moved off in the direction he had come from.

Sheila blinked her multiple eyes at Ru-Lee, gave a spidery shrug, and lumbered away in Nevlon's direction. Shivering, Ru-Lee bent to lift the bundle of clothing from the damp grass. Suddenly, something damp and cold touched her rear end causing her to yelp and jump sideways. Clutching her clothes, she spun around just as a soft furry form shoved against her bare legs nearly knocking her over. Once she realized it was D.G. assaulting her, laughter spilled up from her chest. She tousled his ears and rubbed his back as he wriggled and pushed against her happily.

"Okay, okay! I have to get dressed!" she giggled. "I'm glad to see you, too!"

He grinned, his tongue lolling out to one side. His eyes filled with pure joy as he sat on his haunches and watched her.

Sighing and grinning, Ru-Lee turned her attention to untangling her bundled clothing. She freed her trousers first and pulled them on before quickly slipping a dark blouse over her head without unbuttoning the buttons. As she dressed she snuck glances in the direction of Nevlon and Sheila. She could hear the soft murmur of Nevlon's deep voice and see the small nod of Sheila's silvery head, but nothing gave any clue as to the nature of their conversation.

She wracked her brain trying to remember a time when Nevlon had ever taken Sheila aside to converse on anything without her—she couldn't. A chill of foreboding slid down her spine like ice, speaking of death as it went. Her breath caught in her chest, and her heart seized with panic. D.G. whined and rubbed against her leg as they watched Sheila slowly lower herself to the ground near Nevlon's feet.

Ru-Lee forced herself to breathe slow and deep. She shook her head and let her hand drop to D.G.'s silken ears, "I'm sure it's nothing, D.G. ---right? Just my imagination…."

D.G. rumbled in his throat in response and bobbed his head as if in agreement.

She sighed deeply and stepped towards the clearing, "Well, let's go see what's next."

As she approached Nevlon and Sheila, she noticed that Sheila had curled her long spider legs beneath her as she lay in the cool grass, her head resting on the ground. Her numerous eyes stared straight ahead and she didn't appear to notice Ru-Lee's approach at all. Nevlon stood with his arms crossed upon his chest, gazing down at Sheila's inert form, concern etched in the night-softened lines of his face.

Ru-Lee approached cautiously and touched Nevlon's arm whispering, "Is she alright? What happened?"

Nevlon blinked, as if rising from a trance, and turned to look at her as if she was the last person he had expected to see standing next to him. He sighed and shook his head. "She will be fine…I think. I had to give her some unsettling news…I am afraid she isn't taking it very well."

A knot of apprehension formed in the pit of Ru-Lee's stomach, "What news?" In the darkness, it was difficult to make out the emotions that might be hiding behind Nevlon's eyes—his most revealing feature. She had always been able to read him, but the night surrounded them and swallowed up all understanding. Her chest constricted, her breath becoming strained and shallow, as she waited for his answer.

Nevlon nibbled at his beard, contemplating her for several agonizing moments before finally responding, "I spoke with Triya before I came this evening. She has had a vision—several, actually. One of these visions concerns the role Sheila is to play in defeating the Warta."

Ru-Lee's throat constricted, "What role? What must she do?"

Nevlon's voice was soft and low when he replied, "She has been chosen to replace The Guardian."

Ru-Lee struggled to calm herself, forcing her breaths to long, slow rhythms. She tried to recall all that she knew of The Guardian, Gertrude: she remembered Aylon teaching her that it was Gertrude's strength which provided their world protection by sealing all of the gates, and she recalled something about the Heart---how could that have anything to do with Sheila?

"I don't understand—how can Sheila replace The Guardian? She is a mist-elf….isn't Gertrude a stone spider with earth-bound powers?"

Nodding, Nevlon responded, "Yes, Gertrude is a stone spider---a very large stone spider—with considerable earth-powers. She has been the final protection for the Heart for many years. The dwarves protected the outer areas of the entrance to the Heart, while Gertrude acted as the final obstacle to any who would approach unbidden. Her magic, and that of her predecessors, also strengthened the spells which were imbued within the gates. Those spells blocked the Warta and their offspring from re-entering here.

"When the human wars threatened our world, Gertrude was called upon to extend her powers to seal all of the gates completely. She was only able to do this by sacrificing herself and fusing her own powers with those of the Heart. She was quite old then--now her strength is failing. That is why the shadows are able to slip through.

"Sheila has been chosen to replace Gertrude, but in a new capacity—one which even Triya was not completely clear on—at least one which she didn't share with me."

Ru-Lee shook her head, "Okay, I get that Gertrude protects us and that her strength is failing—but how does this have anything to do with Sheila? She isn't a stone spider like Gertrude—how can she take her place? I thought it had to be another stone spider....one of Gertrude's line...?"

Nevlon tugged at his hat brim sighing, "That assumption was, apparently, flawed. A new Guardian hasn't been needed in so long that those who knew the process have all died away. We have become complacent in our belief that Gertrude would continue to live and protect this world forever. Of course, that was foolish."

D.G., who had been standing behind Ru-Lee listening and watching, slowly crept unnoticed towards Sheila. He nuzzled her face and lay down next to her large body, head on his paws.

Confused, Ru-Lee asked, "Who chooses?"

"The Heart—and the Heart has, apparently, chosen Sheila."

Ru-Lee could hear the others laughing across the clearing. She listened for a moment, her heart in her throat. Swallowing hard, she asked, "What, exactly, did Triya say?"

Nevlon stroked his beard and gazed up at the sky thoughtfully. Still watching the net of stars hovering peacefully above, he replied, "She said, 'Sheila, with Ru-Lee, must form the lock for which there is no key. In shifted form, she must give her all to contain evil and take the Aged One's place'."

"Wait! 'with Ru-Lee'?? What does that mean??" Ru-Lee stammered.

"It means that Sheila must freely accept her role and you must help. You will be the one to seal her fate—if she chooses to accept it herself. I don't fully comprehend all of it, but that is the gist of things."

Ru-Lee gazed down at Sheila and D.G., panic constricting her heart. She felt sick and dizzy. Could she really condemn her friend to a fate that meant she was to 'give her all'? What did that actually mean?? Slowly she shook her head—she wouldn't do it. Sheila wouldn't ask it of her. At any rate, Sheila didn't look like someone who was willing to sacrifice herself for anything right now—and didn't Triya say she had to accept her fate willingly and knowingly? No—things would be okay. Everything would work out, and this nonsense about Sheila sacrificing herself would be forgotten.

The soft shushing sound of footsteps in wet grass broke through Ru-Lee's consciousness and roused her from her thoughts. Aylon's strong arms slipped around her waist, "Are you alright?" Aylon whispered softly in her ear.

Ru-Lee blinked and slipped her arm around Aylon's shoulder, thankful for her grandmother's warmth and concern. She swallowed and breathed deeply, "Yes, I think so."

"Good, I brought clothes for Sheila…she can shift now—I figured she was waiting."

Ru-Lee didn't have the heart to tell Aylon what Nevlon had shared with her…it would make it all too real, and she was not ready to accept any of it. She was determined to find another way—some other option for Sheila.

She forced a smile and said, "Thanks. I am sure she will appreciate it."

Aylon held her gaze for a moment before shaking her head, "Secrets…always secrets around seers and dragons." She sighed and slipped her arm from around Ru-Lee's waist as she moved towards Sheila. Gently touching the spider's back, she murmured quietly to her. Sheila lumbered slowly to her feet, as if it was a struggle to raise herself from the ground. Aylon draped some clothing gently across her shimmering body and stepped back as Sheila slipped silently into the edge of the brush surrounding the clearing.

As Trieca, Jace, Davlin, and Relmar boisterously approached, Relmar placed a comforting hand on Ru-Lee's shoulder. A wry smile settled on her face as she looked away from him. She could feel a gentle weight settling around her thoughts as Nevlon's mind shielded her thoughts from Relmar and vaguely wondered why—was it to protect Relmar, or to prevent him from interfering? Relmar tilted her head back to look in her eyes, a quizzical look on his face. She shrugged and shook off his hands, stepping away. Whatever the reasons for his actions, Nevlon had always taken care of her and the boys---she trusted that he knew what he was doing now.

"Turn around, boys!" Aylon ordered as she returned to the group and stood, hands on hips, facing her husband. "Care to share anything?" she asked accusingly as she glared at Nevlon's bewhiskered face.

He blinked innocently and shook his head answering, "Not particularly."

The air around Aylon began to crackle and small sparks of electricity snapped around her hair causing it to puff up around her head giving her the visage of an enraged chicken. Her voice became menacingly soft and low, "Old man, what is going on?"

Before Nevlon could answer, a deafening rumble exploded into the night, shaking the mountains to their core. The ground trembled and the peaks sent large boulders rolling and bouncing down around their feet.

Pug screeched and launched himself skyward. D.G. growled and snarled at the undulating turf around him. Sheila came darting out of the brush towards Relmar. Ducking and weaving to avoid falling debris, she dove into his protective arms. He held her tightly to him, relief flooding his eyes. Nevlon grabbed Aylon and Ru-Lee, tucking them close beneath his cloak as he hunched over them. Trieca, Jace, and Davlin struggled to keep upright. Jace stumbled and went down, swearing profusely. As he scrambled to his feet, he thought he saw movement in the grass near the forest, as if dark forms were darting through the underbrush, but he brushed it off as an overactive imagination as the ground heaved and rolled beneath him once more.

Above the din, Nevlon's deep voice ordered, "Follow me!" Struggling for footing as they dodged and darted around falling boulders, Nevlon led the group towards the camp of the Travelers.

## Chapter 62

It was awkward running next to Nevlon, his arm around her shoulders. Ru-Lee felt her blood pounding in her ears as she tried to keep up and remain under his defensive cover. D.G. kept close on her heels. Running low to the ground, he nimbly avoided obstacles, growling and snarling at the unstable footing as he went. Aylon had freed herself from Nevlon's arm, but held tightly to her husband's hand, keeping pace on his opposite side. Relmar and Sheila clung to each other a few steps behind Ru-Lee and to her right, Relmar lifting and carrying Sheila when it was most expedient. Davlin, Jace, and Trieca trailed off to Ru-Lee's left, jumping over and dodging obstacles in their path. Pug glided through the sky ahead of them, his loud screeches heralding their approach.

As she ran, Ru-Lee felt her body temperature rise. Her vision blurred and the world around her glowed red, viewed through burning hot pupils. Tree limbs tugged and tore at her clothing and a swooshing roar filled her ears, drowning out all sound except the voices fiercely growing in her mind.

*"It is time!"* they roared.

She shook her head angrily, refusing to acknowledge them. Her skin crawled and prickled, stretching tighter over her frame that suddenly seemed awkward and gangly. She felt the Warta spirits' desire to take dragon form filling her soul—their desire becoming her own. She tripped and went down, scraping her knees and gashing the palms of her hands. Nevlon lifted her up and blood ran down her arms. Her nostrils flared at the metallic scent, and a low growl escaped her throat.

"Hang on, Ru! Don't let them make you shift yet—we are almost there!" Nevlon's voice shot through the roar in her head, jolting her mind.

She turned to look through the red haze that clouded her vision into his strong, bristly face, lined with concern.

Nodding, she gritted her teeth against the shift, even as she felt scales forming lightly on the surface of her skin.

The gravelly voice of the Aged One battered at her strength and resistance, *"There isn't time for this foolishness! Our brethren are through the barriers—we can feel them!"*

The blood in her veins boiled and surged, swelling vessels to near bursting. She felt the bones in her face growing—the spikes of her tail catching her clothing as her body began to extend.

She groaned and growled, "NO!" , but fangs split through her expanding gums making the sound less recognizable as a word of denial. Nubs of wing bones sprouted from her shoulder blades, pressing up into Nevlon's bicep.

"*%#@!!" Nevlon swore and jerked his arm from Ru-Lee's expanding shoulders. "She's shifting!" he shouted to Aylon.

"Release her and let her be! She will lose too much strength if she fights it now, and she can't afford to!" Aylon yelled over the din of the tormented mountains. She pulled Nevlon away as Ru-Lee crumpled to all fours on the tremulous earth, struggling to draw air into her transforming body. D.G. stopped next to her, watching her anxiously. The tops of the trees in the surrounding forest began to bend and sway.

"Over here!" Nevlon ordered the others, drawing them to relative safety behind a large boulder a short distance away. They had passed into the outer edge of the Travelers' camp and were near a string of frightened horses tethered at the forest's edge, snorting and rolling their eyes in terror. A small group of Travelers, young and old, had seen and heard their approach, Triya among them. They quickly worked to calm the frantic equines and move them to safety while shooting curious and frightened glances over their shoulders at the transpiring scene. Speaking softly to the now-rearing, screaming animals, Triya directed the travelers to lead the beasts to the far side of the camp away from the mountain. Once they were gone, she joined the group huddled behind the stone.

Thick air and searing hot winds whipped, snapped, and popped the tents around them, uprooting some and tearing others, tossing them through the air like children's toys. Campfires flared, spewing red sparks that lit up the darkness and threatened to ignite the dry vegetation of late summer. The wind spat the embers through the night, biting and stinging all those in its path. Nevlon and Aylon stood, arms upraised, battered by flying debris. Their voices rose in unison as they murmured incantations to calm the fires that threatened to grow, but they could do nothing about the growing winds that bent and twisted trees sending off flying limbs that bounced across the still-undulating ground. The wind clawed and yanked on clothing and hair, twisting it around the faces and bodies of the people in its path. It swirled and spun around Ru-Lee and D.G., seeming to call forth the dragon into the waning night.

# Chapter 63

Scorching winds caught the tattered edges of Ru-Lee's clothing as it ripped free from her expanding, shifting body. She shrieked in pain as her chest spread, dragon fire and smoke spilling into her lungs. D.G. danced away, avoiding her dagger-like claws that raked the ground where he had been standing.

Ru-Lee roared. Smoke and flaming lava filled the air. The ravaging winds ripped the smoke from her lungs, cast the lava away from her, and toppled several tents while burning gaping holes in others.

Frightened, Pug darted out of the air and dove into Jace's stomach like a tossed football. Jace curled his arms protectively around the small mass of quivering feathers as Pug burrowed in for safety.

A tremor ran through the Dragon Mountains once more, smoke belching forth from several cave openings. Shouts, screams, and the sounds of battle filtered down to them through the howling wind.

Within a vortex of dust, wind, and debris, Ru-Lee extended her now-transformed body to its full length. Wings spread wide, she opened her enormous maw and bellowed her challenge to the unseen foes waiting in the depths of the mountain, scattering the debris, and calming the wind. Without waiting for an answer, she coiled her body into a tight crouch and launched herself skyward toward the midsection of the mountain, the main cave entrance that led down to the Heart--and the intruders.

Hidden behind their stony protection, Nevlon gave Aylon a sideways grin, and kissed her gently on the lips. She smiled at him and shook her head as he began to shimmer, shift, and take wing in one swift movement. Quickly riding the turbulent air currents, he rose above Ru-Lee and kept pace, gliding to meet their foe.

Jace handed a still-frightened Pug off to Relmar, disengaging the small bird's talons from his fingers. He glanced at Davlin inquiringly. His brother nodded in unspoken agreement and the two swiftly shifted into bear and cougar form, trailing D.G. as they raced to join the battle that could now be clearly heard on the shifting winds. Trieca wordlessly followed, his long legs eating up the ground as he promptly disappeared through the brush and trees that skirted the Travelers' camp

Sheila turned to Aylon and tentatively asked, "Should I shift now?"

Aylon shook her head, "No…Relmar needs you for the time being. You will know when it is time."

Relmar tilted his head sideways at Sheila, his brows knitting together in consternation, "What are you talking about?"

Aylon turned to Sheila, puzzled, "Doesn't he know?"

"No—not everything. My presence seems to block his sensitivities—a part of my ability to calm, I guess," Sheila replied, sheepishly shrugging her shoulders.

Irritated, Relmar narrowed his eyes at Aylon and asked, "Know what?"

Ignoring him, Aylon furrowed her brow in confusion, "But that should only be in affect while you are in human form. Didn't he read Ru-Lee, when you were shifting?"

Sheila glanced sadly at Relmar who was beginning to scowl, "Apparently not—or, at least, not enough."

"What the *&^%%@# am I missing here?" Relmar bellowed.

Aylon grunted and moved the two in front of her, "Watch your language!" she admonished. "You are missing no more than I am, to be sure. It's just that I have spent enough time around seers, dragons, and my husband, to sense when things are being withheld from me—and I can guess fairly well at what those things might be." Placing her hand on Sheila's back, she continued, "You must make sure to clear the air soon!"

Sheila nodded solemnly, "I know…." as Aylon propelled her and a reluctant Relmar towards the mountain.

"For now, you two are needed elsewhere—Get moving!"

Still confused, and non-too happy about it, Relmar tried without success to question a now-solemn and silent Sheila as they ran through camp in pursuit of the others.

Triya still stood near the boulder, her eyes glazed and unseeing, staring after the departing combatants. The braided rows of her flaming red hair twisted in the wind around her dark head like angry snakes; her skirts billowed and flapped around her, filling the heated air with her intoxicating scent.

Aylon sighed, shook her head, and gently grasped Triya's arm urging her brusquely forward, "It's a wonder any of us have a hold on our husbands with you around! Come on—we have work to do!"

At Aylon's touch, Triya blinked, rising quickly from her trance. "What do you have in mind?"

"Not sure—I'll let you know when I get there and find out what's needed."

"I have some supplies in my tent that might be useful," Triya offered.

Aylon slowed to a stop and turned to Triya suspiciously, "Like what?"

The seer smiled cryptically, her white teeth flashing in the night, "Large cats."

Puzzled, Aylon followed Triya's brightly-colored skirts weaving across the disheveled campsite, avoiding the suspicious gazes of the women, children, and elders who were surveying the damage caused to their homes.

# Chapter 64

Deep in the dark recesses of Mount Shavla, muffled mechanized grinding and hammering could be heard vibrating through the walls on the south side of a cavern so large that all of Illiand would have fit inside. Hoping to capture the advantage of surprise, the defenders of this space had doused all torches, plunging themselves into pitch black. The efforts of brownies and elves to hinder the progress of the intruders on the human side of the mountain had bought the defenders time, but the trespassers were determined and were now nearly through.

Hulking forms with slit and lidded glowing eyes peered into the gloom—sharp claws impatiently scraping on the stone floor. Smaller stout figures crouched behind rock formations and pressed themselves into the stone walls becoming nearly invisible—labor-hardened hands tenderly caressing weapons made for death. Lithe bodies slipped through the shadows passing whispered instructions and encouragement to their companions and murmuring powerful words to wake the rivers of liquid that ran deep in the veins of Mount Shavla. Furtive brownies clung to rock ledges and overhangs, anxious to join their brethren in the fight to protect their home. The air in the cavern crackled. Anticipation crawled across the floor and tingled on the skin. The heat of many bodies made the air clammy and cloying.

Villagers and Travelers formed a second line of defense, along with a few Dahgsna Dragons, whose wingspan could not be fully accommodated within the inner walls without causing harm to those they fought with. Small contingents of men huddled against walls of the openings to the various tunnels that led up from the lower regions to the main entrance chamber.

A short passage on the east side led to an antechamber that had been set up to provide immediate care for the injured. Several dwarves sat just outside its entrance, grumbling at their poor fortune not to be directly involved in the fighting. The massive form of the dragon, Arnue, glared at them, the scales on his tail scratching annoyingly across the floor as his tail twitched in feline-like irritability making his displeasure at his post known to all within hearing.

"Would you hold that thing still!" hissed Threlm. "Bad enough we gotta' sit 'ere in the dark wi'out the prospect o'fightin'—ye don' need ta' do that!"

Arnue growled, a low rumble that rolled through the air like a ripple on water.

"Bah!" Threlm exclaimed and squirmed uncomfortably as icy water dripped from the ceiling and ran down his neck.

Before he could complain further, the inner chambers of the mountain thundered and shook. Loosened stones tumbled from the ceiling and the floor heaved tossing the dwarves across the ground into the relatively stable form of Arnue. The dragon looked down at them with disdain as clouds of smoke and dust rolled out of the larger chamber. Screams and shouts filled the air joined by the clash of battle. Dragon roars and yells of pain rousted the chosen medic-dwarves and they charged into the dark cloud to offer what assistance they could. Moments later, Threlm and his companions struggled back towards Arnue with their charges of injured elves, men, and dwarves.

As the medic dwarves labored towards the antechamber opening, fanged demons burst through the smoke behind them, clawing at the injured and nearly dragging down the dwarves who swung their weapons seeking to protect their charges. Startled at the onslaught, Arnue jumped sideways and shot flames at the demons, engulfing them in fire and singeing the dwarves who bypassed the antechamber and hurriedly charged towards the main opening out of the mountain.

XXX   XXX   XXX   XXX   XXX

The first rays of the morning sun cast a soft pink hue into the sky where the mountain peaks kissed the night. In this twilight, the graceful form of a large dragon could be seen winging towards Mount Shavla at dangerous speeds. Without slowing, Ru-Lee's body slammed into the side of the mountain near the main opening at the top of a winding stone trail.

She clawed and scrabbled to maintain her hold and climb into the cave entrance grumbling to the Warta Spirits within her, *"I told you to slow down! You didn't take the wind into account! Why don't you just let me handle this?"*

The Ancient One's laughter echoed within her mind, *"Stop complaining! No harm was done. You are not skilled enough at navigating to handle landings—recall the incident by the lake?"*

Ru-Lee grunted as she flapped her wings to lift her body up into the cool, cavernous opening that would lead to the Heart. *"That was an accident!"* she defended. *"I had never flown before—or landed—you have to account for a lack of knowledge! I noticed you were no particular help that time either!"*

The mountain trembled and rumbled as clouds of acrid smoke rolled out to greet her and she nearly lost her footing again. A large eagle screeched, gliding down a safe distance away from Ru-Lee on the entrance ledge. As it landed, its body shimmered and shifted to reveal the crouched form of Nevlon. He straightened up and glanced sideways at her, eyes twinkling and shoulders shaking with laughter.

"Nice landing," he smirked.

Ru-Lee snorted and tossed her head, refusing to answer.

Through the haze of smoke, several small forms could be seen running and stumbling towards them, coughing, sputtering, and swearing. Many struggled to carry injured humans, elves, and dwarves between them, the strain of their loads evident on their faces.

"*%@& dragons! Always spewing smoke, ash, and fire! In close quarters, no less!" a burly, bewhiskered dwarf leading the group grumbled loudly.

Brushing at his singed whiskers, he nearly stumbled into Ru-lee's clawed foot. He stopped short, and rubbed the soot from his eyes. The stout figures of those behind him came to an abrupt halt, staggering into each other and nearly dropping their burdens. The grumbling dwarf slowly allowed his bloodshot gaze to travel up Ru-Lee's scaly body to her enormous, horned head. He growled and stamped his foot.

Swinging a battle mace menacingly above his head, he shouted, "If you an' yer's don' watch what yer doin', yer gonna fry us! Then where will ya' be, eh?"

Quickly stepping forward, Nevlon inserted himself between the dwarf and Ru-Lee, "Calm yourself, Threlm— this one's just arrive—she isn't responsible for your charred beard," he soothed.

"Charred beard's not all I got!" Threlm yelled as he turned around to reveal a blackened and smoldering hole in his pants. "*&#%@!@ Dragons!!! That's Arnue's doin'! I knew he were too close fer comfort, but did anyone listen? NOOO!" He batted at his beard once again, knocking soot and fried hair into the surrounding air.

The echo of metal rang through dark of the tunnel behind the dwarves. Ru-Lee snorted, her eyes dilating in anticipation of battle. The flames beneath her skin roared to life, dancing wildly across her body.

Threlm and the others peered at her, inspecting her curiously. "Never seen one like 'er before," he grunted, squinting suspiciously at Ru-Lee.

Ignoring him, Nevlon asked, "How fares the battle?"

"All 'ell's broke loose in there! Can't see much 'cause o' the smoke and dust, but there's some creatures in there that I never saw before!"

"Where did the injured come from?" Nevlon pressed.

"They were 'urt when the wall broke--attacked by whatever came through.  We was movin' 'em to an anteroom out of harm's way, but Arnue got spooked an' spewed flames all over the *%#$ place!  Had to evacuate."

Nevlon sighed, "Did you see what spooked Arnue? He doesn't usually panic, in my experience."

Threlm grunted and peered around Nevlon's legs as a large blonde bear and a lean cougar stealthily crept up behind the man.  He narrowed his eyes at them, glanced up at Nevlon's face and asked, "They yers?"

Without turning or acknowledging the presence of Jace and Davlin, Nevlon pressed, "Yes—did you see any of the attackers?"  D.G. panted up beside the cougar and sat down on his haunches regarding Threlm and his companions with curiosity.

The dwarf glowered at the canine and grunted again, "Not sure exactly....Somethin' come out of the smoke follerin' us an' tried to get some o' the injured out—Arnue smoked 'em an' got us, too a bit."  Motioning for the others to follow him, he started past Nevlon.  Over his shoulder, he growled, "Go in and see fer yerself—We gotta get these un's down to the gnomes.  They won't come in the caves 'cause of the dragons—too many 'ave been food an' all."

Casting suspicious sideways glances at Ru-Lee, Davlin, D.G., and Jace, the dwarves hefted their burdens and moved past Nevlon towards the wide, winding pathway chiseled into the side of the mountain. Glaring down at the passing dwarves, Ru-Lee huffed smoke through her nostrils, engulfing the short warriors who flung obscene insults back at her.

Trieca, Relmar, and Sheila were racing up the path to catch up to the others.  They were forced to the side against the stone wall so the small procession could wend its way towards the gnome encampment near the base of the mountain.  Pug, impatient to join Jace now that the wind had died down, nipped Relmar's thumb hard enough to draw blood.

"Hey!" Relmar yelled and jammed his thumb in his mouth, releasing the bird so abruptly that he fell to the ground in a feathered heap. Before Relmar could recover him, Pug fluffed the dust from his feathers and took flight. Gliding silently over the passing dwarves, he sailed up to land gracefully on Jace's head. The bear grinned wide, rumbling a bear-like chuckle as he glanced back at Relmar sucking on his thumb and glaring up at him.

*"I'm going in—can't wait any longer!"* Ru-Lee snarled in Nevlon's mind. *"The Warta are impatient—and so am I."*

"Follow me," Nevlon ordered, turning to a wide passage leading west.

Ru-Lee narrowed her eyes and peered into the darkness. *"Why that way? The battle is straight ahead?"*

"Exactly—if we go this way, we can come in from the side, bypass the scrum of forward fighting, and, maybe, be a bit more help to our friends."

Looking sideways, Ru-Lee shrugged at Jace, Davlin, and D.G. before lowering her head and lumbering after Nevlon.

## Chapter 65

Men poured into the jagged opening in the wall of the cavern, coughing and sputtering as they passed through the cloud of dust, dirt, and falling rock. As they entered the cavern, they stopped momentarily, a look of surprised confusion and suspicion on their faces. That look immediately changed, painfully morphing their features into sharp angles of twisted hatred. Horns sprouted from their heads, and fangs grew from snarling muzzles. Their bodies twisted, changing into muscular, clawed, four-legged beasts. The beasts sniffed the air, scenting their prey—for that is how they viewed any who would stand against them.

Behind the transformed demons, an elegantly tall figure strolled through the rubble towards the opening, past the now-dead piece of machinery that had been used to drill through the rock. The self-satisfied smirk on his face nauseated the elves and men hiding in the darkness—they held their breath, waiting to see what would transpire.

The man surveyed the scene before him. His eyes grazed over those who had entered ahead of him. He nodded, his sinister smile widening slightly. Purposefully, he stepped through into the cavern and stood expectantly. A full minute passed—nothing happened. The air within the chamber thickened—a confused scowl wrinkled his aristocratic brow.

The brownies leaned precariously forward from their protected ledges, watching as the demons sniffed the air, snarling and snapping at the emptiness surrounding them. Suddenly, the man's scent filled the beasts' nostrils. They slowly began circling around him, drool slipping down their jowls to spill onto the floor in acidic pools.

Fury darkened the man's eyes; his lips curled as he snarled at the advancing demons. One of them slipped behind him, and swiped at the back of his leg with its gnarled claws. The man roared in pain, blood running into his shoes and spilling over to darken the stone floor. The demons circled closer, the odor of the man's blood strong in their nostrils. The man tried to grab a spiked club that was slung across his back, but it slipped from his fingers and clattered to the floor, the sound echoing through the chamber. He looked at his hands, puzzled. Before his eyes, his appendages were changing—his arms no longer ended in hands, but extended into sharp talons. His eyes widened in shock, then narrowed shrewdly just as the vessels around them burst, coloring his vision red. He screamed in agony as his body shifted---stretching and extending to become an enormous Warta Dragon whose bulk filled the opening. His roar spewed fire across the cave above the heads of the circling demons who cowered before him.

Instantly, the mountain rumbled, the ground trembled, and the defenders launched their attack. Battle cries echoed off the walls. The air filled with fire, smoke, and dust that rolled out of the cavern through every available opening, seeking escape. More men streamed through from the human side of the gaping hole, instantly transforming into ferocious, mindless demons. Many fell and were ripped apart by their brethren as they clawed their way to the defenders.

Brownies shot poison-tipped darts into vulnerable demon eyes and ears. Some hit their mark, dropping their victims instantly. Others bounced off the thick skin to be trampled beneath cloven and clawed feet.

Men wielded axes, swords, and crossbows, spilling putrid green blood that made slick pools on the stone floor. Elves shot bows loaded with dragon-lit arrows, finding every vulnerable area on the bodies of their enemies---but more kept coming. Some were felled as they transformed, a look of confused surprise frozen on their faces. A small cluster of elves stayed near the outer walls, hands splayed out on the rock, mouths silently working, eyes half-closed as they worked to summon the power that flowed through the mountain.

Two large Harta Dragons clashed with the Warta Dragon, filling the space with smoke and flames. Falling scales, torn loose during battle, littered the floor to be crushed beneath the weight of the skirmishing dragons. The Warta ripped and clawed at the scales on the neck, chest, and underbelly of the dragons that fought against him, seeking to expose the soft flesh and the jugular vein that would allow him to end their lives. His wings flailed uselessly in this space, knocking down more stones from the ceilings and walls, and filling the air with choking dust.

As the two Harta circled in again, the Warta swung his thick tail wide, knocking one to the ground. Instantly, he lunged, plunging his talons deep into the soft underbelly. He extended the razor-sharp blades and twisted, cutting through muscle and tendons. Flexing his digits, he pulled, beginning to drag the entrails out of his enemy. The second Harta caught the back of the Warta's neck in massive jaws and clenched down hard, wrenching her head to the side. She snapped her head back and forth, causing the Warta to release his downed victim—too late to save him. Men, elves, brownies, and demons alike scrambled out of the way of the struggling behemoths as the Warta pushed the battle deeper towards the tunnel that would lead him to the Heart, hauling his opponent with him as he struggled to free himself.

Near the outlet of the tunnel leading to the main entrance cavern, the Dahgsna Dragons waited in the dark to capture oncoming demons within their strong talons and disembowel them with their fangs like an eagle gutting a fish. Men and elves fell screaming in the darkness throughout the beehive of tunnels that ran through the mountain, ripped apart by the bloodthirsty demon swarms that seemed never-ending.

The innermost sanctum of the mountain decried the mêlée within it, growling and belching forth steam as if in protest. Hidden streams of life-giving water boiled, bubbling slowly upwards from her bowels, called forth by the elves.

In the deep recesses of the mountain, running along her veins ahead of the boiling waters, thousands of furry creatures scurried forth, beady eyes gleaming hungrily. They slipped along the widening tunnel walls, seeking their opponents. Their dark-accustomed eyes narrowed as they spotted the first of the combatants. With loud cries of war, they charged. Attacking from behind, they scampered up legs and plunged tiny swords into jugular veins, spilling hot blood from the deep wounds. Their victims could only gurgle in shock, never knowing their murderers. The horde moved on—blood thirsty and ready for more.

# Chapter 66

Acrid smoke filled the passageway Nevlon led the small group through. The thick darkness was briefly illuminated with intermittent flashes of orange and red dragon fire that filtered around corners through the haze. Jace and Davlin, in their animal forms, lowered their heads and prowled close to the ground in an effort to get below the toxic fumes that hung in the upper levels of the route. Nevlon held the edge of his cloak pressed against his nose and mouth, his eyes watering from the stinging vapors. Pug burrowed into Jace's neck. Digging his claws deep into the blonde fur, he tucked his head beneath his wing for protection, giving the appearance of being nothing more than a fluffy lump on the unconcerned bear.

Ru-Lee's dragon body drew the odorous vapors deep into her lungs and smiled. Within her, the Warta chuckled, *"Ah—that feels good! Smells like old times!"* Their contentment and anticipation rumbled through her chest causing her scales to vibrate and hum. The flames within her skin danced higher and skimmed over her body, casting an eerie light around her that wove and darted across the wide walls.

A low voice behind her asked, "Are you purring?"

Startled, Ru-Lee halted as the others continued on unaware. She whipped her head around on its long neck to peer into Trieca's sparkling eyes, a kerchief tied tightly around the lower half of his face against the smoke.

*"Where did you come from?"* she asked, projecting her thoughts into his mind.

He blinked and shook his head in irritation, "Behind you, obviously! I wish you wouldn't do that....it is disconcerting."

She huffed hot air across his face blowing his hair away from his forehead and replied, *"Tough—it's the easiest way to communicate in this form!"* Tilting her head to see around him, she could make out two figures carefully making their way hand-in-hand along the dark passage, *"Is that Relmar and Sheila?"*

"Yes," he answered without turning. He stepped forward past her long tail just as the ground beneath them heaved once more. The walls pitched and rolled causing him to stumble against her haunches. Placing a hand on her warm scales, he continued, "We'd best get moving— any idea where we're going?"

*"To war---don't you recall? Do you mind not touching my bum? I don't think we are that close!"* she answered sarcastically. *"The other ways in are blocked by combatants---Nevlon thinks this way will be best."*

As Relmar and Sheila caught up, Ru-Lee nodded her massive head in their direction, then turned and trundled on wordlessly behind Nevlon, Jace, D.G., and Davlin. No one spoke as the sounds of battle grew louder, echoing off the walls around them, filling their ears. The agonizing screams of the injured and dying men, elves, dwarves, and brownies were punctuated by the roars and growls of the dragons and the vicious bloodthirsty snarls of demons. The scent of burned flesh hung strong in the air.

Ru-Lee cringed and tossed her head as other dragon voices seeped into her mind. She could hear them all—the Dahgsna as they ripped and slashed at the enemy that threatened to overrun them and those they grappled with; the Harta as they fought and rallied their brethren scattered throughout the catacombs of passageways, caverns, and tunnels; and the Warta—filled with hatred and revenge.

A deep growl rumbled forth from Ru-Lee's chest, her muzzle curling in a ferocious, uncontrollable snarl. Her eyes burned brighter, the flames on her body spreading across her skin as if she were one huge bonfire. The growing heat from her body forced Trieca, Relmar, and Sheila to step back against the cool stone walls.

Dim and dancing light swam around a bend ahead of them and the floor vibrated with slamming bodies. Nevlon stopped, holding up his hand as a signal to the others. Davlin, D.G., and Jace softly padded to his side and he signaled Davlin to slip forward around the corner. Keeping his body low to the ground, Davlin slunk soundlessly forward, the tip of his long tail twitching nervously. Jace and D.G. sat side-by-side on their haunches, noses twitching wildly as they swung their heads from side to side gathering information through their sensitive nostrils.

Ru-Lee growled in irritation as the Warta Spirits within her rose to fill her mind. *"Reach your mind out to our brethren—but do not let them know you are there. We must know who we are dealing with before we meet in battle."*

*"Why?"* she snarled, narrowing her eyes at the turn in the tunnel.

*"There are many Warta descendents in the human world....it would be useful to know which ones we are to fight,"* they answered, evasively.

Ru-Lee lowered her head and snorted softly, adding small puffs of smoke to the already-thick air. *'They know something—something they don't want to share, and there isn't time to wheedle it out of them!'* she thought angrily. Frustrated, she dug her claws into the hard-packed floor causing long white lines to appear, barely visible in the dim light.

*"Fine!"* she snapped. *"I'll see what I can do....though I have never tried with anyone other than D.G. and Sheila. Are you sure I can?"*

The rough voice of the Ancient One rumbled through her bones, *"Of course we are sure! You are one of us now---and we are all connected. Just take care that they do not detect you—not until we are ready."*

*"Will you be able to see what I see?"* she asked, curiosity and suspicion battling within her.

*"Some—most, yes. But we must be cautious. We do not know if they will be able to detect our presence or if they will only sense yours. Either way, it is best if they do not know about either----yet."*

*"How do you suggest I go about this? Do I just open my mind to what I already hear and allow it to come in?"*

*"NO!!"* the bellow was so loud within her mind, it was like a physical blow to the head. She ducked and cringed. Nevlon and Jace turned to look at her in alarm, but she only blinked back at them innocently.

*"No need to yell!"* she snarled, once the others had returned to watching for Davlin. *"What do you suggest then?"*

*"If you open your mind, they will know you are here---we are here! Any advantage we may have of surprise will be lost! You must follow the trail of their thoughts back to them—go gently. We will try to block your mind from theirs so they won't sense your presence, but you must proceed with caution."*

Grunting in feigned understanding, Ru-Lee closed her eyes and concentrated on stretching her thoughts forward. Beside her, Sheila blinked in surprise as she realized what Ru-Lee was attempting. Relmar glanced at Sheila questioningly, but she ignored him as she watched her friend intently, concern etched on her delicate face.

Ru-Lee gently touched D.G.'s psyche as she sent her own past him and out, seeking the Warta combatants. It wasn't difficult to find them, she had only to follow the thread of mental echoes that spilled into her. She let her mind slip into the largest Warta, the ones whose thoughts were strongest. In an instant, her psyche was flooded with hate and fury. Images of cruelty and feelings of joy in slaughter inundated her causing her stomach to churn. The skin beneath her scales tingled and the spikes along her neck raised in fear, dread, and disgust.

Her mind recoiled trying to retreat from the onslaught, but the Warta Spirits blocked her way, urging her forward, *"A name! We need a name!"* they whispered cloyingly.

Mentally, she returned, cautiously slipping deeper into the mind of the enormous Warta Dragon as it fought a large Harta Dragon, bearing it through the lines of defenses, crushing those in its way. She crawled deep within her enemy's mind, stealthily seeking a name---a title.

She went too deep! The Warta Dragon sensed her presence—reaching out with his own psyche, he lashed out. Back in the tunnel, her body recoiled violently, causing it to stumble against the wall as she rapidly returned to herself. She screamed, the sound, lost to those deep in battle, reverberated through the passage. Nevlon, D.G., and Jace spun around; Trieca, Sheila and Relmar cringed against the wall; Pug popped his head up, spinning it around to regard her with large surprised eyes.

"*Behkna!*" The name was hissed through the Warta Spirits, spreading like venom from a snake through her body and mind.

"*You knew! You knew and you said NOTHING!*" she railed at them, shoving herself furiously upright.

"*Suspected—yes; knew—no,*" came their subdued reply.

Ru-Lee drew in her breath ready to expel her anger in lava and fire, but Sheila's soft touch on her shoulder and gentle voice in her mind reminded her of their close quarters. Instead, she coughed loudly and fought to restrain herself, gnashing flakes of lava furiously between her teeth.

The ferocious sounds of battling beasts echoed through the tunnel. A feline's yowl and the nearby sound of gnashing teeth split the air. Instantly, Davlin bolted around the corner. He crashed into Jace and D.G., sending Pug rolling across the floor between Ru-Lee's massive front legs and staining Jace's blonde fur with crimson blood that streamed from a deep gash on his shoulder. Nevlon stumbled backwards into Ru-Lee's chest, cursing as his hat slipped down over his eyes. Ru-Lee curled her lips, nostrils flaring as the scent of blood and demons filled the air.

Rannue charged after Davlin, sweat pouring down his lean face. He pulled up short just before running into the writhing mass of fur that was Davlin, Jace, and D.G.

attempting to disentangle themselves. His eyes widened as he took in the massive form of a dragon blocking his way, her teeth bared. Without thinking, he swiftly notched an arrow, stepped back, and drew his bow on Ru-Lee in one fluid movement, oblivious to the others surrounding her.

"Wait! Rannue---she's not Warta!" Nevlon yelled, righting himself and rushing to get in front of Rannue's arrow.

Rannue narrowed his eyes and darted his glance to Nevlon before suspiciously returning his gaze to Ru-Lee. He slowly lowered his bow as he took in the scene before him, nodding to his son and Relmar, and giving Sheila a slight look of curiosity.

Shaking his head, he replaced the arrow to its quiver and drew a long, thin blade. "It's about time you showed up! We were beginning to think something had happened to you," he grunted. Tilting his head sideways, he looked up into the glaring eyes of Ru-Lee. "I haven't seen one like her before, Nevlon. Where did she come from?"

"She's new here," Nevlon replied evasively. "What's happened so far?"

Before Rannue could answer, claws rasped on the stone floor behind him. Loud snuffling noises mingled with the battle sounds coming from around the bend—the sound of a beast hunting its prey.

Darting a quick look behind him, Rannue shoved Nevlon against the wall and hissed, "Got any ideas on the best way to kill a demon?"

*"I do—get behind me!"* Ru-Lee ordered, her thoughts echoing loudly in their minds. Pug screeched and flew up from the ground between her legs, circling just above Ru-Lee's head in the narrow passage before gliding down to sit land softly atop Sheila's head. Using her front feet to slide Davlin, Jace, and D.G. to the side as if they were bread crumbs on the floor, Ru-Lee stepped around Nevlon and Rannue. A deep growl rumbled in her chest as she lumbered past Relmar, Sheila, and Trieca. Placing her enormous body between her friends and family and the

oncoming threat, she crouched low. Her muscles rippled and her snout wrinkled pulling her lips upwards to reveal rows of sharp fangs, dripping with dragon venom. The putrid scent of demon spawn, like that of brimstone and rotting flesh, filled the air as their enemy came closer. The others did as she ordered and scrambled behind her knowing there was nothing they could do to help in their narrow confines.

As the flames danced higher across her flesh, her thoughts echoed in the minds of her companions, *"It's time I played my part."*

She could feel the Warta Spirits churning within her, like caged beasts gnawing at their confinement. Their voices surged forth in her mind, *"It is time we ALL played our parts."*

# Chapter 67

As the morning sun began to crawl across the Travelers'' nearly-deserted campsite, Aylon and Triya pulled back overgrown vines and entered Mt. Shavla's web of tunnels through a hidden doorway just below the main entrance. They had followed a narrow, rock-strewn and brushed-in path that had seen little use in recent years. Triya believed it had served as an entrance for the dwarves many years before when dwarves were said to have kept themselves separated from the Dragons. Over time, the two races had come to an unsteady truce, and many of the lower, smaller tunnels had been abandoned. Triya explained that she had discovered this opening years earlier and used it to find solitude when the Travelers were camped nearby.

The stone doorway slid closed behind them, grinding and groaning from disuse. Triya held two torches while Aylon nimbly struck a flint to light them. The wadding smoldered, sputtering slowly to life. In the weak and wavering light, Aylon could barely spot the sleek rear ends of the two enormous black panthers that had been hidden in a large cage inside Triya's tent. Their long, sleek tails hung low just above the dusty floor as they stood, listening intently to the soft sounds of creatures retreating in the darkness ahead of them.

Passing the torches to Aylon, Triya twisted her hands, winding leather thongs tightly up her wrists. The other ends reached out into the shadows to attach to collars fixed around the necks of the patient felines. One, the large male whose name was Orzo, turned its head to regard the women. His eyes reflected the red light cast by the torches giving him a demonic look that sent chills down Aylon's spine. The beast slowly licked his lips sensing her discomfort and appearing to enjoy the fact that he was the cause. He yawned wide to reveal gleaming white fangs, as if to let her know that he could, indeed, eat her if he so chose. The female, Orzo's mother, ignored him.

"Tell me again why you have these animals??" Aylon asked, wrinkling her brow in consternation.

Triya chuckled, "They were a gift from a young prince in Pushnah."

"But why?"

Glancing sideways at Aylon, Triya responded matter-of-factly, shrugging, "He liked my dancing."

Aylon shook her head, "What do you plan to do with them?"

"They will serve a purpose—you will see," Triya smiled cryptically.

A sigh escaped Aylon. She closed her eyes a moment, sending up a silent prayer before following Triya and her charges along the cool corridor.

The tunnel climbed upwards widening into a large hall with openings extending into the dark in all directions like arms on a many-limbed sea monster. The air here was thick and muggy. As they made their way through the hall, the mountain heaved again, emitting an odd gurgling sound that drifted up from its bowels. The ground rolled and the two women stumbled against the cold stone wall.

Aylon stopped and stooped down. Holding both torches with one hand, she placed the other hand on the ground and closed her eyes.

"What is it?" Triya asked, turning to watch Aylon. In front of her, the felines had come to a halt and stood impatiently. Their tails and noses twitched as they surveyed the darkness in front of them and waited for their mistress.

Aylon rose, brushing her hands on her clothing, "The ground's warm---the mountain is coming alive—we need to move quickly. Which direction?"

Triya nodded her head to the right, "That way—it leads up to the main entrance. We are needed there."

"We had better get a move on then."

As they moved forward, furtive scurrying sounds filtered down to them from the passageway. The panthers slowed their pace. Their bodies moving in unison, they crouched low to the ground; the tips of their tails twitched sharply back and forth; their eyes narrowed, noses working furiously to identify the source of the noise.

"Douse the flames!" ordered Triya as she slipped silently between the cats making her way to the front of their long, sleek bodies.

Puzzled, Aylon quickly ground the heads of the torches into the dusty stone floor, filling the air with pungent smoke. Waiting for her eyes to adjust to the lack of light, she whispered, "What are you doing?"

Triya's low voice answered, "Releasing our friends."

Startled, Aylon gasped and crammed herself against the wall, "You're what???!"

"SHHH!" came Triya's hissed response. Her urgent whispers continued, "This passage leads to the main entrance and the Heart. There is fighting there that these cats must assist in—they will be very effective weapons."

"And how will they know who to eat and who not to?" Aylon hissed back.

"Trust me, they will know. They have been trained well."

Aylon stood, her heart pounding in her chest as she tried to distinguish the forms of Triya and the cats from the shadows around her. Unsuccessful, she closed her eyes and leaned her head back against the cool stone, straining to hear sounds of movement over the rush of blood in her ears. She thought she could make out the soft rustle of Triya's skirts and the scuff of leather slippers against the well-worn floor. Triya whispered soft-purred words that Aylon couldn't make out. Then there was the metallic sound of clasps releasing from the collars and the drag of the leather thongs as they were gathered up. She could not hear the felines, but she could sense their mass moving stealthily away from her. Realizing she was holding her breath, she slowly exhaled and opened her eyes. She could barely distinguish Triya's form holding the leather straps in her hands as she crouched low in the tunnel—the cats were gone.

The faint sounds of fighting drifted down the tunnel as the two women worked their way quickly up the passage. Their hands guided them along the cool stone surface and Aylon prayed they wouldn't accidentally run afoul of the predatory felines. Regardless of Triya's assurances, she didn't trust the cats not to attack anything that moved. Shivers ran down her spine as the air was rent with screams of agony, confusion, and pain. Triya shuddered and stopped abruptly causing Aylon to run into her.

"The cats have found their prey?" Aylon asked, concerned.

Triya shook her head grimly, "No—those are the screams of men. My panthers do not attack men; the enemy attacks men."

# Chapter 68

The demon came sniffing and snuffling deeper into the tunnel, swinging its smashed snout in the air to the left and right, seeking the scent of its prey. Acidic drool dripped from fangs that jutted forth from its jowls, pooling on the floor with soft hissing noises that mingled with the scraping of its gnarled claws. Its fiendish nostrils flared, filling with the aroma of its quarry's blood. It neither wondered why nor how the mountain lion had come to join the fray—these things did not matter. The only item of importance was the kill—and kill it would.

So intently was the beast concentrating on its victim's trail that it did not at first notice the smell of another dragon. As it moved deeper into the channel, it slowed allowing its eyes to adjust to the deeper darkness void of the flashes of dragon fire that lit the outer chamber. Skulking curiously around the bend in the passageway, its dim mind attempted to place the new scent that seemed to fill this space and emanated from the animal whose skin bore dancing fire that did not smoke.

The lips of its upper jaw peeled back from black gums. A low snarl gurgled forth from its throat, filling the thick air with the stench of the beast's breath. Halting, it narrowed its burning red eyes as it tried to focus on the hulking form of this new adversary whose body blocked its path, keeping it from its prey. The growl deepened as the demon hunched low, preparing to strike at this unknown opponent. It launched its body toward this new enemy, snarling and snapping as it went.

Ru-Lee's strike was swift and deadly. Snatching the beast out of midair with her deadly jaws, she slashed its underbelly with her claws, impaling the animal. As she dragged her talons through its body, entrails spilled out, putrid green blood pouring down Ru-Lee's front leg. The demon twitched and twisted a few seconds more, then died, still held aloft.

Snapping her head to the side, Ru-Lee tossed the demonic body against the wall and curled her lips back in repulsion, scraping her tongue across her teeth to rid herself of the foul taste of evil the beast had left behind. Her ears rang as the lust of the kill surged through her body. Turning her head away from the gory scene in front of her, she used her claws and carefully swept the demon's innards away from her.

Nevlon slipped beside her and patted her shoulder. "You'll need to burn the demon blood from your mouth, and quickly, before it seeps into your system."

*"Won't that alert our enemies?"* Ru-Lee asked, rolling her tongue around in her mouth and grimacing at the bitter taste the demon had left behind.

"Doesn't matter now—they already know, don't they?" Nevlon replied looking up into her fevered eyes.

*"I suppose they do,"* Ru-Lee conceded. She opened her jaws and blasted a quick burst of dragon fire sideways, turning her attacker's remains to ashes. *"They are all connected, you know?"* she continued, puffing smoke through her nostrils in disdain.

Behind her, Davlin, Relmar, and Jace could be heard retching. *"You had better not get any on my tail!"* she snarled in their minds.

Nevlon moved forwards in the tunnel, feeling his way along the wall towards the bend when quick flashes of light cast grim shadows along the passage. "I guessed as much. Do you know why?"

*"Yes—they, the demons, are all Warta descendents! There is one that is stronger than the rest. Somehow, he figured things out—remembered them or was told them, I don't know—but he found some way to steal the powers of the other Warta so that he is the only one that returns to dragon form! The others are left to be his minions—so long as he can control them,"* she spat. *"If he hadn't done whatever it was that he did, none of them would have returned to full dragon form when they passed through*

302

*because the bloodlines are so diluted. He wanted power—all of it. He still does."*

Rannue and Trieca carefully made their way next to Nevlon. "That was a nice move," Rannue commented to Ru-Lee. "Nevlon, when we have more time, you will have to fill me in on who our new friend here is and where she came from. Right now, we need to get moving. More will be headed our way soon and we would do better in a larger area where we can all fight freely. Do you have a plan?"

"Yes," Nevlon responded over his shoulder as he walked wordlessly back to Sheila.

"Yes?" she asked as he approached, her soft, melodic voice surreally out of place given the ghastly death the space had recently born witness to.

Nevlon placed his hands on Sheila's shoulders, concern lining his face, "You must make your way to the Heart. You know what to do once you reach that place, right?"

Sheila bowed her head and lowered her lids, gently squeezing a puzzled Relmar's hand, "Yes. I was able to communicate with my sisters while I lay in the field. They relayed most of what is needed. The rest will be revealed once I reach the Heart."

"Will someone please explain what is going on?" Relmar snapped. "You know, I used to think that it would be wonderful not to be able to hear people's thoughts, but this is annoying!"

Sheila turned to him. Placing her hands gently upon his chest, she looked up into his hazel eyes. Pug, still perched atop her head, watched the two with growing curiosity looking like a comical bobble-hat. The fire from Ru-Lee's body shimmered through Sheila's silvery hair making it sparkle as it cascaded over her shoulder.

"We all have our jobs to do here, you knew that when we set out." She smiled and caressed Relmar's cheek. "You do your job and don't worry about me and mine. I will be fine, and so will you."

Relmar scowled, his brow furrowing as he gazed down at her. His hands slipped down to Sheila's hips and he lifted his gaze to Nevlon accusingly, "You are blocking me, Nevlon—and you're shielding Ru....why? What is it that you don't want me to know?"

Sheila raised herself up on her toes and coyly wrapped her arms around Relmar's neck. Smiling mischievously, she tilted her head up and softly kissed his lips. As soft groan escaped him as he closed his eyes, forgetting his irritation, concerns, and the ensuing battle.

Slowly releasing him, Sheila stepped away and murmured, "Remember, we do what we must for those we love."

She turned her back and nimbly scrambled up Ru-Lee's scaly body to seat herself just behind the shimmering iridescent wings ordering, "Let's get moving, Ru. We have work to do."

Moving cautiously forward, Ru-Lee answered so only the mist-elf could hear her. *"We will see."*

"Do you have the fire stone Aylon gave you?" Nevlon asked the dazed Relmar.

"Huh?...Oh...no—I think it is still in the lake somewhere," Relmar stammered absently.

Nevlon chuckled and dug into the pouch at his waist to produce a blood-red stone that was slightly smaller than the one Aylon had given Relmar. "She really shouldn't do that to people—she has an unfair advantage, you know," he said as he placed it in Relmar's palm.

Murmuring softly, Relmar gazed at the back of Sheila's head as she perched atop Ru-Lee's back, his hand closing distractedly around the stone.

Davlin padded past Relmar and Nevlon, limping slightly though his wound had ceased bleeding. Jace snarled and shoved Relmar aside in disgusted irritation as he and D.G. moved forward in Ru-Lee's wake.

As Sheila moved further away, the glazed look in Relmar's eyes dissipated. He blinked and looked at the stone in his hand.

"Is this another firestone?  Where did you get it and what am I to do with it?" he asked Nevlon.

Nevlon placed his right hand on Relmar's elbow and guided him behind his brothers, "It was a gift.  You will use it to gather and control fire—your own and that of others.  You can use it to destroy and protect as needed. You will know what to do when the time comes."  He paused thoughtfully before continuing, "Can you hear the thoughts of the Warta descendants?"

Relmar watched Ru-Lee's tail dragging ahead of him in the dim light cast by her body, "No—not clearly, at least.  I have to work to hear anything while Sheila is in human form.  When she shifts, I am sure I will hear and feel more than I'd like."

# Chapter 69

Along the wall of a large tunnel, just above the spot where Aylon and Triya's channel joined it, the bloodied bodies of four men were barely discernable beneath a swarming mass of black rodents that rushed over them. The bodies of these men, so recently murdered, were still warm. Beneath the rushing feet, the surprised whites of the dead men's eyes were barely visible in the dim light—wide with shock.

Two dark forms slunk quickly up the passage following a scent that made their noses twitch and their eyes narrow. Muscles rippled beneath their satin fur as they moved soundlessly through the dark tunnel. The sound of scurrying feet and tiny claws filled the air ahead of the felines with a chatter-like hum as hordes of rodents in the intersecting passageway rushed past headed towards the main opening of the cave. More bodies funneled into the main mass merging from small cracks and fissures along the walls that led upwards from the lower recesses of Mount Shavla. Further up this channel, the horde of small creatures divided itself into two halves to run up the sides of the tunnel, eyes flashing and glowing red in the darkness.

As the large panthers burst from their passage and charged into the back end of the mass of mice, the gloomy darkness was shattered with the screeches, screams, and squeaks of frightened and dying rodents. Many were swallowed whole, others were bitten in half, their bodies tossed against the stone walls. Some were squashed beneath massive feline paws, leaving slippery wet globs on the floor.

Hundreds of the black mice halted their ascent and turned on the panthers, miniscule swords and sharp teeth burrowing deep in the silken fur. The bulk of the small creatures continued on towards the main entrance.

The big cats yowled in pain and anger as they were overrun by the multitude of small bodies. Rising up on

306

their hind legs, the felines snapped and snarled at their attackers, plucking them off and tossing them away like ticks. They smashed their bodies against the stone floor, using their own weight to crush the mice. Their tails flashed through the air, sending rodents sailing against walls and into their brethren, cracking their skulls and breaking their tiny bones.

Finally, having freed themselves of their assailants, the panthers surged upwards in pursuit of the rest of the black horde. Only a few mice still breathed. Curled into balls near the walls, they appeared to be nothing more than clods of dirt—except for the slight shivering of their black bodies and the glisten of blood trickling across their fur, leaking their life into the stone. They would not breathe much longer.

Further up the tunnel, more screams could be heard, mingled with the gurgling noises of those drowning in their own blood. Men were dying now, surprised and overcome by the first wave of murderous rodents that overran them and slit their throats. Their death songs were shared by the mice at the rear of the bloodthirsty horde as the two black panthers released their souls from the earth.

# Chapter 70

Every muscle in Ru-Lee's body bulged and tensed, rippling under the flames that danced frantically across her body. Her eyes narrowed and her field of vision blurred red around the edges, the heat rising in her body. Blood pounded in her ears drowning out the sounds of the battle lurking just around the bend. Her mind and soul were overcome by the combined wills of the Warta Spirits. Their anticipation and hunger for blood heightened her senses. Her nostrils flared, her breath shallow and rapid, a low rumbling growl thrumming in her throat. She crouched lower and crept closer to the bend in the tunnel, unsure of what she expected to find. The Warta Spirits flashed gruesome images through her mind. Unsure of whether they were trying to prepare her or taunt her, she shook her head, attempting to rid her mind's eye of the scenes.

Sheila's soft voice sifted through the voices of the Warta souls inhabiting her body and mind. *"Calm yourself and breathe, Ru,"* Sheila counseled softly, shielding her thoughts from the parasitic beings within Ru-Lee. *"You will need your wits about you, as well as those of the Warta spirits—but you must be in charge for I do not think they will have your interests at heart."*

Ru-Lee grunted in response. Gathering in a deep breath, she slowly exhaled, willing her breathing to return to somewhat normal levels.

*"Can you do anything about your body temperature?"* Sheila asked, shifting her body to keep the smallest amount of flesh in contact with Ru-Lee's sweltering scales.

Ru-Lee chuckled slightly and shook her head, *"I haven't figured that out yet...sorry. You may have to shift in order to protect yourself."*

*"I think I will be fine for awhile. I will just hang on."*

Rounding the final bend, Ru-Lee came to an abrupt halt. The growl in her throat swelled and her lips curled back. She drew herself up as far as the tunnel ceiling would allow and glared down at the sight before her. *"You might want to re-think that."*

Davlin, Jace, and D.G. were nearly bowled over by Ru-Lee's tail as it snaked rapidly back and forth between the walls in agitation. Sheila leaned forward between the horned spikes on top of Ru-Lee's head and peered down sucking in her breath at the sight of six snarling, drooling demons blocking their way. The carnage beyond the beasts was partially shielded from sight by dust and smoke, but the sickening heavy smell of blood and gore hung thick in the air.

In the heartbeat of a second, the beasts launched themselves at Ru-Lee's head, neck, and chest. Ru-Lee surged forward to meet their onslaught, the bloodlust of the Warta Spirits crashing down her defenses. Shielding her neck and chest with her massive, armored head and deadly fangs, she caught the foremost fiend by the head with her jaws and tossed him into his cohorts. Boiling lava shot out of her gaping maw, frying the outer layer of the demons' tough skin before bouncing off to disappear in the battle that ensued beyond the tunnel opening.

Sheila instantly transformed, clothes flying. Pug screeched and took to the air, gliding back into the tunnel to circle above Jace. Rolling into a large silvery ball, Sheila bounced off of Ru-Lee's spine and bowled into Jace, Davlin, D.G., Rannue, Trieca, Relmar, and Nevlon. Pug screeched again, his cry piercing the air as Sheila sprang to her feet and briefly glanced at Relmar before darting towards Ru-Lee, quickly skittering up the wall past her friend's massive dragon body.

"WATCH IT!" Nevlon shouted, shoving the others out of the way as Ru-Lee's tail came crashing down where Jace had been crawling to his feet. Nevlon was caught a glancing blow on his foot as he danced back. "We need to get past Ru and out of this tunnel if we expect to be of any use—and if we hope to do so without getting crushed."

Jumping sideways to avoid the ever-moving tail, Rannue glanced at Nevlon suspiciously, "Wait….did you just call that dragon 'Ru'?"

Rolling his eyes as he helped Trieca and the others right themselves, Nevlon replied, "Yes…I will explain later—provided we all survive."

Rannue set his jaw and shook his head, but remained silent as he bent to assist Relmar who was crouched on his hands and knees, gasping and struggling for breath. "Nevlon!" Rannue called in alarm, squatting down to peer into Relmar's face. "What's wrong with him?"

Nevlon and Trieca ran to Relmar with Jace and Davlin close behind him. Nevlon knelt beside Relmar and placed his hand upon the young man's head. Speaking softly, he stretched out his mind to shield Relmar from the onslaught of emotions and thoughts that poured into him the moment Sheila shifted.

"Help me get him up," Nevlon ordered wrapping his left arm around Relmar's waist and Relmar's right arm across his shoulders. "He will be fine in a few minutes—just a bit overwhelmed right now."

Relmar shuddered painfully as Trieca and Nevlon lifted him. D.G. whimpered softly.

"You can say that again," Relmar whispered, slowly opening his eyes. Glancing at the shifted forms of his brothers he grinned, "I'll be fine—it's Ru that needs our help. These Warta are nasty creatures—be careful." Turning to Nevlon he grinned grimly, "Thanks for shielding me….I think I can handle it a bit better now. At least I am ready for it now. I can stand and you can release your shield—I'll manage. It just caught me off guard."

"Are you able to focus enough to draw on the stone's power?" Nevlon asked as he released Relmar.

Relmar breathed in deeply and drew the crimson firestone from his pocket. Eyeing it, he responded, "I think so….what do you want me to do with it?"

At that moment, Ru-Lee's roar split the air, rattling stones from the tunnel ceiling. It was a battle cry—a challenge to all comers. The small group of men and animals ducked and ran to the relative safety of the passage's stone wall to avoid the falling rocks. Beneath Ru-Lee's enormous front feet, clenched in her claws, the remains of shredded demon bodies could be seen. Putrid blood oozed from the corpses, pooling on the hard floor. Sheila stood over another, its body twitching violently as she injected venom deep into its neck.

Ru-Lee screamed her challenge again, a sound so menacing and loud that the men covered their ears and the animals cringed. Pug, apparently feeling emboldened by Ru-Lee's size and force, joined his voice with hers before gliding down to land on the back of Jace's neck, burrowing in as if settling into a tank before a battle.

Ru-Lee's challenge was answered, but not by demon voices. The voice that answered was that of the Warta Dragon, still battling the Harta that harangued his existence. His roar filled the cavern and Ru-Lee moved forward to meet him, spewing lava as she went.

Moving quickly along the wall with the others behind him, Nevlon shouted to Relmar, "Use the stone to draw forth the fire within you and create a wall that will allow us to slip past the Warta Dragon and his demons. You may be able to drain off some of his fire powers as well, but the rest will have to come from you." As they stood staring out at the deafening melee, Nevlon beckoned Trieca and Rannue forward, "Trieca, stick with your father—you will serve best there."

Trieca nodded and drew his bow before disappearing into the scrum of the fighting with Rannue.

Drawing Jace and Davlin to him, Nevlon murmured, "You two stay close to Sheila and Relmar. Protect her and help her get to the Heart." They nodded and D.G. sat on Nevlon's foot to gain his attention.

Nevlon grimaced, "OUCH! D.G., get off my foot! That's the one Ru got with her spiked tail!" Nevlon jerked his foot out from under D.G.'s haunches and glared down at the canine, "I need you to stick to Sheila. There's nothing you can do for Ru-Lee in this fight, but you can help Sheila reach the Heart."

D.G. grumbled and trotted over to Sheila, curling his lips in disgust at the demon body that lay near her still twitching.

"Relmar, you must get Sheila to the Heart—its imperative that she make it there. Don't let her get sidetracked in this mess."

Relmar narrowed his eyes at Nevlon, "You are still blocking me, aren't you? What aren't you telling me, Nevlon?"

Nevlon sighed, "Sometimes there are things that are best left unknown." Pushing up his sleeves and murmuring incantations as he went, Nevlon turned and stepped out of the tunnel. Electric shock waves thrust forth in front of him knocking back all combatants that were in his way and making a path for the others.

Relmar, Davlin, D.G., Sheila, and Jace—with Pug on board--slipped to the left of the tunnel opening, avoiding the dead and dying as they attempted to slip, unnoticed, past the fray towards the Heart.

# Chapter 71

Ru-Lee's heart filled with hatred and rage—rage so old and hatred so deep, she knew in her mind that it wasn't her own--it consumed her all the same. The rage drove up her body temperature, radiating heat waves that burned those who jostled against her as she progressed through the throng of fighting bodies.

Once out of the confines of the tunnel and into the spacious cavern, Ru-Lee arched her neck and spread her iridescent wings. She flexed her claws and bellowed again, showering the combatants with molten lava that bounced off the ceiling. Men, elves, dwarves, brownies, and demons alike cringed, yielding to her massive form—those that didn't were swept aside or crushed, depending on whose side they fought for or how quickly they moved. Many of the defenders paused to gape—some at the cost of their lives as the demons took advantage of the distraction to mix their lifeblood with the dust on the floor.

The screams of the dead and dying mingled with the throbbing rush of blood pounding in Ru-Lee's ears. Demons rushed at her from all sides to be quickly dispatched by her lightning-quick claws and gnashing jaws, tossed through the air like flotsam on the waves. Their blood dripped from her jaws and coated her talons. She roared again, shooting flames and lava towards the ceiling of the cave to rid her mouth of the putrid, poisonous taste of demon blood.

As the fire dissipated, she vaguely wondered where it had come from, recalling that only molten lava had heeded her call earlier. She hazily wondered if this was something the Warta Spirits had brought out in her—a question the Warta souls did not answer, their energies focused solely on locating their enemy---the Warta Dragon called Behkna.

Suddenly, her mind sizzled and the scales along her spine raised and rattled, like goose bumps rising along human skin. The flames beneath her hide flared, upping her body temperature yet again, causing her fevered eyes to water. A vile voice, oozing unconcealed evil, permeated her mind and echoed through her body.

*"What are you? What do you want here?"* the Warta Dragon hissed.

Through the smoky haze, the entangled shapes of the Harta Dragon and the Warta Dragon wrestled. Ru-Lee watched as the slightly smaller Harta Dragon was forced to the ground beneath the Warta's weight.

*"We are your end!"* the Warta Spirits growled, charging forward to ram Ru-Lee's body against Behkna's shoulder, knocking him off of the Harta Dragon just as he opened his jaws for the kill.

Curling his lips and wrinkling his snout in a loud snarl, the Warta Dragon ran his tongue across his fangs, righting himself to meet this new attacker. The Harta Dragon, bleeding from numerous gashes across its body, struggled to drag itself out of the line of fire as the spirits moved Ru-Lee's body to protect the Harta from further harm. Lowering his head, the Warta, Behkna, inhaled deeply. Narrowing his eyes, he glowered at this new challenger. Acidic saliva dripped from his jaws and his snout curled up in a vicious snarl.

Inside her body, Ru-Lee struggled to separate herself from the Warta Spirits, but their fury was unrelenting and all-consuming. Ru-Lee's heart and mind flooded with the raw emotions of the dozens of souls that now shared her body. Hatred and bloodlust took over, blinding her to all but the Warta Dragon that sized her up across the debris of the battle that raged around them. A high-pitched ringing whined in her ears, drowning out all other sound. She felt the Warta Dragon's mind search hers out, as the souls within her repelled his efforts.

*"We? You look to be one—Are there others like you hiding in this place?"* Behkna growled as he lowered his head and slowly sidled sideways, looking for a weak point he could attack on this new foe.

*"Like you, we are many within one body,"* the spirits answered cryptically as Ru-Lee lowered her head and began to circle opposite Behkna, lips curled back to reveal fangs loaded with venom, another new development in her seemingly ever-changing body.

Behkna seemed not to notice as the poison dripped to the stone floor with sizzling hisses, creating small fissures in the hard rock. He stopped his sideways motion and cocked his head, regarding his opponent with narrow slitted green eyes. *"I am only one—there are NONE like me!"* he snarled vehemently.

The spirits within Ru-Lee laughed, their voices mocking, *"True—there is only one called Behkna, but you have created this new body of yours with the blood and souls of thousands."* Suddenly, the voices turned fierce, filled with rage, *"You have joined the cores of many of your own brothers, allowing your soul to devour them so that you could gain strength both in this world and the world you inhabited from your birth. You are NOT of this world---what you have become does not belong here! How did you learn of your ancestry while you still lived?"*

The Warta Dragon narrowed his eyes, glaring at Ru-Lee through the hazy darkness as if his very gaze could dissolve her heart. *"Who are you that you know these things?"* he growled, his voice low and measured.

The Ancient One's voice now rose above the others, its deep gravelly tones resonating throughout the cavern, not just within Ru-Lee's mind or that of her foe. The spirit of this ancient soul filled her body, pushing the other Warta Spirits out of the way and overtaking Ru-Lee. It drew her body up to her full height, the natural armor-plating on her chest scales shimmering in the light cast off by the flames dancing across her body. *"We are the ancestors of those who came before you. We have watched you within the human world. We have seen what you have become, what you have caused to be in the other world, and what you have done to your brethren. We know what you wish to do here. We are giving you a chance to redeem your actions—a chance we never received. You must stop now, or you will never find peace—alive or dead. Your soul will never rest."*

Fire blazed in a tunnel to the left of the two dragons. Cries of fighting carried with it the scent of blood and death, but the behemoths did not shift from the cavern. Behkna's acidic tones filled with sadistic laughter, *"Peace! A thing I have never sought! There will be peace only when I have left this earth!"*

*"Not even then,"* the Ancient One responded quietly. *"We ask again—how did you learn of your origins while you still lived?"*

Behkna began to move again, his voice now silken and filled with self-importance, *"I worked in a lab with humans, torturing small creatures for the military—finding new ways to inflict pain. Some humans like that, you know, inflicting pain. I enjoyed my work...it was....rewarding.*

*"One day, we got a new batch of rodents in—all black. Some were quite large and appeared to be somewhat intelligent—imagine my surprise when the largest of them tried to speak to me! Of course, it wasn't anything that I understood, but it was words, nonetheless."*

Ru-Lee danced out of reach just as Behkna lunged at her shoulder, fangs bared. He chuckled, ran his tongue over his fangs, and continued speaking as if he hadn't attempted to attack her, *"After a few weeks, I was able to understand some of what the mouse was saying—he understood more of my language than I did his, but we were able to communicate--after a fashion.*

*"He told me fantastic tales of another land where 'my people'—my ancestors—were great rulers and his people were our assistants--assassins and informers--really wild stories...but entertaining, nonetheless.*

*"He filled me in on the history of this place and the banishment of my ancestors. I didn't believe it at first, but, after awhile, some of it began to make a sort of sense. He helped me find others, like myself that had certain...quirks.*

*Some of them didn't even have a clue that they were different. Those were the easiest to lure in.*

*"I was able to convince my supervisors that we needed these individuals to further our research. We accessed their DNA and I was able to isolate certain genes and anomalies that appeared in all of them, as well as myself. The rest was simple. I siphoned off the part of them that I suspected would transform—the dragon part, and infused it with my own DNA. I left them with some small changes that would allow a shift, but would not allow them to become a dragon—there can be only ONE true dragon, you see."*

Crouching low, Ru-Lee answered, *"Unfortunately, it won't be you."* She lunged forward, catching Behkna in the chest with her horned head and slamming him back against the cavern wall. Rock and dust cascaded around them as they ripped at each other with their talons and twisted their necks together, jaws snapping. They tumbled through the cave, crushing cadavers as they went. The other combatants did their best to avoid being trampled by the enormous dragons, attempting to move their fights to the wide tunnels and anterooms leading away from the cavern where there was little fear of being trodden by the beasts.

Ru-Lee curled her claws into Behkna's shoulder and flapped her huge wings, lifting him off the ground. The space was choked with swirling debris. Sparks bounced off the walls, and dust devils spun, thickening the air. Behkna slashed through the leathery webbing of Ru-Lee's left wing. She screamed as they crashed to the floor, rattling the ceiling. Huge boulders tumbled down upon them, bouncing off their armored scales. They ripped free from each other, rolling apart and sending all beings running for safety as the peak of the mountain caved in on them.

# Chapter 72

The bright light of midmorning streaked into the gaping hole that had been the peak of Mount Shavla to filter through the settling dust and debris left behind. Silence weighed heavy in the cave, broken by the cries and growls of the battles still raging in other parts of the mountain.

Three Dahgsna dragons and several dwarves who had been stationed near the main entrance providing a second line of defense against the onslaught of demon spawn, pushed into the main cavern through a side tunnel as the dust began to clear. Demons that had retreated to the relative safety of the cave walls to avoid the cavalcade of stones now circled in towards the newcomers. The possibility that their master may have been dispatched by the falling stones did not dampen their thirst for blood. Several clambered atop the rubble, growling a challenge to the new foes in this cavernous arena.

The Dahgsna Dragons grinned, spread their wings, and launched themselves over the dwarves towards the snarling fiends. Snatching the enemy in their talons, they shot upwards into the morning sky, bellowing in triumph. They soared high as the demons twisted and screamed in fury and frustration, unable to reach their attackers or free themselves. The Dahgnsa climbed nearly straight upwards to a dizzying height, bent their heads to snap the neck of their cargo, and released the limp bodies to drop back into the mountain. They roared in unison as they circled to the rim of what once was the peak of Mt. Shavla and landed, peering hungrily at their enemy milling below.

The remaining demons stalked the dwarves, saliva hanging in gelatinous threads from their jaws in anticipation of easy kills. From a side tunnel, a battered and cloaked figure emerged--Nevlon. A soft murmur of unintelligible words strung together in a chant as the man walked closer. The rear-most fiend stopped its forward progress and turned to investigate the source of this new

318

sound. The man stopped and slowly raised his arms, the chant growing louder and stronger, echoing off the cave walls. The Dahgnsa curiously watched from above, waiting to see if their services were needed.

As the sound of the incantation swelled to fill the space, most of the demons turned towards Nevlon—only two continued towards the stalwart dwarves who stood ready for their attack. The stones below the beasts began to shift, causing some to lose their balance and scramble to get off the pile quickly. They did not move fast enough—the man's voice rose to a crescendo and the air thundered with an electric force that blasted the demons into the air, thrusting them against the walls and removing the topmost layer of rock from the buried dragons.

At the same instant, Ru-Lee and Behkna burst from the debris sending boulders and stones flying through the air. Nevlon dove to the safety of another side tunnel, the dwarves darted back the way they had come, and the Dahgsna kept watch from above as Behkna renewed his attacked on Ru-Lee.

The Warta Dragon caught Ru-Lee's neck in its jaws and closed his crushing fangs around her armored throat, choking her and pressing her body back until she lay on her side. His teeth were unable to penetrate her scales, but they pressed tightly against her windpipe. She flailed and clawed, catching his underbelly with her hind talons. Feeling her claws dig into Behkna's gut, she thrust deeper, flexing her digits as she went. He wrenched on her neck and growled, thrusting her away from him as he released his grip. Her talons sliced free of his belly, rivers of blood spilling over the rocks beneath him.

He staggered back across the rubble and against the wall, glaring and gasping. Out of the corner of her eye, Ru-Lee caught a glimpse of movement—quick, dark shapes darted across the floor from one of the smaller tunnels to run up Behkna's back. One of the small furry forms scampered up the Warta Dragon's spines to the top of his head near his ear. Behkna tilted his head sideways, eyes narrowing as he listened.

Suddenly, he hissed, *"Enough of this! I have more important things to attend to than you!"* He twisted his body as he dove sideways into the wide tunnel opening down which the dwarves had so recently disappeared.

Ru-Lee lay on her side gasping for air, momentarily dazed and confused by the events that had just transpired. As she lay there, the Dahgsna dragons swooped down to gather up the bewildered demons that were slowly rousing after Nevlon's blast. Grasping the stunned beasts, the dragons dug their knife-like talons into thick flesh and carried them away to be dismembered and destroyed before they could cause any further problems.

Ru-Lee struggled to her feet and shook her head attempting to clear her mind before diving into the passage after the Warta Dragon. The muffled sounds of fighting echoed in the tunnel ahead of her, causing her heart to race. Behkna's scent mingled with the stench of blood and death, filling her nostrils. The Warta Spirits within her flooded her heart with hate and fury, calling for Behkna's death. Her lips curled involuntarily, baring her fangs as a low snarl rose in her throat. Her mind throbbed with a willingness to comply with the wishes of the souls that inhabited her body--no longer caring if those wishes were hers or theirs alone.

The tunnel was close and confining and the air vibrated with the emotions of those ahead of her. Fear, fury, bloodlust, and hatred wove together in a tight web, making it difficult to distinguish the emotions of her enemies from those of the individuals she sought to protect. The passage twisted and turned, descending sharply. Trickles of warm water rippled and shimmered as they cascaded down the walls and ran in small rivers down the edges of the tunnel, pooling in low spots on the stone floor to make the rock slick as ice.

Ru-Lee slipped, crashing into the wet stone. Her hot scales hissed and sizzled as water from the wall washed over them.

The voice of the Ancient One grated in her mind, *"He's headed for the Heart."*

Righting herself, Ru-Lee moved forward and growled, *"And just what will happen once he gets there? Will he get stronger?"*

*"We don't know—but he must be stopped! Nothing good will come of him reaching the Heart!"*

*"Great!"* Ru-Lee grumbled as she lost her footing yet again and went sliding into the wall along the wet floor. *"There seems to be a lot more water here than necessary!"* she grunted, slamming into the wall where the tunnel made a sharp turn. *"Any ideas why?"*

*"You can ask your elven friends when you see them again---they always did like playing with water,"* the spirits replied in disgust.

Screams reverberated through the tunnel, shattering the darkness ahead of her. Rounding another corner, Ru-Lee caught the slight glimmer of scales on a tail as it glided quickly out of sight in front of her.

*"It would seem that Behkna is clearing the path,"* the spirits growled.

Ru-Lee held her tongue and charged forward, her heart pounding with fear--hoping her friends and family were not among those whose shrieks pierced her ears.

# Chapter 73

Relmar focused on the firestone, attempting to draw the fire forth from it as he raced along the edge of the cavern wall with Sheila and his brothers, partially hidden by smoke and dust. Occasional bursts of dragon flames illuminated the haze to reveal the grappling shadows of fiendish beasts, glittering steel from drawn weapons, and mutilated bodies of the dead and dying. From somewhere in the murky battle, Nevlon's powerful electrical waves crackled through the air, fracturing Relmar's concentration and causing his hair to stand on end and his skin to prickle as it vibrated through the cavern.

Relmar's brow furrowed, his jaw set, and beads of sweat dripped down his nose as he glared in frustration at the stone. Sheila sidestepped into him, herding him away from and around two swarthy dwarves that were ferociously battling a medium-sized demon. An elven arrow buried itself deep into the fiend's throat as they swept past. Startled, Relmar glanced through the haze to catch a momentary glimpse of Trieca notching another arrow. Beside him, Rannue swung his sword, beheading one of the demons that threatened to overrun them. In the next instant, the father and son were hidden from sight, swallowed by the smoke and dust.

Sheila's melodic voice broke through his mind as he tried to refocus, *"You cannot get fire from the stone—you must use the stone to draw on your own internal flame,"* she admonished softly. *"The spark lies within you."*

Jace stumbled into Relmar's back, ducking as a stray arrow zinged over his head to clatter harmlessly against the stone wall.

Clenching his teeth, Relmar growled in response to his youngest brother's unspoken feelings, "You want to try getting fire from a rock, Bro?"

Jace curled his lips back to reveal his fangs and snorted derisively.

322

"Whatever!" Relmar snapped. "You can take it up with Nevlon when we see him—if we see him—right now, just stop thinking so I can concentrate---shouldn't be too tough for you!"

Jace glared at Relmar and smacked him in the shoulder with his hard head before turning to help D.G. and Davlin fend off one of the demons that had slipped up behind them.

Relmar held the firestone tightly in his right hand as he ran near Sheila. Pulling it to his chest, he tried to force his mind inward to draw forth the flame he hoped resided in his soul. Slowly, the stone began to warm in his grasp. Heat spread up his arm and flooded his chest. He momentarily wondered why the warmth seemed to originate in the stone, but it seemed of little consequence. The heat raced to his core and poured through his body, radiating waves of warmth around him—the stone in his hand glowed red, drawing out the fire that flared in his heart. His eyes burned and the scene around him took on an eerie glow. He blinked, trying to clear his vision. Suddenly, the flames in his body flared to life and ripped through him. He screamed in shock and pain, stumbling into Sheila. A wall of flames burst from his raised hand, shooting out several feet on either side to form a protective shield between Sheila, himself, D.G., and his brothers. The shield protected them from the battle on one side, the stone wall offered protection on the other. Only their front and flank were left exposed. Speed and Sheila's deadly venomous fangs were enough protection for the front, leaving the others to guard their backs. Demons that had been closing in on them on what had been their exposed side now snarled and snapped, retreating from the flames and attempting to circle around behind the group to avoid the fire's heat and sting.

Davlin, Jace, and D.G. held them off, using their claws to inflict as much damage as possible as they tried to keep up with Relmar and Sheila and stay behind the shield. D.G. engaged the demons head-on, snarling and snapping to distract them while Davlin slipped around beside or behind them. Swiftly reaching beneath their unwieldy bodies, Davlin sliced through their thick hide and spilled their entrails, their putrid blood spurting onto the ground. Jace ripped his long claws down an attacking demon's throat while Pug darted off his neck to dive at the beast's face and blind it with his talons. These tactics were repeated several times as the group dodged their way through the mêlée of battle, leaving wounded demons in their wake to be devoured by their brethren.

The crunch of Ru-Lee's head smashing into the Warta Dragon echoed around them and they doubled their speed hoping to avoid being crushed. Sheila slowed slightly and tilted her head as they approached each passageway leading away from the cavern, listening intently. She seemed to know what she was looking for as they passed several small tunnels and the large passage to the main entrance, slowing slightly at each one.

She edged close to listen at the edge of yet another channel, as the voice of one of the Warta Spirits spoke through Ru-Lee, shaking the walls. The combatants in the cave cringed, moving closer to the walls and slipping down side tunnels, hoping to escape the behemoth's wrath.

The dusty haze, smoke, and darkness hid most of what was happening from view, but Relmar's fire revealed the enormous, shadowy form of Ru-Lee, pulled up to her full height, the Warta Dragon, crouched low and menacing in front of her. He hoped Sheila decided on their route quickly—the cavern did not seem to be a good place to hang out.

*"This way!"* Sheila hissed in his mind as she darted down the narrow tunnel she had been contemplating. Relmar, Davlin, Jace, and D.G. quickly followed, glad to be away from the giant dragons and the eminent battle between them.

The group plunged into the dark silence of the passageway. The dancing light given off by Relmar's flames played upon the wall, illuminating their course.

Behind Relmar, Davlin's lightening-quick claws disemboweled a demon that had recklessly followed them, its body lurching against Jace. The furious fiend lashed out, digging its razor-sharp claws into the bear's thick haunch fur, grazing across his already scarred hind-end. Jace howled and rounded on the beast, slashing its throat with his own knife-like claws and thrusting the demon's body away. Others that might be following would slow their pursuit to finish off the wounded one in their path, giving the group more time to reach the Heart unfettered.

Sheila set a break-neck speed, her spider legs scampering wildly in the semi-darkness. Relmar allowed the flame emanating from the stone to die back slightly, becoming an illuminating flame in his hand rather than a shielding fire. His breath came in hoarse gasps as he struggled to keep up with his charge. D.G., tongue hanging out, ran easily alongside him. Davlin's lithe body glided noiselessly through the tunnel, seemingly oblivious to the injuries that allowed small rivers of blood to slide down his legs and sides. Jace brought up the rear. Huffing loudly, he kept pace, trickles of blood from various wounds making dark stains on his blonde coat. Pug burrowed into Jace's neck fur. Digging in his talons, he scrunched his head deep into his shoulders and clung to the bear as the group raced forward.

Rounding a corner, the floor seemed to disappear beneath them, arcing sharply downward. Jace let out a startled growl as he missed his step in the dark and trampled D.G.'s paw; Pug screeched and freed himself from Jace's neck, launching his feathered body towards the low ceiling; D.G. let out a yelp, sidestepping into Davlin and knocking his feet out from under him; Davlin yowled, his body becoming entangled with Jace and D.G. as they crashed into Relmar and Sheila, knocking their legs out from under them and extinguishing Relmar's light; Sheila toppled onto her round back, adding her flailing legs to the mass of bodies that was tumbling downward in the dark. Pug glided silently over the struggling mass of bodies and fur, watching helplessly as his friends careened out of control.

Jace, D.G., and Davlin tried in vain to slow their descent, their claws scraping long pale lines in the stone walls and floor. Relmar clasped the firestone in his hand, trying to focus his mind enough to summon the flames as he worked to brace his body against the tunnel walls with his legs and arms. The firestone flared to life in his palm and Relmar suddenly realized Sheila was no longer falling with them. He rolled onto his stomach and jerked his head, darting his gaze in every direction as he tumbled. His right foot caught momentarily on the floor, forcing his body slightly upright and backwards again. The fire went out once more and he closed his eyes, clenching his muscles as he prepared himself to crash into the stone wall.

The crash never came. Instead, his descent was halted by something springy and damp. Before he could open his eyes to inspect this new development, Jace, D.G., and Davlin smashed into him, forcing the breath from his body.

"OFF!" Relmar groaned beneath the mass of fur. "GET OFF!" He pushed and shoved at the large furry bodies until the others had moved off of his chest and he could breathe again. He tried to stand, but found he was stuck to the substance that had stopped him. Pug glided down to land on his stomach, cocking his fluffy head to one side curiously. Feeling the firestone still in his hand, Relmar quickly summoned its light to reveal thick white strands of sticky netting holding them fast. Jace, Davlin, and D.G. had rolled off of Relmar to find their fur stuck firmly in the web.

A soft, tinkling voice cascaded through their minds, *"Sorry about the stickiness, but it was the only way to slow everyone down."* Sheila's luminescent eyes eerily reflected the firelight as she scurried towards them from the ceiling, carefully navigating along the webbing.

326

"Didn't know you could do that," Relmar grunted as he and the others struggled to free themselves.

*"I have used webbing before, when I was smaller, but I wasn't sure it would stop you. I am glad it worked,"* Sheila responded with a spidery grin.

"Any idea how we get free?" Relmar asked, closing his eyes and stilling his body in resignation.

*"Not sure—I have never let anything go before—not on purpose at least."*

Jace laid his ears tight against his head, curled his lips and snarled at this, flexing his claws.

*"Don't worry, Jace—you would probably give me heartburn---although the thought is tempting!"* Sheila chuckled.

"Um, can we focus here? We need to keep moving, right?" Relmar asked, rolling his eyes and glaring at his youngest brother.

Sheila approached him and carefully lifted him free of the sticky entrapment. *"See those two threads there?"* she asked, pointing one of her legs at two lengths of netting that appeared thicker and dryer than the others.

Relmar nodded.

*"They are not as sticky...shine your light below them and you will see that the tunnel levels out a bit just beyond us. If you drop down from those threads, you should be safe."*

Relmar cautiously crawled along the parallel rope-like threads, slipped his body between the netting, and dropped softly to the floor. Keeping the fire held aloft, he watched Sheila release Davlin and D.G., with minimal hair removal. As she made her way to Jace, a low growl rumbled deep in his throat. His ears pinned tight to his head, he tossed and jerked his body trying to free himself.

"Just let her work, Jace!" Relmar ordered as Jace struggled against his bonds causing D.G. to slip and fall to the stone floor with a sharp yelp. Davlin was able to crouch low and dig in his feline claws until the movement of the web ceased and he could safely drop down near his brother and D.G.. Pug had taken to the air again as Sheila worked on Relmar. He now winged through an opening in the webbed net to land on Relmar's shoulder. His large eyes gleamed as he watched his friend, Jace's panic palpable in the air.

Jace curled his lips back to reveal his long teeth, but stilled himself and waited for Sheila to release him. She tugged and pulled with her legs, working delicately. Jace growled softly whenever his fur was pulled too roughly, but he was firmly held in the gooey substance covering the strands of the web. Sheila stepped back and regarded him for a moment before moving back in. Tipping her head sideways, she lifted his shoulder with her front legs.

Relmar grimaced as he watched Sheila's long pinchers work like shears along the strand beneath his brother's shoulder. "She's going to have to cut your fur, Jace---don't move!"

Jace's eyes nearly bulged out of his head. He yelped, jerked away from Sheila, and shifted instantly.

"Oh no she isn't!" he yelled. "Just pull me free—I'll shift back when I am out of this thing!"

Sheila clacked her pinchers together and grinned as she non-too-gently pulled him free, leaving bits of his skin behind on the web. He quickly scurried across the ropes and dropped down next to his brothers and D.G., the fire shimmering off his bare butt.

"Not one word!" Jace snarled to Relmar who was grinning widely, barely able to contain his laughter.

Davlin sat on his haunches and licked his front paw, pretending not to notice Jace, but there was no mistaking the feline smile that split his features. D.G. grinned widely. Tongue hanging out of his mouth and eyes crinkled, he grunted his laughter. Pug just blinked, his wide eyes revealing nothing of his sentiments.

Jace huffed and shifted back to bear form quickly, while Sheila navigated her way around the web to join them, being too large to squeeze through the netting.

"We should leave that in place, maybe," Relmar suggested, surveying the net that shimmered above them. "It might catch a demon or two."

*"We can, but I haven't sensed any following us—have you?"* Sheila, her voice soft in his mind.

"No—but it doesn't hurt to be cautious," Relmar responded. He turned the light of his fire towards the lower end of the tunnel and listened. "Do you hear that?"

A low thrumming song vibrated as soft as silk through the darkness. It bounced off the walls and ceiling in rolling waves, washing over them in a mesmerizing way that seemed to pull them forward.

*"Yes,"* Sheila answered, moving quickly past him towards the sound. *"I think it is the Heart."*

The small group moved cautiously forward following Sheila deeper into the mountain—none but D.G. seemed to notice the warm trickles of water that gently caressed the tunnel walls, gliding down to form slippery pools on the steep stone floor.

# Chapter 74

Startled screams and confused curses ripped through the air in the entrance cavern as thousands of vicious black mice wielding tiny sharp swords attacked the unsuspecting defenders of Mt. Shavla.  The attackers charged up pant legs like fire-ants, slicing into the main arteries that run deep in the thigh and hacking at the tender parts that reside in the groin.  Some scrambled up their foes' bodies to rip open their jugular veins before their enemies realized what was happening.  Many defenders were overrun by the hordes of ferocious rodents to be buried in their writhing black mass.  Others swatted, kicked, and flung the furry beast away, popping off their heads when possible.

A large Harta Dragon swept his tail across the floor, clearing it of hundreds of mice, as well as the bodies of the fallen.  The remaining rodents brandished their swords.  Roaring a battle cry, they attacked the Harta Dragon.  Clambering up his scaly tail and legs, some sought to reach his head and blind him with their weapons.  Others appeared to be attempting to find his vulnerable underbelly, but kept sliding down his armored legs to be squashed beneath his feet or sliced in half by his talons.  Turning furious golden eyes upon his attackers, the Harta regarded the angry mass briefly before spewing dragon fire that roasted some of the rodents, turning others to ash.

A stunned silence momentarily filled the cave entrance as the dragon huffed, clearing the ashes and fried rodent bodies from his glowing scales.  A few men, elves, and dwarves who had been too close to the Harta when he blasted the mice blinked dazedly before tossing smoking hats to the ground and feeling for sparks in their own hair and beards.

The respite was brief as more black bodies poured into the space vacated by their brethren, resuming their attack.  A small contingent of rodents peeled out of the group, slipping unnoticed down a side tunnel.  As the last of this small cluster disappeared, two black panthers burst from the same tunnel the mice had just vacated, scattering small furry bodies as they went. Their own bodies hidden in the darkness and chaos of battle, they proceeded to wreak havoc on the trailing attackers, unnoticed by the defenders they sought to help.

Aylon and Triya followed, cautiously peering into the smoky darkness, the sounds of pain and dying reverberating in their ears.

Aylon looked sideways to Triya, "Do you have a plan here?"

Triya slowly shook her head and airily replied, "No—we are no use here. Nevlon will need you at the Heart. We must go there."

Aylon sighed heavily. 'Fine---do you know the way?"

Triya blinked and looked at her with a sidelong smile, "Don't you?"

Aylon's shoulders slumped momentarily and she pressed her palm to her temple, shaking her head. "You give me a headache!" she groaned. Lifting her head, she gazed into the hazy battle and closed her eyes, listening. She had heard that the Heart sang to you, if you were listening closely—but how was she to hear anything over the din of battle? She opened her eyes and glared at Triya.

"You're the seer, find the way!" she growled.

Triya shrugged and looked around. Tilting her head to the right, she pointed to the tunnel opening just to the left of theirs, "That one appears to be a good choice."

Dragon fire blazed though the cavern, barely missing the two women as they raced to the next passageway and dove for safety. Scrambling to their feet, they hugged the stone wall and ran into its darkness, listening for the Heart's song that would guide them into the mountain's depths.

# Chapter 75

Deep in the bowels of Mt. Shavla, Ru-Lee splashed through the darkness, barely able to make out the shadowy shapes of other tunnel openings and the bodies of the dead and dying that had been left behind by Behkna. She quickly touched each with her mind as she swept past hoping she wouldn't find any of her party among the scattered remains. Finding none of her friends and family, she pushed their pain aside and pressed on. Her lungs burned and her heart pounded loudly in her chest as she ran trying to detect the Warta Dragon's mind ahead of her in the dark, but she found nothing—nothing but the agony of those around her.

Ru-Lee became dimly aware of a low melodic hum echoing off of the tunnel walls--the Heart's song. It thrummed through the air, barely audible over the roar of blood in her ears. As she slid around yet another turn in the tunnel, Ru-Lee saw a faint glow illuminating the glistening walls ahead. The trickling sound of water joined with the melody of the Heart, gently numbing her senses. She shook her head attempting to clear her mind of the music's mesmerizing pull, but the yearning of the Warta Spirits pushed her forward. She snorted, grappling to maintain a hold on her consciousness, aware that Behkna could be waiting just out of sight.

*"Get a grip!"* she growled to the spirits as they propelled her body ever closer. *"Can you sense him? Can you read Behkna's mind? I've lost him!"*

The Ancient One answered, his voice low and subdued, *"He is ahead—we cannot hear him, but we feel him. He is lost in the Heart's presence--confused."*

*"You don't sound much better yourself,"* Ru-Lee grumbled, sliding into the wall as she rounded yet another corner.

Warm golden light engulfed Ru-Lee as she burst from the passageway into a large cavern that appeared to be linked to several other tunnels all around its walls. She pulled up short, sucking in her breath. The Heart's song flowed through her, vibrating along her spine and ringing off of her scales. It swelled in her mind, nudging out all thought and filling her soul with longing. The voices of the Warta Spirits were silent within her, allowing the energy of the Heart to course through them as well.

Light radiated from the center of the space, spilling out from beneath a glowing orb. As Ru-Lee gazed at the sight before her, she realized that the orb was the enormous body of a stone spider—Gertrude, The Aged One….the Guardian. Ru-Lee blinked and looked closer. The spider's body was not the smooth shining white of Sheila's, but grey and rough. There were cracks and bumps covering its surface, as if time were breaking it down. Gertrude's head lay upon folded legs, her many eyes filmy with age as they tried to focus on something to the left of the tunnel from which Ru-Lee had emerged.

Ru-Lee slowly turned, as if in a trance, following Gertrude's gaze. Behkna stood against the wall. He shook his head vigorously and pulled it back on his long neck, blinking wildly. His breathing was rapid and shallow, as if in shock. His mouth hung open, saliva dripping from his jowls.

*"What's wrong with him?"* Ru-Lee asked the Warta Spirits.

Their voices were soft and muted as they replied, *"He is confused. He has fused the powers of so many to himself, that he does not know who, or what, he is."*

Ru-Lee blinked and breathed deeply, *"I don't understand…"*

*"The Heart, and its Guardian, reveal who and what we truly are--our strengths and our weaknesses—it expands on them. Our true natures are brought forth and strengthened. That is why, when humans pass into this world, they find they have talents that were hidden from them in their own world. The Heart draws out their talents, powers, and abilities. It strengthens them."*

*"That's a good thing, right?"*

*"It can be....but it works without discrimination. The power of the Heart will strengthen ALL talents, powers and abilities, both good and evil."*

Ru-Lee crouched low, bringing her body close to the wall, *"That could be a problem, couldn't it?"*

*"It could be, for you, at least."*

Perplexed, Ru-Lee asked, *"What do you mean 'for me'? Aren't we working together on this?"*

The Warta Spirits chuckled, *"For now we are. Remember, we are made of the same stuff as Behkna. He is just more....ruthless than we dreamed of being in our lifetimes. That is why you need us. You, on your own, do not possess enough evil and hatred to do what must be done.....but we do. Can't you feel it growing within us?"*

Ru-Lee stilled her mind and listened to the murmuring voices of the souls within her. Their true natures swelled in her body, threatening to crush her own spirit. Vile hatred and evil poured into her heart like a caustic liquid, overshadowing her being. The poison-filled fangs that the Warta Spirits had brought forth in her mouth dripped in anticipation as she watched Behkna struggling with himself. Her own desires and thoughts, though strengthened by the nearness of the Heart, were held in check by the parasitic souls that she played host to.

The Ancient One's gravely voice, menacingly low and now free of the Heart's trance, whispered in Ru-Lee's mind, *"We must take him down before he gets control of himself. He will kill the Guardian and make himself ruler and destroyer of this world and its inhabitants if we do not act quickly."*

A wicked grin, not her own, split Ru-Lee's maw; her eyes narrowed malevolently as her tongue slid around her fangs, tasting her own poison. Deep within her psyche, her mind and soul cried out against the cruel anticipation forming in her heart, only to be squelched by the malicious desires of the Warta Spirits that had stealthily begun to inch her body towards their dazed opponent.

Behkna's breathing steadied and his body hunched slightly as he glared at Gertrude's glowing form in front of him, oblivious to Ru-Lee's approach. Small dark creatures seated between his horns and ears on either side spied her. One of them whispered a warning into the beast's ear. Behkna growled and whipped his head in Ru-Lee's direction, spewing fire. Ru-Lee lowered her head, letting the fire lick at her protective scales, her body seeming to absorb its energy. The flames within her flared, dancing wildly across her skin. The Warta Spirits laughed sadistically, their own voices mingling together eerily as they emanated from Ru-Lee's body. They opened her maw and blasted Behkna with fiery lava that drove him stumbling back against the smooth cavern walls. The creatures that had been perched upon Behkna's head were knocked off or burned to ash in an instant.

One of furry bodies rolled into Ru-Lee's massive front claws. She wrinkled her nose and bent to sniff it, wondering what sort of creature it was. As it lay dying, it opened its eyes and defiantly stabbed her in the snout with a miniscule sharp sword. She jerked her head back and snorted, frying the mouse—for mouse it was---with a burst of fire that turned it to a small pile of ash. Ha-Fart! The Creature had been Ha-Fart, the Shaooganah that had travelled with them! Traitor! The words screamed in her mind and she heard the echo of the Warta Spirits' laughter.

*"What did you expect? The Shaooganah were ours long ago...the groveling beasts always desire to rise against those above them!"*

The room around her shimmered and swam red before her. Her own fury and indignation mingled with the emotions of the Warta Spirits', allowing their hatred to pour through her. Her scream of rage reverberated throughout the cave causing the Guardian spider to turn her head and regard Ru-Lee with milky eyes.

Ru-Lee charged Behkna, planning to unbalance him and drive her poisonous fangs into his unprotected underbelly. She had wounded him there earlier--his blood now seeping onto the ground to form a dark pool in the water beneath him. She dove beneath him, crashing her shoulder into his and seeking his open wound. Her poisonous fangs found nothing and her jaws snapped closed on air as the crushing weight of Behkna's hind foot landed on her neck, pinning her head to the wet floor.

Ru-Lee's body thrashed violently, clawing at Behkna's side and back and lashing his head repeatedly with her spiked tail while her front legs pushed against his neck and head to hold off his deadly fangs. Scales were ripped from Behkna's body to fly through the air like large shimmering raindrops, landing with soft splashes on the water-covered floor.

As Behkna pulled his head back to strike at her, Ru-Lee managed to wrap her tail around his snake-like neck. She yanked her tail back and shoved her legs against him, thrusting his body away from her and slamming it into a tunnel opening. She scrambled to her feet, gasping for air and shaking her head violently. Her eyes narrowed, zeroing in on the Warta Dragon. The space around her disappeared, her vision flooded with blood-red hatred. A deep growl rolled from her body and she launched herself, fangs bared.

Behkna rolled and twisted as Ru-Lee's jaws grazed his neck, spilling acidic poison onto his scales. He danced out of reach and whipped his tail through the air, narrowly missing Ru-Lee's head.

*"You are a nuisance!"* he growled, diving in to rip scales from her chest.

Ru-Lee spewed lava in his face, forcing him back. *"You have no idea what a nuisance we can be!"* the Spirits within her replied.

Behkna belched fire, scorching the wall in front of Ru-Lee and boiling the water around their feet. Gertrude stood, clacking her pinchers and extending her fangs. The humming music of the Heart took on a menacing tone, growing and filling the room as it rose to a crescendo. Gertrude turned her body towards Behkna, the light beneath her swelling to engulf her body in a protective encasement.

Behind Ru-Lee, a black mass of rodents slipped unnoticed into the cave. Several darted beneath Ru-Lee's body and scrambled up her tail towards her head. The rest scurried towards the Heart, cautiously approaching the perimeter of bright light

"*We have company,*" The Ancient One hissed in Ru-Lee's mind. Feeling the tickle of tiny feet on her spine, Ru-Lee twitched her scales, sending several of the mice rolling to the floor. Behkna roared, feeding the flames of her body with his own fires and frying the mice that were unprotected on her body. One, however, managed to make it up near her ear and prepared to drive his sword deep inside as she lunged at Behkna, smashing the side of her head against his chest and crushing the unwanted passenger against Behkna's scales, leaving a gooey mush in its place.

The remaining mice gazed in awe at the area encasing the Heart and the Guardian, apparently unsure of their next move. One inched closer, as if in a trance. He raised himself up on his hind legs and boldly reached out as if to touch the light. The light caressed his fur and he was suddenly sucked into it, vanishing with a terrified high-pitched squeal that was lost in the music of the Heart and the din of the battling dragons. The other rodents retreated, scurrying back to the tunnel they had emerged from and disappearing into the darkness.

Behkna and Ru-Lee rose up on their hind feet, snapping, snarling, and grappling for deadly purchase on the other's body. Behkna flapped his huge wings, berating Ru-Lee while he tore at her belly scales seeking a weak spot. He found it and tore a long shallow gash down her midsection. Blood rippled to the surface, oozing down the inside of her leg. She screamed and sunk her fangs into Behkna's shoulder with a vengeance that snapped some of his scales and drove her poisonous venom deep into his flesh. He bellowed, arching his back in agony as the toxin

337

entered his bloodstream. Ru-Lee held on, pumping more and more poison into Behkna's system as his body twisted and writhed, seeking release. Behkna thrashed violently, jerking back against the wall and pulling Ru-Lee's venomous fangs free of her jaws, still imbedded deep in his shoulder.

Ru-Lee crouched low, watching—ready in case her opponent attacked her again. Behkna glared at her, his eyes filling with panic and rage.

*"This isn't finished!"* he hissed. Pushing himself away from the wall, he lunged forward.

Ru-Lee sidestepped, striking his back with her horned head to deflect his charge and turning her body to fight, expecting Behkna to spin around and come for her again. He didn't turn. Instead, the behemoth dove towards the center of the cavern and the light exuding from the Heart. As it swept over him, his eyes shot open in astonishment and fear. He tried to turn, but his speed and size carried him in and he was swallowed up, his terrified screams echoing through the cavern and the tunnels.

XXX    XXX    XXX    XXX    XXX

Across from the roaring, clashing dragons, shielded by the blinding light emanating from the Heart, Sheila, D.G., Davlin, Relmar, Jace, and Pug tumbled free of a water-slide-like side tunnel in a jumble of bodies, legs, fur, and feathers, sliding to a stop just short of the pulsing light surrounding the Guardian.

Relmar groaned, squeezed his eyes shut tight, clasped his head in his hands and struggled to his knees, the thoughts and emotions of those around him flooding through his psyche. Sheila quickly untangled herself from the others and slowly approached the pillar of light as if in a dream, her body glowing and growing.

As Behkna dove into the light on the opposite side of the pillar, Nevlon burst into the cavern to Sheila's left, splashing ankle-deep through the slowly rising water. He cast his glance from side to side, taking in the scene before him and swearing under his breath. He shook his head angrily then raised his arms and began to murmur an incantation.

Opposite Nevlon, Aylon and Triya cautiously emerged from their own tunnel. Behkna's screams reverberated against the walls and the Heart's song thrummed loudly in their ears, but Aylon could just make out the low, sing-song voice of her husband invoking the magic that might contain the power of the Warta Dragon for a short time.

She turned to Triya and nodded towards Ru-Lee, "It has begun. She will need you to nudge her on this—do what you must or we are lost."

Triya nodded and quickly ran towards Ru-Lee, her colorful skirts flashing brilliantly in the shimmering light. Aylon set her jaw and stepped closer to the throbbing light. She lifted her arms, and joined her voice to Nevlon's to strengthen the magic they planned to weave around the Heart's chamber.

Within the bright pillar, Behkna's body could be seen twisting and writhing in pain, caught in Gertrude's massive pinchers. Blinding light blasted upwards through Behkna as Gertrude held him fast, writhing in agony. The light filled Gertrude, surrounding her and filling her with strength. The bodies of the two foes swelled and glowed, filling with the pulsating, shimmering light of the Heart's magic.

XXX   XXX   XXX   XXX   XXX

Jace, D.G., and Davlin, had detangled themselves and stood staring at the spectacle before them. Pug sat perched on Jace's shoulder, blinking in the nearly blinding light. Relmar had managed to gain his footing and stood watching Sheila, comprehension slowly dawning in his eyes.

The whooshing sound of a body careening down the waterslide behind them broke through their consciousness, causing Jace, D.G., and Davlin to instinctively jump sideways in alarm and readiness, dragging Relmar with them out of harm's way and nearly knocking him to the ground once more. At Jace's sudden movement, Pug flew upwards and circled above the tunnel opening, ready to dive down and strike at the intruder.

The defenders did not have long to wait—within seconds, the twisted and thorny body of a demon shot out of the mouth of the tunnel, spraying water high into the air. For a few seconds, it lay on its back, stunned and confused by the brightness surrounding it. But it recovered quickly as D.G.'s snarls and growls filled the air. The hackles on D.G.'s back stood on end as he stalked around the fiend, baring his teeth and licking his lips, drawing the beast's attention away from the others. The demon fell for the bait. It lunged at D.G., unknowingly exposing its underside to Davlin's razor-sharp claws. The feline dashed in and sliced the beast's stomach wide, spilling its putrid blood into the chamber's warm water. D.G. danced away, unharmed and growling.

The wound barely slowed the demon. It spun around, catching Davlin across the head with its huge front paw and sending the cougar flying through the air to land with a splash near Ru-Lee's tail, unconscious.

Jace roared in fury. Charging the demon, he rammed his huge body into the fiend's side. Teeth ripping and claws tearing, he opened wound after wound in the thick skin surrounding the beast's neck and shoulders, forcing it backwards towards the pillar of light. Pug dove between the blows, expertly ripping out the enemy's eyes with his sharp talons and flying out nearly unscathed, losing only a few tail feathers in the endeavor. The creature howled in pain and snarled its defiance and fury, fighting back and refusing to die.

D.G. stayed back, knowing that Jace's wrath must be avoided, but his sharp barks of encouragement bounced off the walls and blended with Behkna's screams, nearly drowning out the Heart's song and the sound of Nevlon and Aylon's magic being slowly woven around the chamber.

XXX   XXX   XXX   XXX   XXX

Relmar's eyes narrowed, his brow furrowed, and electric sparks crackled in the air around his head, yet he stood watching Sheila slowly approach the bright column of light in the center of the cavern.  His mind refused to accept what it was seeing, and his soggy feet stayed rooted to the floor of the watery cavern as his family and friends waged battle around him.  As Davlin's body was tossed through the air in front of him, the trance was broken.  He growled and leaped forward, placing himself between Sheila and the Heart.

"NOO!" he screamed, thrusting his arms away from his body to block her.  Flames shot out from his hands, forming a fiery wall behind him.  Surprised, he momentarily glanced sideways at his fingers, but quickly returned his gaze to Sheila, "You can't do this!"

Sheila stopped and regarded him with blinking eyes. For an instant, her orb-like body shimmered as she shifted before him.  The light of the fire mixed with the Heart's glow on her skin as she slowly approached him, her silver hair cascading down her back and spilling over her glistening breasts.  She raised one hand to his chest, touching his cheek with the other and sending electric waves of heat through his body.  His eyes half closed as he leaned his face into her delicate fingers.  The shield of flames behind him raced outward across the water and around, meeting behind Sheila to form a dancing ring of protection that hissed where it met the liquid that rose around their feet.

Gently, Relmar's hands touched Sheila's soft shoulders, his fingers softly touching her silken hair.  His hands slowly slipped down her body to her hips, drawing

her to him as she caressed his cheek. Silver tears slid
down Sheila's face as she slid her hand around his head
and lifted her lips to his. Their eyes closed as Sheila's
body melted into Relmar's, momentarily dissolving the
world outside of their ring of flames.

They stayed together for several seconds, Sheila
blending her mind with Relmar's so that he might fully
understand what must be. Tears ran in rivers down both of
their cheeks as Sheila finally stepped back and looked up
into Relmar's eyes.

"You see?" she sighed, her voice soft and melodic. "I
must do this---I really have no choice...nor do you."
Softly, she reached up and wiped the tears from his face.

Relmar swallowed and the flames danced lower
casting odd shadows on the water. He slowly shook his
head, still trying to deny what she had shown him.

"You know it must be....no other can do this. My
heart is yours always. Remember that. Keep me with you
in your heart and you will be safe."

Relmar opened his mouth to protest but was cut short
by a deafening scream of terror and deep rumble that
shook the mountain at its roots. The mountain growled and
the walls of the chamber heaved around them as if in
anger. Sheila slipped out of his grasp and shifted as he
struggled to keep his footing in the water that sloshed
around his knees. The ring of flames sputtered and died
and Relmar spun around as something soggy and heavy
bumped against his legs. Davlin's naked body, no longer
in mountain lion form, floated against him, unmoving.
Panic seized his heart as he heaved his brother's head and
shoulders free of the water and laid his head on his chest to
listen for a heartbeat.

Jace had finally succeeded in thrusting the snarling
demon into the pulsating pillar that surrounded Gertrude
and Behkna. It screamed, its body instantly fusing with
Behkna's. The Warta Dragon's eyes snapped open in
shock. A sickening smile spread across it muzzle as its

342

body grew, swelling with the essence of the being it had absorbed.

As the mountain protested, deep blue light shot upwards from the Heart, blasting into the bodies of the beings held above it. The light filled Gertrude, emanating from her body in all directions and bathing the cavern in a peaceful calm. That peace was deceptive. Deep inside Behkna, the light was squelched, strangled by the evil within the beast. A putrid black smoke roiled out of his every pore to be trapped within the space behind the binding shield that Aylon and Nevlon were finally able to weave around Behkna and Gertrude's struggling forms.

The mountain shook again and the trickles of water running down the walls of the cave became cascading rivers. Jace and D.G. joined Relmar in attempting to revive Davlin and keep his head above the slowly-rising water. Pug glided down to rest on D.G.'s head, apprehensively watching the figures within the shield above the Heart. Sheila scurried over to Ru-Lee who stood with her head bent, listening intently to Triya's urgent directions.

*"It is time,"* Sheila whispered in her friend's mind as she approached.

The Warta Spirits had relinquished control of Ru-Lee's body when Behkna entered the pillar of light surrounding Gertrude. Now she glanced at Sheila and growled, shaking her head. *"There has to be another way!"* she protested.

Sheila closed her eyes and sighed, *"You know there isn't. We can't wait. Even now, Gertrude loses ground. Aylon and Nevlon's shield won't hold for much longer, especially once the Guardian fails."*

Looking up, Ru-Lee saw Gertrude's aging body pressed up against the side of the shield. The cracks in her large grey body were longer and wider than they had been when Ru-Lee first entered the cavern. The movements of her legs were slow and weakening by the second.

Ru-Lee glared angrily at her long-time friend, her eyes filled with pain as she slowly accepted the inevitable. *"How?"* she snarled.

"Sheila must join with the Heart—to do that, she must enter the Heart's chamber...." Triya interjected. "The protections of Aylon and Nevlon have been woven in such a way that beings can pass through from the outside—once in, they are trapped."

The Heart's song still vibrated in the air around them, like a heartbeat heard from within a mother's womb. The murmured voices of Nevlon and Aylon mingled with the music as they sought to maintain the protective shield that held Behkna prisoner.

*"What part do I play?"* Ru-Lee snapped.

"Once Sheila has joined with the Heart, Behkna will attempt to kill her by destroying it. You must seal her--- and him---within the Heart." Triya replied softly.

Ru-Lee lowered her head to gaze into Triya's eyes, glaring, *"Are you insane? I will NOT trap her within the Heart to deal with that monstrosity on her own!"*

"You must---and you will," Triya responded firmly.

*"No—I won't,"* Ru-Lee snorted, curling her tail around her body and laying down in the quickly deepening water. The Warta Spirits churned within her, their blood-lust still unsatisfied.

*"Enough!"* Sheila yelled, her voice edged with irritation. *"There is no other way, Ru! We both know it, and time is gone! If you seal me in, I will be able to stop Behkna. If you do not, he will escape---and I will die, as will many more. Since I am not born a Stone-Spider, I lack the natural protections that they have. Even in shifted form, I do not possess their same powers. In order to act as Guardian, I must become one with the Heart and be sealed within its chamber. You are the only one who can do that! You must use your gifts to save me, for I will do this."*

Before Ru-Lee could respond, Sheila thrust herself through the protective shield surrounding the combatants and dove below them into the chamber that held the Heart. Charging after Sheila, Ru-Lee burst through the shield into the compacted area within. She found herself suspended above the Heart's chamber, her back tightly pressed against the surrounding shield as she worked to keep out of Behkna's reach. The air was thick with black smoke that filled her nostrils and constricted her vision. Behkna, still held in Gertrude's weakening grasp, snapped at Ru-Lee and attempted to slash at her through the haze. She ducked and crouched low, peering into the blinding light that poured from the chamber below her.

In the center of an enormous gemstone that glowed and throbbed with life, Sheila lay on her side curled into a gentle ball, surrounded by the Heart's glow. She was no longer in spider form, but that of a beautiful, elegant, woman. Her long shimmering hair spilled about her delicate feminine body—her true form. A contented smile played softly upon her lips as she turned her gaze upwards and winked at Ru-Lee.

Behkna, realizing what was happening, wrenched himself free of Gertrude, smashing her now-brittle body against the inner walls of the shield—the Heart's song weakening to a hum around them. He roared and dove for Sheila, saliva dripping from his jaws as he sought to rip her to shreds. Ru-Lee twisted beneath him, blocking his attack. He pinned her over the opening to the Heart, slashing mercilessly at her underbelly.

The Warta Spirits within her surged through her body once more, forcing her soul to the deep corners of her psyche. Her heart filled with their hatred of Behkna and all that he stood for. The flames on her body flared higher, raising the temperature in their tight quarters. With sadistic satisfaction, the spirits noticed Ru-Lee's poisonous fangs still imbedded deep into Behkna's shoulder, the flesh around them already degrading and oozing fetid puss as the toxins did their work.

The two dragons battled furiously within their tight quarters, ripping and slashing at each other's flesh and sending loosened scales flying through the air. Behkna dug his talons deep into Ru-Lee's stomach. She screamed and snapped her jaws closed around his neck. Her fangs sunk into Behkna's now-exposed flesh, finding his jugular deep within his throat. His life blood poured into her mouth and she shook her head, forcing her fangs deeper, oblivious to the pain in her body. The Warta Spirits' sadistic glee filled her heart as her enemy's blood trickled down her throat.

Beneath the struggling dragons, the Heart pulsed, its light changing colors with each beat, its song growing ever stronger. Sheila's soft voice, tinged with Heartsong, slipped into Ru-Lee's battle-fevered mind, *"You must seal Behkna in the chamber with me."*

Ru-Lee's soul revolted, *"NO! I can finish him—then you will be free!"*

Behkna's voice tore through her mind viciously, *"You cannot finish me! Even if you remove my beating heart, my soul will remain! I will rule this land and destroy all within it!"*

*"You will not,"* the Ancient One's gravelly voice responded. *"We will defeat you and leave you here to rot, for WE will be free!"*

The Warta spirits violently twisted Ru-Lee's body beneath Behkna's crushing weight. The force and speed of the roll cast his form away from Ru-Lee and tossed him into the opening to the Heart's Chamber. Blinding light immediately burst forth from the Heart, engulfing Sheila and Behkna and slamming Ru-Lee's body upwards into the ceiling. She squinted, struggling to see what was happening, but could only hear Behkna's growls and screams as the light blasted through his body once more.

Within her mind, Ru-Lee heard the Warta Spirits speaking softly to her, *"We are sorry for the loss of your friend, but we must do what is needed to be free."*

Instantly, and against her will, her jaws were opened, spewing lava and fire into the Heart's chamber, sealing it closed and plunging the cavern into darkness and ominous

346

silence. The protective shield collapsed allowing water to pour in, instantly cooling and hardening the heated stone. Nevlon, Aylon, Triya, Jace, Relmar, D.G., Pug, and a dazed Davlin stared open-mouthed as Ru-Lee's body crashed down upon the lava-covered opening, her heart filled with panic.

*"WHAT HAVE YOU DONE??"* she cried, furiously clawing at the solidifying stone.

The Warta Spirits were somber in their reply, *"We have done what we came to do. Now we are free. We leave you in your grief and thank you for your service."*

Numbly, Ru-Lee felt the spirits leave her body one-by-one. They slipped away up the tunnels in soft gray clouds, barely visible in the dim fire-light glowing from her body. Large tears ran down her muzzle landing with soft splashes in the water around her. Her own blood spilled from her wounds, trickling down through the water to slip into the pores of the lava-stone seal. The pain in her body no longer mattered—her mind and senses were numb. She lowered her head and curled her body into a tight ball above the Heart's sealed chamber, her heart aching. Lowering her abdomen against the rough stones, she felt the warmth of the lava rock painfully prick into her torn flesh and welcomed the sharp edges of agony that gave substance to her grief.

The mountain rumbled around them again, as if a monster was awakening in the earth. The ground heaved and rolled and the water in the cavern bubbled, heating to a nearly unbearable temperature.

"We have to leave—NOW!" Aylon shouted, guiding the others away from the cavern's center. "Nevlon, which tunnel?"

"This way!" Nevlon yelled, dragging a still-dazed Davlin to the passage he had come down.

D.G., with Pug still perched on his head, paddled over to Ru-Lee and whined. Pawing at her body, he urged her to move, but she did not respond—oblivious to their peril. Relmar stood staring at Ru-Lee, blinking as if he couldn't

347

quite take in what had happened, accusations etched across his face. Aylon splashed through the water and spun him towards Nevlon.

"Move it!" Aylon shouted, urgently shoving Relmar towards the tunnel. "We need you to make some light for us!"

Relmar's leaden feet dragged through the water, all-but ignoring Aylon's pleas for speed and light. The floor of the cave suddenly heaved again pitching Relmar and Aylon face-first into the still-rising water. Relmar's knees struck the rock floor sharply, gashing the flesh. The sharp pain and the slap of the water on his face roused him from his daze.

Relmar surfaced sputtering, brushing his hair from his face. He pulled Aylon up and ran towards Nevlon as the walls twisted around them. A soft melodic hum floated through the air. He stopped and turned at the tunnel opening, confused. Light filtered through the lava seal below Ru-Lee, refracting through the water above it to illuminate the cavern with dancing beams. The ground swayed again. Ru-Lee roused and backed away from the Heart's chamber, eyeing it suspiciously.

With a loud rush, light-infused water gushed forth in a geyser from the Heart's chamber, spilling away on all sides as it smashed into the ceiling to form a spectacular fountain. The water splashed down the walls from a million tiny cracks, running faster and fuller, flooding the space. Suspended in the center of the Geyser, Sheila smiled at Ru-Lee and glanced below her. Ru-Lee followed her gaze. Peering through the fountain-like cascade, she saw the lava-encrusted form of Behkna, floating between Sheila and the Heart.

As the water swirled, the shape of a woman rose from its surface—Sheyna---her liquid voice echoed softly in Ru-Lee's ears, "The Warta Dragon is contained and will cause no more harm. Sheila and the Heart will protect our world for a long time to come—once you have completed your part in this."

Ru-Lee cocked her head to one side, puzzled, *"What part? I did what I was told—I sealed Sheila in a tomb with Behkna. It is done finished."*

"Not quite," Sheyna replied softly. "You must perform one more task…Sheila will blend her magic with your fire and lava, encasing her for all time within the column of water in which she now floats. She will appear to be sleeping—in suspension—but she will be listening to the heartbeat of this world through the water that is its life-blood. You must hurry—soon the mountain will flood its caverns and tunnels to cleanse itself of the evil that has invaded it this day. The Elves have called the water forth, and I cannot hold it at bay."

Dejectedly, Ru-Lee gazed at her friend and whispered, *"Sheila, I do this with a reluctant heart."*

Sheila smiled out at Ru-Lee, her silvery hair swirling around her body. Softly, her musical voice caressed Ru-Lee's mind. *"I know, but I thank you. Do it now!"* she whispered.

Ru-Lee closed her eyes, unable to look upon her long-time companion as she condemned her to her fate. Fire and lava hissed and crackled as it met the watery pillar and joined with Sheila's magic to form a glittering, sealed, ice-like column that stretched from the Heart's chamber up to the ceiling of the cavern. Within the column, Sheila and the Warta Dragon hung suspended above the Heart itself, surrounded by pulsating, glowing light. The muted sound of the Heart's song thrummed softly through the air filling the cavern with a gentle sense of peace.

That peace lasted but a second as the mountain prepared to expel all intruders from its bowels. Water forced itself in from every unseen, stony pore. It rushed up around the column in the cavern's center, quickly rising to dangerous levels that threatened to drown the small group.

Overcome with emotions, Ru-Lee's legs shook beneath her. Her heart felt like lead within her chest and her muzzle dipped into the water. The sound of Aylon's frantic yell roused her. She turned to find Aylon and the others waiting at the mouth of a wide tunnel, struggling to keep their heads above the fast-rising water. Her heart seized at the sight, fearing she might lose more of the people she cared for most. Quickly, she spun around and swam towards them through the heated liquid.

Each found a purchase on Ru-Lee's scales and horns, hoping to use her body to stay afloat—or at least make it to safety. Jace had shifted back to human form and now lifted D.G. up high onto Ru-Lee's back where the canine could clasp one of her horns in his jaws. Jace threw an arm across D.G. and clung to Ru-Lee's slippery scales. Triya and Aylon criss-crossed their arms around Davlin's shoulders, assisting him in finding a hold that would keep him from slipping away as they made their way up the passage. Relmar draped his arms across Ru-Lee's hips, hooking his fingers beneath her warm scales. Nevlon threw himself onto Ru-Lee's back. Squeezing his legs, he dug his heels beneath her scales and pressed his body to hers.

Ru-Lee dove into the tunnel, propelled upwards by the force of the waves and preceded by a frantically flying Pug as he attempted to stay out of the water. Ru-Lee's passengers gasped and choked repeatedly as she swam upwards in the strong current that smashed them against the passage walls at every turn.

After a wild, torrential ride, the group was expelled from the tunnel into the main entrance cave of the mountain. Water erupted from all the other passage openings at the same instant, sending hundreds of beings, both living and dead, tumbling into Ru-Lee, out of the wide opening, and down the mountainside in a muddy, gory jumble.

Ru-Lee resisted the force of the water and the detritus it carried. Not wanting to roll down the mountain to be further bloodied and bruised, she spread her wings and launched her body upwards into the blazing morning sun, her cargo clinging precariously to her wounded hide, her injured wing barely holding her and her passengers aloft.

# Chapter 76

Orange, red, and purple mingled brilliantly as the sun set on the Travelers' campsite. Ru-Lee, now in human form and assisted by Trieca, gingerly walked along the outskirts of the encampment. Curious children darted away, eyeing her with awe and suspicion. She wrapped her left arm protectively around her aching midsection and leaned heavily on Trieca, wandering aimlessly away from the large tents that had been erected near the base of the mountain to house the wounded. Trieca, his right arm in a sling, gently supported her with his left. D.G. trailed a few steps behind. Large shaved spots on his haunches and shoulders revealed angry gashes that had been repaired with long lines of dark stitches.

The battle inside of Mt. Shavla had take place five days past. Since that time, women had come from the village of Ikna to assist the Gnomes in repairing the wounded that had been expelled from the mountain in the flood. Acrid smoke from burned Demon carcasses hung heavy in the air as men and elves worked to dig the last of the graves in the field near Lake Satcha where the fallen defenders of the Heart would rest, Trieca's father among them. In an enormous, odd-shaped tent on the west side of camp, Nevlon and Aylon were meeting with the Council of Keepers pleading---Ru-Lee assumed---for her life.

Loss of blood, shock, and fatigue had taken their toll on Ru-Lee as she flew away from Mt. Shavla over the Traveler's camp five days earlier. Near the north edge of these temporary housings, she had almost blacked out. She had lost control of her wings, nose-diving towards the earth. Landing face-first, she smashed several tents and nearly crushed three men that hadn't managed to get out of the way fast enough when she plummeted from the sky. Luckily, her crash caused no further hurt to her passengers as they bounced and rolled into the debris of damaged tents and campsites. Her last memory was of the pounding of feet on the ground as men, women and children ran to offer assistance.  As she completely lost consciousness, her body shifted back to human form, and her secret was revealed.

Though she had been grievously injured by Behkna, the skills of the Gnomes had worked together with her naturally-healing dragon powers, seeming to heal her outward wounds quickly.  Though still weak, on the third day she had been tersely asked to shift so that she could return to Mt. Shavla and use her lava to help repair and seal the gaping hole made by the Warta Dragon and his minions.  The job took nearly all of her strength to complete to the satisfaction of the Dwarves who were overseeing the job.  She had returned to camp completely spent but hopeful that this request for her assistance meant that her powers had been accepted and she would be safe from any recriminations from the Keepers.

It had been a false hope--the next day, she was ordered to remain in camp in human form until her fate could be decided.  She had immediately retreated within herself, sobbing long into the night, grieving her losses and silently decrying the injustice being perpetrated upon her. Deep within her soul, a small dark voice growled in fury. Her grief and despair left no room for her to wonder why or where that fury came from.  She had awakened drained but resigned, resolving to make the most of the day.

Nevlon had asked Trieca to stay with her.  The young elf had taken this charge seriously and accompanied her as she spent the morning visiting with Jace and Davlin, trying to divert her mind from her concerns.

Within the healers' tent where Jace and Davlin were recuperating, Pug had planted himself on Jace's headboard and refused to leave, screeching and snapping at the Gnomes that had tried to shoo him away.  They had finally relented, placing soft white cloths around the area below Pug to act as drop cloths for anything he might leave behind.

The brothers were in good spirits and healing nicely. They showed off the new scars that criss-crossed their bodies, comparing their severity and counting their numbers to see who had the most. The Gnomes said it would take time for the poison ingested while fighting the demons to dissipate, but it appeared that they would soon recover with few ill effects.

Ru-Lee hadn't told them about the meeting of the Keepers, not wanting to spoil their good cheer, but Jace had seemed to sense something was wrong. He kept cyeing her sideways, thoughtfully, as if considering what might be the source of her melancholy. Not wanting to field any questions, Ru-Lee had pasted a smile on her face and avoided meeting his gaze. When she felt she could no longer uphold the ruse, she had excused herself saying she needed fresh air and a walk.

Her heart weighed heavy in her chest as she left the encampment and headed for the forest's edge, allowing her feet to carry her where they would. A horse snorted near her causing her to start slightly. She looked up into its soft eyes and sighed. Others horses were tethered in the shade of the trees noisily tearing grass from the turf and grinding it in their jaws, unaware of her pain and worry. In the distance, she heard the chink of picks and shovels as workers struggled to dig graves in the rocky earth.

Trieca shifted uncomfortably near her. "Are you sure you want to continue?" he asked softly.

Ru-Lee nodded wordlessly in reply and moved forward, slowly rounding the edge of the trees until the field beyond was visible. It was littered with boulders that had fallen in the earthquake, its surface riddled with cracks that had split the surface as the earth had heaved. Fresh dirt formed dark mounds over the dead that had already been put to rest. Men and Elves, exhausted from their toil, continued to work, oblivious to her presence.

Just inside the line of trees, a lone figure stood watching the progress with slumped shoulders---Relmar.

"Has he slept?" Ru-Lee asked Trieca, nodding her head in Relmar's direction.

Sadly, Trieca shook his head, "He says there are too many voices—too much emotion. His senses have been heightened since his time near the Heart—without Sheila to act as a buffer, I don't know how long he can hang on."

At the mention of Sheila's name, tears pricked at the corners of Ru-Lee's eyes and her throat tightened. She swallowed, trying to maintain control of the overwhelming sadness that threatened to wash over her. Heaving a deep sigh she gazed up at the sky. Soft clouds drifted slowly past, seeming to form the shape of a large white stone spider. She blinked and shook her head, attempting to control her emotions.

Ru-lee, with Trieca and D.G., approached Relmar, moving slowly and quietly beneath the forest's canopy. Relmar turned, watching their approach. In the dim light, Ru-Lee could see dark circles ringing his eyes. His sunken cheeks and sallow skin shocked her. She hadn't seen him since they exited the cavern of the Heart's Chamber, but had expected him to have fared somewhat better than this.

"You don't look well," Ru-Lee chided softly. "Have you seen the healers?"

Relmar snorted in irritation, "Of course! They won't leave me be! Always shoving this or that concoction down my throat!"

Ru-Lee's brows knit together—this temper was not like Relmar. "They are just trying to help. That's their job, you know."

Relmar sighed and his shoulders slumped forward, "I know—it's just that there's nothing they can do. The emotions don't stop—even when everyone sleeps, they still feel.....and so do I. I feel everything—more than everything. Their anxiety, turmoil, sadness, and anger—all their fear—I feel it all."

D.G. lay down next to Ru-Lee, panting. "What about their joy?" she asked. "Don't you feel their happiness and joy?"

Disgusted, Relmar answered, "Far too little! Not nearly enough to take the edge off!" He was quiet a

355

moment, watching the gravediggers fill in the last grave. "I miss her---there is a gaping hole deep within me that I fear will never heal. I am empty---without purpose." Suddenly he wheeled on Ru-Lee and Trieca, "WHAT IS MY PURPOSE!!" he yelled. D.G. jumped to his feet, a low snarl in his throat. "WHAT AM I MEANT TO DO WITH THIS SO-CALLED 'GIFT'?"

Ru-Lee blinked, taken aback. She had no idea how to answer her cousin. His pain was palpable, his confusion painful to see. What could she say? Before she could formulate an answer, Triya approached from behind them, speaking softly to the horses as she passed, her scent preceding her and mingling pleasantly with the pine and earth smells around them. Two large black panthers glided alongside her causing D.G.'s snarl to turn to a full-throated growl, his hackles standing on end. The felines ignored him with an air of arrogance as they drew near.

"Ru-Lee, they are ready for you now," Triya said, her rich voice a gentle salve to Ru-Lee's jangled nerves.

As Ru-Lee turned, Triya lightly touched her arm and leaned in, whispering softly in her ear, "All will be well— you have done what you must here. Now, you must follow the path laid before you. Watch your back, and take care to listen to the voices within you---there is darkness lurking everywhere."

Ru-Lee's brows knit together as she stopped for a moment to look quizzically into Triya's face, but the seer's eyes revealed nothing to give more clear meaning to her words. Triya smiled cryptically and turned towards Relmar, the black panthers melting into the shadows of the trees.

## Chapter 77

Darkness had fallen by the time Ru-Lee entered the huge angular tent where the Council of Keepers were meeting to determine her fate. Her heart pounded in her chest as she slowly walked to the center of the space, the tent flap falling softly closed behind her. She had left Trieca and D.G. waiting outside with some Elven guards, concern etched on Trieca's Elven face; now she urgently wished her friends were by her side to help steady her shaking legs. Candles flickered on small tables around the sides of the tent and from a lamp hung high in the middle illuminating the faces of the Council leaders. On one side, three Elves sat upon tall wooden chairs. Next to them, three large white Stone Spiders lay, their legs folded beneath them, their eyes watchful. Across the tent stood two large dragons---one Harta female, one Dahgsna male—watching thoughtfully as she approached the center space. Aylon and Nevlon joined her in the center. Taking up positions on either side of their granddaughter, they each placed a protective arm around her--Aylon giving her waist a gentle squeeze and Nevlon holding her shoulders so tightly, she was glad her wounds there had healed.

The oldest Elf stood to speak, leaning on a large wooden staff as he rose. Ru-Lee couldn't recall his name-- his features were long and ancient, his body stooped and trembling. The voice that emanated from him did not match his frame, coming soft and musically to Ru-Lee's ears and soothing the edges of her anxiety.

"Ru-Lee, it has come to our attention that you possess all four of the earthen powers, and have for some time now. This, in and of itself, would be problematic at best— but we believe it could be manageable. However, we have also been told that you have the ability to shift shape into that of a Dragon....a Water Dragon, if I am correct—one that has the power of fire as well. Is this true?"

Ru-Lee swallowed and nodded, unable to trust her voice.

Out of the corner of her eye, she saw the Harta and Dahgsna dragons nod and shifted their feet uncomfortably. The Elf continued, "You, my dear, are a truly unique and amazing creature. We were blessed to have you on our side in the battle against the Warta Dragon, and we thank you for your service."

The stone spiders stood and nodded vigorously, their eyes bobbing crazily in the candlelight reflecting off of their small heads. Ru-Lee wrinkled her brow, confused by the direction of the Elf's words. What was happening here? She raised her eyebrows and glanced sideways to Nevlon and Aylon, but neither looked at her.

The Elf was speaking again, "However, we have a problem. The abilities you possess, and the form you are able to take, represent a great amount of power in one being—too much power."

Ru-Lee started to speak in her defense, but the Elf raised a gnarled hand and continued, "Your heart has been shown to be pure and many have spoken on your behalf. Please understand that you have been well represented. We truly believe that, currently, you would not cause intentional harm to our world.

"Unfortunately, the future cannot be seen clearly, even by those who possess the gift of sight. The fact remains that, if you were to be corrupted, we would all be in peril. We do not know if our defenses would be enough to defeat you—in fact, we believe that they would not. There are many lives that could be at stake here. This is an unacceptable risk, which poses yet another problem...."

Ru-Lee lowered her head, shaking it slowly back and forth. Her heart dropped in her chest as if filled with lead and her legs threatened to give way beneath her. Visions of her eviscerated body swam in her mind as she wondered how they would choose to end her life. Despair flooded through her as she struggled to maintain outward control---- but deep within her heart, a small corner of her being seethed in fury, urging her to shift--to rise up against these beings in anger. Shocked at this reaction, she wondered,

*'What's wrong with me?'* She had never before been an angry, aggressive individual—where was this rage coming from?

The Harta dragon's voice invaded her thoughts, projected throughout the tent for all to hear, "The problem is, we don't wish to destroy you or cause you harm.....and we aren't sure we could even if we desired to."

Ru-Lee raised her gaze to look into the wise eyes of the Harta. Her voice was small and weak as she asked, "What will you do then?"

"Nevlon and Aylon have indicated that there may be a need for you to cross over to the human world to assist their contact there---your mother," the Harta answered.

Startled, Ru-Lee snapped her gaze sideways and caught a glimmer of a smile tugging at the corner of Aylon's mouth.

"If this is agreeable to you, you will be allowed to go and seek your family on the other side."

Ru-Lee struggled to process this information. She glanced at her grandparents trying to ascertain the meaning of this news, but neither would meet her gaze. "Will I be able to return?" she asked.

The Dahgsna answered here, also projecting his voice so that all present could hear, "Nevlon has made it clear that, should you wish to return, you would be able to contact him in the same way he has communicated with your mother. He would bring your request to us. At that time, the terms of your return would need to be negotiated—we need to find out if we have the ability to control your powers without your consent. Without that in place, it is possible that you might never return."

"Do you agree to this?" the ancient Elf asked.

Ru-Lee straightened her spine, set her jaw, and responded dryly, "I don't suppose I really have a choice, do I? If I don't, you will have to try to find some way to end me—and that wouldn't be any fun for anyone, would it?"

The Elf chuckled, "No, I don't suppose it would. Done then—you will depart this world in three day's time; time enough to tie up loose ends. Good luck to you," he said softly, bowing before slowly walking past her and out of the tent.

The dragons followed wordlessly, their tails dragging long lines in the soil as they passed. The last to leave were the Stone Spiders. The largest approached her and gazed up into her face, her soft voice gently touching Ru-Lee's mind. *"If ever you need anything, you may call on me and my sisters. We will assist you in any way possible—remember, WE and those of our bloodlines are the keepers of the gates. Sheila hears us, and you—she will always help and be there for you...as will we."*

Soft tears of thanks leaked out of Ru-Lee's eyes as she nodded her acceptance. Stoically she watched the Stone Spiders move away before collapsing in Aylon's arms, sobbing in confusion and relief.

## Chapter 78

Night settled its cool blanket over the Dragon's Teeth Mountains as Ru-Lee, her family, and Trieca descended into one of Mt. Lrosya's wide, deep tunnels. The Elven rulers had released Trieca from his obligations to the royal guard and he had decided to join Ru-lee. He had never passed through the gates before and hoped for a new adventure to soothe the grief of his father's loss. Ru-Lee hoped for peace.

Nevlon and Aylon led the way to a torch-lit grotto that held a hidden gateway into the human world. Dwarves had long-ago set the torches into the stone along the passageway and within the cave. Earlier in the day, a Harta Dragon had come down to light them. Smoke from the flames floated near the ceiling, burning their eyes and making them water.

"We are taking you to the last place we were able to make contact with your mother," Aylon called over her shoulder.

"How long ago?" Ru-Lee asked, hiking her provision-filled pack higher onto her shoulders and deftly rubbing D.G.'s head as he kept pace beside her.

"Three weeks or so," Aylon responded quietly, worry straining her voice.

Behind her, Jace grumbled as Relmar stumbled into him and Pug clacked his beak, irritated at being jostled while he perched on Jace's shoulder. It had been eight days since the battle in the Chamber of the Heart, and still Relmar hadn't slept. He had lost weight and his clothes hung loosely about his frame. His haunted, red-rimmed eyes twitched, and his movements were jerky and disjointed. Sparks flared intermittently around his head whenever his temper slipped—which was often. He stumbled through his days like a zombie—the same way he now stumbled through the tunnel between Davlin and Jace. The younger two brothers had decided to join Ru-Lee on in her pseudo-banishment to help if they could....Relmar followed simply because he had no idea what else to do.

Ru-Lee quickened her pace to catch up with Nevlon, a question burning in her mind. "Nevlon, we have all recovered sufficiently for the journey—all except Relmar. I know the Heart reveals our true nature, expanding on our strengths and gifts. It is easy to see what it did with Relmar—what about Jace and Davlin? What about me? I don't feel any different," she whispered.

Nevlon smiled, "Your gifts are so much intertwined with who you are that I would be surprised if you did feel any difference—other than a possible strengthening of convictions. It is the same with Jace and Davlin. Their gifts are related to the forms they take when they shift. Jace's are a love of life and food, strength, and courage. Davlin's is patience, grace, strength, and wisdom. Trust me—these have grown since their time near the Heart. Relmar's gifts are related to the soul; fire, which he didn't even know he possessed; empathy—to the point of keenly feeling others emotions; and the ability to hear the thoughts of others. These can tear a man apart if he is unable to come to terms with them and manage them. His time in the human world should help, since his gifts will be changed there---at least that is my hope, though one can never be sure."

"Do you think mine have changed?" Ru-Lee asked, thinking about the rage that seemed to flare unbidden in her heart.

"They have been strengthened, of course," Nevlon replied, looking sideways at her. "There may also have been parts of your soul that were awakened by your proximity to the Heart—parts you didn't know you possessed."

This answer did nothing to dispel Ru-Lee's discomfort and she chewed her lip thoughtfully as they passed out of the tunnel into a large, cool cave. A small pool in the center reflected the torchlight, glittering back at them. Ru-Lee could feel the gate's magic vibrating within her core. She closed her eyes and smiled as its music slipped into her soul.

Aylon gently touched a large, smooth archway etched on the stone wall, her hand passing through it as if it were air and not rock. This gate had been unlocked so that they could pass through freely. Aylon smiled sadly, satisfied that all was ready. She turned to Ru-Lee, "On the other side, you will find yourself in a chamber much like this one. From there, you are on your own. You may find help there—the ones that were there for your mother; or you may find that they are gone and you must fend for yourself. It is dangerous—watch who you trust and take care of each other." She hugged Ru-Lee to her as a tear slipped out of her eyes. Ru-Lee returned the hug, not trusting her voice to speak.

Releasing Ru-Lee, Aylon moved on to the brothers, then to Trieca, giving whispered instructions and heartfelt hugs as she went. As she passed D.G., she rubbed his ears and smiled, "You know what do to, don't you—you've been doing it for a long time. Take care of her." D.G. bobbed his head and grinned, his tongue hanging out one side of his mouth as if this was a silly thing to say.

Nevlon, always uncomfortable with good-byes, gathered all three of the brothers into one giant hug before moving on to Ru-Lee. He squeezed Ru-Lee so tightly she thought her ribs would break. Before he released her, he softly rubbed his bristly beard against her cheek, mingling his tears with her own.

"Ughhh!" she groaned, struggling to free herself. "I'm going to miss you too! I will find some way to keep in touch," she giggled as Nevlon released her. "Wait—how were you able to speak with my mother? How do we contact you?" she asked, curiously.

Nevlon threw back his head and laughed, "Remember---the gates don't block spirits or animals! Where there is a will, there is a way—we will be in touch!" With that, he pushed her and her cousins through the gate to find a new life—and her mother—within the human world. D.G. yelped and Trieca laughed as they dove after their friends.

Made in the USA
San Bernardino, CA
20 February 2017